C000220332

AUTUMN'S RISK

AUTUMN TRENT SERIES: BOOK SIX

MARY STONE

Copyright © 2021 by Mary Stone

All rights reserved.

No part of this book may be reproduced in any form or by any electronic or mechanical means, including information storage and retrieval systems, without written permission from the author, except for the use of brief quotations in a book review.

❀ Created with Vellum

To my husband.
Thank you for taking care of our home and its many inhabitants
while I follow this dream of mine.

DESCRIPTION

No risk, no reward . . .

After five months of training at Quantico, Dr. Autumn Trent is ready for her first day on the job as an official special agent with the FBI's Behavioral Analysis Unit. She left for training with a heavy heart, feeling responsible for all that happened to her best friend and fellow agent, Winter Black. Now, her heart is just as heavy, but her spirit has grown stronger as she and Winter continue their fight against evil.

She's only home a few days when a woman with a paralyzing fear of water jumps to her death from a waterfall. Was it suicide or was something much more sinister at play? Autumn's team is sent to small-town Beechum County to investigate what becomes a slew of suicides and the cult connected to it all.

Desperate to prove she can still read people after misjudging Justin Black and putting Winter in danger, Autumn offers to go undercover. Isolated from her team, she soon discovers that under the guise of love, evil lurks under the cult's surface. An evil that threatens not only Autumn's mind but her life.

Autumn's Risk, the sixth book in Mary Stone's Autumn Trent Series, is a spine-tingling thriller that will keep you guessing to the last heart-stopping page.

1

Natalie Garland grinned as the early morning breeze whirled through the car windows, fluttering her hair and filling her lungs with the crisp pine scent. Cruising down the shadowed highway with the first hints of sunlight outlining peaks and dips in the mountainous horizon, she remembered what life was like before. The person she had been...but more so, who she still was, even now.

She belted the next line in time with Kelly Clarkson. "What doesn't thrill you makes you wrrooonger..."

She'd loved this damn song as a kid. Granted, along with her middle school bestie, she'd taken some creative liberties with the lyrics, but she still loved it.

Their changes only made the tune more sentimental.

That was one of the best discoveries she'd made as she'd crawled out of the hell her life had nosedived into two years ago, following a horrid series of heartbreaks. Natalie had realized that she was still Natalie, despite everything she'd lived through.

She'd always been a bit wild. Independent. There hadn't been many boring moments growing up because Natalie found adventure everywhere. It was nice to know that all her personal devastation hadn't wiped that girl away.

She was altered, she could admit, but essentially the same. And as cheesy as the cliché was, what hadn't killed her truly *had* made her stronger.

As Natalie sped past an ancient green road sign announcing Rutshire, the weight of the world lessened a little bit more. She was a mere few miles away from home, and the pain that had accompanied her when she fled the confines of that tiny Virginia town was no longer her constant companion.

She *wanted* to be here. She'd chosen to come here.

She was ready to face the ghosts of her past. Ready to face her family again. Ready to move forward.

Bariiing-bariiing! Bariiing-bariiing!

Grabbing her phone from the passenger's seat, she took her eyes off the road for a second to glance at the screen. Bradley was calling. Of course.

Bradley Garland, her cousin and city councilman of the mighty blip on the map that was Rutshire, had always been an early riser. She'd never understood his affinity for mornings when they were younger.

She understood it now.

Mornings had become her favorite part of the day over the past couple years. Viewing the sun rise had transformed into a sacred experience she felt deeply honored to witness. Learning to appreciate the grandeur of the ordinary had been a paramount part of her recovery from the drugs and alcohol she'd struggled with so terribly. Nature had helped release her from the postpartum depression that had seized her by the neck following her miscarriage.

Natalie tapped the speaker button. "Four-fifty-eight in the morning? Why am I not surprised?"

Bradley's laugh filled the car. "Early bird catches the worm, dear cousin."

It was so good to laugh in response. "For some reason, that fact never held much sway with me."

"Yeah, you have a point. Mornings got a little shafted on the slogans. But look at you...up and at 'em with the best of us."

Natalie rolled her eyes as she steered the car to hug a curve in the road. "As a former night owl, I resent that remark."

"Sorry, Nat. Your vampire license has been revoked." Bradley delivered the news in a solemn voice.

She liked that sentiment. Nothing good had happened after the sun went down over the past two years. Far too many old and destructive habits were easier kept in the dark of the night. Every addict knew that.

"So." Bradley cleared his throat. "You're on the road? Just like we talked about?"

Her headlights illuminated the thick tree lines to her left and right, which were just beginning to show the varying shades of July in the dim light. "Just like we talked about," she confirmed. "Almost to the falls, actually. Going to catch the sunrise from my favorite peak before I head into town."

Bradley gasped in feigned indignity. "How many times did I beg you to go for a morning hike with me at Dogwood Falls growing up? You *always* turned me down. That cuts deep, Nat. *Super* deep."

She laughed, enjoying the way the elation bubbled up from her throat and overtook the peaceful morning air. "I'll carry the guilt with me to the grave."

"Yeah. Right." His dramatic snigger tickled her, making her snigger along. "But seriously, you sound good. Happy." The relief in his voice was unmistakable.

Natalie slowed her car, preparing for the sharp right turn

into the entrance of Dogwood Falls. "I *am* happy. Things are looking up, cuz. I'm coming home."

"And how does that return make you feel?" Bradley needled in his gentle way.

She would have jabbed him in the ribs with her finger if they'd been face-to-face, just like she used to do when they were little. "You should have been a shrink. That's total shrink talk."

He let out a dry chortle. "Well, as your local city councilman, I do get to deal with a lot of disturbed people far, *far* too often."

Natalie pulled her car to a stop in the gravel parking lot she'd often frequented during her adolescence. "I never should have put so much distance between my parents and me. No good came from cutting them off, but I wasn't thinking clearly then. Losing the baby…that really threw me offtrack. Threw me off *the planet*. But I'm back. I'm better."

"I can hear it in your voice." Bradley's optimism seemed to grow in direct proportion to her own. "Can't wait to have you home again. We've got two years of small-town gossip to catch you up on. And I'm sorry, but I'm massively relieved that you got away from those people."

She sighed, pulling her keys from the ignition. "I swear. Clean break. I'm done with them. I want to reconnect with my old life. My *real* life. Even if it's flawed as hell."

"We're all flawed, Nat. Don't go thinking you're special or something." He chuckled, but she perceived the affection in his words.

"Apparently, I'm going to have to convince *Rod* that I'm not that special." She huffed, shaking her head in mild frustration.

Bradley groaned his disgust. "Don't tell me ole Nim-Rod is back at ya again. Pardon my French, but he's a complete and total piece of shit if I ever saw one."

"You know, I took French in high school," Natalie reminded her cousin. "The proper terminology is *morceau de merde*. Much classier that way. And…yeah. He's been trying to get in touch with me repeatedly. Thinks we should give our relationship another shot. But there's no future there. Rod hurt me in a way he can never take back or make up for."

"Damn right, he did." Her cousin was almost growling now. "He left you alone when you were pregnant *with his child*. He left you *because* you were pregnant with his child. Do you know how many times I've run into that sonofabitch around town and wanted to pummel his stupid face in?"

Natalie closed her eyes, not wanting to relive that particular moment right now. There was something about remembering the cold, dead stare in her boyfriend's eyes when she told him of her pregnancy that dropped a shadow of despair on the brightest of moods.

Mornings were too special to taint them with thoughts of Rod Norris, so she mentally shook them out of her head. "I can imagine, Braddy. I can imagine. But hey, I'm at the falls, and if I don't get moving, I'll miss the sunrise."

"Fine. Good. Go." Bradley seemed to sense her need to avoid that subject. For now. "Dinner tonight at Rosie's?"

"Seven sharp. Be there or be…not there." Natalie pushed her driver's side door open and giggled again, loving that she could be a dork with her cousin. He'd never judged her. Never did anything but love and support her, even when she couldn't love or support herself.

"It's a plan. Love ya, Nat."

"Love ya, Braddy." She ended the call and dropped her phone in the front pocket of her backpack, which stocked with water, granola bars, nuts, and a first aid kit.

There was a time when hiking was just an unappealing form of exercise, and the peaks of Dogwood Falls were good for one thing and one thing only…making out with Rod.

But those days were long gone. She enjoyed the physical exertion now. The snapping of twigs and crunching of leaves beneath her feet, the chorus of chirping that filled the forest, and the sensation that with every step she took, she was restoring pieces of her inner self.

The hike was a steady climb. One she was familiar with. An hour later, she arrived at her chosen peak, the highest point at Dogwood Falls. A narrow rock cliff, worn mostly smooth by centuries of rainfall, jutted out straight over the river and stopped just short of entering the massive downpour. Hikers could get just close enough to feel the spray of cascading water, but not without experiencing the alarming reality of being suspended in the sky with nothing to guard them from slipping over the edge.

Natalie was proud of herself for coming here, all alone, to the top of the falls. She'd always had a slight fear of heights, but that was nothing compared to her outright phobia of water. Throughout her recovery, she'd worked diligently to make peace with this force of nature, focusing on the beauty of water instead of its dangers.

She had a rather good reason for her fear. At only eight years old, she'd nearly drowned in the Atlantic Ocean while vacationing with her parents. The first day had been Epcot and funnel cakes, the second day a traumatizing brush with death.

Wandering out in the ocean water by herself, timid and careful, she'd still managed to walk straight toward a sudden drop-off. Her swimming abilities at that age were questionable at best, and she'd only been saved because a fellow tourist farther down the beach had caught sight of her entering the ocean and disappearing in a split second.

He'd sprinted and dove into the water, retrieving her tiny body and bringing her safely back to shore. The catastrophe had barely been avoided.

Her parents, protective and watchful as they almost always were, had missed the entire event. Little Natalie was right there, and then she wasn't.

The idea that she could lose her life in the blink of an eye, even when in the company of the people she trusted to protect her, had left her with nightmares and panic attacks for years. Those had passed for the most part, but the terror of deep water...rivers, oceans, lakes, *all of it*...had followed her right into her twenty-second year of life.

Overcoming the addiction she'd fallen prey to since losing Rod's baby twenty-eight weeks into her pregnancy had opened the door to conquering *all* of the demons in her life, not just the alcohol. Natalie had attacked her fear of water, determined to take back her power.

She was now completely sober and had made great strides in reclaiming the joys of nature she'd experienced as a little girl, before the Florida incident. Though she was much better now, she'd accepted the fact that sobriety and living free of fear were two battles that would more than likely be lifelong.

Addicts didn't just stop being addicts. They stopped feeding their addiction and fought like hell to keep it at bay. Forever.

There was no way she'd ever forget those terrifying moments of struggle and terror in the ocean that day, but as long as she remembered to search for the beauty that was present in water, she'd be okay.

Right now, she stood roughly eight-hundred feet in the air amidst the thunderous roar of the falls, and she wasn't scared.

She *finally* wasn't scared.

Natalie sat down, ready to witness the sunrise and drink in the wonders of nature and freedom. Pleasant tingles along her arms reminded her once again of just how happy she was with life these days.

Sadness threatened to swamp her as the memories came flooding back. Much had been lost. Time with her parents, the love she'd felt for Rod, and the worst...the hardest to reconcile her heart with...the baby.

But she'd survived, recovered, and returned as strong as steel.

In her therapy, she'd learned that it was okay to be sad. That sadness was a reminder of how important someone or something was to you, and tears didn't mean that a person was weak.

She'd also learned that it was okay to be angry too. She allowed that emotion to come and go as she thought of the man who'd so very badly broken her heart and trust.

Rod had loved this very peak. He'd insisted that messing around up here in the sky with the falls booming around them made him feel like an animal. Wild.

Why did you have to turn out to be such a douchebag, Rod? Why?

Never in a million years would she rekindle her relationship with that man, but she had to admit, even now, that there had been a certain enjoyable savagery to those moments with Rod, though she'd certainly never ventured far out on the cliff. All activity had taken place at a very safe and respectable distance from the dangerous edge.

The small distance between her seat and certain death in this moment would have given her seizures back then.

Not all change was bad.

A twig snapped behind her, and she jumped, heart pounding as she turned to scan the trees behind her.

Darkness stared back. The sunrise was in motion, but there wasn't enough light yet to make out much of anything beyond shadows.

Hiking alone in the still-dark hours of the morning, hm? She could almost hear her mom saying the words. *Probably not your best idea ever.*

After half a minute of silence, Natalie's shoulders relaxed, and she laughed at her silliness. She was in the woods. Of course there would be rustling in the trees. Probably just a squirrel or a bunny.

This was an epic moment for her, and she wouldn't lose it to terror of the unknown. She'd lost enough of her life in that manner. Besides, on the slim chance a larger animal was out there, she had mace in her backpack.

She tugged on the navy straps, bringing the bag closer to her in an instinctive moment of awareness. There. Right beside her. Zipper opened and everything. Just in case.

Now, enjoy the damn sunrise!

How could anyone not get sucked into that sky? Sun rays shot across the darkened mountain range in bold golden streaks. The horizon almost appeared to be on fi—

Snap! Snap!

Natalie's fingers clenched around the metal cylinder containing her mace as the rustling grew closer. Too loud for a bunny. Too big too. A tall shadow moved, and she stopped breathing. Definitely not a rabbit. Bear?

Rising to her feet, her hand trembled as she wrestled the switch to the on position. Her mind raced through every bear fact she could recall.

Black bears can be scared off. Loud noises, making yourself look big. Not grizzly bears, though. Loud noises just piss them off more. With them, playing dead often works best. There aren't any grizzly bears here, though, right? Right?

Determination pushed through the fear, silencing the frantic thoughts. Her hand steadied on the mace. She'd spent too much of her life playing dead already. Black bear, grizzly, or Sasquatch, she didn't care. Whatever predator was out there, she'd stand her ground and fight.

The shadow emerged and took shape. Thinned out to reveal a human form. Her frozen lungs thawed as some of her terror subsided.

No claws. No sharp teeth. Just another person. Unexpected? Yes. But probably just another hiker out to enjoy the early morning show. Either way, she could handle herself now. She'd been through too much to—

"Hey, Nat."

The man stepped closer, and her tension drained from her muscles. *Oh, thank god.*

"What are *you* doing here? You nearly scared me half to death. I thought you were a bear for a second."

Natalie dropped the mace back into her bag with an irritated sigh. How on earth had he known she was up here? Bradley never would have told a soul, not that there were many to tell this early in the morning anyway. Had she been followed?

He held up both hands, looking earnest. "I swear to God and all that is holy, I had no idea you'd be up here. What are the freaking odds? I come here sometimes to think. And watch the sunrise, of course." There wasn't even a hint of a lie in the tone, but Natalie felt far from convinced.

She lifted an eyebrow. "It's a pretty damn big coincidence."

The innocent act continued with a small lift of shoulders. "Life's full of 'em. That's what I've learned, and I've learned *a lot.*"

Natalie turned the idea of meeting this exact person at the highest peak of Dogwood Falls so early on a Thursday morning over in her mind. People did do a lot more outdoorsy stuff in the summer months, especially around here. The falls were a huge draw, but so were the campground and hiking trails and horse trails and…

In the end, she mentally shrugged. His presence was unfortunate, maybe, but it was also feasible that the run-in was accidental. The most obnoxious accident ever, but still. Not out of the realm of possibility.

"Fine. Surprise, I'm here," she joked, attempting to cover the awkwardness of the situation with a little dry humor.

This earned her a laugh. "I see that. And what exactly would bring *you* here today?"

Why did the question hit like an accusation? There was hostility in the words that she couldn't quite place or explain. She hadn't done anything wrong.

"Honestly? This just felt like the perfect place to end one chapter of my life and start another." Natalie sat back down and rested her chin on her knees, returning her gaze to the sky. "These falls mean a lot to me."

"Right." Her impromptu guest seemed to relax as well. "I get that. Lots of old times here."

She nodded. "Old times, and hopefully new times as well."

"You know, I feel terrible about everything you've gone through." Genuine affection edged the words. "Losing the baby must have crushed you. Nobody deserves that type of pain. I wish it had worked out differently."

Natalie raised her head and locked eyes with him. "Me too."

"Natalie…this chapter you're about to start…will you be starting it with me?"

The question held another unspoken inquiry, which she answered in a firm voice. "I'm going home to *see my family*." No need to paint an unclear picture here. She was back for one reason only. "I want to be with them again. Reconnect."

A loud sigh of disappointment carried across the bluff.

"You seem different." Intense eyes homed in on her face. "You seem more distant than the Natalie I know."

She knew he didn't understand, so she tried to be as gentle as possible, even though she really wanted to scream. "I think I have good reason to be. I've decided we should cease all contact, okay?" The words fell out of her mouth unplanned, but she stood behind them regardless.

Just let me stare at the falls. Let me be with the sunrise. Go away.

"But we've...the times we've shared." Stunned words from a horrified face. "We've been close, Natalie. We know each other's secrets. You can't seriously mean to just drive into Rutshire and never speak to me again. Come on."

Natalie locked eyes with him. "I mean to do exactly that. We *were* close, but now...I want to reconnect with my family. That is *all* I want, okay?"

"Ole Bradley the councilman one of those beautiful reunions? Did he convince you to do this?" There was no missing the hostility now.

Anger flamed in her chest. "The reasons for my change of heart are none of your concern." Taking stock of the harshness in her own voice, Natalie attempted to level herself. "I'll never have a single bad word to say about you, okay? I'm here for a *fresh* chance at life, and this is the path I've decided to take. I know it's not *your* number one pick, but it's also not your choice."

She refocused on the sunrise, more than mildly perturbed to be partaking of the spectacular show with company she hadn't asked for. But a few deep breaths, and she was back in that mesmerized wonder at the kaleidoscope of colors splaying across the sky.

"I understand, Natalie. I'm going to miss you terribly. Things just won't be the same." Sorrow seeped into his words.

She would have felt bad two years ago. She would have felt bad six months ago. But today was her day. Her emotions didn't belong to anyone else, and she refused to hand them over in the midst of her joy.

However, any moment wasn't too soon for this "coincidental run-in" to end. After a minute or two passed and she still wasn't alone, Natalie decided it didn't matter. The sunrise was beautiful to witness, alone or otherwise, and today was a new start regardless of this unforeseen bump along the road.

She'd endured worse "surprises" in life, after all.

For the next ten minutes or so, she tuned his presence out, drinking in the colorful sky. Once the oranges and pinks faded into clear blue, the time had come to leave. Hoping she wouldn't have an unwanted companion the entire hike back down, she gathered her things and cast a final glance the intruder's way. "Goodbye."

The word sent power surging through her veins. *She* was in charge. Mistakes had been made, but she'd grown from them. This was a new track, stretching out to the proverbial sunset like a—

A hand clamped firmly on her arm, and she stiffened with annoyance. Some people could just not take a hint.

She didn't bother turning around. "Look, I don't mean to be rude, but we're done here. I'm ready to move on—"

Her sentence ended in a shriek as he began dragging her toward the edge of the cliff…toward the heart of the waterfall. "Stop, this isn't funny! What the hell are you doing?" She fought to keep her footing as her hiking boots skidded through the loose dirt.

Instead of replying, his other hand clamped over her mouth.

Icy fear surged through her veins, and for a single instant, Natalie froze. An instant later, her survival instincts erupted.

She kicked, pulled, tried to bite her human gag. She could fight her way out of this. She *would*. She'd always been smaller in stature but fit. Strong.

Or had been...up until the miscarriage. And the alcohol. Now, she was feeble. Her muscles were already tiring out. She needed regeneration. She needed *home*.

The hand disappeared from her mouth, allowing sweet air to rush inside her lungs. The relief sweeping through her was dizzying, making her sway on her feet.

A prank. A terrible, stupid prank. Or else he was trying to scare her into going back.

Once they returned to safe ground, she would rip him a new one. First, she needed to catch her breath.

Before she could, his free hand grabbed her opposite arm and dragged her farther, forcing her perilously close to the edge. The dark blue waters swirled at the bottom of the falls, charging over jagged boulders with a speed that made her stomach plummet and her mouth go dry.

She stood very, very still. Too petrified to twitch a single muscle, let alone fight.

"Please." Calm. She would plead her case in a calm, concise manner, and she would live. The rest would be sorted through later. "Please let me go. I'm not a threat to you. You have my word. Just let me go, and we can both walk away. I'll never tell a soul this happened."

Natalie summoned enough courage to turn her head slowly, locking eyes with the much stronger human who literally held her life in his hands. Surely looking at her would remind him of the affection and bond between them.

The eyes gazing back at her were cold. Hard.

This can't be happening. This isn't going to happen.

"I wish things could have been different, Natalie. I still care about you. I will *always* care about you, but I just can't let you ruin everything. I won't." The emotion was gone now.

No anger, no love, no sorrow...only a robotic emission of words.

Blood rushed through her ears, pounding to the beat of her galloping heart. "No! No. I won't ruin anything. I promise you! You can't—"

Mid-plea, he shoved Natalie backward, flinging her from the peak. Arms flailing, she kicked her feet, but there was nothing beneath them. Nothing but air.

A moment of weightlessness. Of soaring. Gravity took over and she plunged straight down. Wind whistled in her ears as she nosedived into a hell she'd never imagined.

I'm sorry, Brad—

Natalie's head struck rock, and pain exploded in her skull. Icy spray misted her skin, and she drew her last breath to the deafening roar of the waterfall she'd been so excited to experience that morning.

Mercifully, the swift death saved her from the horror of the churning water that swallowed her body, shoving her down into the darkened depths below.

2

A utumn Trent rested her head against the sofa cushion and ran her fingers through Toad's thick fur. From his upside-down position in her lap, the peculiar little Pomeranian mix wriggled and moaned, gazing at her with his snaggle-toothed grin. Some might deem Toad's underbite unattractive, but she didn't care. He was her faithful companion whenever she was home. He always forgave her absences with instant demonstrations of love via face licks and tail wags.

Toad had a lot to forgive as of late.

She scratched the dog's chest. "Sorry, buddy, twenty weeks was a long time to be away. You probably thought I'd deserted you."

When Aiden Parrish first pulled her into a fast-tracked position with his Behavioral Analysis Unit, the Special Supervisory Agent made it clear that if Autumn wanted to become a true FBI agent, attending the training academy was a must. But the idea of traveling to Quantico to fulfill the requirements and the reality of it were two entirely different things. Even now, the fact that she'd completed the course felt a little unreal.

Done. Her training was done, and today marked her first official twenty-four hours as Special Agent Autumn Trent, working with the FBI's BAU out of the Richmond Field Office.

Satisfaction rippled through her body. Special Agent. That title had such an invigorating ring to it. She'd never felt more accomplished, capable, *powerful*…

After earning a Ph.D. in forensic psychology as well as a Juris Doctorate, Autumn had plenty of reasons to be proud of herself before this latest feat. Even so, she'd wanted this job. The title. All the danger and excitement that went with being a federal agent.

As with any of her previous accomplishments, she'd set her sights and climbed until she reached her goal. Now was the time to witness all her work meld together on a career path that she'd fought for, piece by hard-earned piece.

When she'd first arrived home from Quantico last week, she'd taken a few days to tie up loose ends with her old job and get her paperwork in order at the Bureau. Before attending FBI training, Shadley and Latham had been her employer, and she'd contracted out to work with the FBI. That arrangement was done. Mike Shadley was no longer her boss, and his firm wasn't her backup plan.

The FBI was her employer now. Her *only* employer. And being a special agent was her job. Period.

Excitement and nervousness rushed through her body, swirling together to form a potent concoction that made her light-headed and jittery in the best possible way. Autumn had worked her ass off to get here. She was more than ready for a fresh start.

Peach meowed from her lounging spot on the kitchen

counter. The ginger tabby was much less forgiving than Toad, refusing all attempts at cuddling.

Even as Toad stretched across Autumn's lap, exposing his belly and relishing the rubs that followed, Peach narrowed her feline eyes at her owner. The expression on her furry face reeked of the same resentment she'd exhibited since Autumn's return, but now there was an almost human quality in the tabby's gaze too. A malicious gleam.

"Ah, Peachy. Please stop staring at me like you're going to kill me in my sleep."

Autumn chuckled at the thought. Peach would forgive her in time. Probably.

Three swift knocks at her apartment door informed her that Special Agent Winter Black had arrived. This was their first morning run together, and Autumn braced herself for an ass whooping. Unlike her, Winter had been running on a daily basis for years.

Autumn threw open the door with a gusto saved only for her best friend. Twenty weeks away was a long damn time, and they had an insane amount of catching up to do.

Of forgiveness to work through.

And guilt. So much guilt.

Autumn forced a huge smile on her face, and Winter's smile matched her own.

Autumn faltered, though, a gasp coming close to escaping her lips when she took in just how skinny Agent Black was in her shorts and t-shirt. Without her Fed jacket to hide under, Winter appeared bone thin.

Her thigh muscles had all but disappeared, leaving her legs half their old size. Her arms had also decreased in circumference, and her collarbones jutted out beneath the thin, breathable fabric of her workout tee.

It was a shock because five months ago, Winter had been

a healthy size, her body always presenting an impression of fitness and strength.

The glossy black hair that Winter's criminally insane brother had cut short brushed the tops of her shoulders now. No sign of the waxy red streaks Justin had forced upon her remained, but it still made her look so different from the woman from before.

But as Autumn's stomach began to knot with worry, a bad hairdo was the least of her concerns. Justin Black had committed a long list of atrocities against his sister at the start of the New Year. He'd kidnapped her as part of his escape from Virginia State Hospital, the state's only maximum-security treatment program, and left a bloody trail of terror in their wake.

Over the course of the three days and two nights that Justin had held Winter captive, he'd heavily drugged his sister, forced her to murder two innocent people, shot her in the arm, and had been minutes, if not seconds, away from blowing her and dozens of others to pieces via a suicide vest.

The physical wounds were bad enough, but Autumn's apprehension over her friend's recovery had always centered more on the psychological trauma she'd experienced throughout that harrowing forty-eight hours.

It didn't end there.

Even after she'd been rescued from that vest, Winter's every movement had been scrutinized by all of law enforcement and the press for weeks and months.

Paid leave from her job.

The possibility of criminal charges.

Threats of a civil suit from the victims' families.

Though Winter had been found guiltless for the Stewarts' deaths, the media had attempted to tear her apart...up until the press changed their minds and turned Winter into a hero.

That, more than anything, had been what saved the agent from losing her career.

Staring at Winter's bony frame now, Autumn couldn't help but wonder how badly her friend still grappled with the aftermath.

"Ready to do this, Agent Trent?" Winter bounced on the balls of her feet, but her gaze darted around, shifting between the hallway toward the entry door and the awaiting concrete.

Autumn hesitated. Should she call off the run and pull Winter inside for a deeper conversation instead?

What did you expect? She was almost blown up by her brother less than six months ago. Of course she's still working through the aftermath. If the worst outcome is that she lost some weight, she's doing great.

Winter stilled her motion, and her smile started to disappear. "Is something wrong, Special Agent Trent?"

Autumn shrugged off her misgivings and flashed her friend a bright grin before bending to tighten her laces. "I don't think I'm ever going to get used to hearing that." She'd been Dr. Trent for quite a while now.

"You will. Trust me, you will." Winter held the door wide-open and bowed, ushering Autumn through the door like royalty. She couldn't hold the pose for long before they were both cracking up.

See? You worry too much. Winter seems fine. Good, even.

Autumn exited the apartment, and Winter closed the door behind them. They walked toward the sidewalk in a silence that felt comfortable and even more than a little happy.

Reunited, and it feels so good.

Except, now that they were outside, there were other sensations flowing through Autumn that didn't quite fit into the "good" category. Winter wasn't just skinny, she was pale.

And while pale was a typical description for her friend, Winter's extreme level of pallid in July in Virginia caused a warning to ping in Autumn's head.

"So, how the heck was it?" Winter beat her to the first question as they broke into a light jog.

Autumn waved a hand in the air. "A breeze. Add some daily piña colada to that place, and it's basically just a resort."

Winter laughed but quickly returned to her timed breathing. "I do seem to remember a beachfront and cabana boys."

Her reply made Autumn laugh so hard that she stopped to catch her breath. She sure had missed her friend. "Okay. We can't do this *and* run. Catch up time after?"

Winter raised her eyebrows dramatically. "What? I'm sorry, did I just hear you say we should exercise *first*? Did they replace you with an alien? A robot?"

"I'll have you know," Autumn straightened to her full height and puffed out her chest, "I *enjoy* running now. And I've even started doing my Krav Maga again."

Winter propped her hands on her hips, which only enhanced how slim she'd become. "I'm proud of you. Now, put your money where your mouth is and show me just how much you 'enjoy' running."

Without warning, she took off at a sprint. Autumn followed suit.

Ten minutes and a mile and a half later brought them to a city park that Autumn had nicknamed "Turnaround Park." Instead of the touch, turn, and go method she'd been using since returning home, they opted to sit in the grass and stretch so they could catch up.

"You weren't kidding. Got a little oomph in that step now, huh, Trent?" Winter stretched a long, thin arm toward her toes.

Autumn massaged her tight calf muscle, staving off any unforgiving leg cramps. "Told you so. Quantico was no joke.

I almost understand why Chris was so pissed that I hadn't gone yet when the rest of you had."

Special Agent Chris Parker was a fellow member of the Behavioral Analysis Unit and the most vocal voice against Autumn's streamlined entrance to the FBI. Granted, Chris was vocal about almost everything. Smart as he was, the man seemed to specialize in finding the worst in any given situation.

However, twenty weeks of heavy training and a personal understanding of the obstacles every other agent was forced to hurdle before handling cases had given her insight into Parker's complaints.

Quantico wasn't just physically challenging. The mental training and testing were rigorous and exhausting too. From firearms familiarity and marksmanship technique to managing counterterrorism, weapons of mass destruction, and criminal investigations, enormous amounts of information and skills had been crammed into Autumn's brain in a short period of time.

She was much better equipped for the high-stakes cases she'd been privileged to assist with pre-Quantico. Training had provided a framework that would help guide her through difficult on-the-job decisions, taking some of the burden off her overactive heart.

She hoped.

Special Agent Trent was a bit tougher than Dr. Trent. Autumn had sensed the change in herself over the course of her training and tried to embrace the alterations.

Nothing would ever silence her heart. She knew that, and so did anyone familiar with her personality. The tools she'd acquired to temper her emotions were sure to be advantageous in the field, though.

"Parker has issues. I wouldn't give anything he's said to you in the past much thought." Winter's expression hardened. "Chris is concerned with Chris. Not the team. Not the FBI. He lives in Parkerland, and he likes it there."

Her friend's tight jaw and distant stare made Autumn wonder if Winter had been on the receiving end of any of Chris's biting commentary over the last few months. Or worse, if Winter had been made privy to the fact that Chris had pushed the idea—hard—that she'd *willingly* gone with Justin. Helped her brother break out. Murdered civilians of her own free will.

"I can't argue with that." Now that the sun was higher in the sky, the hollows beneath her friend's cheekbones and the dark crevices under her brilliant blue eyes were more evident. "How are you holding up?"

Winter visibly tensed and continued to direct her gaze toward the treetops. "I'm okay. Cyber found the full video of the Stewart murders pretty damn quick. Leave it to Justin to feel the need to post the entire horror show on the dark web. He really wasn't joking about snuff films being his bread and butter."

The clips of videos that Justin had emailed to the press during Winter's captivity had only shown Agent Black breaking the necks of Greg and Andrea Stewart, along with a shot of their deceased teenager lying on the floor of a blood-splattered RV. There had been no audio, and the footage had sent the media into a frenzy. Reporters instantly pushed the narrative that Winter had partnered up with her serial killer brother.

The truth became clearer when Justin strapped her with explosives and left her stranded in downtown Washington, D.C., in the middle of a crowd of thousands there to attend a vigil. She wasn't his accomplice, but she'd nearly been his firework display show.

That evidence coupled with the unedited video feed of what actually happened to the Stewarts—Justin forced

Winter to kill the parents in order to save their two young children—had kept Winter clear from murder charges. However, Autumn was sure that nothing would protect her friend from the self-deprecation that followed taking the lives of two innocent human beings, even if she'd done it to save them from the torture Justin would have put them through had she resisted.

To make matters worse, Justin had killed one of the children anyway. He shot Nicole Stewart in the head right there in the RV, despite leading Winter to believe she could save the thirteen-year-old.

The younger sibling, Timothy Stewart, was still missing. Justin had abducted the eight-year-old, the two of them seeming to disappear into thin air.

Without a doubt, Winter felt responsible for failing to save Timothy from her disturbed brother, as well as for her inability to prevent Nicole's death. Not that any of that was her fault. Her brother had kept his older sister a prisoner by use of physical restraints, drugs, and emotional duress.

"Your name would have been cleared one way or the other, Winter. You're a good agent. A good *person*." Autumn ached for her friend. The position she'd been shoved into by her brother was impossible.

"Hey," Winter lifted a shoulder, "at least I got a vacation out of the mess. The leave of absence they stuck me with during the official Bureau investigation was more than enough time for my arm to recover." She tapped her bicep in the spot Justin had shot her. "And Osbourne's had me doing desk work ever since to make sure I was 'fully rested and able to return to the field.' Good as new and ready to get the hell back out there."

Max Osbourne was the Special Agent in Charge of the Richmond Violent Crimes Task Force and Winter's technical boss. If SAC Osbourne wanted her at a desk, she'd be at a desk. But Autumn wondered if Supervisory Special Agent Aiden Parrish hadn't also had a hand in extending Winter's recovery period so long.

Autumn trusted Aiden. If he thought Winter wasn't ready for action, he almost certainly had damn good reason to believe so. What had Aiden witnessed in Winter all these months while Autumn was away? The physical changes were obvious and concerning enough by themselves.

"You're sure you're ready?" Autumn attempted to mask the gravity of her apprehension. Her friend didn't appear to be sleeping or even eating properly.

Winter met her gaze, a touch of fragility showing in her eyes for the first time that day. "How is anyone ever ready to do anything after an experience like that? I mean, I've gone through all the psych panels. I've checked every box required to prove my competency. You know, after proving my innocence." She laughed, but the harsh sound was mirthless.

"You had nothing to prove there, Winter. You *were* innocent. You *are* innocent." Autumn wanted to hug her friend but hesitated, unsure if Winter would feel violated by her touch.

A hug from Autumn Trent wasn't just a hug. Not since she was ten years old and her abusive drunk of a father caused her a traumatic brain injury with a blow to the skull on a table corner. Emergency brain surgery had been required to save her, and she'd awoken with a startling new "ability" of sorts. The simple touch of her finger to another person's skin sent currents of their emotions streaming through Autumn's core.

Winter was aware of the "sixth sense" that Autumn possessed and would therefore understand that an embrace would reveal her emotional cards. All of them.

Autumn wasn't sure such an intrusion was welcome quite yet.

"Innocence is relative to viewpoint." Winter's throat bobbed as she swallowed. "I'm a federal agent who killed two good people. The Stewarts were a nice family. Greg and Andrea were the kind of parents any kid would be lucky to have. They helped Justin and me out for no reason at all other than just blindly caring for two strangers' welfare."

Agent Black's head jerked around to glance over her shoulder as though a bee had stung her. She turned back a few seconds later like nothing had happened. The movement seemed sporadic at best, but Autumn brushed it off. They were sitting in the grass on a hot July morning in Virginia. Bugs were everywhere.

"Their innocence doesn't cancel out yours." Autumn could barely contain the urge to clutch Winter close. She'd known her friend would struggle to forgive herself, but witnessing the raw truth right before her eyes was heart-wrenching.

Winter pulled her knees to her chest and rested her forehead on them. "Maybe I shouldn't even be an agent anymore. Being 'cleared' doesn't change anything. The guilt...the guilt is just eating away at my insides. I don't know how to make that stop. I'm not sure I deserve for that to *ever* stop." Her hands shook as she plowed her fingers through her silky black hair.

Stress. It's the stress. That's why she's so thin and pale and shaky. She's overwhelmed.

Each successive time Autumn reassured herself that her friend was okay, she believed it a little less. "Anyone who went through what you did would struggle not to blame themselves. That doesn't mean you have to give up your entire career. You have to allow yourself more time."

"I made a list," Winter raised her head, folded her arms across her knees, and placed her chin on them, "of what I would do if I weren't an agent. Private investigator was number one. I thought about that before this ever happened. I'd be a good PI." She nodded, as if to convince herself.

"You'd be an amazing PI. You'd be an amazing at a lot of other things too. But it's too soon to throw in the towel, Winter. I really believe that." Five months wasn't close to long enough to process the ordeal that Winter had experienced.

Winter lowered her hand and ripped up a few blades of grass, mindlessly twisting them in her fingers. "Time doesn't even feel real anymore. There's no future date when this will just…go away. I know what you're saying. It'll get easier, but easier isn't enough. I want to feel free again. I want to feel the way I did before Justin took me that night."

A few tears spilled onto her cheeks, and Autumn's heart twisted. In a flash, she grabbed Winter and pulled her into a firm embrace. Beneath her hands, her friend was even frailer than she appeared. Her shoulder blades protruded like wings from her back.

The torrent of emotions hit next, flooding Autumn with tsunami force. Noxious waves of confusion, anger, and guilt rushed into her body. The pain flowing from her friend was beyond sadness…beyond regret. Winter was *drenched* in despair.

While struggling to catch her breath, Autumn sensed another feeling mixed in with the others. Something else…a yearning of some kind. Winter needed…

Winter abruptly pulled away. "Sorry. I know you're getting an onslaught of crap out of me right now. No reason for both of us to feel this way." She brushed the tears from her cheeks and stood.

Autumn rose from the grass too, vehemently shaking her head. "That's not true at all. If you're hurting, I'm hurting. I'm going to help you through this. As a friend and even as a therapist if you want. I know you already have one, but I'm here for you in all the ways. *All of them.*"

"You're a good friend." Winter was already heading away from the park. "Now, let's find out if your tough newbie butt can make it back as fast as we got here!" She tapped a button on her watch and took off.

Autumn chased after her. The conversation had gone too far, hit too deep for a casual Monday morning run. Autumn understood the hesitancy, but she also hoped that Winter's walls weren't up this high at all times. Part of getting through this tragedy was dependent upon letting the pain out.

Facing the monster, so to speak.

There was no going around that step.

They ran without speaking, their silence only broken by the thudding of their shoes on cement, giving Autumn time to regret her offer to assist with Winter's therapy. In hindsight, she felt ridiculous. She was one of the reasons Justin Black had escaped and pulled Winter through the depths of hell to begin with.

She could have kept the two Black siblings separate, yet she hadn't.

That mistake had allowed Justin's breakout as well as Winter's traumatization. Furthermore, it didn't speak highly of Autumn's abilities. Why on earth would Winter want her as a counselor of any sort?

Guilt weighed heavy on Autumn's head, making the last part of the jog even harder. When they neared her apartment building, they slowed and walked the last short distance. Both of them were slick with sweat as they reentered her home and began stretching while the quiet continued to hover. Winter stared at her, seemed to debate within herself for a moment, and then opened her mouth to speak—

Buzzing from both their phones broke the silence first.

Autumn grabbed her cell from the coffee table. "Aiden."

"Me too." Winter swiped at her screen.

"A briefing…" Autumn began.

Winter checked her watch. "In one hour. Crap. I gotta get home and shower. See you there?" She walked toward the door, wasting no time.

Autumn nodded and waved her goodbye. "See you there." She tried not to notice how violently Winter's hand shook as she grabbed for the door handle and let herself out.

Stress. Stress does that to people.

The reassurance wasn't any more comforting this time around.

Kicking herself into high gear, Autumn headed straight for her own shower. The bathroom mirror reflected her red hair and bright green eyes back to her. Everyone recognized her by now at the field office, whether they were in the BAU or not, but she wanted to appear…*extra* professional on her first day as an official agent.

Whatever that meant.

Rushing around her apartment and preparing for the day, thoughts of her second first impression were quickly replaced by other much more troubling issues.

Winter was not okay. Not even close. And while Autumn hadn't expected to return to Richmond and find her best friend completely past the traumatic experience she'd endured, she hadn't expected to be met with this bony, distressed ghost of Winter Black, either.

Special Agent Noah Dalton, another member of the FBI's Richmond Violent Crimes Task Force and Winter's live-in boyfriend, had to be concerned as well. There was no way in hell he was okay with his girlfriend's current state.

She'd find a way to talk to him privately at the office. Aiden too, if possible. They'd have the insight she needed to round out her approach on how to address Winter's plight.

Everything was going to be okay.

Except for that little boy Justin stole.

She flinched, pausing with one leg in her dress pants and one leg out. Timothy Stewart, assuming he was still alive, was more than likely living a worse nightmare than any of them could ever imagine. Justin wasn't only a serial killer. He'd been *raised* by a serial killer. His blood relative, Douglas Kilroy. The Preacher.

Kilroy had kidnapped Justin one night when he was only six, murdering the little boy's and Winter's parents on his way out. He'd intended to kill thirteen-year-old Winter too, but the bash on her head hadn't finished the job. Just like Autumn, Winter had woken up from emergency brain surgery with an odd new ability.

Their unusual sixth senses were one of the major bonds between Autumn and Winter. No one else could fully understand the blessing and the curse of such "gifts."

Autumn finished pulling on her pants and buttoned them, remembering how she and Winter had also bonded over their stories of sibling loss. Like Winter, Autumn had a sibling she'd been parted from suddenly. After her parents were deemed unfit to keep children in their custody, her little sister, Sarah, had gone to live with her biological father while Autumn went into the foster care system.

Autumn was determined that some way, somehow, she would find Sarah, in spite of her thwarted efforts up to this point. She would never stop searching.

As she buttoned up her crisp white blouse, her gaze caught on a bright pink sticky note on her dresser.

A.L. Press Charges

A.L.

Adam Latham.

An image of the revolting man flashed through her mind, and she tried not to gag.

Just one more thing to take care of. No big deal.

She grabbed a brush to tame her tresses, reminding herself that, like it or not, tending to the Adam Latham matter was her responsibility.

Adam was one of her former bosses at Shadley and Latham, but after he'd assaulted Autumn while "mentoring" her on a case, Mike Shadley had severed all ties with the man. Mike was a good guy, so Autumn had given him time to change his firm's name before taking legal action.

Now that the name change was official, Autumn was ready to press the assault charges. Not taking action after her boss came on to her in a hotel room and then slapped her for turning him down was doing a disservice to women everywhere.

Men like that had to be exposed.

This week. I'll call Mike this week and let him know my plans.

Autumn grabbed her purse, planted a kiss on Toad's nose, and attempted to give pissy Peach a scratch behind the ears. The scratch was denied, but Autumn had expected as much. She was nearly out the door before she remembered to feed her little creatures first.

She filled water bowls, poured kibble, and dished out salmon pâté with impressive speed. At the rate Toad and Peach were eating, she'd have felt like a complete jerk forgetting to feed their hungry little mouths.

Recognition struck after she stepped out of the apartment and secured the front door.

Hungry. That's the word I was searching for earlier.

Autumn stood on the porch without moving. The thought had come from nowhere, but she was able to connect the wires immediately.

Before Agent Black had pulled away from Autumn's hug in the park, she'd intuited that Winter longed for something. But now, Autumn understood the need was more of a hunger sensation. Something Winter yearned for so badly that it was consuming her.

There were so many things that Winter might want, but remembering the way she'd teared up at the park and said, *"I want to feel free again. I want to feel the way I did before Justin took me that night,"* struck Autumn as monumental.

More than anything, Autumn was certain that bruised and broken Winter Black wanted redemption.

She strode toward her car, determined she would help Winter find just that. Her dear friend didn't have to fight alone. Autumn would—

"What in the…"

Autumn's jaw dropped. She stopped in front of her car before circling it slowly. All four tires were slashed, and the sides were keyed. But the hood…

She squinted against the sunlight and read the inscription scratched into the metal with complete bafflement.

"Your Greatest Fan."

3

A iden Parrish tapped his phone screen and alerted all the agents to the upcoming meeting before stepping into the conference room where SAC Max Osbourne and Associate Deputy Director Cassidy Ramirez were waiting. The three had been getting together for early Monday morning meetings on a regular basis to update each other on pertinent information as well as divide the teams for cases.

Today's main topic of discussion was obvious. Autumn Trent would be serving her first day as an official agent, and Winter Black would be returning to the field after months of desk work and recuperation.

Aiden set his briefcase on the table and settled into one of the many plastic chairs. "Cassidy. Max." He gave each a courteous nod and received the same.

"Agent Black." Cassidy wasted no time in broaching the subject that was of utmost concern to them all. "She's set to return to the field today, but I would like to know your personal opinion on the state of her well-being. There's talk amongst the office that she isn't perhaps as recovered as we would hope at this point."

Aiden didn't want to shade Winter's ability to move past her ordeal with Justin, but Aiden wasn't willing to lie outright about anything or anyone. He chose his words with care. "She's been cleared by her medical doctor, the Bureau shrink, and the Office of Professional Responsibility. She's still seeing a therapist on a bi-weekly basis, and in private conversation, Agent Black has also assured me that she is fine. Ready."

It was a big fat lie.

Winter didn't appear to be "fine." On the contrary, she was beginning to remind him of a war refugee. Weight loss that he'd assumed was temporary had only increased. The dark circles under her eyes, which they all experienced from time to time given the stresses of their jobs, were deep. Constant.

Plus, the behavior quirks. On more than one occasion, he'd witnessed Winter look over her shoulder with sudden, frantic urgency. After the trauma of her abduction, there was every likelihood that Agent Black was internally set to "high alert" at all times.

Everything he'd observed in her, physically and otherwise, was explainable. Less than half a year ago, she'd endured a life-changing event. Winter Black would never be the exact same person she was before Justin had taken her. Aiden didn't expect that.

But he had expected *some* improvement. Five and a half months should have been long enough for signs that she was moving in the right direction. To Aiden's careful eye, though, she appeared to be anything but recovered.

However, she'd dutifully checked all the boxes and jumped through the numerous hoops that the Bureau had set before her. Winter had and was still doing everything she was supposed to do.

Her innocence was a proven fact, and highly trained

medical professionals had deemed her fit for action. There was nothing in writing keeping Agent Black from a full return to duty.

Even the media.

Though the press had tried to chew her up and spit her out in the beginning, they'd turned an about-face and supported Winter when the families of the Stewarts refused to toss Winter under the bus for the loss of Greg, Andrea, and Nicole.

Uneasiness slithered down his spine. Good or bad, Aiden didn't give a damn what anyone else said. He knew Winter too well. He'd been an agent on the case of the Black family's tragedy and had first met Winter when she was a devastated thirteen-year-old girl, faced with the murder of her parents and the disappearance of her brother.

Aiden had watched her thrive and also hit rock bottoms in the past. If he had to give an opinion on where she stood today behind that tough exterior armor she'd always worn, he would mark her down as closer to the latter. Not *at* rock bottom, but damn close.

The timing of sending Autumn away to Quantico had been unfortunate. Whatever bond the two women shared was strong, and the support of Agent Trent could only have helped as Winter waded through her recovery.

Plus, Autumn may have been able to provide insight into Winter's mental health that would have enabled him to know how to proceed with Agent Black. How best to help her.

Autumn would have kicked my ass for even asking.

Aiden leaned back in his chair and swallowed a sigh. That last part couldn't be more true. Snitching on her friend was something he knew all too well his redheaded colleague would refuse to do. Such a request and conversation would have quickly gone south.

"We all know there's a difference between proving you

are indeed well, and actually *being* well." Cassidy folded her hands together and locked her dark eyes on Aiden. "Is she truly ready, Agent Parrish, to be in the field on an active case? I don't want you to regurgitate facts I've already read on paper. What's your honest opinion?"

Aiden squared his gaze with the ADD's. "She's not one hundred percent, Cassidy, but she's doing everything she's supposed to do, and I feel that, over time, she'll work through it."

Max cleared his throat. "I'm not so sure. Winter's tough as nails, no doubt. But Justin Black is the one person in this world who could get in her head and really do some damage. I think he did exactly that. The harm he caused may very well be irreversible."

Both Max and Cassidy stared at Aiden. As the Special Agent in Charge of the Violent Crimes Division, Max was technically Winter's boss, but all three of them knew that Aiden was the closest to Agent Black. The pressure of the call fell on Aiden's shoulders, and he found the weight to be an impossible conundrum.

That unsettled sensation crawled down his spine again. Like worms, sliding just underneath the skin. He didn't think she was ready. At least not in the sense of the word that his colleagues wanted her to be. Winter was struggling. Fighting.

That was just it. She was fighting, and as long as she didn't give up...

His jaw set. Leaving her alone, keeping her at that desk any longer...those decisions could backfire worse than letting her return to the job.

"I want to bring her along for this mission." He hoped he looked more certain than he felt. "I'll keep an eye on her. She may benefit from being out in the field. She thrives on that action, and if it's too much for her, that fact will be made clear rather expediently."

"Your call, Agent Parrish." Max leaned toward him, his gray eyes stern. "But that call comes with accepting all responsibility should Agent Black come to any harm."

Aiden tensed, indignation rising in his chest. "I won't allow that to happen, SAC Osbourne." The nerve of the man was irritating, considering the depth of responsibility Aiden already felt for Winter. To insinuate that negligence of any kind would happen under *his* watch was ludicrous.

"You're right. You won't." Max's warning was clear.

Aiden turned to Cassidy. "I'd prefer to have Agent Trent on my team for this case as well. This will be her first outing as a trained federal agent, and as the person who brought her into the Bureau, I'd like to observe her performance after going through Quantico."

Neither Cassidy nor Max seemed to have an issue with this request.

"Agent Black and Agent Trent are very close." Aiden seized the opportunity to remind them. "That could prove beneficial to them both this first case back."

Cassidy raised her eyebrows. "Is this even a real case?"

It was a good question.

"Not sure yet. Our presence has been requested by a city councilman in Beechum, Virginia. Initially, we're going to identify whether or not the FBI's presence is warranted."

"That sounds like a decent plan, Agent Parrish." Cassidy offered him a straight-faced nod. "I agree that keeping Black and Trent together is a wise move for now. But Max is right. The responsibility, as well as the consequences, will fall on your shoulders."

Aiden's chest clenched with simultaneous triumph and concern. "Of course."

"You can take Agent Parker with you as well." The corners of Max's mouth twitched. "I have no need for him this week."

Aiden nearly groaned out loud but managed to keep the sound inside his mouth. "And I do?"

"He's a part of *your* unit, Parrish." Max grabbed his coffee mug and drained the contents, probably to hide a grin.

Ass. There was no arguing with the SAC's statement, though, as much as Aiden wished otherwise. Lately, he'd started to realize that Chris Parker's skillset did *not* balance out his shit attitude and quarrelsome tendencies. Every agent came with a unique set of character flaws because all humans did.

Except Parker's flaws were extreme. The troublesome agent seemed to gun for Aiden's last nerve every time they worked together, which was often. Too often.

"Okay, gentlemen, let's focus, shall we?" Cassidy appeared to be fighting off a giant eye roll. "There's something else I wanted to discuss. We have a leak somewhere in the Bureau."

Max snorted, grinning at her as though she were an oblivious rookie. "Every agency in the damn world has leaks. Also, grass is green, and the sky is blue, in case you haven't heard."

Cassidy Ramirez was far from being an FBI newbie. She'd climbed her way to her position over the course of three decades. While she hadn't gone completely gray like Max, she did have several shimmers of silver gracing her jet-black hair.

"Insightful as always, Agent Osbourne." Cassidy shook her head. "This is a *big* leak. Someone who is privy to top-secret information, which narrows the suspect list down quite a bit. I'd like for you to keep your eyes and ears on alert until we find the hole."

Aiden raised an eyebrow. "And then what?"

Cassidy gazed from Max to Aiden and back again, her expression dark. "We plug it."

The meeting adjourned, and Aiden headed to the breakroom to grab a fresh coffee before the next briefing. As he was pouring the brew into his mug, his phone buzzed. He set the pot down and pulled the device from his suit jacket.

Autumn.

One swipe opened the text and revealed two pictures of Autumn's Camry. All four tires had been slashed. Another text followed. *I'm going to call AAA.*

Aiden hadn't yet processed the information before another picture came through. This picture showed a scratched message on the hood.

Your Greatest Fan

He rubbed his neck as he attempted to make heads or tails of the damage. *Your Greatest Fan.* What in the living hell did that mean?

No ideas came to mind, so he gave up and returned the call.

"Good morning, Agent Parrish." Autumn sounded flustered. "I hope your day is going better than mine."

"Don't call AAA," he ordered. "I'll have some techs come out and search the car to make sure there's nothing more sinister involved here than some key damage. They can bring it in, and we'll do a search for evidence and prints too."

Autumn cleared her throat. "You really think it's something to be taken that seriously?"

Aiden hesitated. Car vandalism wasn't uncommon. Sometimes the act was random, other times a bit more purposeful. But rarely did acts of that nature escalate into dangerous situations, as far as statistics went.

Yet, Dr. Trent seemed to defy the most concrete of probabilities on a regular basis. The truth was, he did think something more serious might be transpiring. That gut instinct, coupled with an undeniable desire to protect the woman, urged him to err on the side of caution.

He massaged his neck again, frowning. On the other

hand, he hated to worry her. Autumn had traveled a rough road before leaving for Quantico. Nearly being suffocated to death by Albert Rice, then coming so close to losing Winter along Justin Black's gory path to freedom. Today was supposed to mark a fresh start for Agent Trent.

Popping that bubble hadn't been a part of his expected itinerary.

"Wait until your car has been claimed and call an Uber." He sidestepped her question. "Get here as soon as possible. I'll hold the meeting off until you arrive."

"Okay."

As soon as Autumn ended the call, he sped out the break-room door toward Cyber to ensure the proper assistance was dispatched.

Aiden strode through the Virginia Field Office with one main thought barreling through his mind. A thought he'd experienced so frequently since meeting Autumn Trent that it almost seemed natural at this point.

How much danger is she in?

Accompanying that question was another one that also revolved around Autumn. Though much simpler, the second query induced a deeper, more personal anxiety than the first. An odd, panicky sensation that roiled his stomach and made him want to turn and run in the opposite direction.

Utterly absurd.

He called himself out as he crossed the remainder of the distance to the section that hosted Cyber. Supervisory Special Agent Aiden Parrish never fled from bad guys of any kind, but when it came to a woman by the name of Autumn Trent? He was apparently too chicken to man up and stand his ground.

That second question tortured him off and on for the rest of the morning.

When are you going to tell her how you truly feel?

4

S pecial Agent Mia Logan arrived early to the Richmond Field Office for the meeting SSA Parrish had called, as was her habit. On her way to the BAU conference room, she ran into Aiden. Her boss's usually impassive brow was creased with worry as he rushed past with an abrupt, "The meeting will be a little late," shot in her direction.

She tracked his progress down the hall before shrugging and heading into the conference room. The delay didn't bother her in the slightest. There was always more paper-work and research to be done in this line of work. No agent was ever "caught up."

Mia took a seat at the long, rectangular table and opened her laptop, but after only a few clicks, she decided to grab a water from the vending machine. No one passed her in the hall this time, and the breakroom was likewise empty. On her solitary walk back to the conference room, Mia began to wonder if an apocalypse had happened, and she simply hadn't been informed.

Once again, she shrugged off the oddity, determined to

enjoy the unexpected change of pace. Quiet was a welcome surprise, even if the gift did come complete with zombies.

She checked her phone as she sat, and her sense of peace shattered with that one look. A missed call from Sloan Grant.

Lovely.

A bitter taste filled Mia's mouth. Sloan was an agent in the counterterrorism unit of the Richmond Field Office. She was also the individual who had diffused the bomb strapped to Winter Black at the Washington, D.C. vigil. On Aiden's orders, Mia had made the phone call to bring Sloan and the bomb squad in.

That day was the first time she and Sloan had spoken in three years. Mia hoped another three years would pass—if not thirty or three hundred—before they ever spoke again.

Why is she calling me now?

Mia let her phone go to voicemail and was pleased when no new alerts dinged from her screen. Even listening to Sloan's voice in a message would be...painful. Like shoving a hot poker into an old wound until it opened up and bled again.

Maybe she needs help. Maybe something is wrong.

Worry fluttered inside her, but only for a second. Sloan's problems weren't any of Mia's concern. If the call was work emergency-related, Sloan wouldn't be calling her. She'd contact Aiden instead. And if the reason for her intrusion—Mia couldn't frame the attempt at contact as anything else—was *not* work-related, then Mia didn't care to know what Sloan wanted at all.

Mia twisted the cap off the water bottle and took a long gulp. Normally, she'd do anything for anyone, but Sloan Grant wasn't anyone. Sloan was the reason Mia's brother was six feet underground.

Back here again, huh?

Mia wished that she weren't, but she was. For three years,

she'd fought off the idea that Sloan had more or less killed Ned. And just when she'd reached a point of peace—of believing that she had forgiven Sloan regardless of the fact that she couldn't possibly *forget*—the bomb situation had occurred.

She still recalled the rage that roared through her veins like fire when Sloan had answered the bomb squad call. A fury that, up to then, Mia hadn't even known she'd possessed.

What she did realize, in that moment, was that she hadn't forgiven Sloan.

More than that. Mia didn't want to forgive her.

She leaned back in the chair as the events came tumbling back. Ned and Sloan had dated for two solid years before her brother had proposed. Instead of giving a yes or no, Sloan had admitted to cheating on Ned in a moment of "weakness." A predictable break-up fight had ensued, and Ned had taken off in his car.

He first returned to his home and called Mia. The two were close and always had been. Ned had been frantic that day, though. More upset than she'd ever heard him. Nothing she'd said calmed her brother, and despite her begging him to stay put, he'd taken off driving again.

No one had been able to reach him after that. He wouldn't answer his cell. None of his friends heard from him. He was just *gone*, and Mia had only been able to sit and wait with her family.

And hope. And pray.

It had all been futile.

Instead of blowing off some steam and returning home, Ned crashed his car and died. Her brother, her best friend, her constant companion since the day she was born, ceased to exist.

Just. Like. That.

And it was all Sloan's fault. Sloan had injured her brother in such a grievous manner that he'd lost himself in a hurricane of emotion that led to his untimely death.

Mia squeezed her eyes shut, blocking out the harsh glare of the conference room lights as loss suctioned the joy from her soul.

When the day of Ned's funeral had arrived, Mia had wanted to stay home. Her brother wasn't in that coffin. He was elsewhere.

But of course, she'd gone. With one arm wrapped around her sobbing mother, they'd walked through the graveyard toward the spot that Ned's body was to be lowered into. Her father had trailed behind them. Mia had instinctively known that he wanted them to believe he was protecting them... helping to guard and maintain their distance from the other mourners. Giving them privacy.

In reality, he'd been sobbing just as hard and was trying to hide his breakdown from her mother. Mia had hugged her mom close to her side to prevent her from turning and witnessing her husband fall apart.

Of course he was falling apart. He had every reason. And just as she'd always tried to protect Ned, Mia felt it her duty to shield her mother as well as allow her father his moment.

The moment she'd discovered that Sloan was already at the burial site, a flaming knife had cut through her body from head to toe, igniting a hatred that was all-consuming. She'd assisted in seating her mother, waited for her father to join them, and then turned on her heel and marched toward the woman who'd essentially killed her beloved brother.

The conversation that followed...

Mia put a hand over her eyes, willing the film reel to stop and knowing full well that the memories would never cease. Not now. Not ever.

"You shouldn't be here." Mia spoke the words in a calm, quiet manner, but she knew they hit Sloan Grant like a slew of knives.

Sloan whipped her head toward Mia. She was sobbing. Her long strawberry-blonde hair was soaked from holding her umbrella with wobbly hands. The rain didn't matter to any of them. "Of course I should be here. I loved him, Mia." Her voice cracked, and a fresh torrent of tears slid down her cheeks.

"Yes. You loved him. You loved him so much that you sent him straight to his grave." Mia had never said anything so cruel to anyone in her entire life. She was surprised to note that she didn't feel even a pang of guilt for doing so to Sloan now.

Sloan took in a sharp breath. "Please don't say that." There was a pleading note in her words that matched the beseeching expression on her face.

Mia squared her shoulders, glanced at the casket holding her brother's cold, dead body, and returned her gaze to Sloan. "You killed him. You killed him, and that will be the truth every day for the rest of your life, whether anyone besides me says it or not."

She walked back to her parents and sat, smoothing her damp black skirt with great care while Sloan fled the cemetery.

Mia twisted a piece of her dark wavy hair tight around her finger, staving off tears that burned her eyes like smoke. As much as she didn't want to be the kind of person who couldn't let their anger go, here she was. Unable and unwilling to leave the past behind.

Maybe their brief contact surrounding the D.C. incident had rekindled some deep need within Sloan to make things "right." To earn Mia's forgiveness.

All the interaction had done for Mia was remind her of what Sloan had stolen from her.

Never. I will never forgive you. You will never make this right. You will think about my brother's face and what you did to him every day until the day you—

Chris Parker burst into the room, throwing his hands up

in exasperation. "Well, here we go again, bowing down at the throne of Autumn Trent. So damn good to have her back." He slammed his large body into a chair across from Mia.

"I wasn't aware of any bowing." Mia pulled herself from her own hateful reverie and took in the bitter twist of Chris's lips.

Dear god. If you don't get past this, you're gonna end up just like him. Do you want to end up like Chris Parker? Do you want to turn into an angry asshole for the rest of your life?

"The meeting is being put off because of Autumn." Chris stared at her as though she were the dumbest human being he'd ever met in his life. "How could you possibly be sitting in *this* room waiting for *this* meeting and not know that?"

She wanted to roll her dark eyes so hard that they flew out of her head and knocked Chris down like a bowling pin, but she kept her expression even. Dealing with Parker was often comparable to handling a small child. He wanted a reaction, so she rarely gave him one.

"I hadn't been informed of the specific reason for the delay. Is Autumn okay?" She didn't have to fake concern. Mia liked Autumn a lot, and she'd been anticipating her return from Quantico.

"She has *car troubles*." Chris slammed a fist down on the tabletop. "Do you think I could walk into work late because of freaking car troubles? I'd be reprimanded on the spot. Assigned extra paperwork. Forced to mop the damn floors or something."

Mia fought the grin playing at her lips. The idea of Chris Parker swabbing the halls of the field office was on the better side of appealing. Especially if he used his wild, floofy hair as the mop. "I'm sure that's not true, Chris. And I'm positive that if Aiden delayed the entire briefing, he had good reason."

Chris dropped his head backward and groaned. "Jesus,

Mia. The 'good reason' is Aiden Parrish has his head shoved so far up Autumn Trent's a—"

"Do you know anything about this new case?" Mia interjected, hoping to distract Chris by giving him a chance to prove how knowledgeable and "ahead of the game" he was. She also harbored a mild concern that flopping his head around in such a manner would muss that meticulously styled blond hair of his, and she'd be forced to listen to him complain about *that* on top of everything else.

Chris narrowed his eyes. "I don't know the first detail about this case, but I bet you *Autumn* probably has the entire score on a pretty piece of laminated stationery."

Well, that backfired, Agent Logan. You only reminded him that he knows nothing.

She studied Parker's face. He'd flushed deep red, and small sweat beads clung to his forehead. He wasn't just annoyed with Autumn. He despised her.

"Tell me why." She closed her laptop and gave Chris her full attention.

He stared back in confusion. "Why what?"

Mia clasped her hands together. "Why do you hate Autumn Trent so much? What did she ever do to you, personally?"

His lips pressed tightly together while his jaw flexed repeatedly. "Let's just say I'm not her greatest fan, okay? She's a damn teacher's pet, and it's deplorable. Disgusting."

"So," Mia tilted her head, "you don't think Autumn works her ass off for the Bureau? Whether Aiden favors her or not, she puts in the effort and the time. Plus, she brings a lot to the team that was lacking before."

"Lacking, my ass." Chris muttered the words as he pulled his laptop from his briefcase. "We were fine before. We'll be fine after."

This piqued her interest. "After what?"

Noah and Winter's voices carried down the hallway, and Chris went silent, which was more than okay with Mia. There would be something soon enough to set him off again. Parker always had a rant to share. He was the proverbial old man on the block sitting on a porch rocker and yelling at kids for walking through his grass.

Unfortunately, he wasn't done yet. Chris leaned across the table and whispered in what Mia assumed was his version of quiet. "After somebody eventually figures out how messed up and wrong Parrish's favoritism is. All it takes is the right person in the right position of power to get rid of one of them. Or both of them, if we're really lucky."

Mia shook her head. "They aren't doing anything wrong, Chris. People don't get in trouble for *not* breaking any rules. Even if they wanted to date openly," she nodded toward the hallway, where a verifiable agent couple was approaching the room, "there would be no reprimand."

His expression darkened by considerable degrees. "No, but there are always consequences for treating other people like pieces of human shit." He turned away, ignoring her and focusing on his laptop screen.

She'd let the matter go for now, but there was something in Chris's voice that niggled at Mia's gut. He'd always spoken ill of Autumn, yet today there was a malevolence in his tone that she hadn't noted before.

Consequences. That was the term he'd used, and the word set her internal alarms blaring.

What consequences, Chris?

5

Special Agent Noah Dalton kept a discrete eye on Winter Black as she strode into the Richmond Field Office. She appeared confident, and as always, beautiful. As she walked down the hall, her silky black hair bounced around her shoulders, finally growing out from when her twisted brother had chopped it all off and streaked some of the strands bright red.

Not that Noah cared about her hair. Short, long, red, or bald, it didn't matter. Winter would always be stunning to him, regardless of her hairstyle.

The dark strands were still a bit damp now, and he breathed a sigh of relief. That morning at the apartment they shared, she'd told him to go ahead without her, claiming that she needed to take a quick shower after her run with Autumn. At the time, an alarm bell had rung in his head. He'd worried that Winter had lied just to get him out the door.

The worry was ridiculous. Since Winter's rescue from the explosive vest her bastard of a brother had strapped to her chest, their relationship had been very raw and open. There hadn't been any point in pretending things were okay after her ordeal.

How could they be okay? The horror of being kidnapped by a murder-happy brother who'd forced her to kill had traumatized her, while Noah was a wreck from coming so close to losing her forever. They'd agreed to be the total disasters that they were...together...and wade through the aftermath hand in hand.

As far as he could tell, Winter had kept her end of that deal. She held nothing back. He'd been informed of every detail of her nightmare spent with Justin numerous times, whether in calm discussion or through her tears.

And he'd told her all about what life had been like on the other side of the coin. Not knowing if she was dead or alive or if he would ever see her again either way.

Noah had been by her side through every step of her recovery. He tended to her gunshot wound, provided a steel base of moral support through her interviews with the Bureau's internal affairs office, and accompanied her whenever she invited him to her therapy appointments.

He held her at night when she woke screaming, or crying, or shaking. He kissed away her fears and guilt, absorbing her inner turmoil and offering warmth and love as a healing balm for those invisible wounds.

Time had passed, and progress was made. Noah was proud of her...loved her more than he ever had. But something was wrong.

He studied her as she approached, analyzing her stride, her posture, her expression. Desperate to get to the bottom of why his inner radar refused to shut up. Nothing jumped out at him, but still...

Off. Something was off. He couldn't put a finger on the matter. On paper, in theory, Winter was doing well. She'd spent over five months on the path of recovery and had walked steadily on that course like a trooper.

He'd witnessed her do so.

And still, he was convinced that she wasn't okay. All these months of transparency couldn't shut up the small voice in his mind that told him every single day, *"She's keeping something from you."*

They lived together. Slept together. Worked out of the same field office five days a week. They'd spent weekends at her grandparents. Winter talked to him just as she always had. No awkward periods of silence or questionable dark clouds hanging over her head.

But she wasn't okay. And he couldn't put a finger on the reason why.

She walked straight to him, stretched to her tiptoes, and planted a quick kiss on his cheek. "You just couldn't get started without me, huh?" A grin and a playful wink followed the tease.

Noah smiled down at her. "Nothin's the same without you, darlin'."

There was a bit of color in her cheeks today. Her morning run with Autumn, as well as quality time with her "bestie," must have been beneficial to whatever still ailed her.

Good. Let's stay on this route. Fill you back up, emotionally and physically. Relieve whatever is still eating away at you.

Those cheekbones were still too prominent, though, and her body too slight beneath the bulky FBI jacket. Winter's weight loss troubled him, but they'd discussed the matter at length. Her medical doctor as well as her therapist had assured him that after such a stressful event, there was no cause for alarm. He hadn't exactly agreed, as Winter had slowly turned into a toothpick version of her former self.

She *was* eating, though. He saw her. She was sleeping. He laid awake next to her and counted her breaths at night. She dutifully took anything her doctors had prescribed, and she exercised on a regular basis.

What choice did he have but to grudgingly believe the medical professionals? This was a natural side effect of a traumatic event. It would pass.

When? When will it pass? How much slimmer can she possibly get before she disappears altogether?

Today was Winter's first official day back, meaning she wasn't strapped to her desk anymore. She could get back out in the field and do what she loved.

Half of him hoped the return would be good for her, while the other half wasn't convinced that she was ready. But the call wasn't his to make.

Autumn burst through the doors behind them, and his eyes widened. On her first day as an official federal agent, he'd expected her to bounce into the room with a big smile, buzzing with energy. Instead, her frazzled expression and drooping shoulders gave off the impression that she'd just trudged through a lower level of Hades.

Physically, though, Autumn looked the strongest he'd ever seen her. Fit. Toned. Still slender, but with a quiet air about her that promised she could kick some ass if need be.

Noah thought back to his days at Quantico. No one left that place the same as they had entered. Not physically and not mentally. He looked forward to hearing about her experiences at the academy and comparing war stories.

Autumn spotted them, and a strained smile emerged on her face. He didn't buy it, and neither did Winter, who approached her friend with open concern.

"What happened?" Winter laid a hand on Autumn's arm.

Agent Trent pulled her phone from her tote bag, frowning and shaking her head. "This." She swiped at her screen and held the phone up for Winter and Noah to view.

The first three images explained her dilemma. The right-side tires of her Camry were slashed. The left-side tires of her Camry were slashed. And on the hood, keyed into the paint, were the words, *Your Greatest Fan.*

Noah grabbed her phone to make a closer inspection. "What the hell? When did this happen?"

"It wasn't like that when I left this morning." Winter's voice held a bit of her old feisty growl, and he found it oddly comforting.

Autumn lifted her shoulders and dropped them in frustration. "Between the time you left and the time it took me to get ready for work. That's the window."

"I'm not sure the perpetrator understands what 'fan' means. What an asshole." Noah zoomed in on the words.

Winter shook her head. "Oh, they understood. This wasn't some random kids with too much time on their hands. Whoever did that did it for a reason."

"Aiden had some guys come and bring it in for the techs to check out." Autumn reclaimed her phone and dropped the device back into her bag. "They're checking the CCTV on my street, and I know he has them scouring the car for fingerprints and any other signs of…whatever the hell might have happened. Hopefully, we'll find out something soon."

"I wonder if this was Justin's work?" Winter surprised Noah with her candor.

Of course, he'd had the same immediate thought, but after considering the possibility for a moment, he'd shot the idea down. "If Justin wanted to reveal to us that he was in our area, I'm pretty certain he would have done far more damage than that. I think it's safe to say that petty crime isn't really his style."

Winter snorted. "More likely, he'd have left a decapitated body on the hood. Or worse."

Both Noah and Autumn went still. An awkward few seconds passed before Noah managed a weak chuckle.

Autumn summoned a flimsy smile, her green eyes hawk-like as they surveyed Winter's face. The lines between humor and Justin Black were blurry at best. Mostly, though, Noah didn't find much to laugh about when it came to the little psychopath who'd almost killed his girlfriend.

Winter glanced from Autumn to Noah and rolled her eyes. "Guys, I still have a sense of humor. I'm not dead."

Noah flinched at her cavalier statement. No, she wasn't dead, but she'd come close. Too close. Winter missed his reaction, though, because she'd whipped her head around to peer over her shoulder.

He followed her gaze and frowned. Nothing there. He wasn't sure if she was pissed at them or just tired, but she seemed to space out there for a moment.

"I do agree that it wasn't Justin." Autumn's voice appeared to act like a catalyst. Winter jumped and turned back around. "This was someone else. I just hope that someone was stupid enough to pull this dumb stunt off right in front of the street camera."

Noah was still frowning at his girlfriend's odd behavior when her phone rang in her jacket pocket. She pulled the device out and held up a finger. "I'll be right back. Gotta take this."

As she walked down the hallway, Noah and Autumn both stared at her retreating back with similar worried expressions.

Once Winter disappeared from view, Autumn turned to him, seeming to push her concern down by force. "How are you doing? We haven't had a chance to talk since I've been back."

"I'm good. I'm great." Noah hoped she was convinced, as there wasn't anything actually wrong with life right now. Not that he could put a finger on, anyway. "Just happy that Winter is with us and doing...better."

Autumn's smile faltered. "I still feel so awful for not picking up just how severe the warning signs were with Justin. I wish I had—"

"Hey," Noah placed his hand on her arm, "we've done this already. No one is to blame. You're not a mind reader." He'd gone off on Autumn when Winter first disappeared, and he still cringed when he remembered the attack.

As an initial reaction to the shock of losing his girlfriend, he'd become volatile and lashed out. Poor Autumn had been on the receiving end of that fury. He'd held her responsible for not blocking Winter's visits to Justin. For not keeping Agent Black safe from her maniac brother...like Autumn had any control over the state-run facility.

Deep down, though, the person he'd blamed was himself. He'd known how dangerous Justin was. He should have stopped her from going to that hospital. Winter had assured him that she wouldn't have listened to anyone and had even proven that sentiment by *not listening to anyone*.

What happened with Justin was unavoidable, she'd told him. Noah had disagreed.

Besides himself, there was one other person who deserved the blame. The mere thought of the man made Noah's hands curl into fists. "You only met with Justin a handful of times, Autumn. If anyone should have done something, it's Philip Baldwin. He was the one treating that little bastard, and if his damn ego hadn't been so out of control, there would have been video surveillance long before Justin had the chance to escape."

While Justin was a patient at Virginia State Hospital, the medical director had only allowed audio surveillance in the facility for his own personal reasons. It had taken Baldwin a near brush with death and Autumn almost suffocating to death for the prick to rethink his idiotic practices.

Flames rose in Noah's chest. His fists tightened. He hated

Philip Baldwin. Autumn insisted that the psychiatrist was a changed man...that he'd become aware of the error of his ways. She'd also shared that Philip had his own inner demons that affected his poor decision-making.

Noah didn't care. As far as he was concerned, the man's redeeming qualities were slim to none.

"In his notes, Philip seemed to be leaning in that direction." Autumn referred to Justin's patient files that she and the team had pored over, hunting for clues to the Black siblings' whereabouts. "Given a little more time, I believe he would have transferred Justin to the maximum lockdown area of the hospital and revoked all visitations. But he was doing his job, Noah. He was evaluating Justin. That's a process."

Noah tried not to grind his teeth. He didn't understand why Autumn always felt the need to stick up for Baldwin. The doctor had been a complete dick to her when they first met—hateful even—but something about their experience as co-captives of a vengeful hospital employee had bonded the two. Autumn now held a soft spot for Baldwin that was annoying as hell. The man didn't deserve an ounce of her compassion.

"A process that could have been sped up." Noah grumbled his reply, stopping when Autumn's face paled. The memories of her and Philip Baldwin's kidnapping still unsettled her, and they probably always would.

Winter rejoined them, and Autumn's expression brightened like magic.

"Whatcha talking about?" Winter put her hands on her hips, attempting nonchalance.

Noah racked his brain, which had suddenly gone blank, while Autumn stuttered. "Um...uh...um..."

Right. Improv was a definite "no" as far as their alternate career options went.

"Okay. This is going to stop now." Winter wagged a finger first at Autumn and then at Noah. "You guys aren't going to do this. Don't tiptoe around me. I'm back. That means *I am back*. Now, what were you talking about?"

"Justin." Noah mumbled the admission like a naughty kindergartener.

Winter made an exasperated noise and raised her hands. "So why can't I talk about that? I know more about Justin than any of you. I know the truth. Kilroy turned him into a demonized killing machine, and he's a lost damn cause. We need to find him before he has a chance to do worse."

Noah studied his girlfriend's face. She spoke with a convincing matter-of-fact tone that he wanted to believe was a good sign. If her damn cheekbones weren't jutting out so noticeably, he'd almost concede that she was doing spectacular considering what her brother had put her through.

"Are there any clues so far as to Justin's whereabouts?" Autumn queried. "I'm so out of the loop. It's driving me nuts."

For the second time within minutes, Noah gave her arm a comforting pat. "You'll be so caught up in a few days that you'll wish you were back at Quantico." He paused when both women laughed. "But to the best of my knowledge, there's no news yet. Not even a hint."

As he relayed the lack of intel on Justin's whereabouts, anxiety wormed through his gut. He knew the powers that be would track Justin down soon, or at least, he hoped they would. But time was ticking away. Every day that passed was another day young Tim Stewart was at the mercy of The Preacher's protégé. Noah could only imagine what the child had been through…and what current horrors would continue to be inflicted on him until a rescue team arrived.

"This way, Agents," Aiden called to them from down the hall. The briefing was about to start.

Noah followed Winter through the building, noting how she straightened her posture and threw her shoulders back before entering the conference room. She marched straight to the table, taking a seat near the whiteboard where Aiden would most likely be standing.

As he pulled out the chair beside her, Noah caught Chris glaring at Autumn like Satan incarnate had just walked into the room. His back stiffened.

What is that little fucker's problem?

Chris met Noah's glare, and his expression immediately turned neutral before he focused on his laptop. Noah stared at the agent for another second or two before shaking his head and turning away.

Whatever Agent Parker's problem was, he needed to get over it and fast. They'd all been through way too much for that type of childish pettiness.

Then again, if the little shit insisted on acting up, Noah welcomed the opportunity to punch Chris's face if need be.

Beneath the table, Noah cracked his knuckles, one by one, as he waited for the meeting to begin.

6

Aiden positioned his iPad on the podium near the whiteboard. As his team settled in and prepared for the briefing, he scanned their faces, pausing on Autumn.

She sat tall in the chair, radiating strength and confidence. Good. He hadn't been sure what to expect upon her return from Quantico. There was a general change that occurred at the academy…a toughening of sorts that seemed to be universal for the FBI graduates. Autumn being the open-hearted individual that she was, he hadn't been able to imagine what that alteration would look like on her.

And sure, maybe he'd been a little worried that the experience would dim the unique qualities that made Autumn who she was.

While he'd understood and accepted the necessity of Quantico, not just for her future as an agent but also for her safety in the field, a quiet and mildly selfish part of him had hoped she wouldn't change *too* much.

He didn't sense that she was any less of the Autumn Trent than she'd been before Quantico, though. She was strength-ened—that was visible to the naked eye—but not *hardened*. The warm rush of relief this observation triggered also made his neck flush with embarrassment.

As SSA and Autumn's superior, he shouldn't worry one way or the other about such things. But he did, and thus far, berating himself over his feelings for Autumn hadn't changed them.

He adjusted the iPad as Autumn crossed her arms and stared at the tabletop, her brow furrowing. She was obviously frustrated, or maybe worried. He didn't blame her.

More than likely, her mood wouldn't improve once he informed her that the camera facing the parking lot of her apartment building had been knocked off track, pointing at the sky. If the device hadn't been tampered with, her car would have been in the direct line of view.

Techs were still combing her car for prints, but the fact that she'd been targeted was clear. And the forethought the vandal had put into the act made him increasingly uneasy. This wasn't a case of neighborhood kids messing around with their attractive redheaded neighbor.

Something more sinister was in motion here, and the revelation rubbed his already raw nerves. Autumn had *just* returned. The idea that she might already be in some type of danger was infuriating. Their friendship had kicked off with Aiden guarding her from a hitman, for god's sake.

Give the woman a damn break.

Despite the worries circling through his head, Aiden kept his composure. A damn tornado could be whirling his brain cells around, and he'd still refuse to show the slightest hint of disturbance to his team.

Or to anyone else, for that matter.

"Okay, Agents. Let's get started. First and foremost, why don't we all welcome *Agent* Trent to the team?" The words had barely left his mouth before an uproar of clapping and a few hoots and hollers broke out.

Aiden bit back a sigh and waited them out. Children. They were all basically just children with badges.

In the midst of all the hoopla, Chris Parker was the sole holdout, slouching down and appearing less than pleased with the merriment and enthusiasm. He held his hands out to one side, giving a humorless golf clap.

Aiden narrowed his eyes and took a mental note.

Next case, he goes with Max. Let Osbourne take a turn dealing with this asshole.

He considered kicking off the meeting with a briefing on Autumn's car sabotage but decided to wait until he'd heard back from the lab. Best to share the information when he knew the full extent of what there was to share.

They had enough to discuss with the details of their new case. Or...*possible* new case.

Aiden cleared his throat, cutting the last of the celebration off. "Here's what we know so far." He tapped his iPad and the whiteboard suspended from the northern wall came to life, showing a serene image of a waterfall.

"Beautiful..." Mia murmured. A series of similar comments filled the room.

Aiden shook his head. "Not so beautiful if you're jumping into them from the highest peak." He tapped his screen, and the picture changed to a map of a small town. "This is a map of Dogwood Falls just outside of Beechum in Beechum County, Virginia. Multiple trails lead to different levels of the waterfall."

"I'm somewhat familiar with those falls." Winter tapped a disturbingly bony finger on the table. "There's a campground near them as well. Horse trails. Brings in a lot of tourists."

Aiden forced himself not to focus on Agent Black's physical condition...for the moment. He'd circle back to the matter later.

"Four days ago, an anonymous phone call was placed to 911 by a man who claimed to have witnessed a woman jump from the highest peak straight into the falls. This woman," Aiden tapped his screen, and a picture of a young blonde female with bright blue eyes replaced the waterfall image, "was Natalie Garland. Twenty-two years old at the time of death. Her body was recovered by local authorities within an hour of the call."

"And the caller?" Noah narrowed his eyes, already following the track that Aiden and local law enforcement were considering.

"The call was placed from a phone which has since been disconnected. Natalie's family members are claiming that her death is linked to a local cult. This was the call received by emergency services." Aiden pressed a button to play the recorded audio stored on his phone.

"911. What's your emergency?"

Heavy breathing and a raspy voice that was impossible to distinguish as male or female replied. *"I just...I just saw a lady jump from the top of Dogwood Falls. The top. I think...I think she was trying to kill herself."*

"That's Dogwood Falls in Beechum County, correct? Can I get your name, please?"

The line went dead.

"Well, that's suspicious as hell." There wasn't an ounce of overt sadness in Autumn's voice over the tragedy, which Aiden silently applauded.

Keep that heart in check. But also keep that heart, Agent Trent.

Chris leaned back in his chair, his blond floof helmet defying gravity by not budging an inch. "We need to find that caller."

Aiden nodded, relieved and annoyed to find himself

agreeing with Agent Parker for once. "Natalie's loved ones insist she wasn't suicidal. In addition, there's been a recent series of 'suicides' in Beechum County over the last few months. A number of those who have died, supposedly by their own hand, has been linked to the same local cult. Furthermore, they all have friends or family who claim they showed no signs of mental distress prior to taking their own lives."

Noah folded his arms across his chest. "Law enforcement thinks they're drinking the Kool-Aid?"

"Precisely." Aiden searched for the next image, wishing Sun were present to work her usual magic with the computer. He could manage, but that woman had a super-human ability to bend the cyber world to her command.

As if reading his mind, Autumn lifted a finger. "Where's Sun, Bree, and Miguel?" She smiled. "I still have Bree's wedding gift. I can't believe I missed the big event."

Mia tapped her phone. "I have tons of pictures I'll share with you later."

While a few of the agents discussed Bree and Shelby's wedding, Aiden hoped Autumn wouldn't ask where the three agents were again. As it were, Special Agent Sun Ming was working hard beside Bree Stafford and Miguel Vasquez to track down Justin Black's elusive, evil ass. That case wouldn't be dropped until it was over, and it wouldn't be over until Justin was either barred into a prison cell or dead.

Aiden no longer cared which way that psychopath's fate played out.

He gave his screen a light tap to turn the conversation back to the subject at hand. The image changed to one of a large, church-like structure surrounded by smaller buildings that appeared to be part of a complex. "Harmony House."

Chris snorted. "Are you serious? That looks like every

other super-church in the entire country. Not very insidious if you ask me."

Aiden gritted his teeth and homed in on Chris. "I agree. The building itself appears harmless, but we are not being asked to investigate based on appearances. Local law enforcement has requested our presence based on the deaths of numerous individuals who can all be connected to that 'not very insidious' facility. The petition is valid, so we will go."

"You said several suicides." Autumn leaned forward, studying the establishment. "Why would law enforcement wait to call in the Feds until after so many individuals had died?"

"They decided there was no reason to raise alarm," Aiden explained, "because each suicide followed tragic and therefore understandable triggers. One individual had just experienced a bad breakup, another young man had lost his job, and so on and so forth."

Autumn arched an eyebrow. "And Natalie? What triggered her?"

Aiden sighed, recalling the information he'd been given about the young woman. There was no end to the sad stories in this damn world. "She was a recovering alcoholic. Started drinking after she lost a pregnancy. Her suicide is what got the ball rolling. Her cousin, Bradley Garland, is a city councilman in Rutshire, a town just west of Beechum County. He's good friends with the Beechum County councilman, Steve Newman, who made the call to us."

"Bradley doesn't believe Natalie killed herself, and Steve knew that the body count was getting a little out of hand to be a coincidence." Autumn shared her conclusion while scribbling something down on a notepad.

Pride warmed Aiden's chest. Autumn couldn't possibly know how different her demeanor now was. Her confidence and professionalism, while always commendable before Quantico, were now exemplary. "Yes, Newman made the call as a favor to Bradley."

"Let me get this straight." Chris's voice held a familiar note of complaint. "A city councilman from BFE asks us to come sniff around a cult after a few *very explainable* suicides take place, and we're just gonna drop everything and go? That's a blatant waste of the FBI's time and money."

There had to be a parallel universe where Chris Parker wasn't the living, breathing, talking, walking, *dictionary definition* of a pain in the ass. According to scientific theory, anyway. Still, Aiden couldn't imagine such a world no matter how hard he tried.

"Agent Parker, you need to learn to trust your leaders." Aiden's enunciation grew clipped as his patience wore thin. "No, we wouldn't be going solely based on Newman's request. But there is more to consider, and the Federal Bureau of Investigation has been considering it for the last two years. The Harmony House cult was already on our radar for suspicions of money laundering. We will be taking full advantage of this opportunity to dig."

Noah held up a hand. "Has anyone considered that perhaps this was just a tragic accident? Maybe she didn't jump. Maybe she fell. I mean, it sucks, and that explanation certainly won't bring her back or erase her family's loss, but people *do* fall from cliffs and bluffs. Even expert hikers."

"Fair question, Agent Dalton." Aiden pressed his iPad, and the whiteboard went blank. "The M.E. found bruising on Natalie's upper arms that appeared to be grab marks."

"You think there's something else going on. There's more to her story." Winter stared at him with vivid blue eyes that only enhanced the unnatural lack of color in the rest of her face.

"I think we need to find out." Had Winter been sleeping

or eating anything at all? Surely Noah would have raised holy hell if he thought she'd developed some type of disorder.

Dalton hadn't said a word.

"Bradley Garland," Aiden continued the briefing, forcing his concern for Winter into silence for the time being, "had spoken to his cousin just that morning before she went hiking. He insists she was in a good headspace. Sounding positive and optimistic."

A sober expression overtook Autumn's pretty features. "I hate to say it, but Natalie could have been putting up a front for her cousin. Especially if she was that close to ending everything. Family is complicated."

Winter snort-laughed, and the two friends chuckled for a moment. Aiden took it as a good mental sign that Agent Black had recovered her sense of humor. Further evidence to support that she wasn't gone but was actively clawing her way back out of the hellhole Justin had sunk her into.

"So is grief." Mia spoke up for the first time in the meeting. Despite her silence, Aiden wasn't surprised that Agent Logan hadn't missed a beat. "Natalie could have been ready to commit suicide and then changed her mind and then changed it back again. It's impossible to know what she was thinking. But the grab marks concern me. We need to find that caller."

Murmurs of agreement filled the air.

"Beechum is only an hour and a half from Richmond, give or take. We'll be driving. You all have two hours to prepare. We may or may not be gone for a night or two or more. Pack accordingly." Aiden slid the iPad into his briefcase and waited while his team filed out of the conference room.

Harmony House. Sounds like a damn resort for washed-up hippies.

If he'd learned anything throughout the stretch of his

career, though, it was that almost nothing in this world, not people or places or circumstances, were ever as straightforward as they seemed.

Harmony was a blissful term. A *bright* term.

But even the most dazzling light was capable of casting a shadow.

7

I ran as fast as my legs would take me, but I knew I could never move quickly enough. Danger, destruction, and death were behind me. They wanted to embrace me. Pull me back into their fold.

No one outran Death. Not even Jesus Christ.

There would be no resurrection for me. I was aware that once my earthly body gave out, I'd be done. I'd spent my life walking hand in hand with darkness. I would have to pay my dues.

My eternal dues.

There was a price for everything. I had known that then, and I knew it still.

My lungs burned. My legs trembled with fatigue. I couldn't keep running much longer. I didn't even want to.

"Swallow me!" I screamed as my shadow was overtaken and devoured by a much more formidable force.

I peered ahead, aware that the attempt to flee was in vain. This rock beneath my feet was narrowing into a pointed cliff. I reached the edge and stared down at the utter blackness. A vast abyss of never-ending night.

As I balanced on that precipice, terror gripped me with sharp, icy claws. Jump or stand still. It didn't matter. I'd invited the dark to be my companion long ago, and now the inky void surrounded me. I had always understood this day would come...in time.

Chest heaving, I turned my back to the fathomless depths. God would not forsake me. He would enfold me in His loving embrace and save me from this hell.

I held my arms out, welcoming the cross, gasping as the nails stabbed electric pain through my palms. Crucified. I was being crucified. Warm blood trickled from my torn flesh, but I didn't care. No physical injury or pain could rival my spiritual wounds. I was being forsaken, and when this was done, I would be forgotten.

With my arms stretched taut and my blood draining drip by drip, a faceless wraith approached me. He placed a bare-boned finger on my forehead and drew a perfect circle on my skin. Before I could pull away, he pushed.

Wind ripped at my face and clothes, and terror consumed me as I plunged downward into that great void. I waited for the inevitable impact that would break me into pieces. No hope for survival. Only free-falling blind until I crashed into oblivion.

The phantom's voice boomed from above. "There's no end for you. You will scream and cry and suffer. You will keep falling and falling and falling, and you will beg for this to end. You will beg..."

I jolted awake in the battered, threadbare recliner. I hadn't meant to fall asleep, and doing so certainly wasn't a wise idea considering I was still in the middle of operations.

I could nap after this was done. After the work was finished.

My eyes ached, and I rubbed them with my balled-up fists. They burned worse because of the motion, and my frustration mounted. Doing what was right, what was holy, was a task not meant for the masses.

But I could withstand. There were scales to balance. Candles to light to offset the darkness.

Each step along this path...each tiny action would help save them.

For every flame I snuffed, dozens more would burn bright.

I wrinkled my nose at the reek of body odor and mold mixed with the burnt vinegar stench of heroin. I'd be extra happy when this particular holy task was complete, though. If only to spare my sinuses.

Kenneth moaned on the bed beside me. I sat up straight, reached for his eyelid, and pushed upward. His pupils had constricted into such tiny dots that the gray of his irises was nearly all I could find.

"You're doing great, Kenneth," I whispered, patting his arm but taking great care to avoid the track marks.

Kenneth Wilder was my prisoner. He just didn't comprehend that fact quite yet. Considering the top-grade heroin I'd been dosing him with every few hours, there was a strong possibility that the man would never fully grasp the reality of his dire situation.

Overdose was a tricky line to walk. Kenneth needed to die, and he absolutely had to die of a heroin overdose, but spacing out his injections was paramount to convincing the medical examiner that Kenneth's passing was a suicide.

There would be no question, once I was done, that poor Mr. Wilder had fallen off the wagon and gone on a mighty bender. His last hurrah.

Regret plucked at my heart as I patted Kenneth's shoulder. I didn't enjoy this particular death. Not because of his lost potential or the way his eyes would eventually roll back in his head or how much he might stink and rot before anyone found his corpse, but because, in the scheme of things, none of that mattered. I didn't want to kill him because he was my only chess partner.

Chess players were slim pickings these days. The game of kings and queens was becoming a lost art.

Kenneth was the last person on earth I'd expected to find a competitor in, but that was the nice thing about people. They sometimes surprised me in good ways.

Most of the time, they didn't.

Kenneth's eyes fluttered open. Or at least semi-open. He scanned the room as though he were exploring a glorious kaleidoscope of colors.

We were in the shittiest motel left standing on the outskirts of Beechum. Locals liked to refer to it as a sort of "charming antique." I was pretty sure the true story was that no one wanted to bother deconstructing the place.

That was okay. Nature and time would take care of that eventually.

The walls were rotted with age. The "carpeted" floor was mostly bare cement. There was no air-conditioning and only one window, which I'd kept closed out of necessity. Open wouldn't have been any better. The July heat was dreadful and had only intensified the fetid smell.

One window, one chair, one bed, one sink, one shit-crusted toilet to piss in...and an impressive supply of heroin for my good friend Kenneth, who had finally found my face amongst the wonders of his surroundings.

"Hey." He gave me a lazy half-smile. "What happened?"

Oh, dear Kenneth. That would be quite the long story, and you wouldn't remember any of it anyway, even if you were still alive tomorrow.

He wouldn't be.

Kenneth giggled, having registered my odd attire. I was sporting plastic gloves with a matching cap and protective gown.

"Is it Halloween already? I thought it was...I thought it

was…" Kenneth didn't remember what he thought anything was. I doubted he cared either, considering he was sky-high.

You will beg for this to end. You will beg…

I shook the memory off. There was no time to relive the dream, and I understood the meaning already anyway. I was damned. The things I had done were very, very bad. Many would be helped by the consequences of what I'd accomplished, but I would pay all the same.

My crucifixion day was coming.

"Relax, Kenneth. Ssshhh…" I put a finger to my lips. "It's not Halloween, but this *is* a special day of the year."

Kenneth raised his eyebrows and gave me the same droopy grin. "It is?"

"Yes." I smiled back at him. "Today, I'm going to release you."

I'd confused him. He was processing and reprocessing my words, his lips mouthing each syllable. Poor bastard.

"I overheard you talking to your sister on the phone yesterday, Kenneth." I re-tucked the sheet that was draped over his body tight under the mattress. "I'm having a super hard time understanding why you would want to talk to any of your family after they all turned their backs on you. And all over a few fights."

He blinked in a slow, subconscious movement. "They didn't…they didn't want me around. The assault charge… they didn't want me around."

"But that charge got dropped, didn't it?" I shouldn't have needed to remind him, but my heart overflowed with genuine pity for the drugged-up fool.

He vigorously nodded. "Dropped. It was dropped."

"Exactly. They knew that, Kenneth, but they still rejected you. Didn't that hurt? Didn't that just kill you inside?" I laid my hand on his, as I'd done the day we first met.

His eyes teared up. I'd forgotten to bring any tissues, but

that wouldn't matter soon. His fingers shook as he squeezed my hand. "She said...my sister said I could come back. If I stayed out of trouble, stayed on the straight and narrow... that's what she said. She said I could come back. I wanna go back. I wanna go back *now*."

Soon, he'd realize he was a hostage, and then the struggling would begin. I didn't intend to let things progress that far. It was easier for both of us to avoid that type of ruckus. "You already were walking the straight and narrow path. You were walking it with me. Wasn't that good enough?"

Kenneth pointed clumsily at my chest. "You. *You* took me out for drinks. You said we should celebrate my reunion. My reunion with my family. Why would you do that? You know I'm...you know I'm..."

"An addict." I sighed deeply, unable to fathom his inability to understand. "You're an addict, Kenneth, and you could have told me no. Why didn't you just tell me no?" I studied him, mildly interested in his excuse.

His brow furrowed. "I don't know. I don't know why."

Talk about anticlimactic. That was a horrible reason.

"Well, I know why." I squeezed his hand the way he had squeezed mine. Affectionately. "You thought I was supporting your return home, but I was really just showing you that you'll never be ready to go home. You'll always be an addict. You'll keep messing up."

Kenneth started to fidget a bit in the bed. He was having the first inklings of his predicament. "Help me up. Help me outta this bed."

"I can't do that." I stood and grabbed a fresh needle from my backpack. "We're not done partying yet."

He licked his lips and stared at the syringe like the needle contained liquid gold. And for him, I supposed it did.

I'd gotten him drunk enough at the bar that any normal human would have passed out cold, but Kenneth had hung in there like a champ. When I drove him here, he hadn't been alarmed. He knew about this place. Nice little shit-shack motel to party in.

All the local addicts were familiar with these rooms.

And he'd been way too messed up to ask questions.

The first dose of heroin was all he'd needed to lose any last bit of awareness that could cause problems for me. I didn't even have to tie him up.

No bindings. No gags.

His addiction served as both.

That was good. That was very good. No ties meant no marks, and no marks made his impending suicide much more believable.

"Be still, Kenneth." I issued the order as I tied the tourniquet around his arm. He obeyed, but I could sense his panic coming alive. His legs moved restlessly beneath the sheet, and his entire body began to quiver.

I'd cut it close waiting so long for this dose, but the toxic build-up was paramount to the story of his demise.

He sniffled. He was going to cry. I certainly hadn't meant for things to get that dramatic. "I wanna go home. I wanna talk to my sister. I wanna talk to Yvette. Please."

His begging pissed me off. "Talking to Yvette was a mistake. Calling her was the *wrong call*. Do you understand? It was the wrong call. Your sister doesn't have your best interests at heart." My voice was getting too loud, so I gave myself a few moments to calm down before going on. "She would have turned you out again the second you messed up. And you know you'd mess up eventually."

He seemed to ponder that statement. "You're right. I'm an addict. She wouldn't ever love me. Not really." He swiped a trembling hand across his eyes. "I wanna go back. Let's go back. I wanna go back to the fold. I can't be alone again...I can't."

The regret stirred again in my chest. This was the part that sucked. Of course I'd love to drive Kenneth back right this moment and pull out the ole chessboard just like old times. But I couldn't.

"Kenneth," I leaned closer to him, "I wish that could happen, but you broke the trust. All I can offer you now is a peaceful rest. A release."

He squirmed again, attempting to sit up. I plopped myself on his stomach. Between my body weight and the sheet that he didn't realize was holding him down, he wasn't going anywhere.

And he didn't *want* to go anywhere. Not really. He stared at the needle, wetting his lips while I brought it to his vein. Visibly scared but desperate, *desperate* for the hit.

His end was fitting. Kenneth would die while doing what he loved most in this world. He would die *from* doing what he loved most in this world.

And he deserved to. There was no way around that. Not now.

"I really wish you hadn't fallen off the wagon, Kenneth." I put a hand to my chest. "It hurts me inside. I'm sure you hate yourself right now, don't you?"

Kenneth was full-on crying now, both tears and snot streaming down his face. I exhaled, feeling more than a little awkward. Under normal circumstances, I'd hug him. Comfort him. That seemed like a weird thing to do when you were mid-process of killing someone.

"It's your fault," he whispered.

In those few words, I lost the need to comfort the bastard. "My fault? It's *my fault*, Kenneth? It's my fault that you drank yourself into oblivion and offered your vein up like a damn sacrificial lamb? You had a *good life*. You had a good life, yet you were going to turn your back on me and everyone else."

Kenneth shook his head. His eyes were wide, and he'd

stopped sniveling. He understood now. He wasn't leaving this room.

Not alive, anyway.

"Please let me go home. *Please.*"

I held up the needle to give him one last good look. "*This is your home, Kenneth. This is the home you chose over all the rest. Here's your housewarming present, bud." I smiled at him and slid the needle smoothly into his vein, injecting what I knew was a lethal amount of heroin into his greedy body.

He stared at me, and I stared back as pleasantly as I knew how. One blink. Two blinks...

His body sagged, and that was it. No more blinks for Kenneth Wilder.

I gave the room a good visual scan. Between my gloves and hat and gown, I wasn't worried about leaving any DNA behind. I hadn't so much as sneezed in this room.

Kenneth's eyes remained open, and the needle was still plunged deep into his vein.

I shook my head. This was one of the saddest things I'd ever contemplated. Why couldn't someone have just helped the poor guy out? That was all he'd needed.

That's what they'd say when they found him. Shaking their heads as they ruled his death an overdose. Wondering why someone hadn't lent him a hand before he took himself out.

I stood over his still body and pressed my hands together. "Lord, please accept Kenneth Wilder back into your fold and forgive me for this sin." I put my finger on his forehead, which was disturbingly still warm, and drew an invisible circle.

Task complete, I left the room and closed the door behind me. A quick shimmy out of my protective gear set me free, and I shoved the garments into a grocery bag before walking to my car and driving away.

I couldn't help but smile when I thought of the will that Kenneth had signed just a few months back. He'd given the substantial inheritance that his parents had left him over to a local charity. Of course, that money only transferred if and when Kenneth died.

His sister wouldn't like this at all.

But if Yvette knew what was good for her, she'd get the hell over it real damn fast.

8

Autumn took in her surroundings at the quaint Beechum City Hall. While crafted in the same brick and mortar style as every other official government building in existence, the facility was a fraction of the size that most bona fide *city* halls were.

The team had arrived at noon sharp, not a moment after Aiden had promised Councilman Steve Newman they would be there. The general plan was to meet in the councilman's office, but stuffing six Feds into that cramped room was an unappealing option for everyone.

Steve instead led them down an ancient linoleum-floored hallway and into an unused conference room, which was, at best, twice the size of his office. He introduced two of the three individuals who were already present and waiting. "Agents, this is Beechum County Sheriff Winnie Frank and Deputy Simon King."

Deputy King displayed a welcoming smile on a youthful, clean-shaven face, but Sheriff Frank gave a mere nod of her head. The gray that had overtaken most of her once brunette hair told Autumn she was a seasoned professional, while the cold stare from her brown eyes warned that she had no tolerance for bullshit.

Chris probably should have waited outside.

"Pleased to meet you, Sheriff. I'm Supervisory Special Agent Aiden Parrish." Aiden extended a hand, and Winnie grabbed it, giving a single shake. Autumn was certain the woman was less than pleased to meet any of them, regardless of Aiden's warm greeting.

"I'll help you folks as much as I'm able, but you all need to know that my officers and I have the situation under control." The sheriff's icy voice matched her expression. "Simon and I were there when they pulled the body from the river. *You* aren't here at *my* request, and I'd appreciate due respect while you go moseying around *my* county."

Aiden was no stranger to this "you ain't from here" treatment, so Autumn wasn't surprised when his reply was warm and steady. "I assure you, Sheriff Frank, my team will operate with the utmost consideration for you and your officers' authority and stake in Beechum County affairs."

The sheriff didn't appear pacified, but Deputy King's head bobbed in approval. There was a clear winner for Beechum's Most Congenial Officer among the two.

Sheriff Frank leaned against the wall and crossed her arms, surveying the group with a sour pucker to her lips. Autumn predicted that no matter what the team uncovered here, there would be no love lost from the Beechum County sheriff when they left.

Councilman Newman cleared his throat and gestured toward the remaining man. "This is Bradley Garland. He's a councilman one county over in Rutshire, and he's also Natalie Garland's cousin. Bradley ID'd the body for us."

Bradley's face went white, and a visible tremble rolled over him at the memory of making that identification. "Thank you for coming, and please, call me Bradley." He spoke to Aiden but met each of their eyes in turn, taking care to acknowledge the entire team.

"Bradley, my condolences to you and your family for your loss." Aiden stepped toward him. "Please forgive us for our intrusion, but we are going to have to ask you some hard questions."

"That's what I'm here for." Bradley's voice cracked on the last word, his attempt at cheerfulness a total failure.

"Shall we sit, ladies and gents?" Steve Newman pulled out a chair from the long narrow table that owned most of the conference room's floorspace.

Aiden took the seat directly across from Bradley, and Autumn planted herself beside the SSA. This was her first *official federal agent* case, and she intended to miss nothing.

Clasping his hands together, Bradley again attempted a friendly tone. "What would you like to know, Agent Parrish?"

Autumn pitied the man as he swallowed the obvious lump in his throat.

"Well, Bradley," Aiden rested his elbows on the table, "Councilman Newman informed me that you believed Natalie was upbeat—optimistic even—on the morning she perished. While I can't agree or disagree with your assessment, I would like to ask you if you're aware of any reasons why she may not have been as happy as you perceived her to be?"

Bradley's frustrated blue eyes conveyed an obvious desire to defend his stance on Natalie's state of mind that day, but he seemed to understand that the question wasn't meant as an affront. "Anyone who knows Natalie would say she's had a rough time of it over the last couple of years."

Aiden tilted his head. "Would they say she was a troubled woman?"

Bradley held up a hand in mild protest. "I know where this is going, and I get it. Yes, 'they' would say she was troubled. So would I. Nat had a lot of pain to work through, but she *was* in a good headspace that morning. She was ready to start her life over. Face her demons. She *wasn't* suicidal."

"When you say 'demons,'" Autumn entered the conversation with a seamless, gentle tone, "what exactly are you referring to? What did Natalie have to face?"

"She got pregnant unexpectedly, maybe two and a half years ago or so." Bradley's clasped hands separated into clenched fists. "Her boyfriend dumped her because he'd knocked her up, which was bad enough, but her parents were total jerks about the baby too. They're super old-school, and I guess Nat was tarnishing their family name with her illegitimate child. Things got ice-cold, and her parents practically pushed her out the door, whether they understand that fact or not."

Autumn pulled a tissue from her tote bag and slipped it across the table. "But she lost the baby, correct? How far along was she?"

"Twenty-eight weeks." His response was immediate, as were the tears threatening to spill down his cheeks.

Autumn ached for his genuine sadness. "You were close." Her observation sent the tears overboard.

Bradley squared his gaze with Autumn, swiping at his cheeks. "We grew up together. Nat was more than family to me. She was one of my best friends. She didn't deserve any of this." He turned back to Aiden. "And she did *not* kill herself."

Aiden took the comment in stride and shifted gears. "The boyfriend. The ex. Was he still in the picture?"

"You mean," Bradley straightened in his chair, his composure making a swift return, "did Rod Norris show his face again after she wasn't carrying *his* child anymore?"

Autumn was aware that Aiden had taken a purposeful dive into the topic. If Bradley was as close as he claimed to be to Natalie, then he was valuable to the case. They needed his input and therefore needed him to stay calm so he could share any pertinent information he had with a clear mind.

Nothing sharpened a man's focus like his hatred for another man.

"That's precisely what I mean." Aiden's confirmation offered Bradley a hint of comradery, like they were just two regular men discussing a jerk who didn't deserve the air he was breathing. "After she miscarried, did Rod contact her? Visit her?"

"She just told me on that last phone call that he'd been suggesting they give things another try." Bradley wrinkled his face in disgust at the very notion. "But she wasn't interested. Natalie would *never* go back to him after he left her like that...baby or no baby. She was done with him and done with those creepy Harmony bastards too."

Autumn caught the infinitesimal twitch of Aiden's jaw, the sole sign of the SSA's heightened tension. "You're speaking of Harmony House, correct?"

Bradley grunted his confirmation. "Natalie referred to them as a 'community outreach group.' She said they were going to help her find a purpose. Help her stop drinking. Heal her with their magical group powers or whatever."

"Did you detect any improvement after she became involved with the organization?" Autumn knew the answer, but she wanted Bradley's take on his cousin's recovery.

He pulled at a thread on his suit jacket cuff. "Yes, but that's because she stopped drinking. Of course she could only go up from there. She could have sobered up with the local AA or even just with a good psychiatrist. She was hurting. *Vulnerable.* And Damien scooped her right up."

"Damien Parr is a nutjob if I ever met one." Councilman Newman inserted his opinion from his place beside Bradley. The rest of the group had remained silent for the entirety of the interview thus far.

"Right," Sheriff Frank spoke up, "and that nutjob has done a lot of good for the local community. He and his people host food drives, clean litter from the parks, all kinds of neighborly, charitable acts. Seems to me they fixed Natalie up pretty nice as well. Harmony House is the least of Beechum County's concerns."

"You're wrong." Bradley swiveled in his chair to lock eyes with the sheriff. "Natalie told me about a week ago that she was getting an uneasy feeling about Damien. Something about him was off, and she wanted to leave. She wanted to continue her sober life at home with her *family*."

"Natalie was a recovering alcoholic with a crappy past." Autumn barely suppressed a groan when Chris entered the conversation, earning himself a glare from their main informant, as usual.

Shut up. Please, shut up.

Of course, Agent Parker couldn't resist making a bad situation worse. "Her take on Damien Parr could have been severely skewed. She probably got 'uneasy' because she couldn't sneak any drinks onto his property."

You've got to be kidding me.

The atmosphere in the room crackled with palpable tension. Autumn examined her hands and wondered how many of the other agents in the room were also wishing they'd locked Parker in the car.

"She was better. *Sober!*" Once Bradley recovered his voice, he barked his response down the table at Chris. "If she'd wanted to jump off the wagon, she definitely wouldn't have been headed to her parents' house. They're dry as the damn Sahara."

Chris held a finger up. "She *never did* make it there, did she? I think it's very safe to say that wasn't her actual plan."

Autumn caught the angry flash in Bradley's eyes and knew they'd lose him if Chris kept talking. "Bradley, what do *you* think happened to Natalie?" She figured he had to have a theory or idea of some sort, considering his refusal of the suicide route.

"Well," Bradley was eager to answer the question, "why hasn't anyone considered that she tripped? Slipped? Got too close to the edge and fell? It was just before sunrise, so there wasn't much natural light to work with. Even the 911 caller might have misinterpreted what he or she saw at that time of day. That's the last way she'd ever kill herself anyway."

The statement reeked of importance to Autumn. "Why is jumping into the falls the last way that your cousin would choose to kill herself?"

Bradley closed his eyes for a moment, thinking, Autumn assumed, back across the years of his life with his cousin. "She almost drowned as a kid down in Florida. *In the ocean.* That incident scarred her for life, left her with a paralyzing fear of water. She wouldn't have jumped in a damn river."

"But you admit she may have been considering suicide?" Chris piped up again. Mia sat beside him, shooting daggers at her colleague with her dark eyes but remaining calm.

Councilman Bradley Garland stood and walked the room until he was directly across from Agent Parker, placed his hands on the table, and leaned in until their noses almost touched. "No. I do not admit that because *it isn't true.* I knew Natalie. You didn't. She hated water. And she didn't fucking kill herself."

Amazingly enough, Chris said nothing as Bradley continued to stare him down. Parker was much larger than Councilman Garland, but in the moment, that didn't seem to matter.

"An animal." Winter muttered to herself at first before repeating the words louder to the group. "An animal could have spooked her or even run into her and knocked her off."

Bradley turned his attention to Agent Black. "Yeah. A *human* animal." He walked to his chair and sat.

"You think it's possible that someone pushed Natalie?" Autumn waited for Bradley to formulate his answer. The entire team stared at him, along with Sheriff Frank and Deputy King.

"I'd believe she was murdered long before I'd believe she killed herself." He gazed down the table from agent to agent. "What do you people even know about the 911 caller? Has anyone tracked that person down yet? Doesn't that seem suspicious to anyone else sitting in this room?"

Of course, the answer was "yes." Cyber was attempting to nail down the mystery caller as they spoke.

"We're working on that, Bradley, I assure you." Aiden stood and extended a hand across the table. "And we're going to give this case our full attention."

Bradley grabbed Agent Parrish's hand and gave it a vigorous shake. "I can't thank you enough for being here." He wasted no time exiting the overcrowded room.

"I second that, Agent Parrish. It's about time somebody checked into those people." Councilman Newman shot a glare toward Sheriff Frank. "There's no tellin' what's going on behind closed doors at that damn Harmony House."

The exchange made Autumn wonder just how long Steve Newman had been pushing for an investigation into the "community outreach group." If the FBI had taken an interest in the cult two years ago, the locals had to have been expressing alarm for quite some time before that.

Winnie Frank was the lucky sheriff who'd taken on the worst of the debacle, Autumn guessed. And after dealing with the locals freaking out about "those weird folks at Harmony House" for so long, Sheriff Frank was probably exhausted by the topic. No doubt she'd been defending their freedom as well as the good they did in the community for a frustrating period of time.

Her current surly demeanor relayed as much.

"Someday, Steve," Sheriff Frank's hands moved to her hips, "you'll get over the fact that not everybody believes the exact same things *you* do. They're a different sort of group, but that's *their* business. Natalie's suicide isn't an unsolvable mystery that we need the Feds for."

The councilman lifted a shoulder. "Agree to disagree, I guess. We'll find out soon enough. The big boys are in town." He offered her a tight smile and left the conference room.

Autumn was surprised at the degree of sexism in Councilman Newman's comment. He hadn't given off any previous signs that he had issues with women in authority, although he might've just had issues with Winnie Frank.

"Let's get teams assigned and get to work." Aiden no doubt wanted to avoid any escalation surrounding his "big boys" being on the female sheriff's turf. "Agent Parker, I'm pairing you with Agent Trent."

The blatant disgust on Chris's face was equal to the repulsion exploding in Autumn's stomach, but she kept her expression neutral.

Aiden pointed at Noah and Winter. "Agent Dalton and Agent Black, I'd like for the two of you to coordinate with Sheriff Frank and Deputy King to go check out the incident scene."

Relief flooded Noah's face. He probably wanted to keep an eye on Winter and make sure she was really up for the action.

That was the main reason Autumn had wanted to be paired with Winter, but she knew no one would be more protective than Noah.

"Agent Logan, you'll come with me." Aiden turned to Autumn. "Could I have a quick word with you, Agent Trent?"

Autumn nodded and followed Aiden into the hallway, not missing Chris's hateful eye roll and slumped posture.

This is going to be a fun first day.

They stepped off to the side, and Aiden raised his eyebrows. "Well? What's your initial gut instinct on all of this?"

She had the sneaking suspicion that this was a test of some sort. Aiden would, of course, want to know just how much of a difference Quantico had made. Autumn had no intention of disappointing him.

"The water part…it doesn't fit." Autumn envisioned the young woman peering over the edge of the peak. "If Natalie had a true phobia of water, and her cousin seemed more than convinced that she did, choosing to jump into the falls as her suicide plan would be unlikely. Just peering down into the water would have been enough to shock her into survival mode regardless of her previous intent."

Aiden considered this for a moment. "Bradley is convinced that she was happy that morning."

"With all the hardship she'd been dealing with, something could have triggered her between the phone call and the plunge. Her psyche was fragile to begin with." Autumn's brain was twirling in circles, and they all led back to one very blatant and reasonable theory. "Or…the whole thing *was* a tragic accident. She *was* as happy as Bradley thought. But she fell."

The rest of the team filtered into the hallway, rustling around and appearing anxious to get started. Chris's expression had mutated into an angry mask, and Autumn fought the urge to bring the matter up with Aiden.

Why me? Why my first case? He knows Chris hates me…

"You'll handle him just fine, Agent Trent." Aiden's lowered voice broke through her thoughts. "If Agent Logan can do it, so can you."

Autumn eyed Aiden warily. "Mia has superpowers. It's the only explanation."

She enjoyed the twitch of SSA Parrish's lips as he struggled to fight off a smile. "And you don't?" He said the words in a light tone, but his cool blue eyes locked on hers with an intensity that made her stomach flip and her breathing grow shallow.

Audience. You have an audience. The entire team is viewing this.

"I'd really like to know more about the other local suicides." She chose an abrupt subject change, willing herself down a different mental path. "We can check for connections and similarities that local law enforcement may have missed."

Aiden nodded and gestured toward the conference room. "I'll ask Sheriff Frank for the files, although I'm starting to think there might not be a lot to investigate regarding the suicides. That being said, the FBI isn't going to waste an opportunity to dig into Damien Parr's business. That's the actual reason we're here. Don't forget."

Autumn glanced at Noah and Winter and mouthed, "Sorry," before reentering the conference room. She didn't bother to offer Chris the same.

The sheriff and deputy were still present and in mid-conversation. Sheriff Frank's tense stance made her appear even more pissed off than before, and King's previous welcoming smile had diminished to a grimace.

"Can I help you, Agents?" The sheriff's offer dripped with resentment.

"Yes, thank you, Sheriff." Aiden stepped forward and slid his hands into his pockets, so relaxed that Autumn bet he'd hold his cool even if Winnie Frank breathed actual fire in his face. "We'd like to discuss the other suicides."

The sheriff barked a mirthless chuckle as she glared from Aiden to Autumn. "Of course you would. The Feds always gotta be kicking dead horses, right? I am one-hundred-percent certain that none of those deaths are related. Each case was investigated, proper autopsies were performed, and the medical examiner ruled suicide for each and every one."

"I'm not certain you should ever be that sure about anything in our line of work, Sheriff." Aiden managed to deliver the warning in a pleasant manner, though Autumn doubted his manners made one bit of difference.

Sheriff Frank wanted them to leave. Yesterday.

The woman narrowed her eyes on Aiden alone. "I investigated those cases, and I've never half-assed anything in my life, Agent Parrish. I am completely convinced that the deaths are not related...unless I missed a big scientific breakthrough, and they've discovered suicide is contagious."

It was only a matter of time—and a short one at that—before Aiden's request became a demand, and Autumn winced as she imagined how the sheriff would react. She held a hand up, anxious to break the tension before someone exploded. "There probably isn't a link, Sheriff Frank. We're aware of that, and we deeply respect the work you've put into closing those cases. But scanning the files is an unspoken requirement that we have to complete before we can go home."

And god knows you want us to go home.

She held her breath, urging the woman to take the logical step.

Sheriff Frank studied her for a moment before snapping at her deputy. "Go grab the damn files." Simon was gone in a flash, and the sheriff followed shortly after, offering not another word.

"Nice save, Autumn." Aiden dipped his chin at her. "I was expecting one of us to shed some blood before she handed those files over."

Autumn laughed, relieved to release the tension after

their rather volatile meeting. She realized Aiden was staring at her and went quiet. He was smiling...and saying nothing.

"What?" She attempted to inject a playful tone into her demand.

He shook his head and gazed out the window. "Just nice to have you back, Agent Trent."

There were probably a million proper replies to his statement, but in that precise moment, Autumn couldn't summon a single one.

Did you go mute? Say thanks. Say awesome. Say anything.

She opened her mouth to speak, but Aiden was already in motion. He headed for the door, giving her a light clap on the shoulder. "Time to work."

Lips parted in shock, Autumn stared at Aiden's back as he disappeared into the hallway, curling her fingers over the same shoulder he'd touched. An odd, fluttery sensation sprang to life in her belly.

At times, the information she received through human touch was foggy. Complicated.

Not today, though.

Today, Aiden Parrish's thoughts had come across loud and clear.

9

For the majority of their trek up to the top of Dogwood Falls, Noah fretted that the hike would prove too rigorous for his girlfriend's current, emaciated condition. He refrained from mentioning the concern to Winter, though, for fear of being punched. Or tased. Or kicked in the nuts. Instead, he sneaked repeated peeks at her while they traversed the steep and sometimes rocky path and called for frequent water breaks. For himself, of course.

Not that the breaks were much of a fabrication. The early afternoon sun was merciless as it beat down on them. Noah's shirt was plastered to his body and sweat stung his eyes.

For her part, Winter didn't show any sign of weakness. With her face flushed from exertion, she marched along like a soldier, but Noah was still far from convinced that she was okay. Winter Black was excellent at keeping a tough exterior in the face of almost any obstacle.

"At least the sun kept the storm clouds away," she called over her shoulder. "If there ever *was* anything to find, rain would have washed it away."

She was correct. Four days had passed since Natalie's

death. Their odds for recovering any evidence were low after Mother Nature had been in charge of the scene for so long, even if it hadn't rained. Especially since the Beechum County M.E. had ruled the death a suicide, which opened the area back up to public use.

Noah swatted at a bug that buzzed near his ear as they trudged the last bit up the trail. Sheriff Frank and the local police department had done little by way of investigation into Natalie's death after the incident was ruled a suicide. The routine examination of the area for foul play had probably involved little more than some quick "glance around" by officers who figured there was nothing to find in the first place.

They reached the highest peak of Dogwood Falls, and Noah caught his breath, mesmerized by the beauty of the cascading water. A magnificent phenomenon to behold.

A terrifying place to die.

Winter ventured out on the narrow cliff first, checking the path to make sure she didn't disturb any evidence. Noah lagged behind for a moment to drink in her beauty, his heart expanding until the damn thing filled his entire chest.

He wanted to stop time and tell her how amazing she was. How brave. He wanted to grab her face, stare into her striking blue eyes, and convey how proud he was of her for enduring all the horror life had thrown at her and remaining purehearted.

Instead, he held all those tender thoughts in check. Winter was finally back in the field, and the last thing she'd want from him was some sappy declaration of love.

"Drag marks." Winter pointed at the dirt.

Noah knelt to examine her find. It took him a little bit to zero in on the faint drag marks hidden amid the scattered footprints, but when he did, he sucked in a breath. "Jesus.

Were they outlined in red, or did you have a superspeed vision episode that I somehow missed?"

His girlfriend wasn't a normal woman. The traumatic brain injury and subsequent surgery she'd experienced as a young girl had left her with some bizarre "abilities" that Noah never would have believed possible had he not witnessed them himself.

Not only did pertinent clues and objects manifest themselves to Winter by way of a red glow, but she also experienced visions that corresponded to current situations in her life. The visions were preceded by a nosebleed and severe headache. Once the pain intensified to torturous levels, Agent Black blacked out and witnessed a reel of footage that no one else had access to. Helpful during cases at times, but a burden all the same.

"No." She crouched beside him. "Just my gut this time." Her whole body seemed to tremble. From exertion or excitement, he wasn't sure.

Noah's stomach clenched. He wanted the troubling symptoms to be no big deal, but he wasn't that naive. "Are you okay?" The question slipped out in blunt fashion.

She turned toward him, her eyes concealed by sunglasses. "Stop it. Seriously. I'm not glass, and I'm not going to break. I *cannot* stomach everyone being so worried about me nonstop. I'm here, I'm okay, and you all are going to have to lay off the mother hen crap."

Fair enough. He'd earned the snappy reply. "I'm sorry. I know you're doing well. It's hard to stop worrying about you after months of—"

"Worrying about me?" Winter finished for him. "I get that. But you still have to stop." She turned back to clue hunting, and he decided his best move was to join her.

Twenty more minutes of poking around revealed nothing else noteworthy besides the drag marks. Even if there had been more evidence to find, it was gone now. Too many other hikers had trampled the path in the short span of time since Natalie's death. Admitting defeat, they hiked back down to the base of the falls, where the roar of the water was much louder.

"The local authorities never found Natalie's phone." Noah stared into the depths of the choppy, swift-flowing river. "I wonder if it'd be worth bringing in some divers to try and locate it. Could be useful."

Winter took cautious steps across the slick rocks, scanning the terrain's nooks and crannies with expert eyes. "Sheriff Frank already has a warrant for the phone company to obtain all of her communication logs. But having the actual device would be even more helpful."

"We can run the idea by Aiden." Noah flashed her a mischievous grin. "Parrish can run it by Sheriff Frank."

They both chuckled at that suggestion. To be fair, Winnie Frank didn't seem fond of a single one of them, but for whatever reason, she had taken an *extraordinary* dislike to Aiden.

Since Winter's disappearance, things had changed for him and the SSA. Their shared ordeal had forged a tangible bond between them that he doubted would ever deteriorate to their former level of mutual contempt. Noah could no longer claim that he "hated" Aiden Parrish. But he sure as hell could still find the humor in watching the Beechum County sheriff take an immediate aversion to the man.

Winter made an abrupt turn, as though alarmed. Noah opened his mouth to ask what was wrong, but she spoke first. "I say we go find Rod Norris." She began walking back toward the vehicle, her emaciated silhouette growing smaller with each step.

Noah stole one more gander at the falls. He wished he and Winter were on a vacation and had chosen to come to

Dogwood Falls for very different reasons than their current circumstances.

He snorted at his wishful thinking. He'd be shocked if Winter wanted any time off in the foreseeable future. Now that she was finally "back," she'd do everything in her power to stay that way.

As long as she doesn't collapse mid-case.

They had an hour-long car ride ahead of them. Maybe he'd find a tactful way to bring up her weight loss and his concerns for her health, although Noah guessed it'd be a cold day in hell before he was able to pull that trick off.

The rented Expedition's leather seats were blazing hot when they opened the doors, but five minutes with the AC on full blast cooled them down. Once he'd steered the SUV out of the bumpy gravel parking area and onto the paved road, the chilled air and humming tires seemed to lull Winter into a state of rest.

His heart softened as he sneaked a glimpse of her peaceful face. Forget the talk. He'd let her rest. The woman had just hiked two hours in the July heat. Her condition, no matter what she insisted, wasn't good. She needed all the recovery time she could get.

She woke when he slowed the vehicle's speed to match the limits of Rutshire County. Being who she was, Noah was certain the embarrassment of "napping" on the job would mortify her for decades to come.

He pretended not to have noticed, and Winter pretended to believe him.

Noah followed the GPS to Rod Norris's place. He lived in a small white country house about five minutes outside the town of Rutshire. A short gravel lane led to a one-car detached garage, and an aged brick walkway stretched from there to the front door of the house.

Noah and Winter exited the vehicle and headed toward

the residence side by side. They took the two steps up to a small front porch and halted at the door.

He eyed the woman he loved as she stared at the door with blatant eagerness. "You want to take the lead on this one?"

Winter grinned and gave the door two solid knocks. "What do you think, Dalton?"

The door opened to reveal an attractive young blonde. Noah didn't think she could be a day over twenty-one. Their jackets gave them away before Winter could speak, and the woman's blue eyes went wide.

Her smile dropped, replaced by fearful trepidation. "Can I help you?"

Showtime, darlin'.

Winter wasted no time. "I hope so. I'm Special Agent Winter Black, and this is Special Agent Noah Dalton. We're with the FBI, and we'd like to speak to Rod Norris. Is he here?"

The blonde put a hand to her chest and fervently shook her head. "He's at work. He won't be home until five-thirty or so."

Noah checked his watch. One thirty.

"And you are?" Winter's question bordered on a demand.

The blonde tried to smile. "I'm Jessica Canter, Rod's girlfriend."

Noah fought to keep the corners of his mouth from upturning as Winter turned to him. He still couldn't view her eyes, but he caught the perfect arch of her eyebrow above the lens.

Agent Black leaned against the doorframe. "Were you familiar with Natalie Garland?"

The flash of anger in Jessica's eyes was more than enough of an answer. "The suicide girl? Yeah. I knew her a long time ago. She went nuts and left town."

Winter pressed her lips together, either fighting off a biting response or a grin at the news she was about to share with Miss Canter. "That seems a little harsh. People go through things. *Hard things.* Were you aware that Rod was back in contact with Natalie?"

Jessica's fair complexion flared tomato red. She jabbed a finger at Winter. "That is not true. He was done with her a *long* time ago."

"Ma'am," Winter's tone conveyed that Jessica was about three seconds away from losing her pretty pointer, "I'd appreciate if you didn't put your finger in my face. It usually goes without saying, but FBI agents have a very low tolerance for bullshit."

Jessica dropped her hand, but her outrage remained. "Rod hasn't talked to Natalie in over a year. He would never cheat on me. You're liars!"

The power of denial was a fascinating spectacle to behold. Noah stepped forward, attempting to save Jessica from an untimely death. "Miss Canter, I'm sure you've been made aware of Rod's past track record with decision-making. Is it really so hard for you to believe he'd speak with Natalie behind your back?"

"Natalie Garland was a liar!" Jessica was not impressed by their badges. Not at all. "That wasn't even Rod's baby. *He told me.* And you're both full of shit!" She slammed the door in their faces.

"I'm not sure whether I want to laugh or rearrange her bitchy little face." Winter cocked her head, as though truly considering the latter.

While the scene could have proved entertaining, Noah had a better idea. "Let's go look Rod up and find out where he works. Maybe make a nice little midday visit? Everyone loves a surprise meeting with the Feds."

Agent Black threw a thumb over her shoulder at Rod's house. "I mean, we just proved that. Jessica was ecstatic."

Noah led the way back to the Expedition. The fact that Winter had retained her cool while an ignorant woman screamed in her face was encouraging. Maybe he was over-thinking the weight loss. Her doctors believed it was a side effect of the trauma, and who was he to argue? The shakiness probably went along with the stress. Her blood sugar might even be—

"What are you thinking about?" Winter opened the passenger's side door, climbed in, and waited for Noah to do the same on the driver's side.

When he was behind the wheel, he found that she'd removed her glasses and was staring at him with an unfalter-ing, vibrant blue gaze. He floundered for a reply. "Just wondering how many doors we'll get slammed in our faces today. We could set a world record. You think that's in the *Guinness Book?*"

She didn't believe him. He sensed the fact in the tight set of her jaw and the intensity of her eyes. She knew him too well and vice versa. Lying straight to Winter's face—even a harmless white lie—was close to impossible.

His shoulders eased when she didn't press the matter. "Lemme find this sucker." Winter pulled out the iPad from her bag and within a minute had the information they needed. "Rod Norris is a software programmer for Lisco Banks, Inc. Seven-minute drive. Let's go."

Seven minutes wasn't a large amount of time in the big scheme of things, but the seconds ticked by in slow motion for Noah. Balancing the scales between taking care of Winter and not acting like she needed to be cared for at all was an exhausting feat. Months of walking that line were wearing him down.

Noah had promised himself that when Winter recovered,

all the effort would be more than worth it. But what if she never fully recovered? He couldn't pretend forever.

Driving past the city limits of Rutshire, Noah could appreciate the quiet, small-town life more than ever. He and Winter both lived for the job, and neither of them had ever intended to walk away from their careers. Lately, though, he'd started to accept there was a lot he'd give up if it meant making the woman he loved whole again.

The GPS led them straight to the unassuming concrete building that was Lisco Banks, Inc. Noah parked, and they both took a moment to observe the business.

"Pretty basic," Winter declared, letting herself out of the Expedition. Noah had nothing to add to the description, so he followed behind as she made her way to the glass front doors.

Inside, a perky brunette receptionist beamed up at them from behind a large mahogany desk. "Thank you for visiting Lisco Banks. My name is Faith. How can I help you today?"

Faith understood that she was addressing two agents from the Federal Bureau of Investigation only after she had spoken. Noah caught the slight stiffening of her posture but was relieved to note that her composure and friendliness remained.

He shifted into immediate polite and pleasant mode. "I'm Special Agent Noah Dalton, and this is Special Agent Winter Black. We need to speak to Rod Norris. He works here, yes?"

She bobbed her head. "He sure does. I can take you to him if you'd like?" Faith was already on her feet and gesturing toward a hallway.

Poor woman can't wait to get rid of us.

"That'd be great." Noah held out a hand. "After you, Agent Black."

Winter followed Faith, and Noah brought up the rear. They didn't have to go far before Faith opened a door on her right and ushered them in. The room was large and contained eight rows of cubicles.

Faith pointed toward the last row on the left. "Rod's desk is back there. Two cubes down." She appeared to have no desire to accompany them any farther, and Winter gave her a nod of thanks and dismissal before Faith scurried away.

Striding toward the indicated row, Noah scanned the tops of the cubicles. Dozens of heads all glued to computer screens made for a sea of worker bees.

Winter led the way straight to their unsuspecting target, and Noah choked back a laugh as Rod Norris whirled around in his rolling desk chair, nearly falling off altogether when he took stock of the emblems on their jackets.

"Can I help you?" Rod's voice came out as an alarmed squeak.

Winter leaned against the cubicle wall. "Are you Rod Norris?"

He hesitated, then nodded. "Yes."

"Good." Winter offered Rod a wide smile that only seemed to scare him more. "We have some questions for you about Natalie Garland."

Rod's countenance immediately drooped. "Okay."

Noah crossed his arms. "That might not be the right word to describe the position you're in right now, Rod."

Natalie's ex-boyfriend gaped from Noah to Winter. "I haven't done anything wrong. Don't you people investigate *criminals*? I'm not a criminal."

Winter grinned. "Sounds like something a criminal would say. Especially if he murdered his ex-girlfriend."

"No. I *loved* Natalie." He was still scared, but Rod kept unwavering eye contact with Agent Black. "Her suicide is tearing me up. It's just so...*awful*."

Noah sat on the end of Rod's desk. "How about dumping your girlfriend because you got her pregnant and were too much of a coward to face your own damn responsibilities? That qualifies as pretty 'awful' to me."

Rod's brow furrowed in defense. "I was a lot younger then. I was stupid."

Winter snort-laughed loud enough for the entire row of boxed busy bees to jump in their chairs. "Two and a half years ago, Rod? You weren't *that* much younger. And you were more than old enough to know you were making a total dick move."

Rod sat back in his chair, jutting his chin out in defiance. "My relationship with Natalie and our...breakup...those aren't Federal matters."

"No, but Natalie's death is." Noah drummed his fingers on Rod's desk. "You were in contact with Natalie again."

Rod gulped and struggled to maintain composure. "Yes. We'd talked a few times, but that was all. I hadn't even seen her in over a year. And what the hell...? She committed suicide. That's what the cops said. Why are you even here questioning me over a suicide? Are you..." Comprehension dawned on his features, and his mouth sagged in surprise. "Are you saying I killed her?"

"Someone may have killed Natalie." Noah noted the horror that flamed in Rod's eyes. "That's what we're saying. And you had a lot of reasons to want to get rid of that woman before she came back to town. Things would have gotten super awkward pretty quick, huh, Rod?"

He gave a vehement shake of his head. "No. *No.* I wanted to try again with Natalie. I wanted a fresh start. But she..." His eyes glistened with emotion.

"She didn't want you back, huh?" Winter's expression steeled over. "Shocker of the century. Maybe you felt like a moron for even asking after she turned you down? That was probably the first time you realized you can't just treat people however the hell you want without repercussions. Was it, Rod?"

Noah thought their suspect was about ten seconds away from bursting into sobs. The dude was an asshole, but he wasn't acting like much of a seasoned killer.

"I know how to treat people." Rod twiddled his thumbs in frustration. "I know what I did...sucked. I just thought maybe Natalie would give me a chance to make it up to her."

"She didn't, though, from what we've been told." Winter picked up a framed photo from Rod's desk. The image showed him with his arms around Jessica, and they were smiling like the two happiest people on the planet. "So maybe you killed her because she wouldn't take you back. Or maybe you were scared she'd come into town and tell Jessica about everything?"

"I wouldn't ever kill *anyone*." Rod stared at the picture as Winter placed it back down. "And Natalie wouldn't have done that. She wasn't like that. She wouldn't want to hurt Jess. They used to be friends."

Noah's internal alarms fired, and he exchanged a quick glance with Winter.

"Did they?" Winter tilted her head. "Jessica didn't mention that to us when we stopped by your house and talked to her a little bit ago."

The fact that no one was recording Rod's facial reaction following Winter's comment was a shame. The man turned as white as the computer paper stacked behind him.

Rod held up a hand, gasping for air as though he'd just finished a triathlon. "You talked to...*Jessica*...about *Natalie?*"

Noah had to jump in. He couldn't let Winter have all the fun. "Sure did, buddy. And I gotta tell you, that conversation did *not* go well."

Smacking his palm to his forehead, Rod slumped in his chair. "Shit."

"*Deep* shit." Winter's emphasis wasn't necessary, but considering that she probably wanted to kick Rod in the balls, Noah felt she'd taken the higher road. "Now, how about you tell us where you were the morning Natalie Garland died?"

Rod couldn't seem to stop shaking his head. "I didn't do anything to Natalie. I would never do anything to Natalie."

Winter chuckled. "You mean aside from knocking her up and abandoning her, right? Answer the question, Rod. Where were you?"

"In bed." He braved a glance at her face. "I was in bed, sleeping off a wine hangover. Jess and I stayed up late playing chess, and she made me try all these wine samples from some online club thing...I was *not* at Dogwood Falls. I was passed out and sick as hell."

Despite his dislike for the little weasel, Noah believed him. "And Jessica can verify this? She was with you all morning?"

"Yes!" Rod glanced around the office, face flushed with embarrassment or possibly anger. "She lives with me. *Of course* she was with me."

"She was in bed with a hangover as well?" Winter pulled a notepad and pen from her pocket and jotted down what Noah guessed to be gibberish.

"Yes. I mean, no." Rod's exasperation intensified the beet-red hue of his cheeks. "She was in bed with me, yes, but she didn't have a hangover. She drinks wine way more than me. But she slept in with me most of the morning."

Noah tapped the digital clock stationed between his body and the computer. "Time is important, Rod. 'Most of the morning' isn't exactly a rock-solid alibi. She could have left for a yoga class, and off you went to get rid of Natalie. Can either of you say with one-hundred-percent, stand before a judge confidence that you were together *all* morning?"

Rod peered up at Noah, his eyes pleading now. "I didn't hurt Natalie. I loved her. You have to believe me."

"We don't have to do anything, let alone believe a lying, cheating jerk like you." Winter slipped the notepad back into her pocket. "Don't make any plans to leave town. We'll be in touch. Soon."

She nodded at Noah, and the two of them turned to leave Rod in all his miserable glory.

"Wait." The frantic programmer jumped to his feet, making quick work of catching up to them. "Do I need a lawyer?"

Well, you do now, moron.

Winter raised her palms with feigned concern. "I dunno, Rod. *Do you?*"

On the walk back to the SUV, Noah turned over the few facts they'd gleaned from Rod Norris. He was a world-class douche, but they'd already assumed as much before the interview.

More importantly, he *was* torn up about Natalie's death. Noah believed the bastard had a heart underneath multiple layers of ignorance and narcissism. And Rod's story of online wine clubs, chess, and hangovers had been stated in detail without hesitation.

Rod Norris was either an excellent liar, or he was innocent.

Jessica Canter was another story. The woman displayed open hatred for Natalie, as well as an apparent past friendship that must have ended poorly. And she hadn't shown an ounce of sorrow over her former friend's sudden passing. Jessica, instead, had seemed smug. Possibly even pleased.

As they climbed into the Expedition, Noah conceded that he might have gotten ahead of himself earlier with his admiration for the quiet little town.

Maybe the small-town life was overrated after all.

10

D riving anywhere with Chris Parker was a punishment in and of itself. Autumn was aware of that fact long before she sat in the passenger's seat of the Explorer currently assigned to them. Today's journey, however, promised to dole out extra helpings of torture.

The Garlands lived an hour away from Beechum in Rutshire. While interviewing Natalie's parents was of great importance, Autumn wished there was a teleportation device to take them there.

She hadn't been seated more than ten seconds before Chris started in.

"He did it again!" Agent Parker slanted her an icy blue glare from the driver's seat that should have frozen the skin right off her face. "What did I tell you? You didn't believe me in Florida. Do you believe me now? *Do you?*"

"What are you talking about?" Autumn didn't bother to hide the giant sigh that escaped her lips. Aiden was right. She could handle Chris. But she sure as hell didn't want to.

Chris waved his hand around, indicating the vehicle. "We have an Explorer. The other two vehicles are *Expeditions*. Do you not know the difference? Parrish shafted me yet again with the shittiest vehicle."

Autumn recognized the difference. She just didn't care. Their vehicle was as shiny and black as the others. The interior was spotless and came with a loaded dashboard.

He's out of his damn mind.

"I don't know. That wouldn't seem to fit in with your theory that I'm Aiden's 'pet,' now would it?" She fought back laughter as Parker's brows lowered as though he were concentrating on the conundrum. "He assigned *me* this vehicle as well."

Chris drummed his fingers on the wheel for a moment before rebounding in his typical offensive manner. "Who knows what kind of games you two play with each other? A lot of people like that whole sadomasochist crap."

Autumn blinked. Well, that was a new one. "Yes. And they often torture each other by way of less luxurious SUVs." His comment was too ridiculous to bother getting upset. "Good detective work."

She could tell Chris hadn't expected a humorous response. His jaw dropped before he steeled his composure and focused his attention back on the road. She almost laughed again when he flipped the radio to an alternative rock station and cranked the volume up.

If you're trying to piss me off, you're going about it the wrooong way.

Autumn closed her eyes and bobbed her head to the beat, letting Nine Inch Nails take her away. Compared to Quantico, this was a tropical vacation.

The holiday ended, however, at the precise moment Chris pulled the Explorer into the Garlands' driveway and slammed on the brakes. "Why the hell are we even here? Her parents know she's dead. I highly doubt she called them before jumping and gave a detailed explanation as to why she was done with her shitty life."

She sucked in a breath, never quite prepared for how low Agent Parker was prepared to go. Comments like that were the reason Chris Parker shouldn't be allowed to speak with grieving individuals. Or anyone else. Ever.

"We need the entire picture before we can arrive at any conclusions. Safe to say, the people who raised her might have some insight that could prove useful." Autumn flung open her door and escaped the confines of their Explorer before he could voice an inappropriate reply. The summer sun on her face was absolute heaven after breathing the same air as the hateful agent for an hour.

The Garlands' street was lined with immaculate green yards that led to rows of large, traditional houses featuring brick walls, expansive porches, and white columns. The front door of the Garlands' own impressive colonial-style home swung open before Autumn or Chris had a chance to knock. Dan Garland stood in the doorway, arms crossed, with a blatant glare shooting from his gray-blue eyes.

His wife, Terri, wasn't far behind. She was a small woman with short, reddish-brown hair, and her eyes were laced with the grief that only parents who'd lost a child could know. In contrast to her husband, she attempted to greet them with a courteous facade, but the effort was futile.

Autumn's heart squeezed as she took in the couple's pain. They hadn't just lost *a* child, they'd lost their *only* child. The level of devastation was unthinkable.

"Mr. and Mrs. Garland, I'm Special Agent Autumn Trent with the Richmond FBI, and this is Special Agent Chris Parker. We're here—"

"We know why you're here. Bradley informed us." Dan's tone was biting, his resentment clear. "My nephew is the *sole* reason we've agreed to this meeting. You should know that before you start prying into our lives."

"Understood, Mr. Garland." Autumn glanced at Chris beside her, whose mouth was moving in a way that could only mean he was about to release some asinine remark. "May we come in for just a few minutes?"

Dan stepped aside, allowing them entry. Photos of Natalie hung on the hallway stretching out from a large, marble-floored foyer. First, her baby pictures from a cute newborn shoot. Then, the toddler years. Preschool. A grade-school portrait where Natalie's bright smile revealed that she'd lost her two front teeth.

The image caught Autumn in the chest. So adorable and so haunting.

So awful to stare at that happy little face and realize that girl was gone forever.

Then, of course, as the progression continued, Natalie became an adolescent and blossomed into a beautiful young woman. Each year of high school showed a slightly more mature Miss Garland, growing into the—

Autumn fought the urge to slap a palm over her mouth when her gaze reached Natalie's senior pictures. They'd been taken in front of Dogwood Falls. The irony was biting and unfair. As though the falls were mocking the Garlands in their own home.

Terri ushered them into an elegant living room, indicating two cushioned chairs for the agents. She and Dan sat across from them on a silvery-blue sofa, a glass and dark wood coffee table between. No beverages were offered, no small talk made.

"I'm so sorry for your loss, Mr. and Mrs. Garland. Please know that we are only here to help." Autumn pretended not to notice Dan shaking his head while glowering at her. "Can you tell me what Natalie was like growing up? Her personality? Hobbies?"

"She was such a bright child," Terri gushed with immediate affection. "Straight A's and so much promise."

Dan shot his wife a harsh scowl. "And she wasted all of that potential by taking the coward's way out."

Ouch. Autumn hadn't expected such a cruel statement from Natalie's own father. Even Chris stiffened in alarm beside her.

Terri attempted to ignore the comment. "Natalie was a sweet girl. She would have done anything for anyone. She always wanted to believe the best in people."

"Even when we told her what a horrible loser her boyfriend was." Dan's cruel interjection was expected at this point. "Did she listen? No. Didn't even *try* to."

Her composure began to crumble as Terri defended her daughter yet again. "Teenagers don't listen when they think they're in love. That's normal. That's every teenage girl in the entire world, Dan."

"Natalie was better than that." Dan's declaration of his daughter's greatness was somehow devoid of any affection. "She *chose* to be less than she was capable of."

"You always put too much pressure on Natalie! Even when she was just a *child*!" Terri's rage unfurled like a lightning storm.

"I encouraged her!" Dan matched Terri's volume and intensity. "I wanted her to succeed!"

Terri stood, shaking a finger in Dan's face. "You were a taskmaster! She needed a father! She turned to drinking and ran away from us *because of you*! My baby girl *left* because of you, and now she is gone *forever*!"

"That was *not* my fault!" Mr. Garland was roaring now. "She was a big girl, and she made her own bad decisions! We taught her right from wrong! She chose her fate!"

"I will *always* hold you responsible for Natalie's death. *Always!*" Terri broke into a sob and ran from the living room. Her footsteps clumped up the stairs, followed by the unrepentant slam of a door.

An awful, uncomfortable silence followed the echo, apparently one that not even Chris was willing to break. Autumn sat in the stillness, her soul aching for poor Terri Garland. How did a mother ever recover from that amount of pain?

Dan finally refocused on Autumn and Chris, his misery, regret, and anger screaming through bloodshot eyes of the hell he now lived in. It was a hell that no one could fix, and Autumn's heart splintered for the man despite the role he may have played in Natalie's ultimate demise.

"Get out. Get the hell out of my house." After giving the command, Dan marched from the room and disappeared down the hallway.

Chris walked toward the door, not waiting to be told twice. "Let's go." When the front door swung shut behind them, he seemed to freeze on the front stoop. He ducked his head, but not before Autumn glimpsed liquid glistening in his eyes.

Was Chris Parker having an emotional response to the sad scene they'd just witnessed?

For a moment, shock held her in place. She recovered quickly and ventured a cautious step toward him. Preparing to have her head bitten off, she kept her voice soft. "Are you all right?"

Once again, Chris surprised her. Instead of the expected angry outburst, he stared up at the cloudless blue sky and bit his lower lip. "I know what that's like."

"Parents who scream?" Autumn wasn't sure she understood, but she wasn't losing the chance to gain some insight into Agent Parker's inexplicable behaviors.

He glanced down at her. "No. Parents who don't love each other. I know what it's like to be a kid with parents like that. Part of Natalie had to be miserable before she ever got pregnant and began her own personal shitshow."

Autumn ventured another step closer. "You're probably right."

"I am right." His reply was firm but without the normal bite. "My parents were never on the same page. I doubt they ever loved each other. Maybe before I was born. I came from this same exact scenario, minus the finely manicured lawns and pillars." He tapped one of the pristine white columns guarding the front door.

There still wasn't any malice emanating from Chris. Given the sudden pallor to his face, he almost appeared ill. Autumn put an empathetic hand on his shoulder, absorbing the current of information about young Chris Parker that none of his colleagues were privy to.

Poor. Chris's family had been poor. His financial status was well-known in the small town he'd grown up in and had made him somewhat of a pariah in high school. He'd struggled for so long and so hard to be accepted, to do his best and get ahead. His parents were too busy working to put food on the table or fighting with each other to give much by way of support to their son's dreams.

Autumn tensed. But also, he hated her. *Hated. Her.* Despised her because…

Chris pulled away, appearing vulnerable for the first time ever in Autumn's presence. He patted his coif of hair, worried perhaps that his messy emotions had destroyed the work of art on his head.

You know why he hates you. He's upset about how easily you pranced right into the BAU. He worked for years to earn what you were offered almost immediately. Of course that's upsetting.

Autumn didn't need more stolen information to put two

and two together. His reasons for resenting her made sense. A turn of the tables, and she may have resented him just as much.

"Hey," she offered, emboldened by her new understanding, "do you want to just go grab a cup of coffee before we meet up with Aiden and Mia? Sit and talk for a little bit?"

His eyebrows lifted, and for a brief instant, a grateful smile plucked at his lips. A few seconds later, his visage hardened, and the Special Agent Chris Parker Autumn was more familiar with returned. "I don't need your help. You don't exactly have the best shrink record ever anyway."

As Chris stomped off the porch, Autumn let his words sink straight to her gut. Her most regrettable blunder to date was well-known by the entire team. The entire *Bureau*. She'd failed to recognize the magnitude of Justin Black's danger, and that mistake had nearly cost Winter her life.

While Quantico may have improved Autumn's federal agent skills and tactics, all the degrees in the world didn't mean she was a good psychologist.

Chris wasn't wrong. She'd let everyone down in an unforgettable—possibly even unforgivable—manner.

Autumn glanced back at the Garland house one last time before returning to her waiting partner. As soon as she climbed into the Explorer and snapped on the seat belt, she shrank into the cushioned seat, turning her face toward the passenger window.

One overriding thought gnawed at her mind the entire drive back to Beechum, flooding her entire being with despair.

Maybe I truly can't help anyone anymore. Maybe my biggest mistake was in thinking that I ever could.

11

Special Agent Mia Logan followed SSA Parrish through the open doorway of the Beechum County Medical Examiner's office. Dr. Warren Castor, M.E., was ready and waiting with a polite smile and hearty handshakes.

"I can't tell you both how glad I am to meet you." The genuine relief in his voice struck Mia as alarming despite the warm greeting.

Just how bad is this situation?

The welcome from a friendly face eased Aiden's typically stoic features into a relieved smile. "I'm Supervisory Special Agent Aiden Parrish. This is Special Agent Mia Logan. We're here to help however we can, Doctor. Would you mind answering a few questions for us?"

"Of course." Dr. Castor gestured toward two chairs sitting adjacent to his own across a tidy desk. "Any assistance I can provide at all, I'm more than happy to."

Mia sat first, and Aiden followed suit. She noticed the whites of Dr. Castor's eyes were intricate mosaics of thin red lines. The man obviously hadn't been sleeping enough, and who could blame him?

They didn't have time to waste, and Aiden Parrish was the last agent on earth to beat around the bush. "Could you give a rough estimate of the number of suicides Beechum County has experienced as of late?"

Warren grabbed his coffee mug from the desktop and frowned. "Off the top of my head? A dozen. At least. Too many. And the numbers seem to be going up at a rather disturbing rate."

Mia wondered if there was any rate of people taking their own lives that didn't fall into the category of troubling. "You believe all of the deaths to be, without question, suicides?"

"On the surface, yes," Dr. Castor answered without hesitation. "But while the obvious cause of death has been clear in each case, I sense there may be something else going on. Most of the victims spent some amount of time at Harmony House before meeting their demise."

"Are you suggesting Harmony House is somehow *inspiring* these acts of self-harm?" Aiden asked the question to cover bases, as the M.E.'s insinuation was clear. Mia could discern from Dr. Castor's face how concerned he was about the establishment.

He pointed at his computer screen. "I'd have to pull up the files to be sure of the exact number, but Harmony House has come up on so many backgrounds of the deceased that I couldn't possibly deny the correlation between the two. Granted, there were some who were struggling addicts last spotted at AA or NA meetings, which puts them in a high suicide group to begin with."

Aiden rubbed his jaw, seeming to consider the doctor's statement before speaking. "Let me ask you this, Dr. Castor. As a professional man whose time is quite valuable, would you consider an investigation into Harmony House a good usage of the Federal Bureau of Investigation's resources?"

"Absolutely." Warren's grave countenance grew darker

still. "Someone needs to dig around in there, and they need to do it quickly. He's off in a way I can't quite describe."

"He?" Mia's knee-jerk inquiry was needless.

They all knew who "he" was.

"Damien Parr. He's not right in the head." Dr. Castor glanced from Mia to Aiden. "But that's just my personal opinion. I have no statement to put on record. And I daresay you'll form your own opinions soon enough."

Aiden thanked the doctor for his time, and after another round of good-natured handshakes, he and Mia left the office with the confirmation they'd sought.

On their walk back to the vehicle, Mia turned their brief conversation over in her head. Small-town gossip was often exaggerated and seldom worth the air it took to spread, but the opinion of a doctor whose profession centered around examining dead bodies was a different matter altogether. His job involved assessing the terrible outcomes of the rash of suicides with his own two eyes. If anyone were to note an oddity amongst local deaths, Dr. Castor was that man.

"Here's what I'm thinking." Aiden started the Expedition and adjusted the air-conditioning. "We go check into the team's hotel, change into street clothes, and pay an exploratory visit to Harmony House."

Mia replayed Dr. Castor's words. *"He's not right in the head."* If Harmony House truly was a cult and Damien Parr the eccentric mastermind leading the way, two complete strangers dropping in might create a rather large and imme- diate wave.

She buckled her seat belt and locked her door. "Tell me you have a plan because this guy gives me the creeps already. I don't think we'll go unnoticed."

"Nor would we want to." Aiden pulled the SUV back onto the road. "We need to be detected to have an opportunity to ask questions, whether from Damien or his followers."

Mia shuddered. *"Followers.* That word in itself is just wrong."

Aiden chuckled, heading down the highway toward the finest accommodations that Beechum had to offer, the Holiday Inn. "I take it organized religion isn't your cup of tea, Agent Logan?"

"My parents are devout Catholics. I guess it never really took with me. Not my brother either." Her chest cramped, and she immediately wished she hadn't brought up Ned.

"I see." To Mia's relief, Aiden steered around the sibling subject. She wasn't sure exactly how much the SSA knew, but he was well aware that her brother had died in the recent past. And *everyone* was aware that Sloan Grant had dated him. "Well, I think Harmony House will probably be a far cry from your previous church experiences."

Despite the lingering ache beneath her ribs, Mia managed a grin. "No Hail Marys?"

"Ha." Aiden pulled the vehicle to a stop in the hotel parking lot. "More like 'Hail Damien,' from what I understand. Let's check the team in at the front desk, change, and meet back in the lobby in twenty. We'll grab lunch and go over our game plan. Sound good?"

Taking a nap on her standard size bed with the hotel's AC icing the room sounded better, but Mia knew the sooner they got inside the walls of Harmony House—let alone the mind of Damien Parr—the quicker they could uncover whatever madness was taking place and go home.

Mia chose a plain white t-shirt and jeans paired with July-appropriate sandals. She added a touch of mascara and a swipe of lip gloss, attempting to appear more like the average twenty-seven-year-old woman. Wearing makeup had never been her thing, neither as a teen nor as an adult, and especially not as an agent.

Her mother had reminded her on more than one occasion that she was lucky to have dimples and a "cute, cherubic face" because most girls "needed a little help." That had really just been her mother's way of reiterating that Mia could be doing more in the beauty department, but the chiding never fazed her.

She kept her wavy dark hair shoulder-length or higher, yet another matter that her mother had been attempting to "fix" for over a decade. Mia had made clear many times that she didn't foresee herself changing anytime soon, if ever, as far as primping went.

She was just as feminine as the next woman, and maybe she *had* lucked out a little in the face department. There certainly hadn't been a shortage of men approaching her over the years, but the career she'd chosen didn't provide her loads of free time to date.

And that was okay. She'd picked the path where she felt she could do the most good and make the biggest difference. Long before experiencing her own greatest personal loss, she'd always had a heart for the suffering. The voiceless. The victims.

Concealer and curling irons didn't seem important when she considered the innocent human beings enduring pain and torture at the hands of sick criminal minds.

Mia grabbed her purse and gave the bed one last lingering glance.

I'll be back.

Their first-floor suites made the trip to the lobby short and sweet. She spotted Aiden near the front exit and bit her tongue to keep the laughter at bay. The always pristinely dressed SSA had chosen an outfit similar to her own.

Jeans, a light blue t-shirt, and running shoes. He had a baseball cap on his head and could double for a regular suburban dad.

Mia tried to envision Aiden Parrish with a toddler on his

hip and another wrapped around his leg. Laughter sputtered out of her mouth despite her best efforts to control her amusement, and Aiden turned toward the sound.

"Always happy to entertain, Agent Logan." Aiden's voice was as serious as ever, even as he made an attempt at humor. The overt contrast only caused her to laugh harder.

She held up a hand of apology and pulled herself together. "I'm sorry. You look nice. Just…"

"Not so much like a federal agent?" Aiden allowed himself a small grin. "Mission accomplished." He headed for the door, and Mia trailed behind, forcing herself to regain her professional composure.

They drove to a local pizza place less than five minutes down the road. Mia was quietly thrilled, having expected the usual choice of a deli or diner.

"The locals say this is the best slice in town." Aiden slung his door open. "I'm sure they have salads and whatnot as well." He studied her as if waiting for signs of protest at the selection.

He wouldn't get them from her. "This is great. I don't even remember the last time I ate pizza that didn't come from my freezer."

Aiden chuckled and led them through the entrance. "Good. I'm glad you approve because I have ulterior motives for coming here as well."

"Oh?" Mia inspected the homey, casual interior as though the red booths might hold a clue before giving the waitress approaching them a friendly nod.

The middle-aged woman whose name tag read "Marge" had the same *you ain't from here* expression on her face as Sheriff Frank, but if possible, seemed even warier. "Table for two?"

After they were seated in a semi-private booth with a classic red-and-white checkered tablecloth, the waitress jotted down their order and scanned them over one last time with a "harrumph" before retreating toward a door behind the counter.

"You were saying about ulterior motives?" Mia unwrapped her straw and jabbed it through the ice of her water glass.

Aiden adjusted his ball cap and leaned forward, keeping his voice low. "We're going to play a married couple making a casual visit to Harmony House. We're investors. We love a good charity, and we're interested in learning more about what their group does. Trying to get a better idea of the situation before we pump any cash into the organization."

Mia sipped her water as she considered the ruse. "What does that have to do with this place?"

"Well," Aiden gestured around them, "this is a favorite spot for locals. Even the cult locals. I figured it couldn't hurt the believability of our 'situation' for one or two Harmony House members to spy us eating together like a normal married couple before our visit."

There was no world in which Mia could imagine herself married to Supervisory Special Agent Aiden Parrish. They both possessed such calm natures, she figured it would be one of the most silent and boring bouts of matrimony to ever exist.

And everyone knew Aiden was in love with Autumn, even if Aiden didn't admit it yet.

Despite all that, excitement stirred in Mia's chest. The idea of playing a part was new and exhilarating. The closest to official undercover she'd ever gotten. They had no warrant, so any "evidence" they might spot could never be deemed as such, but it was secret agent-ish enough to be fun.

Plus, for once, she wasn't going to be Chris Parker's damage control monitor, and that was a priceless gift in and of itself.

Even as relief swept over her, a pang of guilt hit Mia hard. "I'm not sure Autumn is ever going to forgive you for assigning her with Parker on her first official case."

Aiden's instantaneous, crinkle-eyed smile spoke volumes of his special regard for Agent Trent. The man rarely smiled. Not even when he was smiling.

He lifted a shoulder and gazed out the window at Beechum's bustling small-town traffic. "Agent Trent is tough. She survived Quantico. I know she can handle Parker. I want to make sure she knows it as well."

Mia was positive that Aiden had no idea how much his tone softened when he spoke of Autumn. Neither of them, to her knowledge, had admitted to any feelings whatsoever. But the chemistry was so ridiculously obvious that the denial had become somewhat comical.

"Oh, she can handle him," Mia agreed, happy to glimpse their waitress returning with the coveted slices. The rich, cheesy aroma made her mouth water. "She's been through hell. Autumn's a fighter."

Aiden was silent while their plates were placed before them. Mia noted the disparity between their orders. Her thin-crust pepperoni was the simple classic while Agent Parrish's deep dish was piled high with every ingredient known to mankind.

Pineapples, pepperonis, Canadian bacon, thick red onion strips, anchovies…she was part impressed and part repulsed.

He plucked a banana pepper from the top and pointed it at her in lieu of a finger. "You're a fighter too, Mia. You've been through your own hell. And I want you to know that I fully recognize your worth on this team."

The shock of his comment nearly made Mia choke on her first bite. She sucked down water, but her throat retained the sudden thickness. Like she'd swallowed a rock that had lodged halfway down. "Thank you, Agent Parrish."

"Of course." Aiden speared a chunk of Italian sausage and two green pepper strips with his fork. "But it's important to note, Agent Logan, that there is a rather large disparity between a human being killing another with full intent to do so and horrible, unforeseen accidents happening after unfortunate circumstances have occurred."

Now she understood why he'd brought up her brother, and her hands clenched together in her lap. Part of her wanted to cry, and the rest wanted to scream. The rock in her throat expanded into a boulder, and the burning behind her eyes grew stronger. He had no right. No right to—

"Your loss *is* awful. Please don't misunderstand me." Aiden's voice gentled as he grabbed his glass of soda. "You're entitled to your grief and your anger. Just don't live out your life directing all your pain toward the wrong source. It's easier to have someone to blame. There's a certain closure in that."

Mia stared at her pizza without seeing it, struggling to find something to say. She felt betrayed, as if he'd lured her here under false pretenses, lowering her guard with promises of undercover assignments and silly ball caps just so he could cut her with a surprise attack.

She swallowed the angry tears. No matter how smart Aiden was, his admonition—she understood that's what was being delivered—was flawed. "I have closure," she declared, pushing her plate away. "I know exactly who killed my brother."

"A car wreck killed your brother, Agent Logan. Not a person." He sighed, and she sensed that this wasn't a conversation he'd ever wanted to have, either. "He was taken out by a horrible, tragic accident. She didn't murder him."

"She still killed him." Mia spit the reply before she could stop herself.

Aiden tilted his head and studied her with the serious

Agent Parrish expression she was used to. "She didn't. No one did. And I think deep down you know that."

Sloan's face flashed through her mind. They'd been close before Ned's passing. Friends. And as much as Mia hated the woman now, she knew Sloan wasn't a murderer. Sloan was simply one step in a series of unfortunate events that ended in Ned's death.

The hole in Mia's heart deepened, formed a crater, a vacuum, an abyss. Some days, she wasn't sure there was enough material in the world to fill the empty space. Accident or not, Ned was still dead, and no amount of hashing through the past would ever bring him back.

So no, Mia wasn't ready to forgive Sloan for being that steppingstone. Not now. Possibly never.

Aiden cleared his throat. "I'm well aware that I'm speaking of things that are none of my business, and I promise you that I will never speak of them again. But when I perceive one of my agents—an exemplary, promising agent—threatening her own success by clinging to a hatred that is unwarranted, I believe it my duty to remind said agent that she can free herself at any point in time should she decide to."

Mia's mind returned to the day they'd saved Winter, and she sucked in a breath. They'd needed the bomb squad, and Aiden had ordered *her* to make that call. "You *wanted* me to talk to Sloan that day. That's why you had me call the counterterrorism unit."

"I can neither confirm nor deny." Aiden turned his full attention back to the remaining slices on his plate. "Eat up. We've got a cult to visit."

PARKED in the circular paved lot in front of Harmony House, Mia pursed her lips as she and Aiden viewed the main, three-story building in silence. The structure truly did resemble many of the megachurches that had popped up all across the country over the last few decades. Chris had been right about that.

Flawless gray brick walls and towering glass doors sat beneath an ornate sign that read: *Harmony House, Join the Circle, Be the Change.*

A little extreme and a lot unorthodox, but still not exactly in the category of alarming.

However, the amount of activity surrounding the House was unusual, to say the least. There were individuals walking, jogging, biking, chattering together in groups, as well as a few wandering alone. Mia didn't spot anyone who appeared less than content, and most seemed completely engrossed in the goings-on of their small community.

The complex was not the average "house of worship." If anything, the place could double for a new-age spa that hosted wellness retreats or yoga camps.

As she scrutinized the cheerful faces, Mia cautioned herself not to judge too harshly. The FBI was very interested in Damien Parr and his financial affairs, but even if he did turn out to be as crooked as suspected, his followers weren't to blame.

"Take a look." Aiden placed his iPad on the center console and pulled up a map of the vast Harmony House estate. "Over two hundred acres. That's a lot of land."

The satellite footage showed many buildings, but judging from its position on the map, Mia was positive the structure right before them was the main building.

"We've been able to deduce that the large building," Aiden pointed past the windshield, "contains Damien Parr's home and office, as well as the kitchen, treatment rooms, and other offices for miscellaneous cult members. Behind are a series of cabins where Parr's followers live, followed by the church building and several outbuildings used for equipment storage."

"The place is huge." Mia hadn't been aware of the magnitude of the organization before viewing the images. "There's gotta be a lot of money exchanging hands to keep that much activity going."

Aiden slid the iPad back into the briefcase that he would not be carrying with him for once. He pulled a small gold ring from his jeans pocket and handed it to Mia. "If you lose that, you owe me four dollars and ninety-nine cents."

Mia laughed and slid the ring on the fourth finger of her left hand. The gold glinted in the sunlight and made her flash back to Sloan and how Ned had been so sure they would marry and spend their lives together. "You were right." She opened the passenger's side door with a gentle push.

Aiden opened his own door but paused before climbing out. "About?"

"I know she didn't kill him. Logically, anyway." Mia tightened her grip on her purse strap. "But I'm not sure I'll ever stop *feeling* like she did."

"Everybody starts somewhere, Mia." Aiden nodded toward the awaiting building. "Let's go check this out."

A crack-free sidewalk led from the parking lot straight through the technicolor green grass and to the front doors. The entry had appeared tall from the vehicle, but up close, Mia was convinced the doors were better suited to a castle. As they approached, she had to tip her head back to fully appreciate the massive scale.

Although, at the moment, she felt more like a Munchkin in Oz than a fairy-tale princess.

Aiden pushed the door open, holding it while she entered

a cavernous foyer with high ceilings. He'd barely stepped to her side before several young adults approached them.

They bounded over with beaming faces and enthusiastic gestures, like a pack of golden retriever puppies. Several of them sang, "Welcome!" in unison.

Mia's smile faltered at the unexpected creep factor, but she held her cool. Even when, instead of stopping an arm's length away as social customs dictated, they rushed closer and enveloped her in a sea of hugs.

The surprise contact triggered an inner freak out. Mia's body stiffened, as if preparing for attack. When all the residents did was embrace her and murmur more welcomes in her ear, she allowed herself to relax.

No big deal, just lots of strange bodies pressing all around me.

The last woman sobbed happy tears on Mia's shoulder before releasing her to join the others.

Mia took advantage of the lull to step closer to Aiden, peering up at his face to gauge his reaction to all this. As usual, the SSA's chiseled features betrayed nothing. Still, she bet he was even more squicked out on the inside than she was. Affection and physical contact didn't seem to rank high on Agent Parrish's list of hobbies. In fact, Mia hadn't witnessed the man hug anyone. Ever.

No way was he enjoying the forced proximity now.

"Everything happens for a reason." A teary-eyed woman gripped one of Mia's hands between both of hers. "Fate brought you here, and I'm *so* grateful. My name is Alice Leeson. Please, sit." She waved a hand toward a long, narrow table. It was one of those communal types often found in pubs, where multiple parties could all sit together.

The other young people, most of whom were women, encouraged them to sit and rest, so Mia selected a spot at the end of the wooden bench. Aiden took the empty seat beside her.

Platters of cookies and cheeses and fruits appeared immediately, carried in by more smiling women who emerged from a doorway that Mia guessed led to the kitchen.

She considered a cheese cube, thought better of it, and left the food untouched. Aiden, however, held up a giant chocolate chip cookie and smiled as though he'd never been so pleased.

Remember, you're supposed to be playing along.

Mia grabbed the cheese and popped the square into her mouth, grinning at everyone as widely as she knew how.

She almost jumped when Aiden threw an arm around her but caught herself at the last second. "We've been told such wonderful things about this place, Alice." He squeezed her shoulder. "Haven't we, sweetheart?"

Mia reached for another cube. "We sure have. Amazing things."

Some secret agent you're turning out to be. You've almost broken cover at least three times already, and you haven't even been here ten minutes.

When Aiden gazed down into her face, Mia was ready. She smiled dreamily back up at him. Even gave a little flutter of her lashes. He squeezed her once before leaning back. "My lovely wife and I thought we should step in and behold the charitable work for ourselves."

Alice's giggle was mirthful and light. With her long blonde hair woven into a thick braid that hung over one shoulder and her bright blue eyes, she reminded Mia of a Disney princess, which fit well with the whole castle vibe. "There's no place like Harmony House. We're a charity, but *so* much more."

"Oh, how lovely. What does your organization do?" Mia trilled the inquiry to the bubbly blonde woman. If Alice *was* part of a cult, she seemed incredibly happy about that fact.

Alice clasped Mia's hand again. "We save people. We bring them into the Circle. I was all alone and so confused about my purpose in life. I wasn't sure if there was any purpose at all, and then I chanced upon this wonderful place. At Harmony House, I've found total acceptance and my true reason for living. Love." She released Mia's hand to extend her arms wide. "We're here to spread love."

Aiden pressed a hand to his chest, like he was touched by her statement. "That sounds wonderful, Alice. Tell me, what makes Harmony House such a special place? Where does all that love and purpose come from?"

Alice opened her pretty mouth to answer but stopped as a handsome man with thick dark hair entered the room. He was immediately surrounded and bombarded with hugs, taking his time to embrace every single person as though they were his dear children.

Mia's pulse picked up. She and Aiden had both viewed photos of this man while preparing for this visit.

That was him. That was the cult leader.

She pasted a pleasant smile on her face, trying not to be obvious as she studied the stranger between bites of cheese. Beside her, Aiden was no doubt doing the same thing.

Once each member had a turn to hug him, the man made his way to Alice and pulled her tight before addressing Mia and Aiden.

"Hello, I'm Damien Parr." His smile was genuine, full of warmth. It was so dazzling that Mia no longer wondered how the man had gained such a following. His eyes were a luminous, almost clear shade of pale blue that gave the impression of ice crystals on a frozen lake. The kind of eyes that seemed like they could peer right into Mia's soul.

Magnetic. That was the word. Damien's charm was magnetic.

"I love to find new faces in my House. No one comes to

me by accident. Tell me, my friends, is there anything missing in your lives?"

That hollow opened up inside Mia again as the answer sprang to mind. Ned. Ned was missing. And while the information was private, throwing in a little personal fact couldn't hurt. At least she wouldn't have to fake the sadness—

Aiden took Damien's extended hand and gave it a vigorous shake. "We've heard of all the good that Harmony House does for the community, Mr. Parr. My wife and I are investors, and a large portion of our funds are invested in charities like Harmony House. We'd like to help in any way we can."

Damien's face lit up. Something about the way he looked at Mia made her feel like the most important person in the room. "That's wonderful. What an absolutely beautiful act of kindness. If you'll just come with me—"

"Damien." A male voice came from the hallway.

"I'm so sorry." Damien's smile didn't falter at the interruption. "Duty calls. If you folks would just wait here for a few minutes?"

When he vanished down the hall, Mia deflated a little. Almost like he'd taken some of the warmth and excitement with him.

Careful, Mia. You want to fit in here, but not too well.

She shook off the bizarre sensation and turned back to Aiden, who watched her with a slight crease between his eyes.

"Everything okay?"

Mia nodded and held off a shiver. Even if she could explain the weird magnetism rippling from Damien Parr, she'd probably be too embarrassed to try.

"Okay. I think I need to get up and stretch my legs for a bit. Are you good here with Alice?" He rubbed his mouth, using a finger to point in the direction where Damien had retreated.

The SSA wanted to sniff around, and Mia didn't have any qualms about sitting with Alice for the duration of his hunt. Alice Leeson was a ray of pure sunshine. Easily one of the most amiable humans Mia had ever encountered.

"Just fine. Take your time, honey." She gave his shoulder an affectionate pat and turned all her attention on Alice. "Please, tell me more. You were talking about the love and purpose you found at Harmony House?"

AIDEN KEPT his pace at a leisurely stroll as he entered the empty corridor. All the better to scan each and every doorway he passed.

The first two doors were shut, but the following four were open to varying degrees. Every one of them seemed to lead to makeshift bedrooms. A little farther down, a restroom sign hung above another cracked doorway.

His footsteps were quiet as he continued forward, leaving the murmur of voices from the dining hall behind. To sell his cover story, he kept his hands in his pockets, and his shoulders relaxed. Nothing to see here. Just a rich investor wanting to stretch his legs and take a quick peek around.

He was only a few feet from the bathroom when male voices drifted out the open door. Another step and Aiden was close enough to glance inside.

Damien stood within the space, talking to what appeared to be a very upset young man, who was sobbing uncontrollably. Aiden stood still for nearly a full minute before the cult leader finally spoke.

Damien placed his hands on the young man's shoulders.

"You are a good man, Evan Blair, and this is a *safe place.* Never forget that."

Aiden registered the name and moved just enough to get a clearer look at Evan's face.

His features were twisted as though he were in physical agony. "I just can't shake this guilt. *It won't go away.* All day and all night…"

"There is no judgment in the Circle." Damien pulled the distressed follower into a hug. "You are making all of the right moves, I promise you. No judgment, Evan. None."

Aiden had planned to sneak by to continue snooping, but the statement held him rooted to the floor. The hairs on the back of his neck rose. As warm as Damien's sentiment about no judgment was, some of his reassurances were odd.

What kind of "moves" was Damien referring to?

Whatever the significance, Aiden had stood here long enough. If he didn't want to get caught eavesdropping, he needed to move.

Just as he started to slip past, Evan shifted positions and lifted his head. Aiden's stomach dropped as their gazes locked for an instant.

Shooting the young man an *oops, sorry* face, he pivoted in an abrupt U-turn, retracing his steps as he headed back to Mia. Adrenaline surged in his veins, but he ignored the temptation to hurry his pace. Running away would only make him appear guiltier.

His hands remained in his pockets, his shoulders loose, reminding himself to stick to the script. He had no reason to flee. He was a rich philanthropist, scoping out a potential charity. He had every right to research his investment.

Mia sat in the same place he'd left her, engrossed in a deep conversation with Alice. He dropped into the open spot next to her and feigned interest in their discussion. He smiled and nodded, but his senses remained trained on the doorway.

Less than a minute later, Aiden's skin tingled just before Damien and Evan entered the room. The leader of Harmony House's translucent gaze traveled across several other occupants before stopping on him. Aiden gave him a friendly smile in return before refocusing back on the conversation between the two women. He badly wanted to brief Mia about the run-in but knew that would have to wait.

"My friends…" Damien smiled as everyone in the room turned to him, blissful expressions on their faces. The man seemed to bask in the attention and soaked it up for long moments before locking eyes with Aiden. "If anyone needs to unburden themselves, now is the time. The Circle is a safe place, and all who enter Harmony House are under my protection."

The words were obviously intended to comfort and encourage, but the hairs on the back of Aiden's neck stood up regardless. No choice now but to play the act out.

He raised his hand and waited to be acknowledged. It was a tradition he'd been happy to leave behind back in grade school. The benevolent nod Damien bestowed upon him rankled—under any other circumstances, he wouldn't give two shits about gaining permission from this drugstore Jesus-meets-Jim Jones wannabe—but he didn't allow his irritation to show.

"I'd like to say a few words." He patted Mia's hand. "My wife and I have considered how fortunate we are in this world. We've given much to charity, but we feel we can *and should* give more. There doesn't seem to be any worthier place to contribute to than Harmony House."

A round of cheers and applause followed his statement, and Damien strode toward them, his delight apparent and his arms open wide.

Aiden and Mia both rose to their feet. He inhaled a silent breath and steeled himself to be embraced...*again*... managing to hide his revulsion when Damien's arms wrapped him into a hearty squeeze.

I don't even hug my mother, buddy. Ease up.

"How about a tour?" Damien offered the suggestion while hugging Mia a bit longer than necessary. "I would love to give you both a personal tour of the estate."

Success.

Aiden allowed himself a moment to absorb the cool rush of relief. Until Damien had extended the invitation, he'd worried he and Mia were about to get booted over his hallway blunder. "Thank you, we'd be delighted."

Mia also murmured her thanks, and within the minute, they were being led around Harmony House by Damien Parr himself.

The main house fit with what Aiden had learned through intel. A large kitchen and dining room where everyone could eat together, bedrooms, meditation rooms, and Damien's office. The Harmony House leader didn't show them his personal space, but Aiden took solid note of where it was located within the building.

Parr acted the part of the gracious tour guide, feeding them facts about the good deeds performed at Harmony House as they walked. They exited out of a back door onto more lush green grass, where Damien led them into one of the dozens of small cabins nestled between the trees. "We can build one of these for just two thousand dollars. A home for the homeless. A place of belonging for those who have nowhere to go."

He opened the door and invited them to peek inside. Aiden scanned the interior. One room for living and sleeping, with a tiny, attached bathroom consisting of a shower, toilet, and sink. Not the Ritz Carlton, but better than an overcrowded shelter. To a desperate, homeless, or lost individual, a private, protected space like this was probably akin to heaven itself.

Damien gave them a few minutes to explore and admire the dwellings, then urged them toward the church that had been built in the center of the property. Aiden and Mia went right along with every suggestion, oohing and aahing in all the proper spots and playing the hell out of the happy and loaded investor couple.

After the massive size of the main building, the church structure was simpler than Aiden had expected. Older too. Much smaller, with four rectangular walls and a spacious, open room Aiden guessed was the sanctuary. The soaring steeple was beautiful but looked to be in need of repair.

Damien paused in the middle and spun in a slow circle. "This is where we worship."

Both Aiden and Mia stopped walking too. Harmony House was listed as a religious organization. A wise move for Parr to make as it came with certain constitutional protections, safety nets, and tax breaks. Judging by the simplicity of the church, the building had been erected more for show than anything else. Damien more than likely used the space as a convenient venue for his charismatic speeches and called them church services for good measure.

The man was smart. Certain to cover all his fiscal bases. Whatever show he put on to keep up appearances and alleviate suspicions, Damien Parr would pull it off with flying colors.

Aiden was confident he already understood Damien very well. Classic narcissist. Potential psychopath. Regardless of the god-complex Parr was nursing, he wasn't unique. Aiden had crossed paths with his type many, many times before.

Damien concluded their tour by taking them out to what

he called "the overlook." A large deck with built-in bench seating stretched out over a deep drop in the mountain.

"This space is the pride and joy of Harmony House." Damien held out an arm, gesturing toward the skyline. "The magnificent view is a reflection of the beauty that lives here and the peace we nurture on this land. We hope to spread hope and goodness to as many people as possible."

The view was amazing. Aiden could never argue that. The silhouette of the tree-topped mountain range must be nothing short of spectacular when washed in the bright colors of sunrise and sunset. Quiet, with only the chirps and rustles of the forest to intrude upon the senses, the overlook was a commendable design.

Mia exchanged a subtle glance with him before addressing Damien. "How many people would you estimate that Harmony House helps each year?"

Damien was delighted by the inquiry. He grabbed Mia's hand with both of his, an act that Aiden was positive Agent Logan didn't appreciate even though her friendly smile didn't wane. "That number would be impossible to pinpoint because we help *so many* individuals. We run a daily soup kitchen in Beechum and do bi-monthly food drives. Our outreach groups stretch across Beechum, Rutshire, and many other neighboring counties. We're always seeking out people who need our assistance."

I bet you are, you creepy sonofabitch.

Hidden by his pockets, Aiden's hands balled into fists.

"We provide shelter to any and all in need." Damien sounded like he was reading from a marketing brochure. "There are counseling services offered at the main house, and the entire estate is self-sustaining."

The last bit caught Aiden's attention. A self-sustainable utopia was always appealing in theory, but there wasn't much money in the dream. The cash flow had to come from somewhere else.

"Wow, self-sustaining. That's remarkable." Mia peered over the barrier and down into the darkened gorge below. The wooden guardrail was not even waist-high on him but hit closer to Mia's neck. Aiden fought back a genuine smile and briefly wondered if Agent Logan had ever been turned away from a carnival ride because of her height.

"Yes, it is." Damien's pride was unending, but so was his charm. "Gardens, root cellars, barns for the animals we keep. Some are used for meat, but most are for milk and eggs. We use solar power and water from the stream. Harmony House could thrive even if an apocalypse hit."

Red flags waved in Aiden's head. Forget utopia. Damien Parr was starting to hint at the type of anti-government rhetoric that made men like Aiden twitchy.

He stepped closer to Mia, fixing a wary eye on Damien while maintaining the guise of a curious tourist. "Are you expecting an apocalypse?" He chuckled after making the comment to ensure it wasn't taken too seriously. But he wanted an answer.

Damien's expression darkened. "Everything I've created here flies directly in the face of big government. Politicians and the 'one percent' are striving to suppress the hard-working people of this country. I have no doubt that Harmony House has rubbed the government the wrong way, and I wouldn't be surprised to catch sight of the Feds bursting onto my property at any given moment."

Shock sizzled beneath Aiden's skin. Beside him, Mia tensed. He recovered in the next breath and laid a reassuring hand on her back. "That seems a bit extreme. Why would the government have a problem with you helping people?"

"Exactly." Damien snapped his fingers, and the sound echoed through the valley. "If they were really 'of the people, by the people, *for the people*,' they'd host a parade in honor of what I'm doing here."

It didn't escape Aiden's attention that at some point between self-sustaining and now, Parr had shifted gears. Like all good narcissists, "we" had turned into "I." Harmony House was now *his* creation, the good work being done attributable to him and him alone.

"Perhaps one day they will host a parade. You deserve it, Damien."

The parade Aiden had in mind wouldn't align with Parr's vision, but that was okay. The image of his team storming Damien's compound warmed Aiden's heart more than flower-covered floats or marching bands ever could.

Almost as satisfying was the knowledge that Parr already faced a federal investigation. Beneath all that allure and lovey-dovey, feed-the-world crap lurked a selfish heart and a diabolical mind. Aiden was all but certain.

"You're too kind." Damien preened at the compliment. "Well, I digress. I've chattered a bit too long here. Let me lead you back to the main house."

Scanning the property as they walked, Aiden noted that nearly every person they passed, male or female, paused in their endeavors to gaze at Damien with adoration.

Or more like, they were mooning over the man Damien pretended to be.

The poor bastards. Aiden had to stop watching the display or risk his mask slipping. He found their blind devotion equal parts upsetting and infuriating. Like a damn bunch of lemmings following their leader right off the side of a cliff. Only Parr would never actually jump.

Aiden itched to pull the wool from their eyes and expose this slimy jerk for the grifter he was, but even if he wasn't undercover and could enlighten them, it wouldn't matter.

Brainwashing was a terrible and powerful thing.

They finally arrived back at Harmony House and followed Damien to the kitchen area.

Alice, Evan, and the other people in the immediate vicinity gathered around their leader, clearly mesmerized by the man. The term "followers" had been a wholly accurate description.

On an intellectual level, Aiden got it. On a personal one, he'd never understand.

The chatter died off the second Damien raised his hands. The room seemed to draw a collective breath, and every face turned to him in rapt attention. Waiting.

"*Be* the change," Damien called out.

The reply came in the form of a chorus from every mouth present. "*We* are the change."

Aiden's hackles rose at the robotic exchange, and his entire body stiffened. Any lingering seed of doubt he'd held about Harmony House deserving the label of a cult vanished. These people were brainwashed, through and through.

After a brief lull, the followers resumed their bustling about the house. Aiden seized the moment for a smooth exit. "Thank you, Damien, for the tour and your time. My wife and I will consider everything we've learned here today and get back to you regarding our monetary decision."

Damien Parr's eyes gleamed as Aiden uttered the exact words he wanted to hear.

"I am always available to my fellow man." He gave a dramatic bow and turned to leave, but Mia stopped him.

"I really am interested in how far the hand of Harmony House stretches." The earnest note in Mia's voice unsettled Aiden. "I find your organization fascinating. All the good you do. I can only imagine how many people you reach."

"Tell you what," Damien squeezed her shoulder, "I'll gather up those numbers and send them straight to you. Email?" He grabbed a notepad and pen from the counter.

Mia spelled out the address, giving Damien her personal email for unknown and inexplicable reasons that only amplified the uneasiness in Aiden's gut. They hadn't even given their *names*, fake or otherwise.

But Aiden couldn't express his disapproval without giving up their ruse, so he used the extra few minutes to press a little more.

"How long, on average, would you say is a normal stay for a person who comes to Harmony House?" Aiden fired off the question with little warning. "What happens to these people when they leave? *Do* they leave?"

Damien blinked his icy blue eyes several times in response to the rapid procession of questions. Aiden could sense he'd set off an alarm of sorts in the man's brain, but there was no reason Parr should take issue with answering him.

"Well," Damien clapped a hand to Aiden's shoulder for the umpteenth time, "my table welcomes anyone in need of nourishment. That goes for physical *and* spiritual needs. And everyone is able to stay as long as they wish."

Aiden fought the urge to ask about Natalie Garland specifically. Doing so would blow their cover and gain them no knowledge in the process. Picturing the young woman here amongst these shining, happy faces before plunging into a swirling vortex of river water didn't fit together for *many* reasons.

Maybe his followers were genuine, but Aiden called bullshit when it came to Damien Parr. The man wasn't all that he represented himself to be. There was more in that brain than altruism. Like pride, ego. *Greed.*

His jaw ached as he accepted the frustrating truth. Under their current guise, neither he nor Mia would be able to glean much information on Natalie. Time to reconvene with the team and assess from there.

He took Mia's elbow and steered her toward the front entrance.

Alice bubbled up out of thin air by the door, wrapping her thin arms around them each in a final, unrequested embrace. "I wish you would stay for dinner. I swear every minute you spend here with us will bring you nothing but happiness."

Aiden searched the guileless blue eyes, and for a second, was tempted to shake her.

You poor, lost little girl.

Aiden repeated the thought as Mia expressed her regrets at having to leave. Either Agent Logan was giving the performance of a lifetime, or she really was sad to go.

His stomach knotted. Maybe he'd made an error in bringing Agent Logan to Harmony House. He should have realized sooner. Mia was still vulnerable after her brother's death.

Damien grasped the handle and held the door open wide for them. "You really should stay. My door is always open."

Yet you can't wait to get rid of us. I'm on to you.

By the time they'd been ushered out and settled back into the Expedition, Aiden had two clear goals in mind. One, he wanted to gather as much information on the individual members of Harmony House as possible...especially Evan Blair and his mountain of guilt.

Two, Aiden wanted to make sure that Mia Logan hadn't been snake charmed by the arrogant, manipulative serpent that was Damien Parr.

12

Autumn pulled out a chair next to Winter, who was already seated by Noah at the table in the Beechum Police Station's conference room. Aiden stood near the whiteboard, ready and waiting to get the briefing started.

Deputy King stood behind Mia's chair, and Sheriff Frank once again leaned up against the wall with her arms crossed. While Autumn had grown used to local law enforcement not always welcoming their presence with open arms, the sheriff seemed especially hostile.

Autumn's natural internal response was to root out the reasons why.

"Sheriff, Deputy, Agents." Aiden nodded at them all in turn. "Now that we've all done a bit of digging, we've got a leg to stand on with this case. That means we need to compare notes and get moving. Agent Dalton, I believe you wanted to share some photos?"

Noah strode to the front of the room, iPad in hand. He swiped a few times and then tapped his screen. An image appeared of a cliff with Dogwood Falls in the background.

"This is the highest peak at Dogwood Falls and the precise cliff that Natalie jumped or fell from."

Autumn studied the picture. The scenery was breathtaking, and the thought that a young woman had perished surrounded by such grandeur was absurd.

Another tap of Noah's finger and the picture switched to a shot of the ground near the edge of the cliff. "Winter spotted these first. Drag marks." The next picture was even closer, the drag marks more apparent.

"No." Sheriff Frank left the wall and marched toward the whiteboard. "Those marks could have been made by anything. Do you not comprehend how much wildlife is out in those mountains? *Active wildlife.* And we checked Natalie's shoes. They were clean."

Noah cocked his head at the sheriff. "With all due respect, Sheriff Frank, water does tend to do that to shoes…and many other objects as well."

The comment was funny, but Autumn kept her mouth shut, as did every other agent. Except for Chris Parker. He let out the world's most obnoxious chortle and slapped his leg.

Oh no. Here we go again.

Sure enough, the sheriff turned an angry shade of red. She pointed at Chris and then Noah. "You people are not here to poke fun at us. We've worked our asses off handling Natalie Garland's suicide as well as all the others. If you think—"

"You do realize, though," Noah held up a hand, enraging Sheriff Frank all the more, "that the drag marks create doubt that Natalie did not, in fact, commit suicide, right? And if she didn't, it's quite possible none of the deceased—"

The woman stepped toward Noah and held up her own hand. "I have viewed every single dead body this county has been cursed with. Do you think that's an easy thing to witness? Suicide after suicide? It's not. *It's awful.* But I assure you that the cause of death was very clear in each and every case. I don't make mistakes."

Aiden pushed between them. "We don't have time for this. Interpret the marks as you will. They exist. My agents found them. We will take them into consideration because that is *what we do*." He and Sheriff Frank locked eyes long enough that Autumn began to worry the woman might punch Aiden in the face.

At last, the sheriff backed down and returned to her slouch against the wall. Tension crackled in the room. The mutual disdain was abundantly clear.

"Agent Parker and I met with Natalie's parents." Autumn blurted out the information in the hopes of refocusing their attention on the case, no matter how much ill will was present. "The Garlands seem to have a dysfunctional marriage at best, but we saw nothing to confirm or dispute the theory that she took her own life."

"That marriage is *over*." Chris confirmed the train wreck they'd witnessed. "I'd be expecting their divorce filing at the courthouse, Sheriff." Autumn couldn't tell if Parker was attempting to be a smartass or not, but Winnie took the comment as an insult.

"That's not exactly my department, Agent Parker." Sheriff Frank barked the words at him and stepped forward once again, but Deputy King intercepted and pressed a hand to her shoulder. He whispered in her ear, causing a momentary calm to overtake the sheriff.

Autumn had a premonition that there was an expiration date on that cooldown.

Aiden must have foreseen the same because he didn't waste the moment of truce. "Well, what we caught sight of at the actual Harmony House was quite illuminating, albeit disturbing. Damien Parr's followers all seem very happy to be there, but Councilman Newman was correct. Something is off about that man."

"He's very charming." Mia straightened in her chair. "Kind, attractive, and intelligent. Everyone there *adores* Damien. You can read it on their faces. They worship the man."

Aiden studied Mia for an abnormally long length of time before going on. "Quite the phenomenon. Damien is a narcissist with an overt god complex, and I wouldn't put shady activity past him. We did, however, find nothing that connects Natalie's tragedy to him or Harmony House. Aside from Bradley Garland's insistence that they were involved, we have nothing...so far."

"You think there's more to find?" Winter spoke for the first time since the briefing began.

"I think there's a veritable plethora of unsavory things to find when it comes to Parr, Agent Black." Aiden's frustration was evident. "Sheriff Frank, is there a way to gather more info on the members of Harmony House? There are a few individuals I'd like to investigate. One of them being Evan Blair."

The sheriff lifted a shoulder. "Never heard of him."

"Right. Neither had we." The vein in Aiden's forehead that always alerted the team to his suppressed rage throbbed as he gazed at Sheriff Frank. "But *now we have*, and I'd like to investigate the young man. He was having a private conversation with Damien, talking about his relentless guilt. He's suspicious as hell."

"We do have to keep in mind," Mia interrupted with a firm tone that seemed aimed at the SSA, "that most of the members of Harmony House come from rough circumstances. Evan expressing guilt to the leader of his group—"

Aiden's head shake was curt. "Cult."

After Aiden, Mia was the least easy to ruffle out of the

entire group. Except, no one would believe that right now, with the blatant exasperation pulling her features into a scowl.

"Group," she corrected. "Group members confiding in their group leader isn't all that strange. He would very likely go to Damien to speak of any troubling matters, as would they all. They trust him."

Autumn's frown returned. Terse undercurrents pulsed between the SSA and Agent Logan, which struck her as odd. Had the two most even-keeled agents in their team squabbled during their brief stint at Harmony House?

Sheriff Frank eyed Mia like she was a rattlesnake. "I can try to get a schedule and investigate at the Harmony House events, then put a trace on Blair. He sounds like trouble."

Autumn shifted in her seat, an idea forming that she knew Aiden would dislike. "Having eyes on the inside would unravel the mystery surrounding Damien Parr faster than anything. That's the only way to get a clear read on the guy. Get close to him."

"She's right." Chris's affirmation caused more than one jaw to drop in the room. "If he's as slick as you say he is, we're not going to find out *anything* without putting someone in there. Parrish and Logan have already been, so they're the logical choices. Go back and tell them about the positive effects of your visit. Tell them you want to experience more of the same."

"The idea itself isn't bad." Aiden's comment brought a light to Chris's face that Autumn hadn't known the man possessed. "But Agent Logan and I are not an option for going undercover at Harmony House again. Officially or otherwise."

Chris's face clouded over. "And why not?" He appeared equal parts disappointed and angry.

Aiden sighed and squared his gaze with Agent Parker's.

"When I witnessed that tidbit between Evan and Damien, Blair spotted me eavesdropping."

"You've got to be kidding me." Chris gaped from Aiden to Mia and back again. "We're supposed to be *the best of the best.* You're *in charge* of us, for Christ's sake! How could you be so *sloppy?*"

Someone in the room groaned. Noah, maybe. Autumn wasn't sure because her own shock rang in her ears. Yes, Aiden's mistake had surprised her, but nothing could have prepared her for Agent Parker's reaction.

Autumn's chest was tight as she exchanged a tense glance with Winter. Parker had stepped out of line in a manner that Aiden would not overlook. Not now, not ever.

"Watch yourself, Agent Parker." Aiden prowled over to Chris until they were only separated by inches.

Autumn shivered, glad the SSA's ire wasn't directed at her. Chris was taller, but Aiden was so much scarier.

The smile on Aiden's face held no humor at all. It was predatory. A jaguar licking its lips before pouncing on unsuspecting prey. "I *am* in charge of you, and you might want to remember that before you injure your job security in an irrepairable way."

Chris turned and beelined for the door. "I need to piss," was his angry explanation as he stormed off.

Aiden stared at Parker's retreating form. His clenched jaw and fists revealed exactly how angry he was. "Everyone is dismissed. Out."

No one needed to be told twice. Even Sheriff Frank shimmied out of the room like there was somewhere she meant to be yesterday.

Autumn stayed.

When Aiden realized that she was still in the room, he rubbed a weary hand across his forehead. "Agent Trent, do you plan to ever follow my orders in the foreseeable future?"

She couldn't stop herself from grinning. "Nope."

The corners of Aiden's mouth threatened to turn up into a bona fide smile.

"He was wrong, Aiden." Autumn addressed the issue at hand. "The last word in this entire world that could be used to describe you is 'sloppy.' He. Was. Wrong."

"He's a dick," Aiden muttered, low enough that he may have assumed she didn't quite catch the statement.

Autumn heard it loud and clear. "I think I got to know Chris a little bit better today. He doesn't come from much by way of money or love. That's not an excuse for talking to his boss the way he did. I'm only trying to say that Parker didn't turn out like this without cause."

Aiden peered at her as though he were struggling to control his commentary. "You and Parker have a nice heart-to-heart today?"

There was a roughness to his voice that she couldn't quite pinpoint. *Jealousy?* Her heart skipped a beat before she forced herself to focus. "Not exactly. I just caught him off guard and gleaned a little history from him. He was back to hating me point five seconds later."

The explanation was true enough. Besides, it wasn't like she could offer up how she'd read Chris's past with a touch of her hand.

"A thorn in my damn side, that guy." Aiden didn't make eye contact. He walked to the room's only window and stared at the sky. Autumn came near him, wishing she knew how to convince him.

But he was still upset. The job was Aiden Parrish's life. Failing to be anything less than impeccable as a federal agent was not an option.

Parker had aimed for a sore spot and managed to connect a solid hit. "Hey," she leaned against the table in front of him, "I've heard that blowing cover is a very easy thing to do."

Aiden chuckled, whether he meant to or not. "Worst speed-dater ever."

"I still feel bad about that." Her cheeks burned as she relived the moment when she annihilated the team's cover at Heather Novak's speed-dating event.

"Well, if I'm going to be a cover blower, at least I'm in good company." His serious gaze locked on her. There was a different tension in the air now. "Autumn…"

She saw the harbinger in his eyes and panicked. Whatever words were about to come out of his mouth, she wasn't ready. Not now. Here. In Beechum, Virginia, mid-cult investigation.

"I think I should go undercover." She spouted the idea with near-frantic energy and had to remind herself that this *was* the actual option she'd been mulling over throughout the meeting.

Aiden froze. He shook his head, like he'd just been thrown off course, but returned to her abrupt subject change like a champ. "No. Undercover? Why? I don't like it. No."

Autumn fought back the laughter bubbling in her throat and rolled her eyes. "Listen, Special Supervisory Agent Aiden Parrish, you can stop doing that now. I've been to Quantico. I'm a trained agent. Quit protecting me."

"You're *fresh* out of Quantico." Aiden was still resisting the idea. "This is your first case."

The laughter escaped. "This is *not* my first case, and you know it. Besides, I want to do this. I can study cult leader and follower behaviors up close. And I need to prove that I can still figure someone out…read them…after misjudging Justin Black."

The guilt slicing at Autumn was razor-sharp, but Aiden's face softened. "Is that what this is about? You don't have to prove anything, Autumn. That little jerk pulled a fast one on *all* of us."

"I still want to do this." She refused to back down.

SSA Parrish studied her for a moment, his brows hitched together. "What are the other options? Who else do we have that can go in?"

Autumn wanted to shake the man but retained her calm. Logic would win this one for her. "Well, let's see. You and Mia are out. Chris would probably blow his cover in the first hour. Winter is…" She glimpsed the same concern in Aiden's eyes that beat in her chest every time Winter was mentioned.

"Winter is not in the position to deal with a cult leader right now." Aiden summed up the problem without giving it a label. They agreed one hundred percent on that matter. "What about Dalton? He's a solid choice."

She'd been expecting this last-ditch effort from Aiden, and her argument was ready. "From what I've gathered, Damien was a much bigger fan of Mia than he was of you. I'm guessing he's a bit of a ladies' man. Noah's a lot of things, but he's *not* a lady."

Aiden ground his teeth together. "Yes. That makes it better. Parr shows signs of being somewhere on the sexual predator scale. *Of course*, I want to send you in now."

"I'm a big girl, Aiden." Autumn's voice was solemn, all playfulness gone. "I want to do this. I *need* to do this. *Let me do this.*"

He walked to the whiteboard, staring at the drag marks in the dirt. Autumn observed them as well.

She didn't jump. I don't believe she jumped.

"Fine. You can go." Aiden stayed fixated on the image. "But my official opinion stays the same."

Autumn grabbed her bag strap and stared at his back. "Official opinion? And what might that be?"

Aiden Parrish's expression when he turned around was pinched. Worried. "I just got you back. Why throw you in harm's way so soon?"

Autumn's throat locked as she stared into his face, his words ricocheting through her skull.

I just got you back.

He'd said "I." As in, not the team, but Aiden. *Aiden* had just gotten her back.

A dizzy sensation kicked off inside her, making her feel a little like a kid on a Ferris wheel. Excited and sick at the same damn time. Never quite sure if she'd rather be swinging dangerously from the sky or keeping her feet planted safely on the ground.

The voices of her colleagues drifted in from the hallway, saving her from making a decision. About Ferris wheels or anything else.

For now.

13

Winter raced down a narrow cobblestone street, dodging pedestrians and desperate to catch up with him. Justin was right there in front of her. She had to catch him this time. He couldn't escape again.

She was going to collapse soon. Her legs ached, her lungs burned, and every single time she was within arm's reach of her baby brother, he disappeared...only to reappear farther down the road. Still running.

Always running.

And then he was gone altogether. No warning, no logical explanation. He simply vanished.

She placed a hand over her heart, feeling each pulsating beat but more so, the current of pain streaming from her insides. How could she protect everyone she loved if she didn't stop him? If she didn't kill him?

But how could she kill her baby brother?

Winter turned, sensing something behind her. Something wrong.

A beautiful stone fountain stood proud in front of the Bank of Spain. The architecture mesmerized—

No. Water wasn't flowing from the fountain. This picture was wrong.

Red. Blood.

The fountain was full of blood.

Fear tasted like copper in her mouth. She had to warn them. All these innocent people walking about with no clue as to the monster roaming amongst them. She would stop each and every person. She would tell them. She would save everyone this time.

Winter grabbed the arm of the nearest passerby and screamed as the person turned toward her. There were no features where the face should be, and the head hung at an angle...a wrong angle...a dead angle...

"No! *Stop him*! He's *killing* them!" Winter registered the surroundings of the hotel, the cool sheets beneath her, and the touch of Noah's hand on her own, but she was still trapped somewhere else.

Justin was somewhere else.

"Justin has to die." Winter struggled to escape the dream. "I have to kill him. It's the only way."

"Winter?" Noah's soothing voice interrupted her terror. "Winter, can you hear me? You're okay. You're safe. You're with *me*." He pulled her to him, and she clung, afraid to let go and fall back into that nightmare.

"Dream. I had...I was dreaming. And Justin..." She couldn't catch her breath, as though she really had been running.

Noah squeezed her tight. "Justin can't hurt you anymore. You're safe."

Are you, though?

Her heart crashed against her ribs as Winter jumped away from Noah, whirling to scour the room behind her. That voice. That awful, familiar voice. Justin was here, in this room. With her. He was always with her. He wouldn't stop talking...wouldn't let her be.

She checked the walls, the dresser, everywhere. As always, her brother wasn't there.

Not the physical manifestation of him.

"What are you looking for?" Noah held out a hand to her, beckoning her back to bed.

But she couldn't rest. Not now.

Winter began to pace the room, wringing her hands together and feeling the horrible sensation of bone against bone as she did.

Soon there will be nothing left of you. I know you didn't believe me before, but you do now, don't you, Sissy? You're disappearing one ounce at a time.

She swatted a hand over her shoulder. Noah was studying her, and he was going to know soon. He was going to realize that Justin was *with her* if she didn't talk. Explain.

Distract.

"I was running down a street." She knew she should sit or at the very least stand still, but she couldn't. "Long and narrow and endless. I was so close to him, Noah. I almost grabbed him. He was right there…and then blood."

Noah stood and walked toward her. "Blood?" He took each of her shaking hands and gently coaxed her back into the bed.

"A fountain of blood." She bit her lip to stave off the tears. "I tried to save them. I was going to save all of them…but he'd already killed them. They were dead. They were dead, and they didn't even know it."

There wasn't much aside from holding her and stroking her hair that Noah could do. She knew that. What she didn't know was how to tell him that it didn't help. All his best efforts were falling short.

Justin had found her even as he vanished from her life. Nothing made him go away. No one was capable of making him stop.

You know what makes me go away.

His voice was seductive. Incessant.

Winter shuddered, burying her face in Noah's shoulder. "Where is he? Why haven't they found him yet?"

Noah patted her back and held her close, but even his warm, strong body wasn't enough to hold the monsters at bay.

Not this monster, anyway.

"Your brother is smart, and he has a great deal of money and people who are helping him hide. He's not so easy to find, sweetheart, but we're looking."

"That's not good enough!" She pulled away while her pulse accelerated to a feverish pace. He was hiding something from her. She could feel it. "Tell me what you know about my brother."

"I don't know any—"

Red lights flashed before her eyes. *"Tell me what you know!"*

Noah gulped and attempted to approach her again. "I don't think it's a good idea. You're not on the case for a reason. And you're not...you're not..."

"I'm fine." She grabbed his hand, softening against him and pleading with her eyes. "Please tell me what you know."

He dropped his gaze in defeat. "Miguel called me this morning. He's heard through international lines that someone similar to Justin's description was spotted in Seville."

"Justin's in *Spain?*" Winter's hands clenched the blankets as horror infiltrated every cell of her being. *"How?* How did you guys let him leave the country? He never should have made it past security! How are you going to find him now?"

Noah put a finger on her lips. "You have to calm down. You're shouting. Management is going to show up soon if we stay this loud."

Winter glanced at the bedside table. A plastic-encased sign claimed, *"We're glad you're here!"*

See Sissy? I'm welcome wherever I go! Everybody loves a good old-fashioned serial killer.

She took a deep breath and blew it out, then repeated the process until her heart quit galloping like a thoroughbred. "I'm sorry. But how? How can he be stopped now?"

Noah settled back against the pillows. "Every possible step is being taken to locate Justin and bring him back to the States. You have to trust me on that one."

Winter shook her head, her lower lip trembling. "He shouldn't have been able to leave the country. Not ever. He'll keep killing no matter where he goes. And all of those lives… all of that blood is on my hands. I should have taken him down."

A small sob escaped her as guilt pressed on her skull, shoving her down, down, deep beneath the surface of an inky lake. No one understood. Not even the man she loved.

"You were his hostage." Noah cupped her chin. "He drugged you and blackmailed you with the well-being of every person you encountered. You did everything you could. You know he would have tortured the Stewarts if you hadn't shown them mercy."

Mercy.

Crack.

The sound of their necks snapping rang in her ears. She had tried to make it quick because she had absolutely known what Justin would have done to them…to the girl in front of her parents.

She hated the tears soaking her face, her shirt, the blankets. She'd returned from her ordeal with Justin alive but weakened. Ruined.

Worthless.

"I don't…I don't know when I'm going to get ahold of

myself." She rested her forehead against her knees. "I can control this. I have to control this."

Noah's hand on her back weighed a million pounds.

You really are pretty pathetic right now, Sis. Jesus. Weeeak.

Winter shrugged Noah's hand away, then looked into his eyes. His hurt was more weight strapped to her spine, forcing her deeper into watery depths.

Her pain was tearing him apart, but she didn't know how to save him. Not when she wasn't even treading water herself. "I'm so sorry, Noah. I can't stop seeing their faces. Greg and Andrea. I killed them. I broke their necks and took their lives."

"You saved them from a fate worse than death," Noah soothed, pulling her to him yet again. This time she let him.

Her body quaked as she swiped at her cheek, unable to stop crying. Unable to do *anything*. "He's g-got that little b-boy. He'll destroy h-him." She pictured orphaned Timothy Stewart sobbing on the RV floor, bound and gagged, inching toward his dead mother.

And don't forget Nicole, Sissy. That was the best part.

Brains. The teenage girl's brains had splattered across cheap oak cabinetry—

I regret that, Sissy. I wanted to play with her first.

"We'll find him long before he does that." Noah's voice held a determination and confidence that she wrapped around her like a force field.

Safe. She was safe with Noah.

Are you sure about that?

If Winter knew where her brother was hiding inside her head, she wouldn't hesitate. She'd grab the sharpest knife and plunge the blade directly into her brain. A makeshift lobotomy would be a picnic compared to this.

Anything would.

"He was going to rape me." Winter's whisper was so soft, she wasn't sure Noah caught her words until his body stiffened. "He was ready to...but he got distracted. I wouldn't have been able to stop him. I would have just had to *endure it*. Lay still and die inside and die every single day after..." Anguish crashed over her like a never-ending wave as she started sobbing again.

Noah squeezed her and shook his head. "He didn't. You got away. You're okay. You're going to be okay, sweetheart."

He didn't understand. "I'm never going to be normal again. I'm never going to be myself. I can't find me. I'm *lost*."

A half-truth, but it was all she was willing to share. No one would believe her reality. Her nightmare.

His green eyes glistened with tears as he stared back at her. "You *will* find your way back. You will. And I will be here every step of the way supporting you. *Every. Step.*"

Winter curled her fingers around his, entwining their hands. She knew he meant every word. He would be there. Their bond was unbreakable.

Barf. Please tell me you know how stupid you're being. Our *bond is unbreakable, sister dear. Ours.*

Whatever gift she'd received from her brain injury had come with a hellish curse. Just as she couldn't stop the visions and couldn't predict their occurrence, she couldn't stop Justin. He'd connected to her somehow, invaded her mind like a virus.

Telling anyone that her psychopath serial killer brother was telepathically torturing her would only earn her a nice cozy bed in the psych ward. She'd never been able to tell anyone about her "superpower," and this supercurse was even more unbelievable.

Was Justin really connecting to her, or had she somehow mentally absorbed him? And either way...how did she make it stop?

You know what makes me go away.

Work. She'd continue to throw herself into the job and stop wallowing in sorrow and regret. Maybe she could help locate Justin and prevent her nightmare from coming true.

Eventually, she might even stop hating herself.

Winter made an abrupt beeline for the bathroom. "I'm going to take a shower."

Noah nodded and attempted a smile for her, but he wasn't remotely close to believing she was okay.

She locked the door behind her and went to the shower, turning the nozzles to full blast. After checking to make sure the door was truly locked, she knelt and dug in her bag for her makeup kit, opening it and retrieving the small prescription bottle of pills she kept hidden there. She'd told Noah she was done with the painkillers.

That hadn't been true at all.

Need battled logic as she leaned against the sink and clenched the bottle in her hand.

Just take one, her brother urged in her mind. *I'll leave you alone. For a little bit.*

Winter stared at herself in the mirror. She wasn't oblivious to her emaciated state. The sunken, shadowed eyes, the knife-sharp cheekbones. Her wan, unhealthy complexion. The reflection showed a woman who might be better off just lying down on her death bed and letting go.

You're a ghoul now. A hideous ghoul. Take the damn pill. Take it, and I'll go away.

Justin had injected her with a consistent stream of drugs over their three-day "adventure," and in that short period of time, she'd developed a hunger…a *need* for some type of numbing substance. Her doctors had prescribed a hearty dosage of Vicodin for the bullet wound in her arm, and they never so much as blinked when she asked for a refill on account of her "pain levels still being high."

Addiction was eating away at her body. She didn't need a mirror to know that.

"I'm done. I don't need you anymore." Winter shoved the pills back into her kit. Seconds later, she grabbed the bottle, seized a pill, and popped it in her mouth. She didn't even need water to swallow anymore. Just took it down like a pro.

Good job, Champ. I'll talk to ya soon.

Justin's laughter faded away behind her, but she didn't bother to turn around. He was never there. Justin wasn't following her. He was inside of her, which was worse. She couldn't run from herself.

She held the bottle over the toilet. Flushing them was the right thing to do.

Get rid of them. Deal with your demons. Find yourself again.

But the cruel truth was that the only time she could even hear her own inner voice was when she fed her addiction and drowned out her little brother.

The even crueler truth was, she was scared that without the pills, Justin would drown *her* out. Terrified that one day when she was sinking from the weight of her own guilt, he'd trap her beneath the surface forever. That she was doomed to have him overpower her once more, only this time, he'd take everything from her. Mind, body, soul.

Winter stuffed the pills back into their hiding place and stepped into the steaming shower. She'd stop. She'd get a handle on things again. She *would*.

Just not yet.

14
———

Chris dropped onto one of many wooden benches lining the hallways of Beechum Police Station. He wasn't quite ready to enter the conference room. The briefing hadn't ended well yesterday.

At least not for him.

Aiden and Autumn had cozied right up after everyone else left. He'd stayed in the hallway long enough to ascertain that. They'd probably gone back to the hotel and banged. And laughed about what an idiot Chris Parker was.

Heat flushed through his body. That's exactly what they'd done. He was a big joke to most of the team and well aware of that fact.

Noah and Winter had more than likely done the same. All night.

Was he the only one without an eff buddy colleague? Was this just acceptable behavior now? Didn't anyone take pride *in the job* anymore?

Chris wouldn't screw Winter in a million years. Not even if someone paid him to. She might have returned to the field, but she looked like hell. Bones sticking out everywhere and her cheeks all sunken in.

No thank you.

She was so obviously not okay. The fact she was on an active case seemed *wrong*. Did Parrish want her to die? And did Dalton not have the balls to grab her and tell her she should be hospitalized?

The way this BAU was run, Chris wasn't surprised that Justin Black was still on the loose or that he'd ever escaped to begin with. Train wreck. They were an absolute train wreck. Stupid people making stupid decisions that—

"You're here early." Mia's voice carried down the hallway. Though he'd come to think of her as his unofficial partner, he recognized that after one afternoon spent with Aiden Parrish, Mia was just as big of a suck-up as any of the rest of them.

Chris fought the urge to flip Agent Logan the bird for her betrayal. She wouldn't understand why he was so angry anyway. Mia was a good girl, and that meant she was probably just dying to be "teacher's pet."

Autumn really wouldn't like that.

He'd find a way to slip that into conversation the next time Aiden saddled him with the obnoxious redhead. Maybe rock Parrish's damn boat a little bit. The man deserved it.

"You know," Chris hid his repulsion as Mia sat next to him, "arriving early used to be the gold standard. There was a time when *not* being early was the same as being late. Back when people respected the job."

Mia peered up at him with her giant brown eyes. They were too big for her face. She reminded him of a Beanie Boo stuffed animal. One of his cousins had a daughter who went batshit over those things. Lined them up in her room on shelves and just let them stare at any poor soul who passed by with their ginormous dilated pupils.

"You don't think *anyone* on the team respects the job?" She asked the question as though she cared to know the answer, but Chris wasn't fooled. He'd figured out who Mia was yesterday, underneath all the quiet, calm, and patience.

She wasn't any better than the rest of them. Worse maybe, because she pretended to be different. There was no reason to be surprised. He should have seen this coming.

People sucked. Point-blank truth.

Chris stared blankly back at her. "I think everyone could do better."

Mia grinned. "Including you?" She had dimples when she smiled that made her appear to be twice as happy as a normal person ever should be, and he found them annoying.

"I never lost sight of what this job means," he finally barked back. "I don't need to do better."

"Okay, Chris. Fair enough." Mia's smile disappeared. "But you *do* have to stop giving Aiden such a hard time. He's your boss. No matter what you think or feel, you have to remember who has the power to fire you at the end of the day."

Chris sneered at the wall across from them. "Oh, you think I'm getting fired now?"

Mia slapped a hand to her forehead. "No. But I think if you keep that behavior up, you might walk yourself right onto termination grounds."

"Awfully outspoken today, Logan." Chris knew why. "One day with the big boss, and you're an expert on all things BAU?"

Mia's expression turned stormy. Defensive. He'd offended her. For a split second, guilt needled his chest. But then he remembered her face at the briefing the day before. She'd been all attentive, like Aiden was her new master or idol. Disgusting.

"I'm trying to *help* you." Mia made the claim like she was

the FBI's designated Mother Teresa. "Why is it so hard for you to just keep your mouth closed?"

Chris scuffed at the tiled floor. "Because I know what I'm capable of. I would have done better with Justin. I would have registered what that little bastard was and kept Winter the hell out of that hospital. Have you *seen* her? She looks like a *Walking Dead* extra."

The troubled expression on Mia's face confirmed his suspicions. She *had* noticed. They all had. And yet Winter was out in the field.

Aiden was an idiot. A *reckless* idiot.

Emboldened by Mia's unspoken confirmation that he was correct about Winter, Chris continued, "Furthermore, I wouldn't have gone digging around like a newbie my first visit to Harmony Hills. I would have focused on establishing *trust*. That can take time, but it's worth it. If they'd known and trusted Aiden, even for a few days, catching him eavesdropping wouldn't have been such a big deal. They might have written it off as him just caring about the group members."

"We were there to spy around and investigate, Chris." Mia stretched her tiny legs out, reminding him that she was the size of a child and probably hadn't been able to view anything at all at Harmony House aside from other people's stomachs. "I could have made the same mistake. Easily. Anyone could have."

He considered her for a moment. She really was on board with the *Go Aiden* team now. One of Parrish's little soldiers. Chris wanted to tell her she was better suited for a Girl Scout troop. "I wouldn't have made that mistake, Mia. I wouldn't."

She wouldn't give him the satisfaction of agreeing with him. He knew that. But what did Mia's opinion matter in the big scheme of things?

This wasn't new. He'd been ignored and underappreciated his entire life. For whatever reason, that was his path. "You don't know what it's like to claw your way through life and have your opinions continually brushed aside. I do. Maybe my temper flared yesterday, and you can say I was out of line, but I disagree. Sometimes people only listen when you make them. Aiden didn't like what I said, but he damn well *heard* it."

Deputy King approached. The man's vacant, pleasant expression gave the impression that he was a doofy moron, and Chris fought the urge to tell him so. Why in the hell everyone thought smiling was so damn important was beyond him.

Sheriff Frank was a bitch, but at least she didn't put on a show trying to be "nice." That's not what their jobs were about. Not a single one of them. He could respect someone like Sheriff Frank, even if she was one of the most disagreeable human beings he'd ever met.

She was real. Simon King was obnoxious.

"I've got some info on that Evan boy you all were curious about." Deputy King spoke to them like they'd all been drinking buddies for years. "Got a bit of a history, that one."

As much as he detested the deputy, Chris jumped at the chance to get some important information before Aiden even arrived.

This is why early is the gold standard.

"Let's hear it, Deputy." Aiden's voice carried down the hallway. He and Autumn had arrived just in the damn nick of time and were probably fresh off a morning adventure in Aiden's hotel sheets.

Chris's hatred was a living, breathing monster inside him. He only wished he could pry open his chest and unleash the creature on the happy couple, letting it devour them so he never had to hear their grating voices again.

"Good morning, Agent Parrish." Deputy King tipped his

hat to the SSA. Bile surged into Chris's mouth, and he fought the urge to vomit. "From what I've dug up, Evan Blair is an ex-con with a few petty convictions. But his record's been clean since he started associating with Damien Parr."

Aiden's face hardened at the name. Chris figured Parrish was jealous as hell that he didn't have the same following Damien Parr did. Narcissists could never stand each other.

"Let's take this into the conference room." Aiden made the suggestion, leading the way, and the rest of them followed like sheep.

Chris insisted on waiting until he was the only person left in the hall before he obeyed the command. He'd be careful because Mia was right. Aiden Parrish did have the power to ruin his federal agent career.

That didn't mean Chris was going to tag along blindly and tiptoe around the SSA's pride. But he'd attempt to rein in his insights, which were obviously too spot-on for Aiden to handle.

Noah and Winter walked in, pulling two chairs close together and sitting in unison like one damn human being. Chris tried not to even glance at Winter. He didn't trust his expression to stay blank.

Aiden stood by the whiteboard and cleared his throat. "To recap, Agents, Deputy King has found some interesting information on Evan Blair. He's an ex-con with some petty convictions on his record, but he's stayed clean and out of trouble with the law since he's been under Damien Parr's wing."

Chris couldn't help himself. "Almost sounds like Parr helped the young man better his life." He kept his face neutral, which wasn't easy. But the comment mixed with his stoic expression was going to drive Aiden nuts.

"Harmony House helps many." Aiden directed the words

toward him. "That doesn't make Damien Parr or Evan Blair one bit less suspicious."

"Also," Deputy King interjected, "I placed a call to Bradley Garland. The councilman said Natalie hadn't mentioned anyone named Evan. Not once."

Chris glanced around the room, taking in the reactions. Nods and concentrated stares, but not one person stating the obvious.

He ground his teeth together so hard, he was surprised no one noticed.

She didn't mention him because he has nothing to do with the fact that she killed herself. Wake up and smell the waterfall, my dear fellow agents.

"That's, unfortunately, another inconclusive tidbit." Aiden refused to admit to what *was* indicated by the tidbit. Namely, that Natalie committed suicide, and everyone in the room besides Chris was an utter moron. "We need more. We have to get eyes on the inside like we began to discuss yesterday."

More than one pair of eyes slid toward Chris, and he attempted to meet them all with an indignant scowl. Aiden had dismissed the meeting. Not him. Yet somehow, he was to blame.

Chris pushed the unfairness aside and focused on the opportunity at hand. Eyes inside. Aiden and Mia were out, per Parrish's admitted fuckup. Winter wasn't going anywhere. Autumn was too fresh. Dalton would want to stay attached to his other half, more so than normal, considering she appeared to be dying.

This was his chance. He opened his mouth to volunteer—

Aiden's booming voice blasted through the room. "Agent Trent will be going undercover so that she can use her special training in criminal and forensic psychology to better understand the inner workings of Harmony House and get an accurate read on the group members."

"What?" The protest barreled from Chris's mouth before he glimpsed Mia shaking her head in warning. Not that it mattered. He was too incredulous to hold back. "You've got to be kidding me. She just got back from Quantico, and the last thing she did before leaving was screw us all over by misstepping with a monster like Justin Black. You can't believe she's actually ready for this. *Come on, Parrish.*"

Pain flashed across Autumn's face before she fixed her demon green eyes on him. "You only make *yourself* look weaker when you keep using people's previous mistakes against them."

The laugh that Chris almost let fly was pure bitterness. She couldn't stand when someone reminded the team of her failures. "It's my turn to take the lead. I've earned it. I wasn't even given a chance to work with Justin. This one is *mine.*"

He gripped the table so hard, his knuckles turned white. What in the actual hell was wrong with Aiden Parrish? The man was losing his mind. And Chris had a very good idea as to why.

Autumn glared at him, as close to hateful as he'd ever witnessed. He shot her the same back, hoping she understood that he did *actually hate her.* No questions asked.

Aiden walked toward him, and he understood that he'd overstepped. Again. At least in Parrish's eyes. Heeding Mia's warning might have been a better choice, but how much could one man be expected to take?

"Come with me." Aiden barked the order, and Chris detested himself for obeying like a bad dog.

They stepped into the hall, and Aiden pulled the conference room door shut. "I'm done with this, Parker. You earned your spot on my team. You're here. But you are going to give yourself a major attitude adjustment, or I will be forced to make some team member adjustments. Do you understand?"

Like a child. He speaks to me like I'm a damn child.

Chris straightened his posture and clenched his fists, refusing to play the role of naughty little schoolboy. "I want to solve this case. I *care*. That should be a good thing. I think it's ridiculous for everyone not to be worried about Autumn messing this all up after her performance with Justin. If it was that easy for you to make a mistake at Harmony House, she's definitely going to fail."

Aiden's eyes flashed with anger, but per usual, he kept all his emotion reeled in. "Individual agent assignments on this case, as with every other case we take, are *my call*. You have no say whatsoever in those decisions. You need to watch your step, Parker, because you've skated onto some dangerously thin ice."

The heat in Aiden's typically calm gaze was more than enough of a warning for Chris. Parrish was ready to kick him off the team for this overstep. Hell, Parrish was probably ready to kick him off the team for anything. "I messed up. You have my apology, and I will be certain to fall back in line."

The words all but stuck in his throat, but somehow, he managed to spit them out. This was what Aiden wanted him to say, of course. He wanted his ass kissed and his ego re-fluffed. Chris knew how to kiss an ass. He just hated doing it, unlike the rest of his suck-up colleagues.

"You may be dismissed from this meeting." Aiden nodded down the hall toward the front entrance. "Go pull yourself together and report back to me for your assignment."

Parrish opened the conference room door and pushed it closed while Chris stood in the hallway. Alone and disgraced.

Nothing new, really. Humiliation scalded his face, but so what? That ugly emotion had been a part of his life for as long as he could remember. How many times had he been told off and left standing like a moron by an authority figure? That had been a reoccurring incident since he was a small child. And he'd been a *good kid*. He hadn't even deserved the rebukes.

His father had been disappointed in him since birth. One of Chris's earliest memories was his PE teacher calling in a parent to discuss his "lackluster performance in gym class." He had been seven at the time. *Seven.* And those two assholes sat there going at him like he was a twenty-year-old Olympic gold medal winner letting them both down...

"I just don't know what to do with him, Mr. Parker." Coach Tarski had made fun of him since the first day of second grade when he tripped on his own big feet during a game of kickball. "I try to encourage your son, and I understand that he has some... handicaps to work with."

"My son isn't handicapped, Tarski." His father was immediately enraged. "It's just asthma. Doc says it's a classic case of childhood asthma, and he'll outgrow it in a few years. That's not no damn handicap."

Chris remembered how safe he had felt in that moment. Mean Coach Tarksi wasn't gonna get away with treating Larry Parker's son poorly. His dad wouldn't let anybody push his family around.

But when they left Coach's office and headed out of the school toward his dad's pickup, he found out just how wrong he'd been. Chris managed one full step into the parking lot before his dad started in.

"Do you know how embarrassing it is to have to leave work early so I can talk to your damn physical education teacher? Gym isn't a class people fail, *Christopher. Not in the second damn grade. Aren't you ashamed of yourself?" His father opened the passenger door, let him climb in, and then slammed the door so hard the entire pickup shook.*

When they were driving away, Chris attempted to explain his side of the story. His father must have misunderstood something.

"Dad, I just can't always breathe when we're doing stuff. Coach makes me keep my inhaler in the locker room, so I have to walk really far to get it, and that makes my chest hurt worse. I try hard, Dad. I promise!" He'd started crying, and even at that age, he knew how pitiful he would appear in his father's eyes for doing so.

"You're not trying hard enough, Christopher!" The way his father barked the criticism made him cry harder. "You need to toughen up, boy! I'm working fourteen-hour days, and you're crying about having to walk too far?"

That wasn't what Chris was complaining about. He was trying to tell his dad that he couldn't breathe. But he was saying it wrong, somehow. He was just making his dad angrier.

"Seven years old and already saying the wrong thing," Chris muttered to himself, throwing the Beechum Police Station doors wide open. The July sun didn't brighten a damn thing. Not today. Not for him.

"Chris?" Mia's mouse squeak voice hit his ears from behind him. "Are you okay?"

He wanted to scream. Throw large objects. Why did people do this? Why did they pretend to care when they were so clearly a part of the problem? Mia was an ass-kisser. She added to Aiden's overblown self-importance just by existing.

"I'm great." He refused to turn toward her. "Peachy. Why the hell are you out here? You can't just skip Aiden's briefings, Agent Logan. There are *consequences*."

Mia came down the sidewalk and stood beside him. "The briefing was over. Dismissed. I've been assigned the task of gathering more evidence on the other suicides. Maybe he'll assign you the same."

Chris chuckled and wondered how it had taken him so long to perceive what a dimwit minion Mia was. "Maybe. I guess he could assign me to pick up the litter in the local ditches, and I'd have to jump on it, right?"

"That's not fair." Mia stepped in front of him now,

wanting his full attention down in Munchkin Land. "You have to stop having such a short fuse with Aiden, no matter what you think he's done to you."

His chest burned as he glowered at her. "Oh, should I be more forgiving, Mia? Is that what I should do?"

Her emphatic nod almost made him chuckle again. "Yes. That would be a great place to start."

The satisfaction of what he was about to say was sooo delicious that he didn't even fight the vicious smile spreading across his face. "Forgiveness is a great place to start? You think so, Mia?" His smile widened into a sneer as he went for the kill. "What about you? Are you always so quick to forgive? Do you try to understand and let things go? Or are you a big, fat hypocrite, just like everyone else?"

Her expression froze, and her throat bobbed as she tried to swallow. When she spoke, her voice was soft. "Forgiveness is a virtue I need to work on. I'm not too good to admit that."

She spaced out for a second, but he predicted where her mind was going. Her dead brother and Sloan Grant. Sloan had totally pushed the dude over the edge, and the entire Richmond Field Office knew it. Also well-known was the fact that Mia and Sloan had ceased to be friends from that day forward.

Chris knew he'd hit Mia's sorest spot, and he didn't experience the slightest hint of guilt about it. She didn't practice what she preached, and that was one of the most annoying qualities any human being on the planet could possess.

Truth hurts, Mia. Sorry, not sorry.

"You know what?" Mia placed her hands on her hips. "The difference between my situation and yours is that my forgiveness issues don't *threaten my job*. Yours do. You need to prove you're a part of the team if you expect Aiden to keep you around."

This may have been the first time he'd witnessed Mia angry. He'd accepted a while ago that he didn't have the apparent power needed to piss off Agent Logan. The fact was frustrating but acceptable. At least he could say whatever the hell he wanted without getting lectured.

Until now.

She turned to leave then swung back around with the fury of hell on her face. "Also? There's another huge difference between my issue and yours. *Your brother didn't die.*"

Mia took off after that. He assumed she was making her return to the forest to bake cookies with all the other tree elves.

You're an asshole. When did you become such an asshole?

He was aware of what he'd turned into, and he accepted it as just another simple fact. He was a jerk, but with good reason. *Decades of reasons.* And when people labeled someone else a "jerk," the reason was usually because they just couldn't handle cold hard facts. Truth.

Chris had spent enough of his life trying to appease and impress.

Done. I'm done with that crap, and I don't give a shit how upset Mia is.

He flinched. That wasn't entirely true. Mia was the closest thing to a friend he had on the team and the only one who didn't seem to detest him. He'd meant to hurt her, but maybe he hadn't figured she'd take it so personally. Based on past arguments, she never did.

An acrid taste coated his mouth.

This was about her dead brother. You're worse than a jerk. You're a nasty, soulless, rotten prick, and you don't know how to be anything else anymore.

What was the point in forgiveness and kindness and all of that bullcrap after everything he'd witnessed in this world?

He knew what people were underneath all of the niceties and good manners. They were assholes.

And…he knew what he would never be.

Accepted.

Chris stared in the direction Mia had stormed off in, loneliness an aching hollow where his heart should be.

Ringing from his pocket snapped him out of his bitter reverie.

Chris pulled his phone out and grimaced. Gus.

The reporter called him without fail when he was on a case. The sleazebag was willing to pay for a little insider information, and Chris was careful to never tell him too much. Just enough to make some quiet side cash. Today he wasn't in the mood to deal with the scumbucket, but the two dollars and thirty-six cents in his bank account said different.

Chris sighed and took the call. "Got nothing for ya yet. Check back tonight." He pressed "end" and dropped the phone back in his pocket. The text alert buzzed not even two seconds later. "I swear to god, if this motherclucker is gonna start harassing me through text messages…"

Viewing "unknown sender" sent a shot of anxiety through his body. He swiped the screen and pulled up the message.

You and I share a similar redheaded problem. Would you like to discuss options?

He only knew one redhead, and there was no surprise at all in finding out that someone else couldn't stand her either. At the same time…he had no idea who in the hell the text was from. What if it was a setup?

Or…maybe it was someone with the means to do what he'd been wanting to do for months without casting a shadow on himself. Maybe this was how he could make Autumn pay. For everything.

Standing alone on the sidewalk, Chris wasn't sure how long he waffled. In the end, the anger and bitter disappointment of the last twenty-four hours—no, the last twenty-four years—won out.

He typed three simple letters.

Yes.

15

A utumn sat by herself in the tiny breakroom, cradling a much-needed cup of joe in her hands and slowly allowing the stress from her run-in with Chris to seep away. She'd escaped as soon as Aiden had handed out their assignments and dismissed them. A time-out of sorts.

She sipped the aromatic brew in silence. There were emotions that only hot coffee could soothe, even if it was police station breakroom dispensed.

For the next ten minutes, Autumn allowed herself to relax. No being pissed at Chris. No wondering what in the hell the edginess between Aiden and Mia concerning Harmony House was about. No stealing glances at Winter and fighting the instant, internal freak-out that her friend's obvious unhealthiness inspired.

Ten minutes wasn't nearly long enough, but it helped. By the time she drained her cup, she'd made a plan to seek out Aiden and discuss her impending undercover mission in greater detail. Now that she'd gotten "her way," the butterflies of actually working as a spy were taking over.

Action time, Agent Trent.

She found him still in the conference room, hunched over a pile of papers at a corner desk and deep in concentration. She approached with soft steps. "Boo."

Aiden didn't jump or even flinch, which was just as she'd expected. One of her long-term goals was to catch Agent Parrish off guard and scare the living bejeezus out of him. The feat seemed impossible, but she was determined to crack that code.

Eventually.

"Agent Trent." Aiden granted her a brief smile but was clearly engrossed in the information spread out before him. "This is everything we've been able to find, thus far, on the members of Harmony House. I have to admit our intel is spotty at best, but you'll want to study up regardless."

She pulled out a chair and sat, excitement growing in her chest. "I cannot wait to get in there. Meet Damien and dissect his every move. I want to know how in the heck he recruits his followers almost as badly as what he does when someone attempts to leave."

Aiden slid her a sideways glance. "This is your dream come true, isn't it?"

Autumn grabbed one of the reports, grinning from ear to ear. "It's up there."

"Please remember," SSA Parrish's voice was full of unease, "just because the place has a sweet name and people are mauling you with hugs, Damien Parr is still not to be trusted."

She emitted a haughty huff. "Duly noted. I'm not claiming to be a genius, but the fact that we're investigating the guy kind of summed up that warning for me already. I wasn't planning on...wait." She studied his face more closely. "Did you say *maul with hugs*? Did *actual* humans *actually* hug Aiden Parrish without even asking his permission?"

The imagery was too good. Autumn sputtered into laughter, promising herself that she'd ask Mia for a play-by-play of the torture later.

Aiden's lips pressed together before breaking into a small grin. "I'm not claiming to be a genius, either, but shoving people away in disgust probably would have blown our cover. I was trapped."

He gave a little shudder, which only made her laugh harder. "I would have paid good money to witness that play out."

Aiden pushed a paper to her. "Alice Leeson. She was one of the members we interacted with when we were there. Sweet girl. Completely on board with Parr. She worships the man."

Autumn eyed the pretty, young blonde in the picture. "Mia said *everyone* worships Damien."

"I have a gut instinct that Mia took a bit of a shining to him herself." Aiden's eyebrows lowered in that same tense expression he'd displayed during the meeting whenever Mia spoke of Harmony House.

"She was playing a part." Autumn defended Mia without fully understanding what there was to defend. "Was she supposed to walk away from the place hating everyone? They're people, Aiden."

He frowned at an image of the cult leader. "They're people, and they're *off*. Something is off there. I didn't have enough time to pinpoint specifics but—"

"I'll have plenty of time to do that." Autumn flashed him a bright smile. "Plenty."

This time, Aiden didn't return her humor. His mouth thinned, and he shook his head. "You need to be extra careful. Damien Parr, Harmony House, and every other cult on the planet prey on people like you."

The insult came out of nowhere. A sucker punch to

Autumn's gut. She stiffened, and her smile vanished. "People like me? Tell me you didn't just say that."

"I did." He picked up Damien's picture and held it in front of them both. "This man is a psychopath. Whether or not he has anything to do with the suicides, he's a psychopath. He collects people who are struggling the same way other people collect seashells."

"I'm struggling?" She didn't like the insinuation that she was gullible enough to be sucked into Damien's web like a naïve fly.

Aiden squared his gaze with hers. "You don't want to hear that. No one does. But you said yourself that you're trying to prove your worth after what happened with Justin, and you haven't accepted that the situation was never your fault to begin with. Furthermore, I know you still blame yourself for not having found Sarah."

"That's not fair." Autumn wished she were wearing the mood ring Aiden bought her in Florida so she could smack him with it. "How do you know that my desire for redemption doesn't make me a better, *stronger* agent?"

He leaned back in his chair, considering her words. "I don't. I just want to make sure that you can be one-hundred-percent focused on *this* case, despite the other concerns you're harboring."

Autumn counted to ten and attempted to remember that this wasn't a personal attack. It was Aiden's job, his *responsibility*, to ensure that she was fully present. "I'm going to enter Harmony House with my alert eyes wide open. I'm not bringing my baggage with me. I want to dissect *theirs*."

Aiden grinned and gathered the spread of papers together. "You need to study these people, hard and fast."

She grabbed the stack and raised an eyebrow. "And *you* need to go easier on Chris."

His startled expression proved that he hadn't been expecting such a remark. "Why might that be, Agent Trent?"

Autumn bit her lip. How did she share without giving away what she knew about Chris? "He's just…been through hell." She shrugged. The explanation wasn't enough, but what else could she say?

"We've all been through hell." Aiden growled and gave an emphatic shake of his head. "Chris Parker isn't special when it comes to rough pasts."

Autumn ran the reel of "Chris intel" through her mind again. If she focused, she could slow down the imagery and pick out separate scenes. The one she was stuck on now was a very young Chris Parker sobbing in a pickup truck while being verbally berated by his father.

She was aware she was frowning but couldn't stop. "We all have rough pasts. We don't all have the ability to work through them. And some people don't know how to reach out for help. Chris is trying to handle some demons from his past, and he's doing that inner work *alone*."

"All the more reason to keep a close eye on him." Aiden wasn't budging in his stance on Agent Parker.

Fair, considering the shitshow that had been Chris's interactions with SSA Parrish as of late, but still…Autumn believed if Aiden could see what she saw and know what she knew, he'd soften just an infinitesimal bit.

Her own heart hurt when she remembered the painful criticism she'd felt when she touched Chris's skin. He'd only been a child.

Aiden stood, checking his watch and surveying the conference room. "We should get you ready to go in short order. You're going to need a new wardrobe, Agent Trent."

"Music to my ears." Autumn was more than ready to go track down Winter. A little quality "girls' time" before she went undercover for a few days would do them both good.

She hoped.

"WE DROVE TWENTY-FIVE MINUTES FOR THIS?" Winter waved at the small strip of stores before them. Two boutiques, one secondhand store, a sportswear shop, and a tiny Goodwill.

Autumn was enjoying herself, regardless of the drive to a semi-bigger town than Beechum. They'd made the short trip in part because Beechum had no clothing stores to speak of but also because shopping in Beechum wasn't an option anyway. There was too much risk of being spotted by Harmony House members.

"Hey," Autumn headed for the secondhand store, "it beats hanging out at the Beechum Police Station with Sheriff Frank."

Winter let out a long, low whistle. "I keep thinking she's gonna relax a little, maybe even smile or something crazy like that."

"I wouldn't hold your breath for that one." Autumn pushed the shop door open and was hit with that distinct, musty thrift-store scent. She headed to the closest rack and began thumbing through the hangers. "Whatever reason that woman has for resenting us so much, she's sticking with it hard."

There wasn't a huge selection, but she didn't need one. T-shirts, jeans, maybe some sandals or sneakers. Normal, unassuming clothing that any person would wear on a random day. Regular stuff.

The fact that she had a closet at home full of "regular stuff" was a bit obnoxious. If she'd known about the impending undercover assignment, she could have just packed the appropriate wardrobe.

She shrugged, pushing a few more hangers aside. Shopping was shopping. And getting away from everyone with Winter had been an enjoyable experience thus far. They'd cranked the radio up and rolled the windows down on the drive over, both of them belting out the lyrics to the greatest pop hits blaring from the speakers.

The July heat had been a bit on the warm side for Autumn. She would have preferred the windows up and the AC blaring, but Winter was cold. Her friend trembled and tried to point the vents away from her when they'd first taken off down the road. Autumn had taken pity on her and flicked off the air-conditioning, opting for the windows-down option.

Fresh air was good for both of them, she reasoned. And Winter shaking like a leaf hanging from a tree mid-snowstorm was disturbing.

Autumn considered a flowered t-shirt before pushing it aside. She didn't want this little trip to be about Winter's health. She was certain that forcing any conversation about the matter would cause her friend to completely shut down. Hopefully, spending time together just for fun would help heal some of whatever ailed Winter.

"Please get this." Winter held up a t-shirt that read *Virginia is for Lovers...So Get Busy.*

They burst into laughter loud enough to draw the attention of the older, gray-haired woman at the checkout counter. She attempted a polite smile but kept a careful eye on them.

"I'm guessing that's not the kind of vibe I want to give off right off the bat." Autumn imagined Aiden's face if she were to arrive ready for duty in such attire and snickered.

Winter lifted a shoulder and hung the shirt back on the rack. "Are you nervous?" Her somber voice betrayed her nerves about Autumn's task.

Autumn flashed what she hoped was a reassuring smile.

The last thing she wanted to do was stress Winter out. "Not really. I'm more excited than anything."

It was true. She *wasn't* nervous. Not yet. And while she expected a few butterflies to arrive at about the same time she set foot onto Harmony House property, her fascination with the organization would more than likely outweigh all else.

"That's good." Winter shivered in the chilled air of the store. "Just don't forget that Parr is a massive creep in the middle of all that excitement."

Autumn went still. "Why does everyone seem to think I'm so capable of falling prey to Damien Parr? I'm a *psychologist*. His twisted mind fascinates me, but I'm not about to forget that it's twisted."

She turned away and pretended to inspect a pair of jeans, trying to hide the hurt on her face.

First Aiden and now Winter.

They weren't saying the same words Chris had. They weren't insinuating that she was unable to perform based on her failure with Justin. But all the same, the over-protective card was being played enough to make her wonder just how fragile she appeared in their eyes.

Did no one believe in her anymore?

"I think...it's just that," Winter took a deep breath, "you're wounded. Inside, I mean. That's precisely what Parr feeds on."

Autumn met her friend's vivid blue eyes, taking in the purplish-brown craters beneath them. "I'm not any more wounded than the next person."

The frown on Winter's face was evidence that she'd understood Autumn's comment all too well. She opened her mouth to reply but made a sharp turn instead. She looked like she was searching for someone behind her.

*Just touch her shoulder. Figure out what in the hell she's strug-
gling with right now. Find out what's really wrong.*

Winter made a slow turn and backed away as though she
knew exactly what Autumn's intentions were. She knew
what Autumn was capable of, and Autumn knew that for
unknown reasons, her friend did not want to make physical
contact in the present moment.

"Fly." Winter waved a hand around her head and refocused on the t-shirts. "Damn fly in my ear."

Autumn had the fleeting urge to gift the undercover privilege to Noah or even Chris. She desperately wanted to help
her best friend heal, and Winter's welfare far outweighed her
personal fascination with the case.

She couldn't, of course. Winter would harbor even more
angst were she to learn her condition was the reason
Autumn backed out of the mission. The absolute last thing
she wanted to do was increase Agent Black's distress.

Noah will be with her the whole time.

The fact didn't silence Autumn's fears, but she accepted it
as enough for now.

What else could she do?

16

I stepped out the back door, inhaling the fresh summer air as I greeted a brand-new day. The world was a beautiful place, but this particular piece of land was spectacular. The Harmony House grounds that sprawled like an emerald sea all around me far surpassed the normal definition of "beauty."

Members were out and about as I strolled to the overlook, busy in the sweet morning hours. Some knelt in the dirt, yanking out weeds and tending gardens, while others hung clothes up to dry behind their quaint cabins. Flowers of every color bloomed and livened up the pathways, attracting the fat bumblebees that buzzed from one to the next in search of pollen.

Sometimes the glory of it all was almost too much to bear. Why should any single human be so blessed? My heart swelled, and when I stepped onto the wooden deck that formed the overlook to drink everything in, tears burned my eyes. Magnificent creation that the viewing area was, the surrounding scene of nature was what made the place truly special.

Take away the flourishing trees and bright blue sky, erase the mountains in the distance, and all you were really left with was a giant deck and a very steep drop-off.

I approached the waist-high railing that bordered the edge and peered over, picturing sweet Natalie's face just before she went off the cliff at Dogwood Falls. My heart swelled even more. She was one with the water now. A perfect, harmonious ending for such a troubled life.

In retrospect, I almost wished I hadn't placed the 911 call. Natalie's spirit would always be in the falls, but pesky law enforcement had, of course, pulled her body out of the river.

I gave a regretful sigh. Unfortunate, but the anonymous emergency call had been necessary. The local authorities had to know where she'd disappeared and how she'd killed herself before her death could be ruled a suicide.

The call couldn't have been avoided.

Kenneth's face came to me next. Though their backstories and suicides were entirely different, Natalie and Kenneth had one thing in common.

In those last final moments before their deaths, they'd both been terrified. They would have done or said anything to save their own lives. They would have followed after me like the last shining light in the sky.

The irony being, of course, that it was simply too late at that point for them to change paths.

I shook my head. Sad. Such promise and youth wasted.

Why couldn't they have stuck to the original road to recovery that I'd helped them find? Why wander from the paradise of healing we had inhabited together?

A warm breeze drifted up from the canyon, caressing my cheeks as I recalled what an absolute wreck Natalie had been when she first arrived at Harmony House. Granted, that was par for the course as far as new members went. But her particular story of abandonment, miscarriage, and addiction had torn at my spirit.

The absolute barbaric way in which the poor girl had been treated! Turned away by the man she loved because she was carrying *his child*. Her parents had shunned her as well for marring their "good name." And even after she'd stayed strong through both of those horrific emotional hells, she'd lost the baby.

Convinced she had nothing left, Natalie had turned to alcohol to help her forget. Eventually, she hadn't been able to go a full thirty minutes without pouring some type of liquor down her throat.

Sorrow settled over me, coating my skin like a fine layer of dust. Tragic. The way humans were capable of treating each other was a tragedy. Natalie was attractive, young, intelligent, witty…she hadn't deserved to walk through that valley of despair. And if she hadn't found Harmony House, she quite possibly never would have left the valley to begin with.

She'd lucked out. She managed to drag her shattered, despondent soul to our front doors, and once inside, Natalie Garland had learned what the word *family* could truly mean.

I lifted a finger, pointed at the highest peak in the distance, and circled it slowly in the warm air.

The Circle was a wondrous gift, and Natalie had been a part of the beauty. A *vital* part. I had loved her, and I always would.

Always.

But leaving the Circle…that wasn't an affront I could just let go.

Every word of thanks, every carefree giggle she'd emitted while safe under the wings of Harmony House ceased to mean anything once she walked away from the fold. She'd betrayed the people who cared for her most. She'd abandoned the people who had loved her when the people who were *supposed* to love her had turned their backs.

Another deep sigh spilled from my lungs. As much as I'd loved Natalie, I couldn't let that insult stand. I *had* to release her when she left Harmony House. She was spitting in the face of my love. Endangering the entire group. The others witnessed her leave, and the sight could put crazy ideas into their minds about what life would be like outside of our haven. Outside of our *utopia*.

How easily the human mind pushed aside the horror of the past. The members of Harmony House lived such a peaceful, happy existence here that they sometimes forgot the worst of what happened before we embraced them into our fold and even began believing they could reenter their old lives and bring their newfound joy with them.

So misguided. They didn't comprehend that the light in their souls was directly connected to the power of Harmony House. The beauty that coursed through our connection every second of every day. Unplugging from the source was asinine.

Such a move couldn't end well for the vast majority of our flock. As for the very few who might find a semblance of happiness outside our midst?

I made sure it didn't end well. By releasing them.

I believed that God had taken Natalie back into His fold, and she was much better off there. She'd find true redemption in the afterlife.

But you won't.

Images from my nightmare stirred before my eyes, momentarily obstructing the breathtaking view. I shivered in the humid air. There was no altering my path, though.

Banishment from the kingdom of heaven was the price I would pay. I'd accepted my fate.

I'd *chosen* my future, just as Natalie and Kenneth had.

I kept Harmony House safe and alive by releasing those who threatened to mar heaven on earth. And I would pay for those untimely deaths by screaming in hell for all eternity.

Walking this path was a noble way to live, and I didn't regret my service to the greater good. Not for one second. Sacrifice was necessary sometimes.

Jesus Christ, for instance, knew his crucifixion was essential.

With my head tipped back to the sun, I stretched my arms all the way out from the shoulder. Envisioning my body nailed to a cross.

I wasn't delusional. I knew there would be no resurrection for me. But all the same, I humbly followed His example. There were no better footsteps to follow in this existence.

Harmony House meant everything to me.

I'd believed Kenneth was on the same wavelength after his recovery. He'd come to us so broken and tainted by addiction. His morals had been all but annihilated by his desires.

For a time, he'd been one of the most amazing turnaround stories Harmony House had ever witnessed. His journey gave hope to countless numbers of recovering addicts who were already members of our circle, as well as the new weary faces who stumbled upon our light.

When I overheard him speaking with his sister, all the love in my heart for Kenneth turned ice-cold. Yvette was the one who'd turned her back on him when he'd needed her most. She'd ordered him to leave and never come back.

Taking into account his alcohol addiction and continuous trouble with the law, Yvette had basically sent him to his grave.

Here at Harmony House, we'd given him a new life. A rebirth. We'd walked Kenneth through the steps of recovery and helped him reclaim who he was.

Yet he'd tried to leave.

Remembered shock rippled over me. Of all our members, I'd never once considered that Kenneth Wilder would dream of abandoning the Circle.

He may have believed he could leave, but that was pride whispering lies of the devil into his ear. That was selfishness tugging at his greedy human soul.

And he'd listened to those lies. He'd caved.

The absolute brazen ignorance he was operating under, thinking he could walk away from the Circle and amount to anything on his own...even now, my stomach churned at the memory of such hubris.

He'd agreed to the drinks so easily. Without hesitation. If I was okay with polluting my body with alcohol, Kenneth was okay with it too.

That wasn't a true recovery at all. That was denial.

My duty lay in showing him the truth of who and what he was and would always be.

In the end, I'd prevailed. He'd accepted his beast of a black soul, and in doing so, significantly improved his chances of entering the kingdom of God.

I'd granted him that much, via his release.

Sweet release.

With the sun baking down on my skin, I recalled the first release I'd ever committed. Not for a member of Harmony House, but rather a man I'd hoped could be a member. I'd attended the local AA meeting, seeking out new recruits. One of the attendees had the nerve to show up for the gathering completely wasted and reeking of alcohol.

This man stood on shaking legs and slurred out his introduction. "Hi...I'm Patriiick, and I'm annn...an alcerholic." The group seemed familiar with Patrick, which only made his situation sadder as he proceeded to share, "I dinnn even wanna come o'er herrre tonight but I got merself kicked outta the barrr and lookey me. I camed."

He was helped to a chair and given a steaming cup of black coffee, which I feared would land in his lap. But he managed to hold it and sip throughout the entire meeting. Borderline impressive.

My body had buzzed with the knowledge that we could help this mess of a man. All he had to do was come with me, and I would show him the path to freedom. To peace.

But after the meeting, Patrick—I later learned his full name was Patrick Benjamin Ryder—stumbled out of the church basement he'd been sheltered in for the last hour and straight into a liquor store three blocks down. I'd waited outside, hoping and praying that he'd change his mind.

He didn't.

When Patrick had reappeared with a fresh bottle of vodka, I'd understood what had to be done. This man was a pariah…a leech. He would burden this world every second of his life until the blessed day that he stopped living.

I'd convinced Patrick to walk with me to the local park so we could hang and get drunk together. Or in his case, even drunker. We'd found the perfect bench, deep inside the park. Surrounded by trees and far from the road.

He'd laughed when I pulled some plastic gloves out of my backpack and slipped them on. I told him I had a trick I wanted to show him.

The first part of the trick had involved punching him in the side of the face, which sent his big, clumsy body collapsing onto the grass. The worthless lug was still struggling to sit up when I'd introduced part two of the magic act: sitting on his chest and holding his arms down with my knees.

The saddest part of the entire event was that Patrick

barely put up a fight. He was so far gone that the best he could do was wiggle around like an earthworm.

A sloshed earthworm.

"If you swallow, I'll let you go."

That was what I'd told him before shoving the bottle into his mouth.

For a while, Patrick had held his own. Twenty-four ounces of straight vodka had proven too much, though. Even for an alcoholic like him. Halfway through the bottle, he'd begun to fight the flow. Choking and gurgling, causing vodka to run down the sides of his face.

Wasteful, even in his last few moments of life.

He'd passed out within seconds of finishing the bottle. I'd dragged his body behind a thicket of bushes, making sure he was flat on his back so that anything his system tried to regurgitate would choke him. In his hands, I'd placed his suicide weapon of choice. Dead Patrick had held his liquor bottle proudly.

I'd taken the few dollars he had from his pockets. Every little bit helped the Harmony House community, and I took comfort in the fact that in this small way, Patrick's death might make a difference.

When Patrick was found a few days later, the toxicology report had pointed a clear finger to alcohol poisoning as his killer. His death was ruled a suicide.

No one "accidentally" drank *that* much.

The success of Patrick's release had helped me gain confidence. I realized that I had the power to make hard calls, carry them out, and create a safer world for all. Whether someone I sent on their way to the afterlife died with twenty bucks in their pocket or two thousand…none of that money would go to waste.

Not one cent.

Keeping law enforcement off my scent required me to

release random addicts now and again. Souls who'd never set foot on Harmony House grounds. Therefore, their suicides couldn't be connected to us.

Collateral damage was a small price to pay to keep Harmony House thriving. Any act that benefited the Circle was not undertaken in vain.

The Circle was everything.

After enjoying one last look off the deck into the tree-topped valley, I turned and strolled back to the main house. I ran into Alice in the communal room. She smiled at me from her spot at the dining table, pure joy radiating from her eyes.

With her blonde hair, creamy skin, and heavenly light, Alice might be the most beautiful woman in the entire world.

If I had to describe an angel, I'd describe Alice.

"Hey." I sat as close as I dared. "You ready for the soup kitchen today?"

She grabbed my hand, making my heart flutter. "Absolutely. There is nothing as wonderful as serving those in need."

You. You're that wonderful.

"You're truly happy here, aren't you?" The idea of ever losing her twisted my insides into unbearable knots.

Alice squeezed my hand, her face as guileless as a newborn kitten's. "I've never been so happy and content in my entire life."

"Good." I released a stagnant breath, relieved to hear the words from those delicate pink lips. "Stay in that mindset. Embrace your happiness. The Circle would never be the same without you."

17

After the swift shopping spree with Winter, Autumn spent the rest of her morning poring over intel on Damien Parr and his group of followers. The details of each individual's background were sparse at best. The cult wasn't an open book to outsiders, and she became even more convinced that going undercover was their best bet.

"Wow." Autumn pursed her lips. "Damien is a war veteran who specialized in defusing bombs? Can't say the guy's a dummy, that's for sure."

The only agents left in the conference room besides her were Mia and Chris. Of the two, Agent Logan alone was paying attention.

Mia swiveled her rolling chair to face Autumn. "He definitely seems intelligent to me. I don't think a person could amass that type of following without brains."

"Good point." Autumn continued to read. "Damien Parr was written up several times while serving in Afghanistan before he was discharged. He returned stateside and devoted his life to community service. Hmm. Something *had* to have happened to him during the war to shift his stance. Sounds like he went overseas as one man and came back as quite another."

"Sloan Grant was in the service around that same time." Mia rolled her chair closer and studied Autumn's iPad. "And they both defused bombs."

Autumn fixed hopeful eyes on Mia. "Really? The same time?"

Mia blew out a long breath, looking like she might soon face a firing squad. "I can get ahold of her and find out if she knows any specifics on Parr's overseas experience."

The urge to jump at Mia's offer was strong, but the pink hue infusing the other agent's cheeks made Autumn hesitate. Sloan and Mia's turbulent past wasn't a secret. Not even for a newbie like Autumn. "You don't have to do that. I can try to reach her myself."

"No." Mia shook her head. "I'm a big girl, and I can handle it. You're going undercover. Today."

Autumn chewed her cheek as she studied her friend. Of course Mia could handle it. On that count, Autumn had no doubt. The point was, should she have to? No special ability was required to see that the idea of contacting Sloan Grant troubled Mia. Far more than the agent was letting on. "Mia... I've heard enough about your history to know you probably dread talking to Sloan."

Mia stiffened, but she played her reaction off by lifting a shoulder. "This would be the second time I talked to her in six months. I'm the one who had to call her to come in and defuse Winter. My feelings about the role Sloan played in Ned's death have nothing to do with the Bureau or Damien Parr or Afghanistan. I can compartmentalize."

"Can you?" The blunt question slipped out before Autumn could slide it through a softer filter.

"I can." Mia straightened in her chair. Her chin lifted. "I'm a professional. I'll get it done."

"Really. I don't mind making a quick call before—"

"Autumn?" Mia cut her off. "I want to move past what happened. Somehow. Contacting her is something I *need* to do."

After taking in the determined line of Mia's mouth, Autumn dipped her head. "Okay." Without thinking, she laid a gentle hand on Mia's arm. Intending to offer comfort.

The touch sent images bursting inside her.

Mia...gazing at Sloan...gazing at Ned's coffin. Pain, so much pain. And anger. Fiery, seething resentment.

Autumn's heart wrenched. She yanked her hand away and waited for the emotions to subside. "If you ever need to talk, Mia..." How the woman stayed so kind while carrying around that absolute boulder of ache was no small feat.

Agent Logan stood and smiled at her with warm brown eyes and dimples ablaze. "I know. Now let's get you ready for your covert ops mission."

Mia was right. The clock was ticking, and Autumn needed to transform into the version of herself that would enter Harmony House. She grabbed the bags resting at her feet and headed for the door.

"I'm gonna go change in the restroom," she called to Mia over her shoulder, "but meet me in the breakroom in about ten. I'll let you decide if I'm a convincing enough troubled soul."

Agent Logan gave her a thumbs-up. "Wouldn't miss it for the world."

Autumn made quick time of walking down the hall, entering the restroom, and locking the door behind her. Adrenaline was kicking in. She was more than ready to do this.

She pulled off her dress slacks, replacing them with a pair of worn, baggy jeans. Her blazer and button-down were ousted for an equally loose dark gray t-shirt. From another sack, she retrieved some hair-shaping wax. While meant to assist with style and hold, Autumn slicked enough of the product through her locks to bypass styling and move straight into grease-ball territory.

A beat-up pair of sneakers completed the ensemble. Autumn topped it all off by wiping away the limited amount of makeup she wore on a daily basis.

Barefaced and messy.

She considered her reflection in the mirror. The redheaded homeless and troubled vibe she'd been aiming for stared back at her.

The hand she lifted to the mirror was unsteady.

Sarah.

Was her sister homeless right now? Had Sarah found a roof and a warm bed after fleeing her trailer in Florida? Was she sleeping on benches? In alleyways? In abandoned buildings?

The fact that her sister could be in a situation all too close to the one Autumn was attempting to fake caused doubt to creep through her mind.

Maybe she shouldn't be going on this mission at all. Maybe a good sister would request some time off and go find Sarah. *Actually* find Sarah. What if her sister truly was sitting in some crack house right this second, not knowing where her next meal or cup of clean water was coming from?

The questions kept coming, pummeling her with worry.

What if Sarah had fallen prey to drugs or alcohol? What if she'd become so disillusioned with her hard life that she was contemplating suicide?

Wasn't Sarah more important than any one person at Harmony House? Shouldn't she be top priority?

Autumn closed her eyes and drew in one sharp breath after another. Again and again, until the panic and guilt subsided. Until she could think straight.

When she reopened her eyes, she stared at her reflection with clear perspective. Going undercover on this case didn't mean she cared more about the rampant suicides plaguing Beechum County than she did Sarah. Beating herself up wouldn't change that.

As desperate as Autumn was to find her sister, she had a job to do. A life to live. She'd worked her ass off to get to where she was, and all the guilt in the world wouldn't help her find Sarah.

Even if she dropped all her responsibilities right this second and made finding her sister her sole focus, she wouldn't have the first clue as to where to start searching.

Sarah had vanished. No trail. No clues. No footprints, digital or otherwise.

Autumn hadn't given up on finding her sister. She never would.

Right now, though, other people needed Autumn's help. People who hadn't vanished. Sarah was the most important person on Earth in Autumn's heart, just like the multiple "suicide" victims were important to their families. She couldn't abandon them or her job. Especially to spin her wheels and go nowhere.

After splashing cold water on her cheeks, Autumn exited the restroom and sped down the hall, keeping her head lowered. She wasn't embarrassed, exactly, so much as she didn't want to explain herself to anyone who might actually mistake her for a homeless person.

What she hadn't expected upon entering the breakroom was to find Aiden lounging just inside the door, mowing down his takeout lunch. The remains of a giant BLT sat in a Styrofoam to-go carton next to a mountain of fries.

Mia's grin was all the warning Autumn needed to inform her of the ribbing she could expect at the hands of her colleagues.

She pushed her self-consciousness aside and strutted like a runway model. "Well? How do I look?" A twirl completed the show.

Aiden chuckled, covering his mouth with a napkin. Mia clapped and giggled. "Amazing. Convincing."

Autumn fluffed her greasy hair as she sashayed up to Aiden. "What about you, oh great and powerful SSA Parrish? Will this do?"

He laughed again, but she didn't take offense.

On the contrary, Autumn considered making Aiden Parrish smile to be an impressive accomplishment. Even if his amusement was directed at her.

After a few gulps from his water bottle, Aiden rubbed his jaw and pretended to scrutinize her. "Hmm, I'm not sure. I think we can do more."

"I got it." Mia walked to her, tilted her head, then reached up both hands and roughed Autumn's hair around. "There."

The shit-eating grins on her colleagues' faces informed Autumn that the situation on top of her head was every bit as scary as she imagined. "Do I have your approval *now*?" She raised an eyebrow at Aiden.

Instead of a verbal response, Aiden rubbed his hands over his fries with dramatic flair. Autumn wrinkled her brow as he rose and approached her. *What the heck?*

Before she could ask, he'd cupped both sides of her head between his palms and started rubbing.

She cringed as fry grease seeped into her hair.

When Autumn's entire head felt like she'd dunked it in a fast-food fryer, Aiden stepped back. After a quick once-over, he nodded. "There. That was the touch of magic you were missing. *Now* you're ready, Agent Trent."

Mia sputtered a laugh. After another few moments, Autumn couldn't help but join her.

Served her right for wanting to go undercover.

Once she stopped giggling, Autumn granted Aiden a lingering smile. "I find it comforting that you have a backup career as a beautician awaiting you should you ever choose to leave the Bureau, Agent Parrish."

His grin was back, triggering an answering warmth within her chest. A satisfaction that probably showed on her face. They stared at each other for a heartbeat too long before Aiden turned away and motioned toward the door.

"Sheriff Frank is waiting for us. We need to get going."

"Best of luck, Autumn." Mia's voice was so carefree that Autumn could almost forget she was preparing to immerse herself in an actual cult.

A cult that might have a serial killer within its midst.

Autumn ignored the chill trickling down her spine and gave Mia a carefree wave. Too late for second thoughts now. Aiden and the team were counting on her. "It's gonna be a blast."

She slung her backpack—another beat-down Goodwill find—onto her shoulder and followed Aiden out of the breakroom. They made their way down the long hall.

"Clock's ticking." Sheriff Frank straightened from the wall near the entrance and pushed open the glass double doors. "Let's go."

As they followed the sheriff out of the building, Autumn wondered if the woman wore that scowl everywhere, or if they were the only lucky recipients of her sour moods.

She slid into the back seat of Sheriff Frank's patrol car. Unsurprisingly, the interior was as spotless as the gleaming exterior, the aggressive kind of clean that Autumn would be scared to eat in. The sheriff was in a hurry, reversing out of the parking space while Autumn was still shutting the door.

Their destination was a soup kitchen in downtown Beechum. Sheriff Frank had informed them that Damien and his group were serving there today. If the outing went according to plan, Autumn would wander in and strike up a conversation with one of the Harmony House members, relay her sad, "lost soul" tale, and hopefully be inside the walls of Harmony House before the sun went down.

With Sheriff Frank at the wheel, the drive took less than five minutes. They pulled to a stop curbside a few blocks down from the soup kitchen. Aiden exited the passenger's side, and Autumn climbed out of the back seat, grabbing her stuffed Goodwill bag.

Standing on the sidewalk, trepidation began to set in. In a few moments, she'd be on her own. What if she'd made a mistake? Bitten off more than she could chew? Back in college, she'd never signed up for a drama class, yet here she was. Jumping into an investigation that hinged on her ability to take on a role and fool everyone around her.

Autumn tightened her grip on the bag and stiffened her spine.

I'm ready for this. This is what I've trained for. It's time to show them that I'm capable of more than just screwing things up.

Aiden stared at her with a pronounced frown. His light blue eyes were so full of concern that Autumn averted her gaze. She had enough worries of her own without taking on his as well. Plus, he was too observant by far. If he noticed her hesitation, he might experience a last-second change of heart and call the whole operation off.

"Here." He handed her a black burner phone. "None of your contacts are in there, but I want you to contact me at the end of every day before lights out and at the first sign of trouble. The first *hint* of a sign of trouble. Do you understand?"

Ironically, Aiden's overprotectiveness eased some of the tension from Autumn's neck. She fought an instinctual eye roll. "Yes, Dad. I understand."

"Don't do that." The soft command sounded more like a

plea. "There could be more danger in that place than any of us predicted. I need to know you're safe. Please."

Worry creased Aiden's forehead, and there was no trace of his earlier grin. In the face of his very real concern, Autumn's throat constricted. Pleading wouldn't come easy to a man like Aiden.

"I'll be careful, and I'll call. I'm going to see you soon. Promise." She attempted to smile and failed.

"Why does that not make me feel any better at all?" Aiden held her gaze, intense as ever. Drawing her in like a magnet. Autumn's skin tingled as she became aware of how little distance was between them. Inches, really. Close enough for her to breathe in his cologne.

Close enough that if either of them took one more step, their mouths would collide...

Somewhere down the street, a car honked. Autumn broke the spell by jumping back. This was absurd. She needed to go...needed to move. Get this started and break away from the cool blue stare that threatened to freeze her in place for all eternity. "Goodbye."

He reached for her arm, hesitating with his hand hovering an inch away before finally giving in and patting her.

Autumn tensed as a frenzied, flustered signal slammed into her brain.

Desire and longing and—

The signal cut out when Aiden removed his hand. "Good luck, Agent Trent." His face was an impenetrable mask as he gave her a firm nod and slid into Sheriff Frank's patrol car.

Autumn hurried in the direction of the soup kitchen before the sheriff pulled onto the street. She didn't wait to watch them leave. Part of her was afraid that if she did, she'd turn around and run back to the car.

After turning right at the corner, the soup kitchen was a

straight shot down the sidewalk. Less than two blocks away. Staring directly ahead, Autumn slung her bag over her shoulder and kept walking while her stomach knotted into a tight ball.

Shake it off, Trent. You're about to enter the lion's den.

18

Alice Leeson stood behind the counter and plunged a stainless steel ladle into a deep vat of beef stew. She took extra care to add plenty of meat chunks to each bowl so every stomach would be filled.

Many of the faces in the long line were hollow-cheeked and gaunt. These people were hungry and desperate for nourishment. Feeding their bodies was a blessing, but feeding their souls would be an absolute honor.

She hoped to walk away from today's service with a new friend. Alice considered everyone she met a friend, especially those who dwelled with her at Harmony House. They were her friends *and* her family.

A young mother with two little ones clinging to her was next in line. The poor woman, who looked to be more of a girl, held her bowl up but kept her eyes low.

She's ashamed. But there's no shame in love, and love is what we're serving today.

"Your little ones are beautiful." Alice leaned against the counter and waved at the two sets of shy green eyes peeking up at her.

The woman ventured to meet her gaze. "Th-thank you." The corners of her mouth upturned ever so slightly before she ushered her children away to find a seat at one of the numerous long tables.

Alice smiled, her heart filled with glee at the small positive boost in the woman's demeanor. Any piece of happiness she could share with a hurting soul was wonderful.

A flash of bright red near the entrance caught Alice's eye. She focused in on a woman in baggy clothing standing at the end of the soup line. Her auburn hair was clumped in spots and stringy in others, as though she hadn't showered in at least a week, if not two or three.

The line shuffled forward, and the woman tripped on her own dirty sneaker. She stumbled, bumping into the person ahead of her.

The older woman lifted her head. Alice cringed when she recognized the crabby, wrinkled face.

Oh no. Maude, please behave.

Maude whirled and shoved the redhead backward.

Oh, no. Not here. No no no.

"You wanna watch where you're going, jerk?" Maude barked at the new face.

Alice held her breath, worried that the newcomer would turn tail and run away before filling her belly. Instead, the newbie pushed her chest out and stood her ground. "You push me, and I'm the jerk? *You're* a freakin' jerk!"

The redhead stepped closer to Maude, fists clenched at her sides.

Alice dropped the ladle into the pot and raced around the counter. "Please. There's no need for arguments. There is plenty of room for everyone." She held up her hands as though she were approaching two feral hellcats.

Maude and the redhead both stared at her, waiting to see what she'd do next. Alice nodded at Maude and made a split-second decision to give their visitor a personal welcome.

"Ain't enough room for clumsy jerks like her." Maude turned away abruptly and resumed her previous state of silence in the line.

"Come." Alice motioned for their visitor to follow her. "Let's get you a seat." She led the woman toward a corner of the room where a wide space of bench and table were unused.

"That wasn't my fault." The woman reeked of fast food mixed with dirt. Not the worst smelling person in the room by far, but the poor thing could definitely use a shower. "I tripped. Tripping is an *accident*. She shoved me *on purpose*."

Alice bobbed her head, empathetic and thankful to have prevented any further scuffle. "Maude is a regular here. She's got a bit of a tough exterior, but she's really a sweetheart once you get to know her."

The redhead snorted, shooting a glare across the room toward her new acquaintance. "Right. And I'm the virgin mother Mary."

Her response was fair, considering Maude had given her quite the nudge. Alice offered her hand and a wide smile. "I'm Alice Leeson. I volunteer here with Harmony House. I don't think I've met you before."

"Autumn." The woman seemed to retreat into what Alice guessed was her normal, soft-spoken tone. She shook Alice's hand and tilted her head. "What's Harmony House?"

Those words always filled Alice with a surge of warmth and happiness. "Oh, Autumn. Harmony House is just the most beautiful place on Earth." She teared up at the thought of her home.

This silenced Autumn for a moment. She hunched her shoulders and stared at the floor. "I'm sorry. I didn't mean to walk in here and cause problems. I'm just, I'm *hungry*, and I fell on accident. My shoes are a little big for my feet. But that lady…why are people so mean?"

When she lifted her head, tears glistened on her cheeks.

Alice's heart wrenched. Seeing others hurting so much caused her physical pain. She wished she could help every last struggling soul that stepped foot in the shelter, but she had to be satisfied with the ones she could save. "I know you didn't mean to. Don't cry. Take a few deep breaths and try to just relax. You're in a safe place. How about I grab you a bowl of soup? Wait right here."

She beelined for the counter, bustling between fellow House members and scooping out a full bowl for her new friend.

Damien stood just inside the kitchen doorway. Their eyes met for a brief second, and he gave her a nod of approval. She knew exactly what that nod meant.

Help her, Alice. She needs you.

Alice's chest expanded with a renewed sense of purpose. She knew what it was like to be hungry and alone. After the death of her sister, Maggie, life had plunged to such a low that she never thought she'd escape. She had accepted that no one was going to help her with her problems. People had their own problems to deal with, and that was more than enough for most. She was on her own.

Until she'd happened upon Harmony House. *Everything* had changed that fateful day. Gratitude warmed her soul as she finished ladling the soup. There were no words to describe how thankful she was for her newfound family.

Alice scurried back to the table, setting the steaming bowl in front of Autumn and sitting across from her. The poor woman shoveled spoonful after spoonful of stew into her mouth like she was afraid someone might snatch the bowl away. So fast, Alice feared she might choke.

"How long has it been since you had a nice, hot meal?"

Autumn gulped another large spoonful. "Too long." She continued to inhale the stew at an alarming speed.

Memories stirred in Alice's head. Phantom hunger pangs tightened her stomach. She'd been there. She remembered her hunger growing so severe that her mind had started to slip into delirium. She recalled wanting to die rather than live another day with nothing to eat and nowhere to go. "Well, we'll make sure that's not the case ever again, okay? Are you from the Beechum area?"

"No." Autumn's response was quick. "I just...ended up here somehow. I lost my job, and I couldn't pay rent. I didn't have anyone to turn to, you know? I don't have people I can lean on in life. I never have."

"I understand." The pain in Alice's chest swelled. "Where have you been sleeping since losing your place?" She could guess because she'd played that game before. The *Where Am I Going to Sleep Tonight* and *Hope I Don't Get Murdered* games.

Autumn sniffled and lifted a shoulder, then dropped it in defeat. "I mean, I can usually find a doorway or an alley where I can hide enough to get a little sleep. Sometimes I'm too scared to sleep, though. I'm just thankful the weather is warm right now."

Alice's arms ached from resisting the urge to embrace the woman. Autumn reminded her so much of herself. Before she'd found Damien.

One terrifying night, Alice had awoken on a park bench to two men staring at her. Their eyes had crawled all over her body, their smiles all wrong. Hungry and cruel. She'd known exactly what they'd wanted and that her window of escape was slim.

Clutching the rock she'd always slept with back in those days, she'd slammed one man in the temple. The other she'd kicked in the groin before running for her life. They'd recovered from their injuries far too quickly and gained on her at a frightening pace.

Diving into a leaf-covered ditch and crawling into the sewer pipe had been the split-second decision that saved her life. The men ran past and disappeared, but she'd stayed hunched down in that filthy muck for at least an hour before daring to run in the opposite direction.

An involuntary shudder quaked through her body.

Horrible, horrible days. But those are in the past. I have a new life now.

Alice leaned across the table. "No one should ever have to suffer in such solitude, Autumn. I know a place where you can stay and get a good night's sleep on a *real* bed."

This was always the general moment of truth when hurting individuals either bolted or opened up. Alice held her breath, praying Autumn wasn't a bolter.

Autumn's forehead creased. "You got an extra room just laying around?"

Her lungs eased, and Alice smiled. Sounded like her new friend wasn't preparing to run so much as she was finding it hard to believe in such kindness from a complete stranger. "There are many rooms in my father's house."

The other woman tilted her head. Considering. "I mean, if you're *serious*, I'm definitely not going to turn down a warm bed…"

The response filled Alice's heart with joy. "Sit tight for just a minute, okay?" She rose and rushed through the maze of tables to find Damien.

She found him in the same spot in the kitchen, leaning against the doorjamb. His thick dark hair was tamed and styled. Damien didn't value physical beauty, but he did preach the importance of keeping a tidy appearance.

His gentle brown eyes were locked on her, and she realized that he'd been observing her interactions with Autumn. He must have sensed the same thing Alice did, about the potential and promise Autumn held to become another blissful member of Harmony House.

Even so, Alice would never take his approval for granted. That would be disrespectful. "Damien, I think I've found another lost lamb in need of a home...in need of *love*."

Her leader nodded, placing a hand on her shoulder. "Once again, I am blessed by your keen observational skills. Your natural insight may have just saved that woman's life. Invite her to my house."

To Alice, the light of Damien's approval always felt like a blessing from the Almighty. She glowed whenever he smiled at her. This saintly man had done so much good for so many people...if she could be even a small light next to his beacon, the privilege was great.

"Thank you, Damien." Alice threw her arms around him for a quick hug before hurrying back to Autumn. Her excitement and joy were overflowing, and she had no reason to keep them in check.

Autumn raised her head, having just scraped the last spoonful of stew into her mouth. Alice was struck by her beauty, even with the greasy hair and stew dribbling down her chin. A shower and some fresh clothes would do wonders for her new friend.

"Your worries are over, Autumn." Alice clapped her hands together in delight as she dropped to the bench beside her. "You've found a place where you can finally lay your head and rest."

Across the table, Autumn observed Alice's enthusiastic face. The blue-eyed blonde had been cute on the pages of the report Autumn had studied, but in person, she was positively stunning. No actress on the planet could fake the kind of sweetness that poured out of her. For better or worse, the woman clearly believed that Harmony House was the solution to Autumn's problems.

"I mean," Autumn scraped at her empty bowl like a scavenger, "are you sure? I don't want to inconvenience anyone."

Alice laughed and shook her head. "It would be our *honor* to have you as a guest at Harmony House."

Autumn jerked her chin across the room toward Damien. "Who's that man? Why did you have to ask his permission first?" She hunched lower in the chair, careful to maintain an air of suspicion.

"Damien Parr is our leader." Alice beamed at him as she spoke. "He founded Harmony House to help the lost and the hurting. He made it a place that all are welcome to call home. He's a lovely person."

"He's staring at us." Autumn wasn't ready to give up the jaded lost soul act just yet. "Why is he staring at us?"

Alice giggled. Her eyes sparkled like a little kid who'd just received a pony for Christmas. "Damien is so excited about you, Autumn. He and I both knew the second you walked in that you were special."

"I'm not special." Autumn lowered her eyes to the table as if ashamed. Oddly enough, she was experiencing more than a hint of that emotion at the moment.

"You are." Alice cradled Autumn's hand between hers. "I promise you, once you step foot into Harmony House…meet the members…you'll be in love. And everyone will love you as well. Kindness is our number one priority, and Damien reminds us of that often."

The only emotion pulsing from Alice's hands was a strong current of joy. Autumn took a second to savor the vivid, unadulterated warmth.

This woman was the real deal. Brimming over with love and peace and kindness, and a huge desire to share it all.

A little longer and Autumn started to feel light-headed. The amalgamation of good emanating from Alice Leeson was intoxicating, to the point of overwhelming.

Autumn gently extracted her hand while the other woman continued to beam.

"Should we just call you Autumn? Or…?"

Alice's warm mannerisms relaxed every muscle in Autumn's body. "Nichol. Autumn Nichol."

Giving her actual surname was out of the question, so Autumn had given Sarah's.

Sarah.

The tension returned to Autumn's limbs. Was her sister dependent on soup kitchens for nourishment? Was she surrounded by hundreds of Maudes, or had she found people willing to help her along her path? Or even one person who was willing to show her an ounce of the kindness that Alice was gifting to Autumn?

Would Sarah be happier…better off…finding a place like Harmony House, even if it *was* a cult, rather than stripping and selling her body to survive?

That was if she survived at all. For all she knew, Sarah could be dead already. Her sister's story could be over.

A cold front passed through Autumn, turning her body to ice. Hollowness gnawed beneath her ribs. She wanted to reject the thought of Sarah being dead as ridiculous, but she refused to lie to herself.

Sarah may or may not be dead. As of now, Autumn had no way of knowing.

The next time she locked eyes with Alice, Autumn didn't have to fake a heavy heart or weariness. The truth was enough to take care of that.

Even if her sister was still alive, Autumn's chances for a happy reunion dwindled every week that passed without information on Sarah's whereabouts.

19

Soup kitchen lunch hours ended at two. Autumn stayed in her seat and surveyed the Harmony House volunteers as well as the patrons who passed through for nourishment.

The character she was playing worked to her advantage as far as openly spying went. Alice and every other Harmony House member would expect nothing less than skepticism and hyperawareness from a homeless human abandoned and ignored by society.

Though not every cult member was as beautiful or quite as animated as Alice, they were all without fail friendly, polite, and kind. Autumn noticed a trend concerning the individuals passing through the soup line. Most all of them seemed to be on a first-name basis with the volunteers, and anyone who wasn't was swiftly visited by a smiling Harmony House member after sitting down to eat.

There was a remarkable balance of concern tempered with respect for privacy involved in every conversation Autumn overheard. Damien's followers were careful to ask questions that would not offend while offering tidbits about their "home" whenever possible.

They seemed to sense whether an individual was open to further discussion of Harmony House or if it was best to just let them be and hope they came back again tomorrow. Or the next day. Or the day after that.

Another half hour led Autumn to a startling observation. While male volunteers served from behind the counter and a few more popped in periodically from the kitchen, only the women ventured to speak with anyone in the crowd.

Reluctant admiration flickered in her chest. Smart move on Parr's part, to set up the protocol that way. Unfamiliar men were generally perceived as more threatening than women. If the Harmony House leader wanted to lure in houseless, hurting people, using a woman's soft voice and smile was the safer bet.

Damien Parr had mastered the art of recruitment so well that he didn't have to lift a single finger of his own to grow his movement.

Parr himself disappeared shortly after Autumn received her official invitation. She figured he had a lot to keep his eye on back amongst his followers at the estate. A man like that wouldn't want to turn his attention away for too long.

Once all the visitors had eaten their fill and the last one shuffled out, Alice locked the front door and came to retrieve Autumn. She led her through the kitchen and out the back exit, where two large vans were filling with volunteers. Autumn climbed in behind Alice and crammed herself into an open seat.

At first, her anxiety wasn't all feigned as she clutched her bag to her lap. Over the short course of the drive, though, her nerves eased, soothed by the excited chatter and laughter that spilled through the van.

If Harmony House was a cult, its members sure didn't seem to be suffering for it. These people were all stone-cold sober yet as giddy as kids on Christmas Day.

She began to understand Sheriff Frank's frustration with the open bias against the group. Harmony House members *were* different, but by no means was anyone required to believe as they did. And in a world full of pain and depression, they were happy. The good they did in the community couldn't be denied.

Every person in the van had a glow about them. A smile on their face. Autumn didn't doubt that Damien's reasons for this might be covered in a few layers of slime, but someone like Alice? She was volunteering because she found joy in helping others.

A good reminder that Autumn was there to scope out Damien's financial activity, along with any possible connections between Harmony House and the uptick in community suicides.

What she wasn't there to do was judge the members' personal choices and belief systems.

When the vans pulled into the compound, Autumn gaped out the window at the size and grandeur of Harmony House in real time. Pictures didn't do the immense three-story edifice justice, nor had they relayed the natural beauty that surrounded everything and everyone on Harmony House grounds.

Flowers, fruit trees, and lush green grass splayed out across the landscape with picturesque, museum-wall-worthy colors. Autumn searched for a disturbed face amongst all the gaiety and couldn't find a single one.

The sign above the monstrously tall glass doors read like a motivational poster, only reconfigured for a charitable organization. *Harmony House, Join the Circle, Be the Change.*

Alice whisked Autumn through an immediate tour of all three stories. The Harmony House resident kept up an animated, one-way dialogue while Autumn took mental notes on the layout. She paid extra attention when Alice pointed out the closed door that led to Damien's office. There were answers in that room that she intended to uncover.

Somehow.

The communal room, kitchen, and other first-floor features were all exactly as Aiden and Mia had described. The second and third floors blew Autumn's mind. Almost every room and space available had been converted into small bedrooms. Some of the large rooms were outfitted with several cots and sleeping bags.

When Autumn paused at a large window on the third floor overlooking three rows of cabins that disappeared into the woods, Alice stopped with her. "Anyone who has committed to staying with Harmony House lives in a cabin. New arrivals stay in the house so that they can be nourished and protected by more established members."

Autumn murmured, "How nice," and turned away from the window so Alice wouldn't catch her expression.

Protected. Right. More like Damien Parr's nice way of saying "monitored." No one made it to cabin status before the Harmony House leader was sure they'd drunk the Kool-Aid.

"Here you are. A place to rest." With great fanfare, Alice threw open the door to Autumn's room and beamed like she'd just escorted her into a penthouse suite.

The cramped enclosure had obviously once housed a walk-in closet, with little extra space beyond the single twin bed.

Still, a private room with a bed and a door. All luxuries if Autumn were truly homeless.

Autumn let out a fake gasp and clutched both hands to her chest. "Alice, are you sure? I mean, I'm a complete stranger and—"

"You're a *friend*, Autumn." Alice plopped down on the bed.

"*All* are welcome in my father's house." She patted the mattress, and Autumn obediently sat, placing her backpack beside her.

"I'm very grateful." Autumn's lower lip trembled as she focused on her hands. "I don't know what to say."

Alice patted her back, injecting Autumn with a few more shots of blindingly pure energy. "You don't have to say anything. This is why we exist. This is what Harmony House *does*."

"Could we maybe," Autumn gave Alice a tentative glance, "talk for just a little bit? I'm sure you're busy, but…"

The eagerness in Alice's expression was unmistakable. "Of course we can talk. I do have some chores to do in a bit because we all pitch in here. That's what makes it such a beautiful place. But I will always make time to talk with you if you need me."

"Thank you." Autumn ducked her head to escape the guileless warmth exuding from the other woman. Alice was so selfless and good-natured that lying to her face made a lump lodge in Autumn's throat. However, that trespass couldn't be avoided.

People like Alice were the reason Autumn was under-cover here to begin with. If Damien Parr was a bad seed, he didn't deserve to hold power over anyone as pure as Alice Leeson.

"How did you end up here?" Autumn pulled her knees to her chest, fighting off a gag over the reek of her grease-pot hair. "You had to find this 'safe place to rest' at some point yourself, right?"

For the first time, Alice's smiled faltered. Her lashes lowered. "Right. I guess I was lost, just like the majority of people here were. I don't have a horrible history of lifelong suffering. Many here have been through much worse than me."

When she glanced back up, Alice's blue eyes brimmed with tears.

Autumn's heart softened. Most likely, Alice had experienced plenty of suffering. The woman was just too empathetic toward others to value her own pain.

"What happened?" Autumn checked herself as she sensed her therapist mode coming on too strong. Wanting to help Alice talk through her pain was second nature.

"My sister died," Alice divulged, sadness dousing out her smile. "Maggie. She was in a car accident and…well, she didn't make it, and she was kind of my hero growing up. Older sister, younger sister. You know how that goes."

Autumn swallowed with effort. She did know how that went. All too well.

Alice waved a hand in the air. "I'm okay now, but it was hard afterward. My parents were in such deep grief that they couldn't really help me face my own. I left home and spent some time on the streets. But then I met Damien and all my friends at Harmony House. They really helped walk me through my loss."

"I'm sorry you had to go through that." Autumn wanted to wrap the woman in a hug but refrained.

"It's been almost three full years." Alice's sigh was wistful. "I'll always miss Maggie, but I've honestly never been so happy in my entire life. My life has a purpose now. Every day is a gift."

Autumn ran the numbers, and a vice clamped her ribs. Alice's file listed her age as twenty-one years old. That meant this all took place when she was just eighteen. Right when life was beginning for her, it ended for her sister.

Survivor's guilt, along with emotional abandonment by her parents, could explain why Alice had been so drawn to a place like Harmony House. She'd probably been desperate for someone to fill that parental role for her. To give her the love stolen by her mother and father's grief.

Damien Parr preyed upon the vulnerable. The weary. He'd built Harmony House on the shoulders of pain. He was a succubus who leeched off the good intentions of people like Alice.

Autumn dug her fingers into her calves. If Damien had any skeletons in his closet, and the FBI seemed rather convinced that he did, she would find them.

And I'll rip apart the happiness of every innocent person living here. I'll tear Alice's heart to shreds. If Damien goes down, Harmony House falls as well.

Alice stood and swiped at her face. "I'll check in on you a bit later, okay? I'm going to go do my chores. You get some rest."

"Thank you, Alice. I mean that."

Once Alice left Autumn alone in the room, she seized the opportunity to stretch her arms and legs, ridding her body of the tension that was an inherent part of being undercover. When her muscles no longer felt like rubber bands on the brink of snapping, she settled onto the narrow bed.

This was the perfect time to analyze what she'd learned so far. Well, it would have been, but her mind was too full of Sarah. Alice had found Harmony House after losing her sister. Autumn had found a loving adoptive couple after her father's attack.

What had Sarah found?

Poverty, stripping, and prostitution. She hoped that was where the list stopped, but there was really no way to be certain.

I have to find her. I'm going to drive myself insane if I don't try to find her again.

She didn't know where to start, but wasn't that what the

team did best? Pick up and follow old trails that were never meant to be sniffed out?

Autumn laid her head on the pillow and stared up at the ceiling. Maybe she would talk to Aiden after this case was over and discuss pooling their resources to track down her little sister.

Chris would resent the usage of federal agent time and have yet another reason to call her Aiden's "pet." But she didn't care. If Parker hated her forever, then he did. She could live with that.

She couldn't live with never seeing Sarah again.

The bed creaked when Autumn rolled onto her side. There was a part of her that wished Sarah had found a place like this...had found a friend like Alice.

Damien, of course, was the reality check to that wish. He would have preyed on Sarah's wounds just like he did with every other member of his cult.

The laughter from the van ride over echoed through Autumn's head, making her doubt her own words.

What if Damien is legit and not doing anything wrong at all? What if all he's doing is bringing together broken people and giving them a place to call home?

She flinched at the idea of sharing her uncertainty with Aiden. Her boss was convinced that Damien was crooked as hell. Heck, before she'd arrived, she'd been just as convinced. Now, though...

Alice popped her head in the doorway. "You're supposed to be sleeping." Her wide smile was back. Maybe Harmony House encouraged mindfulness, teaching members to quit dwelling on the past and live in the now.

"I'll sleep. I promise." Autumn gave Alice a thumbs-up and pulled the worn but cozy blanket over her body.

She closed her eyes, determined to follow Alice's lead. Time to stop obsessing over Sarah and focus on the present.

Her plan was to sift through the investigation. Instead, her eyes grew heavy, and she drifted off to sleep.

20

Chris groaned as he slapped the folder shut and tossed a file onto the conference room table. "This guy never even stepped foot on Harmony House grounds. No ties whatsoever."

Mia pulled the papers to her. "Patrick Ryder. If that date is correct, he was one of the very first suicides in the time period we're investigating."

"I'm on board with Damien Parr being a sketchy mofo, but this suicide crap is getting old." Chris grabbed his bottled water and chugged the liquid down. He expected Mia to protest, but she didn't.

"Maybe they really aren't related to Harmony House." Mia met his gaze, solemn as ever. "Maybe we're on a witch hunt."

Not this shit again. Chris narrowed his eyes. "What did you experience there that's got you so soft? You might as well put on a cheerleading skirt and grab some pom-poms."

Mia laughed, another response he hadn't expected. "You said it yourself, Chris. This is getting old. I just haven't found a single clear connection. It's a small town. A lot of people have probably been in contact with Harmony House at one point or another. That proves nothing."

He still didn't like her tone. "You do know that Parr is about as suspect as they come, right?" That bastard wasn't clean, even if his entire following were purebred angels.

"I think we should investigate him." It was plain that Mia chose her words carefully. "And that's what we're doing. Autumn's in there right now."

Chris turned the statement over, analyzing Mia's precise phrasing. She clearly had doubts as to whether or not Parr was the crook everyone else believed him to be. In the meeting, he'd noticed the tiny standoff between Aiden and Mia when discussing their experience earlier that day.

Mia had developed some type of soft spot for Harmony House, and SSA Parrish seemed to dislike it as much as Chris did.

His lip curled. *Women. So easily swayed by their damn emotions. I bet she's got her period. She's being an idiot about this.*

Deputy King charged into the room with wild eyes and a frazzled expression, which Chris highly preferred over the doof's usual goofy grin. "There's a woman in the reception area. She's claiming that her brother was murdered, *and* she mentioned Harmony House. Someone needs to talk to her."

Chris could see that "someone" clearly wasn't going to be Simon King. He exchanged a glance with Mia.

"When does Aiden get back?" Mia kept her voice low to prevent King from overhearing.

Parrish had left to witness a noted forensic medical examiner do a follow-up on Natalie's body. Aiden had called the guy in himself, wanting someone with a trained eye for criminal foul play to examine her corpse.

"I have no idea." Since Mia wasn't jumping in to volunteer, Chris shoved back his chair with an annoyed sigh. Not like he wanted to take on the task either, but someone had to do it. "I'll talk to her."

"Oh, thank you!" Deputy King nodded his head so hard Chris was surprised the man didn't snap his own neck. What an embarrassment. King wasn't a federal agent, but Christ, he *was* a sheriff's deputy. He couldn't have gotten that position by displaying this scared little bitch behavior.

Then again, small towns presented limited options, and Sheriff Frank struck him as the kind of woman who wouldn't want anyone too manly hanging around. She needed to be certain that she had the biggest balls in the county.

Smirking to himself over that visual, Chris followed Simon down the hallway and through the door to the reception area. A plump woman with frizzy brown curls flew at him.

"Are you a Fed?" Her demanding tone made it obvious that if he was, she wasn't intimidated.

Mia was going to owe him big time for volunteering for this.

"I am." He stuck out his hand. "Special Agent Chris Parker with the Richmond Behavioral Analysis Unit. How can I help you, ma'am?"

She gave his hand one hard shake before dropping it. "I'm Yvette Wilder. My brother, Kenneth, passed away yesterday, and they're trying to tell me he overdosed on heroin. But I know that's not true. Kenneth had some run-ins with the law, and he used to have trouble with drugs, but he's been clean for years. Besides, he wouldn't even have been able to afford drugs to begin with."

In his peripheral vision, Chris caught Deputy King sliding out of the room like a quiet little slug. *Wuss.* "Just what kind of problems with the law did your brother have, Ms. Wilder?"

Yvette shook a finger in his face. "Don't you do that. You're trying to dig and reason that Kenneth was a drug dealer or a damn junkie. He wasn't. Not anymore. I had just talked to him the day before, and he wanted to come home. He wanted to break away from that creepy church group he'd fallen in with."

"Which church group is that?" Chris had to be sure. There was no telling how many backwoods religious nutjobs were out here in rural Virginia, recruiting people like the damn military.

"Harmony House." Yvette's face contorted with disgust. "That place. Those people are crazy, and Kenneth was done with them. *Done.* He told me he was coming home, and then he just randomly turns up dead at some crack house motel room? No. They *killed* him. Someone injected my brother with heroin."

Chris took in Yvette's frenzied state and wild gray eyes, understanding how desperately she needed to know that her brother hadn't died at his own hand. "Let me make sure I understand. You think someone from Harmony House killed Kenneth because he wanted to leave?"

"I know they did," she declared with unabashed authority. "And I want justice for my brother."

"Ma'am—"

"Don't. You still think he overdosed." Yvette's voice filled with anger even as her eyes glistened with tears. "I had to identify my baby brother's body. His eyes were still *open*, Agent. He died in terror. I know he did. I know how he felt about those people, and I know he intended to come home."

Under normal circumstances, Chris would have led Yvette to a private room more suitable for speaking with witnesses. But here at the Bumpkins 'R' Us Police Station, spare rooms didn't exist. They were stuck with this sad space and a couple of old plastic chairs, probably stained from the butt sweat of every Jethro, Bubba, and Billy-Bob in the area.

He grimaced as he gestured at the seats. "Let's sit. I want you to tell me exactly what Kenneth shared about the activities he saw within Harmony House walls." Although he'd been speaking with Mia of his doubts about any connection between the suicides and the cult just minutes ago, Yvette's story was setting off internal alarms.

Yvette dropped into a chair. "He talked about that leader as though the man was some godlike creature, and all of his followers were angels of light. It was downright blasphemy, and I told him so. He defended them like he'd known these people his entire life. But then, when I talked to him two days ago, he suddenly didn't like them anymore."

"Did he mention that anything specific had happened?" Chris remembered Bradley Garland's words when they'd first arrived.

"She was done with him and done with those creepy Harmony bastards too." Bradley had insisted that Natalie was on her way home and wasn't suicidal in the slightest degree.

At the time, Chris had openly doubted the claim. Yvette's take on Kenneth was so damn similar to Bradley's, though, that he'd be negligent if he didn't investigate further. In hindsight, maybe he'd been a bit too hard on Councilman Garland.

Somebody had to be the hard-ass bad guy, or they'd be taking on every damn "case" in the country.

Chris Parker was used to retaining a black-sheep status.

"He never told me anything specific." Yvette had softened considerably and seemed moments away from bursting into tears. "Just that he was happy and loved it there...until he didn't. And as soon as he decided he didn't love it there anymore, he turned up dead."

The creepy sense of déjà vu lifted the hairs on the back of

Chris's neck. "Are you stating that you believe Harmony House guilty of foul play in Kenneth's passing?"

"Yes." Yvette clapped a hand on his arm. "Now, what are you going to do about it? What are you going to do to find justice for my brother?"

"I'm going to follow through with his case. If there's a dark side to Harmony House, I'm going to uncover it, ma'am."

Tears streamed down Yvette's cheeks. He squirmed as he gave her hand an awkward pat, wishing Mia were present to deal with all the weepy female crap. After Yvette dabbed at her eyes with a tissue, he took down her phone number and promised to be in touch soon.

When the front door clicked shut after Yvette left the station, Chris finally gave in to the excitement pulsing through his veins. He pumped his fist. *Yes.* This was huge. He had just been given *crucial* information regarding their case. Maybe at long last, he'd get a little recognition for a job well done.

Hell, he might even end up as the agent who solved this entire mess.

Chris called Aiden. Of course, the asshole didn't answer.

Dammit, Parrish.

He scowled at the phone. Aiden was ignoring him, no doubt. What a joke. Chris couldn't stand how easily the man let his personal opinions about the team interfere with how each case was handled. If he ever made it to the position of SSA, he would be sure to check his emotions at the door.

Supervisory Special Agent Parker wouldn't give special treatment to *anyone*. He wouldn't try to screw one of his colleagues. And he sure as hell wouldn't let an inexperienced newbie take the lead on an undercover assignment.

Chris charged down the hall and burst into the conference room. "I think we were wrong." He marched to the table and crossed his arms.

Mia's head popped up from the suicide victim files she'd been stacking. "About?"

"That place." Chris pictured the three-story facility that he'd only seen in images. "Bad shit is going on at Harmony House."

Mia tilted her head, appearing interested and defensive at the same time. "Based on one woman's claims in the reception area?"

Chris shook his head in irritation and sat across from Mia. "Yvette Wilder. Her brother, Kenneth, was found dead yesterday in a rundown motel. They're calling it a suicide, a heroin overdose. But Yvette claims her brother was doing well and hadn't used drugs in years. She said he was *leaving* Harmony House—he was done with them—and coming home. Ringing any bells?"

The horrified circle of Mia's gaping mouth was somewhat comforting. He'd half expected her to burst into a tirade of reasons why Damien Parr and Harmony House couldn't possibly have anything to do with Kenneth Wilder.

"Wow." She shook her head, looking dazed. "That's almost exactly what Bradley Garland said about Natalie…*someone* doesn't want any members leaving."

"Right." Chris pulled his iPad from his briefcase and began typing the interview with Yvette Wilder into the case notes. "I knew Damien Parr was a piece of shit the first time I laid eyes on him."

Mia frowned. "You realize that we have no reason to assume Damien was that person, correct?"

Chris couldn't believe his ears. Even after he'd told her about Yvette, she was still defending that bastard.

"What in the hell did that guy do to you in the five seconds you were around him?" He hissed the words, not wanting the entire station to hear him. "He's a nutjob, Mia. He's a *psychopath.*"

"He didn't do anything to me." Mia's expression turned mutinous. "The people there are happy, Chris. Not fake happy. Not creepy happy. *Happy* happy. And Damien is—"

"Let me guess." Chris clenched his hands in his lap to keep them from shaking. He couldn't believe they were having this conversation. "Damien is charming. Well-spoken. Full of *obvious* good intentions. Too handsome to be a bad guy. Does that sound about right?"

Mia glowered at him but said nothing.

"He's a psychopath with a god complex." Chris typed faster as his frustration mounted. "You've seen this before. This is just the first time you were personally charmed by the snake."

She guffawed, slamming a tiny elf hand on the table. "I was not charmed by anyone. You weren't there. You didn't see what I did."

Chris dragged the back of his hand across his forehead. Caffeine. He needed caffeine. "Agent Logan, I think you saw the exact picture that Damien Parr *wanted you to see*, just like every other person in that damn place. Parrish was the only one who walked out of there without a new set of blinders."

"Wow." Mia sat back in her chair, eyebrows raised. "I think that's the nicest thing I've ever heard you say about Aiden."

"This isn't about mean or nice." Chris growled the reprimand. "It's about acting blind or seeing clearly. You're the former. Parrish is the latter."

His phone rang, cutting the conversation short, which was more than okay with him.

Aiden.

Chris answered the call. "Agent Parrish, you still with that new medical examiner?"

"I am." Aiden issued the confirmation in his usual curt, a-hole manner.

"Keep him there." Chris pictured Yvette staring at her brother's wide-eyed corpse. "We've got another body to investigate."

21

Autumn rubbed her eyes as she wandered down the hall toward the Harmony House communal kitchen. She'd been in the building just a few hours, half of which she'd spent sleeping, but she was catching on to the lay of the land in quick time.

A nap and a shower had done wonders for her energy level. Though waking up in her closet room had been a bit surreal, she was more than ready to attack her mission once again.

Alice spotted her through the kitchen doorway and let out an excited squeal. "We're making dinner. Would you like to help?"

"Sure. Of course." Autumn hurried over to her new friend. Alice was just as joyful about making dinner as she was everything else, and her energy was infectious.

"I'm in charge of the salad." Alice plopped giant tomatoes in each of Autumn's hands. "Do you think you could dice these?"

Autumn hadn't had a free moment to prepare a meal for

as long as she could remember. There was a therapeutic aspect in the process she missed. "I'll dice away."

Set up with a cutting board near a large, farmhouse-style sink, Autumn took her time rinsing the tomatoes so she could survey the room. Women were scattered throughout the space, chattering and laughing as they performed various prep tasks.

Only women, and all of them very attractive. Not super-model gorgeous, but prettier than the average population.

When the women burst into song, Autumn focused her attention on slicing up the tomatoes. She was a lot of things, but a songstress was not one of them, and no undercover plan in the world was going to make her magically sing on key.

A heartfelt rendition of "Somewhere Over the Rainbow" swelled through the room, the chorus of voices admittedly pleasant. Waking up in Harmony House was on par with waking up in Oz. Alarming, bright, and without question, overwhelming.

Autumn fought the urge to clack her heels together and see if anyone picked up on the joke. Something told her this was the wrong crowd for that type of humor.

"You must be Autumn." A smiling young woman with long brown curls approached her. "I'm Roberta. We're *so happy* you're here."

"Thank you." Autumn boasted her brightest smile. "This is such a lovely place."

Roberta clasped her hands together and nodded. "Heaven on Earth. We live in paradise." The woman proceeded to rinse off a small pile of cucumbers in the sink beside Autumn.

"How long have you been at Harmony House?" Autumn continued chopping to mask her interest. Though considering her current situation—in a strange house, surrounded by strangers—blatant curiosity shouldn't be alarming.

A dreamy smile spread across Roberta's face. "I've been here for fourteen months. I wouldn't trade it for the world. This is home…a home like no other."

The woman hummed as she finished scrubbing another cucumber. There were no cracks in her mask of joy.

"What's your favorite thing about living here?" Autumn was careful not to push *too* hard, although, with these women's "heart on your sleeve" policy, nothing she asked seemed to offend or raise suspicion.

Roberta giggled and dropped her rinsed cucumbers into a wire basket. "*Helping people*, of course. I wake up every day so excited to find people in need and show them that they're not alone. No one has to be alone. I am so blessed to have found this place."

Autumn returned her smile, taking the opportunity to scan the woman's youthful face. If Alice was twenty-one, Roberta couldn't be a day past eighteen. How had she ended up here at such a young age? Did her family even know where she was?

"You're blessed to have found it too, and I really hope you decide to stay and join the Circle." Roberta pranced away with her basket, leaving Autumn to stare after her with a perplexed frown.

She certainly isn't a seasoned serial killer. She's just a girl. Sweet and young and impressionable. Vulnerable.

What was she missing?

Autumn chewed her cheek as she slid the knife into the second tomato. One thing she'd noticed was that Damien definitely appeared to have a type when it came to his female followers. Pretty, but possibly more important was their ability to be easily manipulated and controlled.

A striking woman with shiny black tresses approached,

wielding a small bowl of apples. "Autumn? I'm so happy to meet you. Alice has told us such great things about you! My name is Chelsea."

Instead of offering her hand, Chelsea set the bowl down and pulled Autumn into an embrace. The emotions that pulsed into her were similar to Alice and Roberta's. Only Chelsea's affection for the Harmony House leader was more complicated.

The woman hugging her didn't just worship Damien. She believed herself to be in love with him.

"I'm happy to meet you as well." Autumn took a deep breath after Chelsea released her. All these people, with their myriad of emotions, created a bit of a sixth sense overload. She'd never experienced a short circuit regarding her mysterious ability, but that didn't mean there wasn't one in her future.

Chelsea nodded toward Roberta, who was across the room, still humming away while she sliced cucumbers. "Poor Roberta. She was a runaway teen. She lived on the streets, and after nearly starving to death, decided to try her hand at prostitution. We found her that *first* night, before she'd gone off with any man, and asked if she wouldn't rather have a warm bed and some food. She's been with us ever since, happy as a little sprite."

Autumn wondered about the dynamic between the women. She had a strong suspicion that Chelsea wasn't the only follower harboring romantic feelings for Damien. Yet there didn't seem to be a single catty vibe amongst them.

How was that even possible?

Before she could go very deep down that rabbit hole, men's voices boomed into the kitchen. They filed in with their faces glistening with sweat and streaked with dirt. Cheerful, even though they'd obviously come straight from physical labor, probably involving the estate's livestock or crop-bearing fields.

They headed directly to the communal dining table and took a seat.

Autumn stifled a snort as she finished dicing the last of the tomatoes. Women in the kitchen, men out sweating in the fields. The whole thing struck her as a little archaic. Sweet, maybe, but also sexist as hell.

Across the counter, Chelsea's hand stilled on her knife, her attention rapt on one of the men. Autumn didn't need an advanced degree to guess who.

On second thought, maybe the segregation of job responsibilities by sex had little to do with sexism and everything to do with Damien. Maybe their esteemed leader segregated the duties that way because he didn't want "his" women disappearing off into fields with the other men.

Maybe there were *certain* things that Damien Parr didn't, in fact, like to share after all.

Autumn wrinkled her nose. Gross. As repugnant as the idea of Parr keeping the female members housebound as his own personal harem was, that didn't necessarily translate into him being a killer. She had no facts to reach that conclusion. Yet.

What her profile did suggest was that if the suicides were indeed murders, their killer was likely male.

She performed a quick headcount. If the profile was correct, there were a good twenty contenders within their midst.

Another man entered the room. Autumn straightened, recognizing his shaggy brown hair and pale green eyes.

"Isn't it wonderful to see so many hard-working, selfless individuals gathered into one place?"

Autumn startled at the unexpected voice behind her. *Calm down, silly. It's only Alice.*

She turned, pressing a hand to her chest. "Goodness, you startled me! I guess I was too caught up in dicing these tomatoes."

Autumn waited for Alice to reply, but the woman's attention was fixed on something over Autumn's shoulder.

"How are you doing today, Alice?"

Autumn pivoted again to find Evan standing right behind her. Was it just her, or did the members of Harmony House creep around on catlike feet?

"I'm doing amazing." Alice gave Evan a quick hug before motioning at Autumn. "This is Autumn. She might be staying with us for a while."

Evan inspected her with a much more careful eye than any of the women had. His was one of the faces from Autumn's brief morning study session and the "sketchy" individual Aiden had demanded information on.

In person, Evan's hunched shoulders and fidgeting came across as more shy than anything. A little awkward and a lot lonely. When he tucked his chin, his sandy brown hair swung forward in an almost boyish shag. Just long enough for him to hide behind.

"It's nice to meet you, Autumn." Evan had a hard time holding eye contact. "How's your stay been so far?"

"Excellent." She beamed at him and received a small smile in return before he stared at the floor. The man was the dictionary definition of socially inept. For very different reasons than Alice, nothing about him screamed *I'm a secret serial killer*!

She wanted to talk with him more, but the group was disrupted by squealing tires and flying gravel. Heads swiveled to peer out the front windows at the car that had just pulled up. A man jumped out, slammed the door shut, and stormed into the house.

He stalked straight past all the onlookers and down the

hall toward Damien's office. Something about his profile tugged at Autumn's memory.

"I'm going to go use the restroom really quick." She whispered the words to Alice, who gave her a gentle smile and nod. Most everyone in the kitchen and dining rooms were a bit distracted, talking amongst themselves about the stranger who'd just barged into their midst.

Autumn exited out the rear kitchen door before circling around the hallway to where it intersected with the main hall. A quick glance both ways assured her the coast was clear, so she turned right toward Damien's office. The same direction the interloper had headed.

As she walked, adrenaline flooded her veins. Her hands felt jittery.

What, you figured since this move didn't work out so well for Aiden, you'd go ahead and try it yourself? Not your shining moment of genius either.

Raised voices poured from behind the door leading to Damien's office, but she couldn't make out any words. Autumn crept closer until she hovered just outside the door. The thick wood still muffled the conversation.

See? Idiot. Big risk for no payoff.

Her shoulders drooped. Just as she was about to turn away and cut her losses, Damien's shout stopped her in her tracks.

"Rod! You need to sit down!"

The light bulb went off. *Rod Norris.* Autumn had viewed pictures of him in their briefings. She'd recognized the man because he was Natalie Garland's ex-boyfriend.

Could Natalie's ex be involved with Damien somehow? Had the two of them worked together to plot her death?

Approaching footsteps sent her pulse skyrocketing. She scurried to the bathroom, where she proceeded to lean over the sink and stick her hands under the faucet.

After counting to thirty, she dried off and returned to the hallway. The voices had ceased.

Rod was gone.

Dammit.

Autumn gathered her jumbled thoughts. Evan would still be in the kitchen and near done with his meal. The perfect time to make a little small talk. The better she got to know him, the clearer his motives would become.

When she stepped back into the communal area, most of the women had migrated to the dining table. Forks clattered amid laughter and talk as everyone happily shoveled down their dinners. Some were in the kitchen washing dishes and singing yet again, while a few had spilled onto the lawn. Autumn didn't spot Evan among the indoor members, so she followed the flow moving outdoors.

Evan was nearby, leaning against a tree trunk and watching the others move about. Peaceful but alone, and maybe a little sad. Autumn approached him at a leisurely pace so as not to alarm him.

"Hey." She waved a hand in greeting. "Me again."

He gave a polite nod while his gaze darted this way and that, as if searching out escape routes.

Autumn *had* to get him to relax. "This place is crazy pretty. I didn't even know places like this existed."

Evan didn't return her smile. "Damien has made a very special home for us all."

"I haven't met him yet." Autumn feigned fascination with the row of red flowers off to her right. Afraid that too much direct eye contact would send him sprinting for the hills. "But I can only imagine what a wonderful person he is to make all of this happen."

The commentary on Damien she'd hoped to invite never came. Evan rocked back and forth from his toes to his heels, like he was gathering momentum to bolt.

Autumn took a deep breath and tried again. "Do you get to spend much time with Damien, being he's the leader and all?"

He frowned at her. Fidgeting and rocking. "I have to get back to work."

As Evan sped away, Autumn heaved a frustrated sigh. Some spy she was turning out to be so far. First, the eavesdropping fail, now this. Though, in her defense, Evan wasn't the easiest to sidle up to.

"I see you've met our Evan."

The low, velvety voice sending tingles racing across her skin could belong to no one but Damien Parr. Autumn swung around to face him, eager to meet the man who'd created his own world from scratch.

The oxygen caught in her lungs. *Oh, my.*

Handsome. Damien was *very* handsome. Autumn had allowed that he was a good-looking man in his photos, but in person…wow. She'd seen firsthand how handsome he was at the soup kitchen, but up close? He radiated the kind of magnetism that a picture would never capture.

A strange giddiness took hold of her. Suddenly, she better understood what Mia must have experienced upon first meeting the Harmony House leader.

"I have. Sort of." Autumn tugged at a strand of hair and battled a surge of nervous energy, the likes of which she hadn't experienced since the days of middle school crushes. "I just wanted to get to know him. Or anyone. Show the kindness that Alice has shown me…but I don't think he liked me."

Damien grinned, white teeth gleaming in the late afternoon sun. "Evan's a quiet fellow. He mostly keeps to himself. I wouldn't take it personally. I sincerely doubt anyone would be able to dislike you."

Autumn blushed and hated herself for it. "I'm just me."

She met Damien's eyes, which reminded her of crystals. They were such a light blue that they sparkled in the sunlight.

"You're special, Autumn." Damien gestured toward the walkway. "I'm Damien Parr. Harmony House is the dream I brought to life to help the hurting. I'd love to show you around the grounds. Have you been to the overlook yet?"

His question reminded her of Aiden and how the SSA had mentioned the breathtaking view. That was enough to zap Autumn back to her senses. "No, but it sounds nice."

Damien began walking, waving at her to follow along. "Let's go see."

Autumn attempted to scan every person and building she saw for signs of...anything. The gardens and grounds continued to be as lovely and pristine throughout the estate. The central church building was a simple construction. No evidence of anything other than a peaceful community.

"Here." Damien led her onto a man-made deck that stretched out over the open air. "Of course, we surrounded this area with a fence, but we didn't want to make it too high and block out the spectacular view."

He walked straight toward the farthest edge of the overlook. Autumn followed, attempting not to dwell on the treacherous, rocky gorge that plummeted beneath their feet. As Damien had mentioned, a fence formed a perimeter around the deck, but the barrier was low, with large gaps between the wooden planks. Someone could easily slip between them or scale the top...or even be *pushed* over.

A little shiver trekked down Autumn's back. She was thankful when Damien settled onto one of several benches and tapped the space beside him. "Sit. Tell me a little about yourself."

She obeyed, knowing that conversing with Damien was of utmost importance to earning his trust. Once that happened, she stood a better chance of slinking around

Harmony House without him or his followers scrutinizing her every move.

"I don't have a great story to tell or anything." She shrugged. "I mean, I grew up in foster care. Everybody knows that sucks. But I got adopted by a very wealthy family. I should be grateful…"

Autumn sensed Damien's ears perk up at the word "wealthy." He leaned toward her with that ridiculous, alluring grin stretched across his face. "You can be grateful for the good hand life dealt you while also mourning the bad. That's your right as a thinking, feeling human being. There's no shame in being honest about what's hurt you in the past."

She blinked. That sounded like something she would say to a client in therapy. "That's kind of you. I guess I've never thought of things like that."

You're really going to hone your lying skills at Harmony House.

"Well," Damien scooted closer, "that's what I try to do here. I want people to view their world—their past, their pain, their joy—in a different light. I want every human who walks through the doors of Harmony House to understand that they matter, and everything they've been through…whatever they've done or had done to them… doesn't change how important they are. How *worthy of love* they are."

His warm, liquid voice weaved a spell, tugging Autumn closer. She gave herself a mental slap at the last second.

Holy cow. The charm exuding from Damien Parr was something else. A trait that definitely fit with the profile she'd thus far concocted for the killer. If those deaths weren't suicides, then someone had gotten close enough to the victims to take control of the situation and make their murders appear self-inflicted. That was no small feat.

Human nature had a way of kicking in when a threat presented itself. Survival instincts, adrenaline, fight or flight...all of these tools worked together to keep death at bay.

She diverted her attention to the overlook, drawing calm from the mountaintops and trees. One of the common threads amongst Beechum County's suicides was the lack of defensive wounds. Until Natalie, anyway, though the grab marks around her upper arm were mild enough to indicate that she hadn't been gripped for very long.

Not that it would take long to throw someone off a cliff. If they trusted you, that is.

And that was the key. If a psychopath was responsible for the string of "suicides," this mastermind was getting remarkably close to the victims. They'd known the killer. More than that, they'd trusted him. At least in part.

Their murderer had taken them off guard. All of them. Led them to believe all was well...until it was too late to escape.

The mild breeze kicking up from the valley did nothing to stop the goose bumps racing along Autumn's arms.

Damien shifted his weight, reminding her that she was overdue for a response. She summoned a sheepish grin. "You're so kind. I'm not...I'm not used to anyone being so nice to me."

He stretched an arm along the top of the bench behind her, almost but not quite touching her upper back. "Even your adoptive parents didn't show you love and kindness?"

She noted how he didn't stray from the subject of her wealthy family before gathering more information. Money was a key driver for most cult leaders, and Damien Parr was no exception.

"I think they meant well." Autumn hung her head as if saddened. "They just wanted the perfect little girl. They wanted her so badly that they adopted six of us."

Crystal blue eyes grew wide. "Six of you? Six little girls?"

Autumn nodded, her lower lip trembling. "We were supposed to be sisters, but all we really did was compete for their approval. Hours at the piano and the ballet studio...my toes would bleed by the end of my practice sessions. And it didn't matter anyway, because I was the worst dancer out of all of them. I tried to make up for that with the piano playing, but they were only satisfied by those of us who could do both."

"I'm so sorry, Autumn." Damien's sympathetic tone struck a chord deep in her chest. "I hope I can remind you how special you are."

She simultaneously wanted to sob and hand him an Oscar for Best Male Performance. He was smooth. Scary smooth. "At some point, I just couldn't handle the pressure anymore, so when I was seventeen, I ran away. As you can tell, that didn't turn out so well either." Autumn pointed at herself. She was clean after the shower, but her hair was still a bit unruly, and her secondhand clothes served as an ever-present reminder that she was "down and out."

Damien sighed in a dramatic manner that he somehow managed to infuse with genuine sorrow. "I've seen this same exact situation a countless number of times. The people who are supposed to love you instead treat you in such a way that makes you question your innate perfection. They abuse the goodness inside your soul."

His words conjured an image of her biological father. Angry. Drunk. Hateful. He'd nearly killed her...when she was just a little girl. When she was small and innocent and needed his protection and guidance...

Her throat tightened, and a tear slipped down her cheek. She swiped her face in alarm. "I'm sorry. How embarrassing." She wasn't sure why she'd allowed herself to go to that place, that time in her life that could never be painted into a pretty picture even if da Vinci himself took a brush to the imagery.

"No." Damien leaned toward her until mere inches separated them. "You should never be sorry for your tears. They're precious, a reminder that no matter what happened to you, you're still here. You still feel. You've survived this world after it hit you hard."

Without thinking, Autumn lifted her fingers to her cheek, remembering the sting of Adam Latham's hand when she'd rejected his sexual advances.

Damien tilted his head as a frown marred his handsome face. "Someone actually hit you, didn't they?"

Uneasiness stirred in her gut. She inched away. The conversation was getting a bit too real, considering Damien was probably a psychopath and possibly a murderer.

Autumn lifted her chin. "I'm a big girl."

"Yes." His velvety voice wrapped around her like a warm, soothing cocoon. "You're a big girl who's experienced isolation, negligence, fear, and abuse. Emotional *and* physical. And I suspect there's a lot more you're keeping close to the vest. Am I right?"

She stared into the distance, attempting to mentally extricate herself from this man's magnetic web. The difficulty, which she was self-aware enough to pinpoint, was that she *did* have a rather dark past. She was, like Aiden and Winter had both pointed out, vulnerable in the exact areas in which Damien excelled at exploiting.

That's why you're perfect for this job. Show him some of your suffering. Making him believe he has power over you will be the quickest way to gain his trust.

"Of course there's more." Autumn stared at the hands she clasped tightly in her lap. "I've failed a lot of people. I've let them down...horribly. Caused them pain. That's worse than my own pain. So much harder to handle."

A sharp blade stabbed her heart as she thought of Sarah,

the sister she'd not only failed to find but had scared even farther away.

And Justin…she'd failed the *world* with that one, releasing a demented killer into a sea of innocents. Poor Winter resembled the walking dead more than the living after surviving her ordeal with her homicidal little brother.

The blade twisted, shooting pain across her chest. Her fault. That would *always* be her fault.

What if Winter didn't get better? What if she really did waste away and die? What if Justin killed hundreds more people while he toured the world with that poor little boy?

Each question pushed the knife a little deeper. Ripped her up a little more.

Damien's somber stare drilled into her. "You have to release those emotions, Autumn. You have to let them go because they do you *no good*. I spent some time in combat overseas, and the horrific things that I witnessed…" He shook his head. "Well, they followed me home and ate me alive. Until I decided to take a *different* path. To take control of my future and set my past free."

Narcissistic evil genius or not, Damien's take on releasing regret resonated. She'd spent her entire adult life trying to accept what she'd been through and take ownership of her traumas. Not once had it occurred to her that she could have complete freedom from her past.

Even if every other word he'd spoken so far was bullcrap, she believed he'd had a rough time of it overseas. His file alone suggested as much. Who was to say the man wasn't onto something, despite whatever shady dealings he was involved in?

Alice's glowing face popped into Autumn's head. That woman was so happy. Was her state of mind a direct result of Damien's teachings?

"Thank you." Autumn offered the words and meant them. "For this conversation, I mean."

His smile dazzled her. She had to work to mentally shake him off. "You are more than welcome, Autumn." He stood and motioned her to follow him to the very edge of the overlook.

Autumn did, taking another moment to absorb the beautiful view. What an oasis this place was. What a tranquil home for the broken and the—

She froze when Damien stroked her cheek, sending novels of information soaring through her mind. "All of this beauty, but I still think the most spectacular sight on the overlook this evening is you."

Her stomach roiled at the images flashing with technicolor clarity. He was imagining they were alone. He was tearing her clothes off. He was—

Autumn pulled away, stepping closer to the outlook's edge. From this vantage point, the sheer drop was dizzying.

Just the thing to clear her head. "I'm gonna go back to the house. I told Alice I'd help her in the kitchen."

It took every last ounce of her self-control to hide her true feelings.

You're disgusting, just like Adam Latham, and god knows how many more men out there.

All the glorious philosophy in the world didn't change the fact that Damien was, underneath his mask of charm, a lust-filled asshole who had already concocted quite the future for her here at Harmony House. A naked future. With him.

"Autumn." He leaned closer, and she edged away. Until the wooden railing dug into her spine. "The Circle is a safe place. The Circle has no limits. Only love. And if you want to know the unbelievable gift of genuine peace, joining to me is the fastest path to that joy."

Joining *to* him, and not in the spiritual sense. Autumn

shivered despite the July heat, suddenly all too aware that Damien Parr stood between her and solid land.

Her heart raced while she scanned the surrounding area. She needed a weapon. A log. A sharp stick. Her gun.

There was a monster inside of Harmony House's leader. A beast she no longer doubted would dispose of her without a second thought were the action suitable to his plans. That handsome face and charismatic persona masked a lust-filled, predatory soul.

Her gifted sixth sense had shown her a sliver of who Damien truly was. But his followers, exceptional individuals like Alice, didn't have the luxury of that same tool. All they knew was the outer shell of their leader, and on the surface, Damien was an inspiring man.

"I'm going back to the house now." Autumn brushed past him, taking eager steps to reach solid land and put as much distance as possible between herself and the edge of the outlook.

And Damien.

"Autumn. I'm glad you're here. But make sure you remember that being here is a privilege. Not all who pass through the doors stay, and I would hate for you to disappear."

She halted, a chill sweeping across her skin at the threat. Was he alluding to kicking her out? Or hinting at ending her existence altogether? Either way, his displeasure over her dismissal was clear.

Damien Parr was not the type of man who handled rejection well.

Turning toward him, she was shocked to note his smile. Not a trace of malice showed on his face.

He dipped his head. "It's almost time for the evening prayer circle. I truly hope you enjoy it and receive God's enlightenment." With that, he walked away, leaving her to gape at his retreating form in silence.

She *would* join the prayer circle, and her undercover investigation would continue. But not for a single moment would Autumn harbor any more doubts about what kind of man Damien Parr was.

Aiden's instincts about Damien Parr had been spot-on.

Autumn trailed after Damien, taking care to keep a sizable distance between them. The confirmation that Harmony House's leader was a psychopath wasn't surprising. Cult leaders were often diagnosed as such.

So were business leaders, politicians, brain surgeons, and a plethora of other individuals.

Not all psychopaths turned into killers. In fact, not even a notable fraction of them did.

Autumn's task was clear. During her time at Harmony House, she needed to figure out whether Damien Parr's psychopathy was of the common variety...or if his brand of manipulation made him a member of a more exclusive, murderous club.

22

A iden walked through the Beechum Police Station's front doors, frustration running rampant in his mind. The case was getting uglier, but evidence remained elusive.

He'd stood by as the forensic medical examiner did a follow-up autopsy on Natalie Garland and an initial one for Kenneth Wilder. Despite the M.E.'s enhanced skill set and experience, he hadn't been able to find much more than Dr. Castor. This had seemed to both please and frustrate the county medical examiner. As much as Warren Castor took pride in having done his job well, he wanted answers to the influx of suicides.

Upon entering the station's sole conference room, Aiden was relieved to find the space deserted. He hated small talk on a good day, and today was far from stellar. They'd found no clues as to a murder suspect regarding the "suicides," Beechum County had gained yet another dead body, and he'd sent Autumn straight into the belly of the beast.

A subpar day indeed.

Aiden raked his hand through his hair before taking a seat in the far corner of the room. He pulled his iPad from his briefcase and logged in to read the case notes thus far, particularly Chris's interview with Yvette Wilder. The woman refused to believe that Kenneth had taken his own life, which was the textbook response from family members who had learned of a loved one's suicide.

Except the Beechum County suicides weren't the average story. Despite standing in the room and hearing two medical examiners confirm that Kenneth Wilder had died from a heroin overdose and without a single defensive wound on his body, Aiden wasn't convinced.

Off. Something felt off with Kenneth's death. He'd had the same unsettled sensation in that morgue as he'd experienced at Harmony House. And although Aiden was as logical as a man could be, he'd learned a thing or two about gut instincts over the years.

Ignoring them was often a significant mistake. Sometimes catastrophic.

He checked his phone. Autumn hadn't called or texted, but it technically wasn't time just yet. She'd contact him before the day was over, and he would at least be able to sleep knowing she was alive and well…even if she was also in a precarious position.

His muscles tensed as he pictured the building and its welcome sign. *Harmony House, Join the Circle, Be the Change.* Organized religion had never been his cup of tea, but cults took everything a step further.

The way they absorbed followers into their fold and consumed entire lives was uncanny. Many people assumed that the individuals who became involved in a cult typically came from the pool of low IQs, but Aiden's education and endless studies had taught him otherwise.

Being a part of a small group of individuals who lived their lives in a manner that most would consider abnormal, strange, crazy, etc., required a mind that could think outside of the box. Many who entered into an alternative type of life-style were actually quite intelligent and creative human beings.

Brilliant, innovative ideas that improved life for the entire planet could be created in that type of brain-space, but so could unthinkable, malevolent evil.

Aiden rubbed the knot on the back of his neck. In the current moment, he cared less about the misconceptions of cult members and more about the Harmony House followers' intentions toward Autumn.

He really *had* screwed up with getting spotted by Evan so early on in the visit. Parker hadn't been wrong about that, but still. Nothing excused an agent for speaking to their superior in such a way. Nothing.

That, of course, didn't stop Aiden from berating himself in private. Staying even an hour longer on the compound may have given him a chance to get a deeper grasp on the situation. While many of the people he and Mia had encountered appeared to pose little to no threat, Evan and Damien were a different story.

Aiden couldn't stop replaying Evan and Damien's conversation…what little he had gathered of it. What was Evan unable to stop feeling so guilty about? His record was squeaky clean since entering Damien Parr's fold.

Even though Damien had comforted Evan, there'd been an edge of shadiness to his words. Aiden sensed that most of what Parr said and did came straight from an inner sea of greed.

There was no telling what a man like that was capable of.

Aiden pulled his phone from his jacket pocket and placed a call to Cyber in Richmond. He barked the order to dig deeper for existing connections between Damien Parr and any shell corporations, then hung up.

Parr shouldn't have had any money to invest, legally or

otherwise. Harmony House and the land it sat on was, on paper, owned by the Harmony House Charity Group and listed as a religious organization, giving it the charitable 501(c)(3) tax code.

The estate was protected, in a sense, by the classification. But earning a place in that class also meant Harmony House was not a cash-making juggernaut. The grandness alone of the compound was enough to turn the heads of the Federal Bureau of Investigation, but deeds much worse than money laundering could be taking place within Damien's fold.

That's why you have Autumn in there. She'll be able to shed some light on this guy. And Evan. All of them.

Aiden checked his phone again. Still nothing. He didn't know exactly when "bedtime" was at Harmony House, but he was almost positive there was a specified time for sleeping.

Rules, even flexible ones, were just another way to keep control over his following. Damien—and any other cult leader for that matter—didn't want his minions up and about throughout the night hours. There were too many variables involved with such freedom, and Aiden was sure Parr understood that.

Come on, Autumn. Call.

To ease his nerves, Aiden walked to the whiteboard and studied the posted pictures of all the victims. The entire team had been working on a killer profile, but Aiden believed it was time to form a more structured victim profile as well.

The deviant place theory stated that greater exposure to dangerous places made an individual more likely to become the victim of a crime. This fit for a victim like Kenneth Wilder, who'd entered a rundown motel known amongst locals for drug usage and prostitution.

The theory fell apart with Natalie Garland, though. Dogwood Falls was a serene location known for its natural beauty. Natalie hadn't willingly walked into a dangerous situation filled with questionable company.

Aiden tapped his chin as he studied Natalie's photo. The deviant place theory *could* apply to her if Harmony House were to be considered the unsafe environment, which was exactly what Bradley Garland and Yvette Wilder insisted upon. If Damien or anyone else living on the compound was a killer, simply existing in the facility placed them in harm's way.

His stomach burned with acid when he remembered that right at this precise moment, Autumn was within those walls. Potentially in harm's way with his stamp of approval.

He took a step back, frowning at the whiteboard. There were problems with that victimology profile. Not all the deceased had been affiliated with Harmony House. There were some, such as Patrick Ryder, who appeared to have every reason to commit suicide. That man had been fresh out of an AA meeting, where several attendees attested to his intoxication on the night in question.

The poor bastard had kept drinking and drinking until his body shut down. Shut *off*. Anomalies like Patrick served to cut the strings that would otherwise tie the suicides and Harmony House together in a tidy package.

Aiden sighed and pulled his phone out yet again. The evening was nearing eight o'clock. Maybe a little early for "lights out," but Harmony House didn't seem like a party 'til midnight type of establishment.

He stared at the screen, urging the damn thing to ring.

She would call. Soon.

I STEPPED into her room without hesitation because pausing would indicate that I was going somewhere I didn't belong.

No one was in the hallway to spot me. I had no boundaries at Harmony House and refused to act as though I did.

Autumn was out with some of the other women taking an after-dinner walk. I'd waited for the right moment to inspect her belongings and now was the time.

This was nothing new. I made it my duty to ensure no items had been brought onto Harmony House grounds that could in any way be detrimental to our utopia. That was my right as well as my responsibility.

Our newest arrival had brought only a backpack with her. I found the dilapidated thing sitting on the floor at the end of her bed. Who knew how old this bag was or what stories it could tell?

Autumn was incredibly lucky to have found Harmony House.

I crouched down and dug through the items stuffed inside. A couple of dingy t-shirts and a pair of baggy jeans. I wrinkled my nose at the pervasive stench of greasy fast food that wafted from the backpack. Perhaps she'd been sleeping in an alley behind a burger joint before coming here.

"Ahhh." I unearthed a small black cell phone from the depths of the bag. It opened with no password required. An immediate check of her contacts showed she had none. No recent texts. No calls in the call log.

This was a classic example of what I called a "just in case" phone. Many of the lost who came to Harmony House brought something of the sort with them. What none of them understood, at first, was that there was no need for such a device.

Harmony House was overflowing with love and acceptance. There were beds for everyone, food for an army, and beauty all around. No members ever lacked any basic needs.

I pocketed the phone. There was no reason for Autumn to be calling anyone outside of these walls. Ever. She was in the process of joining the Circle. Her past life, her family and friends, anything that happened before she came to us was of no consequence.

She was starting fresh.

Sometimes, it took the newbies a bit to absorb what that meant and the freedom it granted them. But no matter. That was where I came in to help.

I rose and walked to a nearby utility closet. Cleaning supplies, toilet paper, light bulbs of every size, and batteries of every sort. I kept the replacement phone batteries locked in an old filing cabinet just in case curiosity got the best of one of the members.

Sure enough, I found a match for her phone. It was a common make and model, so I hadn't been worried. I pulled the battery from Autumn's cell and slid the replacement back in. She would never detect the difference.

What she would notice was that her phone would no longer charge.

I walked back to her room, buried the phone in the bottom of her bag, and replaced it at the foot of her bed. No harm done.

A bright red strand of Autumn's long hair caught my eye on her pillowcase. I smiled, picked up the strand, and placed it on her pillow in a perfect circle.

Beautiful.

Voices drifted up the stairs from the kitchen. This was the time of late evening when some gathered for a soothing cup of chamomile tea and end-of-the-day chatter. A lovely routine I cherished.

Satisfied with my work, I turned and left Autumn's room. Such a small deed I'd performed, but so important.

I cherished nothing so much as ensuring the complete safety and control of Harmony House members. The Circle was to be protected above all else.

23

An end-of-the-day "songs of thanksgiving" session was the apparent norm amongst the group. Alice led Autumn to the church building, which truly was as unadorned inside as the outside had led her to believe. The sanctuary room held many chairs, but they were all stacked and pushed against the wall.

Group members gathered in a circle on the floor without instruction or protest.

Autumn sat as close to Alice as possible without actually touching her. An influx of Alice's mind wouldn't be a dreadful thing, as she was the kindest person Autumn had ever come into contact with. But focusing on Damien and Evan while also observing the rest of the group members and doing so in a convincing, nonchalant manner didn't leave much brainpower to process anyone's soul.

Not even if that soul was ninety-eight percent butterflies and rainbows.

The Circle, as Damien and his followers called themselves, sang a type of hymn-ish song that Autumn was wholly unfamiliar with.

Since no one would expect her to know the words, she took the opportunity to check out her surroundings. Everyone would understand her inquisitive demeanor. She was new. That's what "new people" did.

Roberta and Chelsea sat side by side, singing their hearts out. Evan sang along as well, but with less gusto. He seemed shy even amongst his "family."

Autumn's heart softened. Maybe Evan had experienced the foster care system like herself. Or abusive parents. Autumn, even now, fought the deep-seated idea that her presence was never quite accepted in full. When the people who had biologically created a child were incapable of showing love to their offspring, a wound was formed that the individual would carry with them into every situation life threw their way. Even as adults.

"You have to release those emotions, Autumn. You have to let them go because they do you no good...I decided to take a different path. To take control of my future and set my past free."

With a shudder, Autumn pushed aside Damien's words to focus on Evan. Whatever Evan Blair had been through, Autumn sensed he hadn't yet recovered. Not deep inside of himself. There was an inner chamber that locked anguish up like a safety vault. Accessing those types of wounds was at times impossible. Disposing of them altogether was a fairy tale.

Evan was struggling, and she wished there was a way to truly help him. A lofty goal when she'd yet to engage him in a real conversation.

She'd been on Harmony House grounds for less than twenty-four hours, though. There was time. Time to possibly help Evan, or Roberta, or Chelsea, or even Alice.

What does Alice need help with? She's happier than you've ever been in your entire life. Do you want to fix her simply because you're incapable of being like her?

The thought stung. Autumn realized she was frowning and made a swift facial adjustment. But one glance at Damien found him staring at her. She doubted his keen eye had missed her expression or interest in Evan.

A loud knock at the church doors interrupted the chorus of pretty voices. Damien nodded at one of his followers, a woman Alice had introduced to Autumn as Dolly Oleson. Dolly strode to the door, confident and brave despite the collection of alarmed gazes that followed her. She grasped the handle and pulled the wood slab, first creating a crack to peer through and then opening the door wide.

Two people, a man and woman, entered the room. Distress was evident in their furrowed brows and down-turned lips.

Alice gasped and threw a hand over her mouth. Autumn frowned. "Alice? What's wrong?"

"My parents," Alice whispered back. "My parents found me." She was on her feet in an instant, charging toward the couple with more fire than Autumn had thought her gentle soul possessed.

The woman, Alice's mother, let out a small yelp and rushed toward her daughter with outstretched arms, but Alice stopped just short of the embrace. Her mother's excited expression turned into a mask of despair, and Autumn's heart fractured for her.

"Ingrid. Kyle." Alice's address was formal. Cold. "What are you doing here? How did you find me?"

Kyle Leeson wrapped an arm around his wife. "It wasn't easy. We've been searching for...for..." The man choked up.

"Over two years, Alice!" Ingrid broke into a sob. "Why would you do that to us after what we lost?"

Alice shook her head once. "I lost her too. You never understood that, Ingrid. Neither of you did."

Ingrid reached out her hand and clasped Alice's arm.

"Please, please come home. We can talk through everything. We'll do family counseling or whatever you want. You can't stay in a place like this, honey. You need to come home."

Autumn glanced at Damien, who remained seated and calm. He even had a pleasant, welcoming smile on his face that appeared to be one-hundred-percent genuine. The man was unbelievable. And more so, he wasn't worried about losing Alice in the slightest.

He knew he owned her now.

"I've found a real home." Alice's soft voice uttered the declaration. "Damien has helped me through my pain and suffering. Harmony House is where I belong. I won't leave. *Not ever.*"

Damien's smile widened. Autumn's hands balled into fists. The man was overseeing the utter destruction of a family. Worse, that grin demonstrated that he was happy letting the Leesons crash and burn.

"This isn't a home." Kyle waved his hand toward Damien's followers, still artfully arranged in their circle. "This is a *cult*, Alice. That man has *brainwashed* you. He's not a saint. He's not a god. He's a horrible person who takes advantage of people in need."

Dolly, the only other standing member of Harmony House, flushed red at the accusations toward her beloved leader. She stalked toward the man. Autumn wasn't sure if she meant to admonish him or stab him.

"He's a good person who helps people in need," Autumn blurted, rising and rushing to Alice's side. "We know how the world judges us from the outside, but that's *the outside*. If you spent a day at Harmony House, you would understand what a beautiful haven it is."

She held her breath, praying that jumping to Damien's defense was enough to make up for rebuffing his advance. If nothing else, she'd stopped Dolly and her murderous glare dead in her tracks.

Kyle's blue eyes, which were an exact replica of Alice's, darkened with fury. The anger faded as he took in Autumn's rumpled state. "I don't know you, sweetheart, but I'm guessing you've got a family out there who misses you like crazy. My daughter doesn't need a haven. She has a *home*." The man was tearing up...breaking down.

Autumn silenced every instinct in her soul that told her to comfort him, comfort Ingrid, try to build a bridge between Alice and her parents, and give this family a chance. "If she felt the same, she wouldn't be here. Alice isn't a child. She's allowed to live wherever she wants, and she chose Harmony House."

Dolly vigorously nodded in agreement, but Alice seemed to falter. "I'm happy here." She placed a gentle hand on her mother's, which was still vise-gripped around her arm.

"But we can't...even *speak* to...y-you." Ingrid's sobs caused her to gasp between words. "We can't even...call you here. They keep you *locked away*."

Tears streaked down Alice's cheeks. The firmness with which she'd greeted her parents was waning. Regardless of her bliss at Harmony House, a part of Alice Leeson wanted to go home.

Was it really so impossible to speak with someone inside the confines of this place? Were all calls, letters, and other attempts by family to reach their loved ones blocked or intercepted? Was that how Damien made sure no one's mind became "infected" by outsiders?

Natalie had spoken with Bradley the morning she died, but she'd also spoken with him the day before when she was still residing at Harmony House. She'd found a way to make outside contact. Had that been the tipping point that led to her death?

Kyle put his hand on Alice's cheek. "You're our baby girl. *No one* loves you more than we do. Come home, and we'll make this right. I promise you, we will make everything right."

Alice opened her mouth to speak, but Damien was at her side before a single word slipped past her lips. He put his arm around her shoulders and gave a gentle pull, interrupting any physical contact between Alice and her parents. "The choice is hers. Only hers. Coming here with your tears and your pleas after Alice's world was turned upside down doesn't change the fact that your daughter has found a life of purpose and peace at Harmony House. *Of course* she can leave whenever she'd like. She can use the office phone whenever she'd like. But it's up to *Alice*. Not you."

Damien squeezed Alice's shoulder, as if to reassure her that he was still on her side, no matter what these horrible people had said. Alice's lips trembled as she raised her chin and looked from one parent to the other. "I'm staying, and you both should leave."

The shadow of defeat that descended onto Kyle and Ingrid's faces was a sight that would haunt Autumn forever. Kyle stared at Alice, blank with grief. "We love you. And if you ever change your mind, you are always welcome to come home. *Always.*"

After one last look brimming with hopeless longing, he turned and stumbled from the building. Autumn was certain he'd burst into tears the second the door shut behind him.

Ingrid stepped to her daughter once more, ignoring Damien's existence as well as the rest of the group. "We *do* know what you lost. *I know what you lost.* No one understands your grief better than us. No one here loves Maggie like we do. And no one *loves you* like we do. We can't...we can't bear to lose another child."

Her mother said nothing more. She turned and followed after her husband, disappearing behind the church door.

Alice broke the silence that followed by stepping away from Damien, keeping her eyes low. "I'm going to my cabin. I need to rest. Forgive me for breaking the Circle this evening." She hurried to the church's back door and left the group of astonished followers behind.

Evan stood. His face was contorted with agony. Autumn wondered if Evan didn't have a bit of a special place in his heart for Alice. He began walking as if to follow her, but Damien intercepted the move. "Evan. No."

Turning back to face his leader, Evan locked a serious, pale green stare on Damien. If Harmony House were an army, Autumn guessed that Evan had just been given a direct command of sorts, and he was not pleased.

Damien ignored him and addressed the group. "I know what you all just witnessed was disturbing. It's always difficult to be reminded of life before Harmony House...before beauty and grace encompassed us in the Circle. Keep your prayers with Alice as she recovers from this vicious blow but respect her sacred privacy. She will mourn, but she is strong. Love will heal her wounds as it has before."

Bobbing heads and "amens" overtook the room as everyone deferred to Damien's wishes. Autumn wondered if anyone ever dared to disagree with their charismatic leader.

Damien held both hands high above his head. "*Be* the change!"

"*We* are the change!"

Afterward, members flowed out the front and back exits. Autumn hadn't caught the "cue," but the dismissal was clear. She moved to follow and noticed Evan standing still, his posture as tense as ever. He didn't appear to be leaving like the rest, and whatever he had to say to Damien could prove useful to the case.

Outside the back exit, Autumn knelt and pretended to tie her shoes, neglecting to push the door all the way closed. She focused her eyes on the make-believe knot plaguing her laces while training her ears on the voices emanating from within the church.

"Alice needs me." Evan's tone was a mixture of resentment and heartache.

"She needs time to herself," Damien countered with his usual charm. "You know the rules."

Autumn leaned closer to the crack.

Rules?

"She's been here nearly three years." Evan's resentment had escalated to anger. "If she hasn't chosen to join with you by now, she more than likely never will. You can't just keep her off-limits forever, Damien."

"Nor would I." The leader of Harmony House spoke as though he were Zeus, and Evan nothing but a human peasant. "Once she has joined to me, she is free to do as she pleases within the Circle. She knows this. She has chosen celibacy for now."

"You've *forced* her to choose celibacy!" Evan shouted. "That's not the same thing!"

Damien emitted a growl. "Do not raise your voice at me, Evan. Not in this holy place. If Alice wanted to be with you, she would take the steps required to make that happen."

"She doesn't want to sleep with you, Damien." He'd lowered his volume, but Evan's rage level had risen. "Alice *worships* you. She's the most faithful of all your followers. Why isn't that enough?"

"I thought *you* were the most faithful of all my followers." Damien threw the statement back.

Evan didn't reply for a moment. "I've devoted my life to you, to the Circle, to Harmony House. I believe in you. So does Alice. Should we be punished for that? You're keeping us apart for no reason."

"The reason," Damien angrily retorted, "is that she has yet to join me. She is a part of the Circle, a blessed part, but until she receives the full glory of my essence, she must conserve her energy. Every day that passes only purifies her all the more. *I* don't mind waiting, Evan. She'll come around. That Ceremony will be *spectacular*. And then, if she wants, she can be with you, and you will take part in my glory as well. Or she can continue with me."

"She won't." Evan's confidence surprised Autumn. "She won't continue with you because she loves *me*. She won't join you because *she loves me*."

Damien laughed. "Has she told you that she loves you?"

A long pause, and then Evan's meek, "No."

"That's what I thought." Damien sighed and returned to his role as charismatic leader. "Evan, you are worth more than hoping for the love of a woman. If Alice truly loved you, she'd do anything. That's what lovers do. They fight their way through. And if she isn't fighting to be with you...well, you deserve better than that. You are an exceptional young man."

Evan had no response to this. Autumn guessed that Damien's words had stabbed a dagger straight through his smitten heart. Damien had cunningly managed to both puff Evan's ego *and* put him back in his place. The man was diabolical. A grand manipulator.

"Does she love *you*?" Evan's inquiry made Autumn ache for him. He sounded as if he were trying to be respectful while also having his dreams ripped apart.

Damien waited a few beats, probably for dramatic buildup. "Of course she does. Did you really ever doubt that?"

There was a long bout of silence, and then Autumn made

out their footsteps fading toward the front door. Relief flooded through her when she realized she wouldn't have to lie straight-faced about tying her shoes for five minutes or take off running like an Olympic track star.

"Be the change, Evan." Damien's parting command was given in a gentle manner that only the best of friends would employ.

Evan sniffed, the sound echoing off the empty church ceiling. "I am the change."

The front door closed, and Autumn stood, knowing she had limited time to teleport herself to a less suspicious resting place. She eyed Damien and Evan heading toward Harmony House and whirled to hurry off in the opposite direction.

Her heart leapt into her throat when she almost crashed into a person. Dolly stood directly before her, arms crossed, with the same fury in her eyes as when Kyle Leeson insulted Damien. "I can teach you how to tie your shoes if you need me to." She raised a chestnut brown eyebrow that matched her chestnut brown hair and eyes.

Autumn forced a light laugh. "Knots. I had knots. But I do sometimes think I should go back to preschool and just start over."

Dolly's skeptical expression relaxed but didn't vanish.

And why wouldn't she be skeptical? You sat at that back door for an eternity.

Dolly nodded at the church building. "That was messy. The nerve of those people. Alice is one of *us* now. We are her family, and we *love* her. Alice is irreplaceable, and she belongs here in this beautiful place."

"I know." Autumn played along, sensing the passion in Dolly's statements. "You can't just walk into someone's home and insult them *in their home*. No wonder Alice left those horrible people."

"Exactly." Dolly unthawed a little. "You did a decent job, standing up for Damien like that."

Autumn ducked her head and offered a shy smile. "I couldn't just sit by and let something awful happen." Awful, as in letting Dolly attack the Leesons, but Dolly didn't need to know that.

"Will you be at the Ceremony tonight?" Dark eyes studied her as Dolly waited to analyze her answer.

Other than hearing Damien mention the word once in his conversation with Evan, Autumn hadn't the slightest idea what "the Ceremony" was. She lifted a shoulder. "I don't think I'm on that level yet."

Dolly smiled with genuine warmth for the first time since Autumn had met her. "I suppose that's true. You just got here. The Ceremonies are special. Private. They're only meant for those who are committed to the Circle."

There was no mistaking the condescension in Dolly's voice. Autumn almost found it amusing, considering she had no idea what Dolly was talking about and had zero desire to attend, aside from information-gathering purposes.

"See you later." Dolly started walking toward the main house, and Autumn seized the opportunity to beeline to Alice's cabin.

At some point, she would attempt to seize Dolly, albeit in the form of a loving hug or encouraging pat on the back. There was more going on in the feisty follower's head than she wanted anyone to know.

Sorry, Dolly, but one touch, and your cover is blown.

Alice lived four cabins down, making the walk short. Autumn tapped on her door and hoped she wasn't intruding. She understood why Alice would want to be alone, but as a psychologist, she knew that Alice desperately needed someone to talk to.

The door opened, and a puffy-faced Alice Leeson ushered

her inside. There were no chairs, so they sat on the bed together.

Holding a tissue to her nose, Alice hung her head. "I'm so sorry. What a scene that was. How *disgraceful*. Damien must be so disappointed in me right now."

Damien needs a good kick to the balls. Screw him and his disappointment.

She wished she could say as much, but she had a role to play. "I don't think that's true. I think he was worried about you. He cares about you."

Alice buried her face in her hands. "I do miss them, Autumn. Sometimes I wonder if I could form a new relationship with them, even if it's on different terms than they're used to."

Autumn recalled Natalie Garland's image taped to the whiteboard at the Beechum Police Station. She envisioned the hall of pictures in the Garland household leading up to Natalie's graduation photo taken in front of Dogwood Falls. The Garlands were destroyed. Just when they were on the verge of getting their daughter back.

"I think you should pray about that first, Alice." Keeping the urgency from her voice was difficult. "You just went through a very upsetting situation. Lots of scenarios will come into your mind, but those are ideas that you need to really process...*alone*...before you act." Autumn wished she could add a warning about not speaking of such notions to anyone. Especially not Damien.

Very possibly, someone within Harmony House viewed having a change of heart as the ultimate cardinal sin.

"Thank you." Alice's sweet smile had returned. "You're a good friend. I'm so glad you came home with me. I think we have lots of great days ahead of us." She hugged Autumn, sending out her usual wave of innocence and goodness.

Autumn struggled to return the smile. What she really

wanted to do was grab Alice by the hand and run straight off Harmony House property. Give her a safe place to sort through her thoughts and decide what *she* wanted.

And possibly put her in witness protection, based on how things had turned out for Natalie.

Alice rose, swiping at her cheeks. "I should go help with end-of-the-day cleanup. I can't shirk my responsibilities every time I get upset."

"I'll meet you down there." Autumn understood that Alice needed a few minutes to freshen up, so she showed herself out with a friendly wave.

Damien approached the cabin at the same time Autumn closed the door. She held her breath, afraid she'd over-stepped by visiting Alice after he gave direct orders to let his upset devotee be, but his smile was as wide as ever.

"What a good friend you are." He placed a hand on her shoulder. "Alice is lucky to have you. We all are. I sincerely hope you will stay, Autumn." He gave her a pat and entered Alice's cabin without another word.

Autumn's unusual ability told her that he'd meant the words. Still, her heartbeat pounded in her ears, and she struggled not to take off running.

A swirl of emotions assaulted her senses like a slap.

Lust.

Love.

Hate.

Damien was obsessed with sex. She'd already known that, but now she knew more.

He *loved* Alice. He was waiting and praying for Alice to "join to him." He'd even considered joining *only* with Alice from that point on out.

And…he was contemplating the option of throwing Evan Blair off the overlook.

Alarm bells clanged in her head as she headed for

Harmony House, walking as fast as possible without drawing any special attention. She made her way through the building, giving polite smiles and nods to all she passed. Entering her bedroom, she closed the door behind her and took a few deep breaths.

She had to call Aiden and update him, although she hadn't exactly figured out how to tell him the method in which she'd gleaned the information.

You'll figure that out. Call him. Now.

Her phone was right where she'd left it, at the bottom of her backpack. She swiped at the screen. Nothing happened. The battery was dead.

"Dammit." Autumn dug around for her charger cord in the depths of her bag, grabbed it, and found the only outlet in the room. She jammed in the plug and connected the device.

Still nothing.

Had someone tampered with her phone?

"We can't even call you here. They keep you locked away."

She rubbed the goose bumps from her arms, telling herself there was no reason to jump to any conclusions. She hadn't been on Harmony House grounds long enough for anyone to begin messing with her belongings or worrying about her contact with the outer world.

Someone may have messed with her cell, or she could just be freaking out based on her already frazzled nerves. Still, as she stared at the black screen, a chill crept through her limbs. How in the hell was she going to get ahold of Aiden now?

She needed to tell him about Natalie's ex-boyfriend's surprise visit. Even more troubling was her newfound worry about how often Damien Parr solved his personal problems by shoving someone off a cliff.

Would she be able to find a way to contact Aiden before Evan's beloved leader disposed of him?

24

S loan Grant hit the last couple hundred yards of her daily jog hard. Her lungs burned, and her quads cramped, but she pushed through the pain. She *always* pushed herself at the end. Testing her limits was something of a hobby since her time spent with the army in Afghanistan.

Go. Faster. Faster.

Her breathing wheezed in her ears as she pounded down the pavement. The extreme pressure of working in a war zone had turned her into a certified adrenaline junkie, and her position as an agent with the FBI's counterterrorism unit fed that addiction well.

Bombs. Her specialty was defusing bombs. Boredom wasn't part of the job description.

Her mind flashed to an image of the explosive she'd faced down yesterday. The other people had run in the opposite direction, but not her.

She'd run *toward* the danger.

Sloan pumped her arms, lungs on fire now as she took the final corner of her run at a catastrophic speed.

In the early morning hours yesterday, she'd been called

into a local high school just outside of Richmond, where a troubled teen had planned to create his own version of Columbine.

Part of the boy's plan had involved guns and ammo stashed in a large duffel bag he'd left in the boys' locker room. The other part was a crudely fashioned explosive device he'd planted in the teachers' lounge.

Luckily, his youth had led him to make some major mistakes, like sharing too much on social media. Law enforcement had been eyeing him for months. And all it took to thwart his intentions was one anonymous call from his girlfriend—who made said call from her own personal cell phone—to the police station warning them of her boyfriend's deadly plans for the school day.

Sloan had clipped the wire herself after a frantic evacuation of the high school.

Save a thousand kids. Save a dozen teachers. You still killed Ned.

Her muscles screamed as she sprinted even harder. Sweat poured down her face, and her lungs felt like she'd swallowed glass. No matter how fast she ran, though, she couldn't outrun the truth.

Ned was dead. And it was her fault.

It didn't matter that she would have died a thousand times over to save Ned from his car wreck, to give Mia Logan her brother back. The haunted, cold stare in her former friend's eyes whenever their paths crossed was enough to shatter Sloan's heart all over again.

Mia and Ned had two years between them, but they'd looked like twins. Big brown eyes. Dark brown hair. Dimples. Mia was as pretty as Ned had been handsome.

And now Mia was an only child.

Sloan staggered to a stop a short distance away from the front steps of her downtown Richmond apartment building, breathless and doubled over in agony. Some days she wondered if she weren't trying to kill herself by running until her heart exploded.

Once the pain subsided and she caught her breath, she straightened and began walking her fatigued muscles out. Five months ago, she'd been called in—*by Mia Logan*—to defuse the explosive vest Justin Black had left his sister wearing amongst a throng of mourners in D.C. There had been a moment when Sloan promised herself that should she not be able to locate the correct wire, she would instead throw herself onto the bomb to save as many lives as possible.

Rather than abandon Winter, Sloan had planned to die with her, absorbing as much of the blast as possible and saving hundreds.

She'd been *so* okay with the idea of exploding into a billion pieces that she'd later questioned whether or not she truly had developed a death wish. She had begun to wonder if it weren't time to consider a new line of work before her luck ran out.

Change was an attractive idea. Starting fresh with something new. She couldn't abandon the adrenaline rush of being an agent altogether, and she was self-aware enough to accept this fact. She'd be bored to tears with a desk job.

But a different unit was worth contemplating. Maybe one that didn't thrust her in constant, close proximity to life-ending explosives at a time in her existence when guilt wracked her body with every breath of air she took.

She paused on autopilot to stretch her quads, her mind still fixated on the past.

Ned wouldn't have wanted you to live your life like this. He loved you. He would want you to love yourself. Forgive yourself.

Her mouth twisted. Would he, though? Ned had loved her *before* she ripped his world to pieces. The few hours that he'd been alive *after* she made her betrayal known, his passion may have very well morphed into pure hatred.

He'd wanted to marry her. The entire second year of their relationship, marriage had been a subject they often visited, despite Sloan's repeated and clear stance on the matter. She wasn't ready for the long-haul commitment because she wasn't quite sure any human was capable of fulfilling those weighty vows.

Her parents divorced when she was six. They'd both remarried and eventually divorced again. Her mother had even performed the whole circus a *third* time with the exact same result.

Marriage didn't seem so much a sacred bond as it did a surefire way to ruin a relationship. Plus, even without marriage, her own heart had already been broken twice.

Her high school boyfriend of four years had cheated on her one semester into his freshman year of college. She'd thought he was her future.

She'd been wrong.

The man she fell in love with during her own college journey had promised her the sun, moon, stars, and more. But after taking three years of her love and devotion, all he'd left her with was more heartache. That particular a-hole had been banging other women for over half the time he and Sloan were together.

This was, of course, a fact she only found out after catching him in bed with one of his many "special friends."

What she'd had with Ned was too good to tag with the pink slip of marriage.

Ned, on the other hand, was certain they were the exception to the rule. He may have been right…but Sloan hadn't been ready to consider that possibility.

The more Ned talked about marriage, the bigger her inner ball of anxiety had become. So big that, on a random weekday evening within that period of self-suppression, she'd gone out alone for dinner and had too many drinks and ended up in a handsome bartender's bed, drunk and desperate to release her pent-up emotion.

Sloan was horrified when she woke the morning after. She'd turned into her own worst fear…a cheating, lying piece of shit.

Ned was never to know. Telling him would break his heart, so she kept the burden of truth heavy in her own. She would suffer for him and remind herself every time his brown eyes gazed at her with love that she didn't deserve this man.

That self-imposed purgatory had worked up until Ned actually popped the question. Instead of saying yes or no, she'd spilled out the details of her betrayal. She left nothing out, even as Ned's face turned into a map of utter despair.

The irony lay in the fact that she'd wanted to say yes. Against her better judgment and all her fears, Ned's proposal had awoken a tender piece of her heart that still somehow believed in the fairy tale.

He'd taken off, angry, destroyed, and assuming their relationship was over. She'd sat alone in her apartment sobbing and assuming the same.

And then he'd wrecked his car, and their love story met a definitive end. So did Ned's life.

And her relationship with Mia.

Sloan entered the building, legs trembling as she climbed the staircase to her second-floor apartment. She walked straight to the fridge and pulled out a bottled water, holding the chilled container to her forehead before chugging the liquid down.

Her phone rang in the pocket of her athletic shorts. Grabbing the device, her eyes locked on the screen in disbelief.

Mia. Mia Logan was calling her on a random Tuesday evening.

Her hand was unsteady as she took the call. "Hello?"

"Sloan, this is Mia. I'm calling on official business for the BAU's current case. Nothing more."

Sloan flinched as the hope stirring in her chest died. So stupid. Of course Mia would only be calling about work. "Okay. How can I help?"

Mia cleared her throat. "Damien Parr. Does the name strike a bell with you? You were both overseas serving in explosive disposal units around the same time."

Sloan sank onto her sofa, going through a mental reel of soldiers she'd met during her tour of duty. Faces flashed in and out of her mind until she landed on one particularly handsome, dark-haired man. "I do remember him. We were in different units, but we worked together once. Why?"

"He might be involved in a series of murders related to his community charity organization. Damien created an estate called 'Harmony House,' which is essentially a cult with a bunch of Parr's followers living on the premises. Did the Damien Parr you met strike you as someone who'd be interested in running a squeaky-clean nonprofit?"

"Well," Sloan scoured her mental files for memories of the man in question, "I guess stranger things have happened. But from what I knew of Parr, he never did anything without an ulterior motive. Very self-interested."

Mia typed away in the background, more than likely adding to the case notes. "Do you know any stories in particular that would back that theory up?"

Sloan laid her head back against the cushions and stared at the ceiling. She was going to need a shop vac and fifteen gallons of air freshener to get her sweat out of the fabric. But what did that matter when she was mid-conversation with her dead ex-boyfriend's sister?

"Black market. The guy was known for doing business on the black market. He didn't believe the government, neither ours nor any overseas entities, had the right to place limits on his personal financial dealings. Doesn't take a genius to figure out that's what got him discharged."

"Thank you for the information, Sloan." Mia's voice was reminiscent of an automated operator. "Have a nice evening."

The call was cut off before Sloan could even say goodbye.

Mia Logan is going to hate you forever, and you deserve nothing less.

Sloan propped her feet on the coffee table. There had to be a way to make amends to Mia for the loss of Ned…but how? The idea seemed impossible.

She couldn't bring Ned back. She couldn't change her betrayal or the last conversation she'd had with Mia's brother. What was done was done.

"I'm sorry" wasn't enough, and it never would be. Time would continue to pass, and Ned would continue to be gone. There was no "fixing" death.

But the thought of living out her entire life as Ned Logan's indirect killer was too much to bear. She had to find a way to make peace with Mia. To earn her forgiveness. They'd been close once, and that had to count for something.

Yes. It counts for the fact that she's able to hate you all the more for betraying her trust.

Sloan's mind wandered back to Winter Black and the explosive vest. A small part of her had been disappointed that she had to crawl away from that situation alive…and full of the same never-ending regrets.

She finished the water, staring off into space as she crushed the empty bottle beneath her fingers.

She had to find a way to get out from under this shadow of the past…before being blown to smithereens became more than just a welcome thought.

25

A lice tossed and turned for hours before giving up all hope of any deep sleep. She couldn't stop thinking of her parents.

Initially, the sight of her mom and dad had triggered a cascade of anger and other negative emotions. After so many months of contentment and bliss, the onslaught of such feelings was akin to being doused with freezing water on a warm, sunny day.

Once the shock had settled, Alice was hit by a wave of memories and softer feelings. These were her parents. The man and woman who had given her life. The only two human beings in the entire world who understood what was lost when Maggie Leeson passed away.

Ingrid, her mother, sobbed so hard that Alice worried for her blood pressure, which had always been a bit on the high side. Her father, Kyle, appeared as though he'd aged at least twenty years...even though less than two and a half years had passed.

She rubbed the heels of her hand across her puffy eyes. She'd hurt them. Terribly. And yes, they'd hurt her as well.

The hell of being a child in mourning with no one to share in her sorrows was still vivid in her memory. She'd been orphaned while still living in her parents' home. Abandoned in plain sight.

However, maybe now the scales had evened out a little. No matter how monstrous their grief was when Maggie died, she'd doubled it by running away herself.

I should call them. I should call them and at least let them know that I love them. And maybe...maybe we can start over. Build a relationship that's fresh and pure.

There was only one landline on Harmony House property that she was aware of, and it was located in Damien's office inside of the main house. His office was never locked. There were no locked doors amongst Harmony House members.

Damien valued transparency and truth. No one had anything to be ashamed of in a place where love was all-encompassing. Therefore, locks were unnecessary. Damien believed they encouraged distrust as well as dishonesty.

Alice agreed.

And though she knew calling her family in the middle of the night wasn't something she should do without permission, she also wouldn't be ashamed if anyone were to find out. They were her *parents*. What could be more understandable than that?

The old-fashioned pendulum clock hanging on her cabin wall showed the hour was nearing two in the morning. Perhaps she was taking liberties by entering Damien's space, but he held a soft place in his heart for her. Hopefully, that was solid enough ground on which to make the decision.

The short walk from her cabin to the main house was lit with silver moonlight, the air filled with magic and promise. As long as love led her steps, she could do no wrong. Damien had said as much.

Alice agreed.

She tiptoed down the dark, empty halls of the main level and entered Damien's office. The phone sat right on top of his desk. Not hidden away as her mother had accused. Harmony House members were allowed to make any choices they deemed right concerning their former lives and the individuals they'd left behind. Damien believed his followers always made the right choice in the eyes of God.

Alice agreed.

She had just picked up the receiver to place her call when a figure emerged from the shadows. She jumped and dropped the receiver back in the cradle. Her hand flew to her chest. "You scared me."

"I'm sorry." He walked slow steps toward her. "That wasn't my intention. What are you doing here, Alice? At this time of night?"

Alice bit her lip. Saying she'd called her parents after she'd spoken with them was one thing, but admitting to it before making any contact was another. What if she'd misunderstood? What if she truly *wasn't* allowed to speak to them without permission?

She would never do anything to disrupt the serenity of Harmony House or its members. This was her family. Her home.

Her brain froze. "I w-was, um…well, I couldn't sleep and…"

There was nothing convincing in her hesitation. "You were going to call your parents, weren't you?"

"Yes." The word slipped from her mouth. "I wanted to talk to them and make sure…make sure they knew I was okay. That was all. My loyalty lies with Harmony House. I swear to you. My heart belongs to the Circle."

"Does it, Alice?" There was a note of disappointment in the tone.

Alice's eyes filled with tears. "I promise you. I *love* living here. I love *all of you.*"

A long silence settled between them in the darkened room.

"I believe you. I won't stand in your way. In fact, if you'd like, I'll give you a lift to your parents' home right now." The figure stepped toward her, smiling now. "Conversations like the one you need to have are best done in person, and I doubt they would mind being woken up by their beautiful daughter."

Her heart soared. "Really? You would do that for me?"

The heavy sigh caused a pang of guilt in her chest. "Alice, I would do *anything* for you. I thought you understood that by now."

Warmth flooded her as she embraced her savior. "I couldn't be more grateful. I'm humbled by your kindness."

"Let's go." A new hoarseness accompanied the command.

More guilt needled Alice. She was upsetting someone she deeply cared about, but she couldn't let the beautiful opportunity pass. To make peace with her parents *and* continue her life at Harmony House was a combination she'd never dreamed possible.

Her spirits lifted as she left the office and followed her volunteer driver.

Every day on this planet truly was a gift.

I'D WAITED FOR HER, knowing she'd come while praying she wouldn't. Alice's heart was so soft. Tender. Naïve.

Forgiving.

Seeing her parents again…seeing them like *that*…was too much for her. I'd hoped to talk sense into her once they were gone, but I'd read the truth in her magnificent blue eyes.

She missed them. She didn't want to leave that relationship in such a blurry, painful mess. She wanted to speak with them.

There was only one way to do that at Harmony House. I knew this. Everyone knew this. We didn't keep secrets here. Secrets were for liars and those ashamed of their actions.

No judgment lived within the Harmony House community. Therefore, shame couldn't exist among us either.

Alice had attempted to lie. I'd cut her off, not being able to bear the agony of hearing a falsehood slip past her perfect lips. But I knew. If she were capable, she would have lied and stuck to it.

She wasn't capable. She was too good. Too pure. The truth would come out of her...probably within seconds. I'd saved her the sin of deception.

Kyle and Ingrid Leeson lived an hour away from Harmony House. Not so far, but not so close. To think they'd been searching for Alice all this time and she'd been just a hop, skip, and a jump down the highway was almost amusing.

Almost.

Now, they knew exactly where she was, and they wouldn't give up. Not those two. They'd keep barreling across our property with their accusations and screams and tears and pleas...the scene could *not* be repeated.

My grip on the steering wheel tightened. How long until one of the other members burst into tears thinking of their own parents? How many would sneak away from us, overcome with fear, guilt, and sadness? All those evils would continually be poured upon us by the Leesons.

I was prepared to release them if it meant saving Alice. I *needed* her to stay. And though sending her parents into the afterlife would be a grievous sin, their deaths would be mere grains of sand on my pile of wrongdoings.

Two more decisions I would pay for, in time. But that penance was coming anyway. Securing the sanctity of Harmony House was the least I could do.

When I saw her tiptoe into the office, I'd known.

Alice was already gone. I'd lost her. She wanted her family more than she wanted me.

Maybe that was why she'd never gone through with the Ceremony. That would be full integration into the deepest levels of the Circle. She would have achieved an echelon of belonging she'd never dreamed of...but it wouldn't include her parents.

Disappointment tasted bitter on my tongue. That belonging *would* have included me, though. I'd hoped that was more important to her than all else.

But I was wrong.

Alice didn't love me. She was just a little girl who wanted her mommy and daddy.

So, I was taking Alice home.

I'd encouraged her to rest on the drive. Such a delicate woman should have been tucked in and warm beneath layers of blankets at this time of night.

After she fell asleep, I stole frequent glances at her. Her head rested against the passenger window, and long, angel-like blonde hair flowed down her back. Some of it hung around her face like a protective curtain.

The agony of the knowledge that I was returning her to her past life, that I would never feel her bare skin against mine, that the Circle would exist without her flawless, smiling face...it was almost unbearable. Like my heart was being ripped from my chest, but I was expected to keep living as though nothing had happened.

I considered releasing myself after Alice was reunited with her parents, but I'd only be switching the hell of a life without Alice for an eternal one.

And Harmony House *needed* my constant protection. I had to keep the paradise we'd built safe and whole. If I gave that up now, all the souls I'd released to this day would have died in vain.

Releasing Alice's parents would have killed her. Taking her home was the only option.

She woke as I pulled the car to a stop in front of the Leesons' substantial suburban house. The smile that spread across her face turned my stomach.

Maybe I was holding out hope that she'd change her mind. I didn't even know if it was possible to step away from the Circle and return, but for Alice, we could try.

Her expression assured me that there was no chance of this magnificent woman reversing her decision. Her heart was here. In that house. With those people.

The truth was in her eyes. Alice always spoke with her eyes.

She turned to me with the giddiness of a schoolgirl. "There's something I want to show you. Come." She was out of the car in a split second, and I followed after her like an obedient dog.

Alice led me to a tree on the far east side of her home. Hung from a sturdy branch, a simple wooden bench swing swayed in the cool night breeze. "This is where Maggie and I would play. We'd take turns pushing and swinging until we were old enough to pump. She'd go high enough that I could run underdogs beneath her. I was always so impressed. I couldn't bring myself to go that high."

A luminescent glow surrounded her. She truly was an angel.

My angel.

I stepped toward her, grabbed her face gently, and kissed the lips I'd stared at for so long. Desire ignited in my body. How I had craved this—

"What are you doing?" She pulled away, shocked and something else. Angry?

Was Alice Leeson angry at me for kissing her after all the time we'd spent together?

I stepped toward her again, needing to close the gap between us. I couldn't stand the distance any longer. "I'm kissing you." I reached for her face, but she backed farther away.

"No." Alice shook her head and held out a hand. "Please. Don't."

This couldn't be happening. "But I love you, Alice. You have to know that I love you."

Her face contorted into some mixture of pity and compassion. "Of course I know. And I love you too. I do. But I'm not...I was never...I'm not *in* love with you. Not in that way."

I'd watched a lake get drained once when I was much younger. The bacteria levels, pH, something hadn't been safe, and the lower the water level became, the sadder I felt inside. Eventually, all that was left was an empty dirt pit. It was giant. Barren. The image had haunted me with its darkness since childhood.

But now...I wasn't staring at a hollow cavern. I *was* the cavern.

I was the abyss. The void.

After this day, I would never be anything else.

I smiled at her, needing to relieve her fears and take in her sweet expression of acceptance once again. "It's okay, Alice. I was mistaken. I apologize. You can't help what you don't feel."

She gave a tentative nod. "I'm sorry."

"Don't be." I shook my head. "Wait here. I've got a present to give you before I leave, just in case you don't come back to—"

"I'm coming back." Firm. Her conviction was audible, but I knew how these types of reunions went. The Leesons would never let go of Alice again.

"Just in case, silly. Hold tight." I jogged back to the car across the lawn, hating every inch of the property. It was all a cage. A cage they would trap Alice in forever.

My Alice.

I eased the trunk open quietly, not wanting to disturb her parents or the rest of the neighborhood. The gift was right there. I'd known the time would come when I'd give it to someone.

I just hadn't ever thought that someone would be Alice.

She waited patiently by the swing, offering her usual smile upon my return. I loved that about Alice. No matter what happened, she couldn't help but stay kind. She truly loved everyone, including me.

Just not in "that way."

It took her innocent mind a moment or two to process what I was holding when I revealed my hands from behind my back. I wasn't sure which shocked her more, but I knew which one would keep her from screaming.

I held the pistol in my right hand and aimed it steadily at her head. The noose was gripped in my left hand.

Her mesmerized eyes went back and forth between the two. "No."

Tears spilled from my eyes. "Alice, I need you to keep quiet. If you keep quiet, I won't kill your parents. Do you understand?"

She nodded, trembling as her own tears streamed down her cheeks.

"Stand still." I threw the noose over the same branch that held her beloved childhood swing and looped it twice. "Don't move. If you try to run, I will shoot you. And then I will shoot your parents before anyone has the slightest idea what's happening. No one will stop me, and they will *die*. I know you love your parents, don't you?"

More nodding. More tears. I shoved the pistol under my belt and tied a knot with the thick rope as fast as I dared.

The knot had to be good. But I needed that gun in my hand.

Alice behaved, regardless. I'd known she would. She was a good girl.

Not *my* good girl, though. As much as I'd yearned otherwise.

I grabbed the gun and retrained it on her. "Step up onto the swing and keep your hands on the chains." Despite the relentless beads of sorrow falling from my eyes, my voice held steady.

"Please," she whispered, grasping the chains and pulling herself up as ordered. "Don't do this. I *do* love you. Harmony House loves you. They need you. They believe in you...in your *goodness*."

I would dissect every word she spoke later and break with every bleeding crack spreading across my heart. But here, now, I had to finish this. Because what I'd realized in these last moments together was that I couldn't let Alice go.

But I could release her.

I pointed the gun barrel at the noose. "Put it on."

Any person in their right mind would have refused, gun or no gun. They would have chanced the bullets on the small gamble that escape was possible.

Not Alice. She was so meek. So humble. So noble and giving. Sure, the gun scared her, but undoubtedly her main motivation was saving her parents' lives.

She held the swing chain with one hand and placed the noose around her neck with the other. She did it as though it were her duty.

We met eyes. My insides wrenched.

Alice. My sweet Alice.

"Why?" Speaking was harder for me now. I was sobbing. "Why did you have to leave the Circle?"

She'd sobered. A single tear spilled down her cheek as she stared up at the moon and stars as though I didn't exist and none of this was happening. "I never left. *You* brought me here. And I would have gone back."

Her words rang with truth, and I went still. Shock was a sharp pressure in my chest. I'd messed up. I'd made a hasty, *horrible* decision. Alice would have ended up back at Harmony House within hours, and with time, maybe even learned to love me.

She would never love me now.

"The light." She smiled as she spoke. "The light is positively effervescent tonight. This world is such a beautiful place. A lovely gift that—"

I moaned in agony and kicked the swing from beneath her feet.

It flew backward.

Alice descended.

Even as I tried to catch her, to stop what I'd started, her neck snapped clean in the listless summer wind.

26

Autumn awoke in the narrow twin bed, disoriented by the cramped, unfamiliar surroundings and the strong scent of bleach until the fog faded from her brain. A cheap plastic clock on the wall in the closet-sized room read four-fifty in the morning. On a normal day, that meant she still had an hour and forty minutes left of sleep, but today was anything but normal.

Her heart pounded as she remembered Damien's mental threat toward Evan yesterday. Did the leader really want to toss his shy young follower off a cliff?

She threw back the thin blanket. "Lights on" time was at six, and while Alice had insisted that the rule was more of a suggestion to keep everyone on roughly the same schedule, Autumn caught the strong vibe that at least ninety-nine percent of the group rose at six sharp.

If she wanted to snoop around Harmony House or the grounds, now was the time.

Creeping down the hallway, she noticed a plume of smoke through the gargantuan third-floor window.

Weird. The gray cloud appeared to be confined to a

section deep within the forested half of the Harmony House estate. She doubted a random fire had broken out in the wet July humidity.

Something was going on out there. Possibly something innocuous, but there was only one way to find out.

If anyone happened to notice her wandering the grounds, she could simply say she was an early riser and wanted to breathe in some of the majestic nature that surrounded them.

Autumn eased her way down the stairs to the ground floor, pausing at the bottom to listen for signs of life. Nothing stirred, so she crept out the back exit.

Once she was outside, the trees blocked most of the smoke cloud from view. A faint glow and hazy smog hung over the forest well past the cabins, though, and the pungent scent of burning wood reached her nose.

As much as she wanted to run toward the distant trees, she couldn't chance someone witnessing her acting so erratic before sunrise. Instead, she kept a brisk pace, pumping her arms like a speed-walker out for some morning exercise.

Her heart grew heavy as she approached Alice's cabin. The poor girl probably wasn't getting a wink of sleep after the upsetting confrontation with her parents. Autumn hesitated by the front door. Should she tap to check if Alice was awake and in need of company?

Pale streaks of light were already starting to streak across the sky. Not much time left until the entire compound would be coming to life, and Autumn had to know what was going on in those woods.

Dolly's words came back to her. *"Are you going to the Ceremony tonight?"*

Technically the night was over, but Autumn supposed any hour before sunrise could be referred to as "nighttime." Was that the scene she was preparing to spy? The Ceremony?

She was about to find out.

Autumn followed the path, trying to make as little noise as possible as she headed for the trees. The smoky, burnt-wood odor grew stronger with every step. Halfway there, the bushes to her left rustled. She froze, heart fluttering like a hummingbird's.

In the pre-dawn light, the raccoon's eyes glowed yellow before the animal turned and raced away.

She exhaled and continued, walking at a steady pace until a male voice reached her ears.

Damien.

Autumn veered off the path and crept into the woods. The path was too obvious and open. She needed to find a safer vantage point, somewhere behind a tree.

She flinched every time a twig snapped under her feet, holding still until she was certain she hadn't betrayed her whereabouts. The glow of the fire grew brighter as she weaved between trees, taking careful steps so as not to trip over the roots.

When she finally crept close enough to peer around a massive trunk into the clearing, some of the tension clamping down on her shoulders eased. No one was going to detect her presence over the madness taking place around that blazing fire.

Her relief was short-lived, however. Swept away as her brain struggled to comprehend the scene before her.

Damien stood by a stone altar. Buck naked, his skin glistening in the fire's glow.

A slender, nude woman lay sprawled out across the altar at his feet. Her dark hair flowed like silk around her head. *Roberta.* A circle of fire surrounded them, and a circle of naked women surrounded the fire.

Autumn's lungs hitched as she dug her nails into the

rough tree bark. Was she too late to prevent another murder? Oh god, was Roberta already dead?

The younger woman stretched out an arm. Autumn's breathing eased a little. Still alive. For now. Something was way off here, though. This entire setup screamed "human sacrifice," or at least pointed to some form of dangerous ritual.

But as she focused on the women's faces, the startling realization hit. None of the participants appeared frightened. On the contrary. Roberta's expression was starry-eyed as she gazed up at Damien, as though she believed herself to be in the presence of a god.

When Damien mounted the altar and straddled the young woman's body, Autumn no longer had to guess what was going on. The women who formed the circle joined hands and began to twirl around the fire, creating a moving wheel of flesh.

Their voices joined to form a chorus. "Join the Circle, be the change. Join the Circle, be the change."

Chelsea and Dolly danced within the carousel of gleaming skin, as lithe and uninhibited as the others. Round and round they went, heads tipped back in abandon.

"Join the Circle, be the change."

In the middle, Damien proceeded to "perform" the Ceremony. His hips bucked atop a writhing Roberta. Bile burned the back of Autumn's mouth when final understanding dawned.

This was Damien's version of turning the women into true followers. Of spreading his glory.

He was spreading his glory, all right. Right into Roberta.

Autumn wanted to run away, but her eyes were glued to the scene. It was like watching a car crash, only one with surprise porn instead of blood and mangled metal.

Soon, Damien's moans joined in with the chanting. The

women twirled faster, in time with the thrusting of his hips. As his animalistic noises gained momentum, the chanting grew louder until everything climaxed into one giant roar.

When the crescendo faded, Damien kissed Roberta on the forehead, then the lips, and gently slid off.

This…this was "the Ceremony."

Autumn pressed her hand to her mouth and fought back a gag. Poor Roberta, brainwashed into believing she was making the holiest of choices. Autumn bet every other woman gathered around to watch the joining of Roberta and Damien had once formed the focal point of the same ritual. Reclining on that stone altar, waiting for the Harmony House leader to "bless" them into the Circle.

Just as some of them still eagerly awaited Damien's visits afterward, to receive special deposits of his "glory."

"…And if you genuinely want to know the unbelievable gift of peace, joining to me is the fastest path to that joy…"

This was his ploy. If her stomach wasn't threatening to upchuck her last meal, Autumn might have applauded Damien for his resourcefulness. Not just any man could create his own harem without making a single member feel preyed upon.

Impressive and also incredibly repulsive. Autumn would consider injecting herself with every last gallon of brain bleach in the world if that might banish the images emblazoned on her retinas.

Because whether or not the members felt preyed upon didn't change the fact that Damien Parr was a predator. Memories of his inner thoughts toward Alice made her stomach churn double-time. He was obsessed with that pure, sweet woman. *Obsessed.* He wanted Alice more than anything or anyone.

Autumn had felt that truth whirling through his body.

She turned away from the fire-lit scene and toward the

woods. Her window of time to hike back to the main house and remain undetected was narrowing. Her steps as she weaved through the canopy of trees were less careful this time. With all the animated chatter and racket coming from the group post-Ceremony, no one would hear a branch snap.

As she climbed over a root and popped out onto the trail, an image of Agent Black filled her head. Winter, bursting from the woods to tackle a naked Damien to the ground. Handcuffing his wrists above his pale ass while ranting about what a perverted piece of shit he was.

The imagery made her smile. It also made her miss her friends.

The undercover world was a lonely place.

Without Alice's companionship, Autumn could only imagine the isolation she would be experiencing. She anticipated Alice's smiling face at breakfast with a deep sense of relief. At least her new friend hadn't "joined" to Damien yet.

Maybe Autumn could show support for her decision... encourage her to hold strong in her stance. Better yet, maybe she could somehow get Alice the hell out of here.

No wonder Evan was so upset. If he was in love with Alice and going through the Ceremony was the only way the two of them could be together per Harmony House policy, it was a baffling phenomenon that he didn't hate Damien Parr instead of declaring himself the most faithful follower.

And Damien...he probably only *thought* he was in love with Alice because the woman had thus far refused his advances.

Narcissists loved to possess what they'd been told they couldn't have. But once they obtained the coveted person, object, etc., the tune often changed. Quickly.

Then again...there was always the possibility that Alice was the exception to Damien's rule. Maybe he'd truly met his match, someone who made him want to be a better person.

She shook her head as she hurried down the last part of the path. Humans were complicated. Statistically, behaviors could be predicted. But statistics were only an estimate. An educated guess.

Autumn crept inside the back door and up the stairs to the third floor before slipping back into her room. Five minutes to six in the morning. Five minutes until the start of another day at Harmony House.

Alice had promised to wake her in the morning, knowing how early the recommended rise and shine time could be for newbies. With this knowledge in mind, Autumn collapsed on her bed.

Six hundred seconds of sleep still counted as rest.

AUTUMN WOKE to chatter and footsteps traipsing through the hallways of Harmony House. She checked the wall clock and bolted upright.

Three minutes until seven. How had that happened? Why hadn't Alice woken her? Even though she'd only known the woman a short time, Autumn didn't get the sense that Alice failed her word.

Ever.

She jumped out of bed and attempted to smooth her shirt and jeans. This was another problem that Alice had promised to help tend to today. She'd told Autumn that Harmony House kept a small stockpile of clothing for new arrivals. Autumn had thanked her profusely, even as guilt stabbed her over the idea of taking clothing from someone in need.

Poor Alice. She hoped the other woman wasn't too traumatized after the public showdown the night before.

When Autumn entered the kitchen, there was no sign of Alice's blonde head anywhere. Roberta stood by the sink, her cheeks especially rosy. Chelsea leaned on the counter, shoulders drooping while she scowled into a bowl of fruit. Autumn supposed it was unsurprising that the woman was a little miffed after the "joining," given her obvious infatuation with Damien.

Dolly stood in the far kitchen corner, stacking freshly washed plates together and placing them on overhead farmhouse-style shelves. Dolly's expression was neutral, but Autumn had already learned that this was Dolly's norm. She struck Autumn as the type of woman who kept track of the members and their activities like an unofficial watchdog.

Autumn arranged her features into a pleasant mask—no small feat after the horror-porn she'd witnessed only a few hours ago—and approached Dolly, who saw her coming and attempted a weak smile in return. Autumn didn't delude herself that the other woman had experienced a sudden change of heart where she was concerned. There were probably just too many people around for her to fry Autumn with another one of her evil glares.

"Hello." Dolly offered a polite nod. "Did you sleep well?"

The question almost seemed like a trap, but after studying Dolly's features, Autumn decided everything Dolly Oleson said probably came with an edge of attitude.

Autumn clasped her hands together. "I slept amazing. This place has…it's almost like some type of magical aura, you know?"

Dolly arched an eyebrow. "I do know. I live here." She added a smile at the end for anyone who happened to glance their way.

"Right." Autumn thunked her palm against her forehead. "I'm so ditzy sometimes. But hey, have you run into Alice this morning? I can't seem to find her."

"I haven't seen Alice since yesterday evening. She stays incredibly busy. She told me once that every minute she does nothing is a minute that she could have helped to change someone's life."

When she spoke of Alice, Dolly's expression softened, and even her voice lost its sharpness. Interesting. "She does seem pretty amazing."

Dolly lifted a stack of plates to the proper shelf. "Alice is the most beautiful creature to ever grace this Earth." She froze for a moment, as if the words had slipped out unbidden before clattering the rest of the plates into the pile.

The pieces clicked into place. Dolly had feelings for Alice. Beyond the platonic love of one member for another.

Autumn forced a bright smile. "Well, if you see her, tell her I'm looking for her, okay? I'm going to go help with chores."

Dolly didn't reply. She continued with her dish stacking while Autumn slid away toward the hallway exit and the stairwell. Yesterday, Alice had informed her with a childlike giggle that Wednesday was "Window Washing Wednesday," so that was what Autumn would do.

Alice had indicated that the utility closet on the third floor held a bunch of cleaning supplies. She'd assist the other residents of her floor with the window cleaning and wait for Alice to show.

Autumn passed Damien's office while another woman entered with a garbage bag. She headed for a wastebasket near the workspace, and Autumn spotted the landline phone on top of Damien's desk.

Aiden.

She desperately needed to get ahold of her boss and make him aware of her phone's status. But the feat was easier said than done. Harmony House was bustling at this time of day. Witnesses everywhere.

And Autumn couldn't think of a single reason why she would have "accidentally" wandered into Damien's private office. Going in there now meant blowing her cover to smithereens in a hot second.

Autumn climbed the staircase, unsure as to her next move. Without Alice, she really had no one to talk to and found it fascinating in her psychologist's mind how quickly she'd become attached to a complete stranger. But at the same time, Dolly was correct. There wasn't a mystery to the immediate friendship.

Alice Leeson *was* irreplaceable. As friendly as the rest of the Harmony House members had been toward her, Autumn didn't have the instant connection with any of them that she did with Alice. And judging from Alice's numerous admirers, the affection was widespread.

After spending an hour spraying and wiping windows, Autumn ventured back to the main floor. Damien would have made an appearance by now, and despite her disgust with the man and the imagery she'd be fighting off until the day she died, he was the only person she was sure would know where Alice was.

She entered the communal room and spotted the leader speaking with a red-cheeked Roberta. She'd taken two steps in that direction when the glass front doors burst open. Kyle and Ingrid Leeson charged into the house, appearing even more stricken than the previous day. Autumn's eyes widened as the two men rushed in behind them.

Deputy King and Agent Parker.

Both of them strode inside with neutral expressions. Chris's gaze skimmed over her without pausing, but his familiar presence alone was enough to flood her body with relief.

Thank god.

Two words she never would have guessed could be inspired by Agent Parker.

"You!" Kyle marched straight toward Damien. "You drove her to this!"

Damien's expression was equal parts angry and confused. "Drove her to what? And if you wouldn't mind keeping your voice down. This is a place of peace and—"

"She *hung herself* because of you!" Kyle grew louder. "I will not keep my voice down! You *killed our daughter*! You killed Alice!"

The anxiety that had been brewing in Autumn's chest all morning boiled over into a searing pain. Her fist flew to her mouth. She shook her head.

No. There had to be some mistake. Alice's father was wrong.

Damien's face drained of all color. "Alice...is *dead*? Alice is dead?"

"Yes, you sonofabitch!" Kyle was screaming now. Tears trickled down his cheeks, and his hands balled into fists. "You drove her to this madness!"

Ingrid Leeson stood behind her husband, silently sobbing. She didn't attempt to speak. Just stared at the floor and shook with grief.

The truth hit Autumn like a hammer. *Alice Leeson was dead.*

"I didn't do *anything*!" Damien turned to Deputy King. "What is he talking about? Is she really...*what is going on*!" Keeping the peace had gone by the wayside as Harmony House's gallant leader shouted at the law enforcement officials before him.

Deputy King confirmed the horror. "Alice Leeson was found this morning hanging from a tree on the Leeson family's property. No signs of struggle or coercion, and no one here is under investigation. It appears she took her own life, but we'll know more after her autopsy is completed. The Leesons are here to collect Alice's belongings."

Autumn began to tremble. Another set of broken, devastated parents. Poor Leesons.

Poor Alice.

Her breathing grew sharp, like she'd swallowed glass.

"This is *your* fault!" Damien roared at Kyle, making everyone jump with the suddenness of the attack. "You and your wife came barging in here spouting your ridiculous guilt trips! Alice was destroyed after you left! *You did this to her!* You made her feel like she had to go back to that loveless home, and she did. Are you happy now? *Are you?*"

Kyle growled and lunged forward until his nose almost touched Damien's. "She was destroyed the second she stepped foot into *your nutjob cult!* You brainwashed my daughter! You stole her from us! *I will end you for this!*"

"Mr. Leeson." Chris clamped a large hand on the man's shoulder. "You need to calm down. We'll get the answers you need, but you have to get ahold of yourself, or I'll be forced to remove you from the property."

Ingrid came alive at that. She skirted Chris and Kyle to stand before Damien. "And if you think for one second that Alice's recent revision to her trust fund is going to stand up in court, you're wrong. You will not see a cent of her money. *Not. One. Cent.*"

From within her shock, Autumn's brain signaled an alert. *Oh, god...had Damien murdered Alice for her trust fund?*

"You think I'm concerned about Alice's *money?*" Damien's voice cracked. "I will be mourning your daughter for the rest of my life."

"No." Ingrid slapped Damien's cheek, shocking them all. "You don't get to mourn our daughter. You killed her. You will burn in hell for this, you unbelievable bastard."

Kyle grabbed Ingrid's arm and pulled her backward before she could assault Damien again. She collapsed in her husband's arms, her wails resuming.

Autumn stared numbly at them all. *Alice would hate all this fighting. So, so much.*

"Let me get you folks outside." Deputy King gestured toward the front door. "I'll drive you back to the station. We will sort this out, Mr. and Mrs. Leeson. I promise you."

"You're not going to arrest him?" Kyle's outrage echoed off the communal room's ceiling.

Deputy King shot Damien a loathe-filled glare. "I'm sorry, Mr. Leeson, but there's nothing that makes the man a suspect. Yet."

"Bullshit." Kyle pointed a finger at Damien. "I will take this to the district attorney. Don't think for a damn second that this is over. We *will* find justice for Alice." He held Ingrid close, and the couple seemed to crumble into each other as they were escorted toward the door by a grim Deputy King.

When Chris glanced at Autumn, she barely pulled herself together in time to mimic holding a phone by her ear and mouth, *"Broken."* There was enough commotion taking place to distract from their swift exchange.

He began to pull his own phone from his pocket, but she shook her head. Chris halted, dropping the device back into his jacket.

She needed a new phone, but absolutely could not be seen with it.

Chris cleared his throat and turned to Damien. "The Leesons would like to collect Alice's belongings."

Damien shook his head. Autumn could see the tears glistening in his eyes from across the room. "We don't own anything at Harmony House. All have what they need. Belongings are a part of your world. Alice had none. She didn't want any."

To his credit, Chris kept whatever smart-ass comment he was most certainly thinking to himself. "The Leesons may take legal umbrage with that statement. I'll leave it be for now, but expect to see us soon, Mr. Parr."

Following Deputy King and the Leesons to the exit, Chris gave a quick nod to Autumn. Her heart sank as he disappeared through the door.

She was on her own. Again.

Only this time, Alice was gone too.

The room was full of frantic discourse. Sobs, moans, and cries of anguish filled the air with a dark fog of gloom. Autumn tried not to picture the scene that the Leesons woke to that day...to no avail.

Beautiful Alice with her long blonde hair swinging from a tree.

Another suicide tied to Harmony House.

Autumn fought back her tears and focused on the fire of rage burning inside of her. Alice had been upset after her parents left but not suicidal. The woman was too selfless to have ever purposely caused such a level of grief for her friends and family.

Scanning the room full of grief-stricken faces, Autumn made a silent vow.

I promise to find your murderer, Alice. I promise to find them and make them pay.

27

Aiden paced the conference room, processing the news of Alice Leeson's "suicide." Sheriff Frank had gotten word of the tragedy before Aiden and his team even arrived at the police station. Winnie met him at the door and informed him of everything she knew.

Ingrid Leeson had spotted their daughter's body from the kitchen window while making breakfast. Dangling from their tree. Time of death hadn't yet been established, but there was an obvious overnight window of opportunity.

Deputy King and Agent Parker were sent an hour north to the Leesons' home to collect the bereaved couple and bring them to the station. No one considered them suspects, per se, but they could possess vital information as the first to arrive at the scene of Alice's death.

Faking a hanging without leaving any defensive wounds wouldn't have been an easy feat for anyone. Though the initial report stated that there were no signs of foul play, Aiden wanted the medical examiner's full autopsy results before he accepted Alice Leeson's death as "just another suicide in Beechum County."

He didn't buy it. Not this time. Coincidence ceased to be an optimal explanation when the remarkable became the norm.

Someone had murdered Alice. He could feel the truth of that in his gut and was convinced more than ever that Harmony House was harboring a murderer. Maybe several.

And Autumn was smack-dab in the thick of it all.

Sheriff Frank walked into the room, followed by Deputy King and Chris. Mia, Winter, and Noah entered seconds after. Everyone was grim and uneasy...with good cause.

Beechum County was becoming a veritable corpse collection site.

Aiden's team all sat around the conference table while Sheriff Frank took her usual stance, leaning against the wall with crossed arms. "All right, Deputy King, Agent Parker. Update us."

Simon took the lead before Chris could open his mouth. "Well, for starters, Kyle and Ingrid Leeson are as upset as I've ever known two people to be, but I guess that goes without saying. They believe Damien Parr is responsible for Alice taking her own life."

"We stopped at Harmony House so they could pick up Alice's belongings," Chris stepped in. "But apparently, no one at that fruit farm 'owns' anything. That didn't even matter. Kyle Leeson was through the door screaming his head off at Parr two seconds after we parked the damn car. Huge shocker here, but Damien denies any wrongdoing and blames Alice's parents for her suicide."

Deputy King cleared his throat. "Turns out they made a drop-in visit the day before, and things got ugly. Emotional and whatnot. Alice wouldn't leave with them, but Ingrid swears her daughter wanted to come home. Meanwhile, Parr says they pushed her over the edge by blindsiding her with that visit and pouring on the ultimate guilt trip."

"Did you believe him?" Aiden focused on Chris. "Analyze that conversation with Parr. Would you say his behavior was sincere?"

Chris lifted a shoulder. "The guy was pretty upset. If he was faking, he should move to Hollywood 'cause he missed his calling. But if he's the sociopath we've been profiling, he *would* be an excellent liar."

"And," Winter piped up from her seat beside Noah, "his emotions could have been the real deal even if he was involved with her death. He wouldn't be the first killer to experience remorse after the fact."

"I don't like this any more than the rest of you," Sheriff Frank approached the table, "but we have to consider the obvious. Hanging someone is a difficult physical task. There would have been close contact, and Alice would have no doubt fought back. Even if she ultimately was defeated, she'd have defensive wounds. And unless someone else has an update I don't, she didn't have markings of that nature on her body."

Aiden turned toward Sheriff Frank. "We won't know that for sure until the autopsy is complete. Don't count that out yet."

Mia raised her pen. "When we visited Harmony House, there was a clear sense of devotion—*adoration*—toward Damien from his followers. If they truly view him as some sort of prophet or godlike figure, who's to say he couldn't just tell Alice to kill herself and have her obey? Maybe he hadn't intended for her to completely go through with the act. It could have been a test of devotion gone wrong."

Quiet settled over the room. There were so many bizarre possibilities that could very well be the true story. Cults were breeding grounds for the outlandish.

"Something else." Deputy King broke the silence. "Ingrid Leeson mentioned Alice having recently made revisions to her trust fund. She wanted Parr to know that he wouldn't see a cent of the money."

Chris snorted. "And then Ingrid slapped him upside the head."

Aiden could hear the bells of lawsuits tolling from the Beechum County Courthouse. He didn't blame the woman, but her slip could prove costly for the Leesons.

"He's not pressing charges," Deputy King assured them. "I called him when we first got here, to cover that molehill before the mountain fiasco could happen. He said he has no intention of pressing any charges against Ingrid Leeson, and he will cooperate with law enforcement in any way necessary regarding Alice's suicide."

"I bet he will." Winter narrowed her eyes. "He's got members dropping left and right *in addition to* suspected money laundering charges, and god knows what else. He's going to play nice from here on out because he knows he's in deep shit, whether he killed anyone or not."

"I spoke with Agent Grant." Mia made the announcement so calmly that Aiden did a double take. "She was overseas around the same time as Damien and even worked with him once. He had quite the reputation for being mixed up with the wartime black market, and she's pretty sure that was the reason for his discharge. She also found it hard to believe that Damien would be involved in any type of charity work unless he had something to gain from it."

Aiden agreed with Agent Grant's summation, but the pride warming his chest was for Mia. No way picking up the phone and calling the woman she blamed for her brother's death was an easy task, but she'd done it anyway.

Mia locked eyes with him. "Someone in her unit told her that Damien thought he had the right to make black market purchases and distribute the bounty as he saw fit, government be damned."

"God complex." Noah verbalized Aiden's exact thought. "The man thinks he's above the law. *All* of the laws."

Winter curled her lip. "Not hard to get why the Bureau's been eyeballing him and his 'charitable' community establishment."

Chris propped his elbows on the table. "Autumn doesn't have a phone anymore. I don't know how, but hers broke. She gave me the impression that she was fine, but she can't reach any of us. I was going to leave her my phone somehow, but she seemed pretty adamant that doing so was a no-go. Or at least as adamant as an undercover mime can be. We were surrounded by those whackos."

Aiden's entire body tensed. On the one hand, there was a great relief in knowing Autumn was all right and that there was a logical explanation for her failure to call.

On the other hand, the idea of her stuck in that place with no way of contacting him triggered a fresh burst of panic in his chest.

What happened if circumstances took a dark turn? He and the rest of the team would have no way of knowing. None.

He stood. "We have to get her a phone. I'm not leaving her in there with no line to the outside world. It's too dangerous." He didn't add that what he really wanted to do was go blow her cover and pull her out of Parr's reach altogether.

"We could go back." Chris leaned back in his chair. "Say we need to question some of the group. We should be doing that anyway. I'll find a way to slip her the phone without anyone knowing."

Aiden noted how professional and *normal* Agent Parker was behaving. If the man could stay in this mode for the rest of his career, he'd be fine. All that'd be left to deal with was Parker's ridiculous blond plumage, and one trip to a proper barbershop could knock that issue out pronto.

"That's not a bad plan." Sheriff Frank pointed at King. "You wanna go back in there and do some questioning?"

Deputy King nodded, agreeable as always. "Of course. You comin' with?"

The sheriff's lips peeled away from her teeth in a genuine smile. "Wouldn't miss it."

A hush fell over the room. Aiden apparently wasn't the only agent alarmed by Sheriff Frank's out-of-character show of good humor. Chris's jaw had dropped, Mia's head tilted as she stared at the woman in fascination, and Noah and Winter seemed to be having an eye-widening competition.

"Okay." The SSA tried to regroup. "Sheriff Frank, Deputy King, and Agent Parker can head back to Harmony House and question its members. Chris, I'm putting it on you to get the new burner to Agent Trent."

Chris sat up straighter and nodded, appearing to be honored by the assignment. At some point, Parker had convinced himself that everyone hated him and wanted him fired, which had never been the case. Aiden had brought Chris onto his team because he believed in the agent's abilities and considered his addition to the BAU an asset. Agent Parker's attitude needed fixing, but most of them had certain demons they were trying to conquer while performing their jobs.

If Chris could hold himself together like this while also sorting through his personal issues, he'd be fine. Aiden's eyes moved down the table to Winter, who appeared to be quite composed herself today. A little of the tension in his stomach eased.

"Noah and Mia," he continued the assignments, "I'd like you to call in Bradley Garland and Yvette Wilder. I want to know more about the financial side to these deaths. Who would have given Parr a profit by taking their own life? The two of you can interview Garland. Winter and I will take Ms. Wilder."

Noah and Winter exchanged a startled look while the rest of the team nodded. Neither of them had expected to be split up, and while he wasn't keen on tearing Noah away from Winter's side considering her condition, Aiden needed to work with her himself to get a clearer picture of what was going on.

"I'll go make the calls." Mia was up and out the door without hesitation.

Sheriff Frank gestured toward Simon and Chris. "Deputy. Agent. Let's head out."

Aiden closed his eyes for a moment and pictured Autumn sitting among the Harmony House followers. She'd have a new phone soon, and his anxiety levels would take an extensive drop.

Agent Trent was going to be fine, and soon, Damien Parr would be publicly outed as the monster he was.

He dragged a hand down his face. Soon couldn't come quickly enough.

AIDEN OBSERVED Yvette Wilder as she sipped water from the Styrofoam cup Winter had given her. The woman wasn't crying, neither did she seem particularly angry. Blank. Aiden thought that Kenneth Wilder's sister appeared blank from the shock of her loss.

He and Winter faced Yvette across a small table in Beechum Police Station's only interrogation room. Generally, there were separate areas designated for questioning witnesses and interrogating suspects, and he was more than a little apologetic for the drab surroundings Yvette found herself in.

Aiden attempted a pleasant demeanor. "I'm Supervisory Special Agent Aiden Parrish, and this is my colleague Special Agent Winter Black. We wanted to bring you back in, Yvette, because we have a few more questions about Kenneth's affairs."

She tilted her head, gray eyes boring into Aiden almost as though she didn't register his presence at all. "His affairs?"

Winter leaned forward, her expression kind but determined. "Did Kenneth have a trust fund that was maybe only transferrable in the event that he passed?"

Yvette's glare sharpened. "Not a trust fund, but he had an inheritance. He would have had full access to it when he turned forty, but I guess that's not going to happen now, is it?"

"And in the event of his death...?" Winter pressed. Her voice was even, and her hands appeared to have steadied.

Good. Seeing her in action calmed some of the alarms that had been clanging in his head.

"He could leave the money to whomever he wanted." Yvette emitted a heavy sigh. "Until very recently, the money would have stayed within the family."

"What changed that, Yvette?" Aiden could guess, but Yvette needed to say the words.

She snorted in disgust. "He signed everything over to a local charity called Stand Strong. He said in the event of his death, he wanted his money to 'mean something.' So, he gave it to those people, who I've never even heard of before. I've already checked into fighting it, but my lawyer says the document is legal and binding. The only way to keep them from taking that money is to prove that they took Kenneth's life."

Winter patted Yvette's hand. "Ma'am, please know we are doing everything we can to bring you closure. This information is useful."

Yvette wrinkled her brow. "The other Beechum suicides...they were trust funders?"

Aiden navigated the question, hating times like these when he couldn't be completely honest with the mourners left behind. "It's an avenue we're pursuing."

"I want to know the second that Harmony House bastard gets taken down." Yvette's eyes pled with Winter first before shifting to Aiden. "Promise you'll call me when he's been taken down."

Aiden hesitated. Promising a mourning family member anything was a bad idea. They still had no proof that the suicides were murders. While Parr was almost certainly motivated by monetary greed, that didn't make him a killer.

An asshole, yes, but not a killer.

"I will call you myself," Winter blurted. "I promise you."

Aiden bit back a groan. *Really, Agent Black?*

Meanwhile, Yvette teared up and yanked a tissue from her purse. "Thank you. My brother had a rough time of it, but he was a *good* person. He deserves justice."

Still shaking his head, Aiden opened the door and prepared to usher Yvette out, but she hurried past him without a word.

Once she disappeared, he turned to Winter and frowned. "Well, Agent Black. What do you tell Yvette if Damien Parr turns out to be innocent?"

Winter pressed her lips together. "He's not innocent."

"Okay." Aiden crossed his arms and leaned back against the cement bricked wall. "Let's say he's guilty. What if we don't catch him?" He studied her face.

Her reply was immediate. "We will."

Instead of pissing him off, the stubborn lift of her chin sent relief washing over Aiden. Winter wasn't one hundred percent yet, but she had her fire back. In this line of work, a bit of flame went a long way.

He smiled, wishing he could find a way to tell her how proud he was. She'd been through hell more than a few times and always found her way back. Even if the current road to recovery was longer and rockier than any of them liked, Winter was walking it.

She wasn't giving up. She was fighting.

"What?" She stared back at him, the question echoing in her blue eyes.

He waved a hand toward the door. "Good work, Agent. Let's go check if Noah and Mia have anything to add to—"

Mia burst into the room, her cheeks flushed. "Natalie didn't have a trust fund, but she did have a savings account that she had willed toward a charity called Stand Strong. The document wasn't notarized by any legal entity, so the Garlands are fighting it. Bradley suspects Parr is behind that business as well, and he's determined that Damien won't get a dollar of Natalie's money."

Winter slapped the table. "That's the same charity Kenneth Wilder willed his inheritance to. His sister said she'd never even heard of it."

Aiden held up a hand while he considered the information. "We need to dig up whatever we can on this Stand Strong organization and *fast*."

Noah popped up behind Mia's shoulder. "Been there. Done that. Stand Strong has ties to a shell company that doesn't trade on any exchanges and has no employees on record."

"Well, that's suspicious as hell. Go on, then!" Aiden clapped his hands together one time. "Dig deeper. All of you."

Noah, Mia, and Winter rushed from the room. Aiden followed at a more controlled speed, the wheels in his head spinning.

The pieces were falling into place. Proving Damien Parr was a criminal finally seemed within their grasp. The

Harmony House slimeball may not have killed anyone, but they were steps away from linking him to the suicides via money. Once that happened, the truth behind how all those Beechum County residents had died might come to light more easily.

Of course, Parr was a crafty son of a bitch. There was every chance he'd realize the authorities were closing in, and a cornered psychopath was a dangerous one.

Aiden's pace slowed as fresh worry pulsed through his veins.

Autumn.

No matter how fast they worked, there was the chance that they wouldn't be fast enough. If Parker didn't get that phone to her, Aiden was considering compromising her cover altogether. He didn't care how pissed off Autumn might be at the intrusion.

A mad Autumn was fixable. A dead Autumn wasn't.

Aiden clenched his jaw and hurried after the others. One way or another, he needed to get Autumn the hell out of Harmony House's shadow.

28

F or the second time in twenty-four hours, Autumn found herself sitting on the hard floor inside the barren church, forming one tiny portion of a human circle. Only now, there was no Alice Leeson beside her to offer friendship and infuse everyone with her effervescent joy.

Damien had gathered everyone together before lunch and led them to the church. Once again, they formed a perfect sphere without a single word of direction.

There was a solemnness today that was absent yesterday. An emptiness that seemed to settle into the very walls. The shock of Alice's death had touched every person in the room, brushing them with sorrow.

As Autumn stared at the spot on the floorboards Alice had occupied last night, her sorrow was accompanied by knifelike pains in her gut. Guilt. She was a federal agent. Here at Harmony House on an undercover assignment to flush out a possible killer. To save lives.

Instead, Alice Leeson had died under her watch. No, she'd died while Autumn had *slept*, all snug in the bed Alice had shown her.

Just one more person you've failed in life. No big deal. Just keep racking up that body count, Agent Trent.

Her throat burned. Her eyes burned. She pressed her hands to her abdomen to apply pressure against the pain. Roberta sat to her left, Chelsea to her right, both of them sobbing openly.

The entire group was a veritable chorus of sorrow.

Damien cleared his throat, causing a hush to fall over his mournful assembly. "Loved ones, today we have suffered a great loss to the Circle. Alice was a dear friend and a kind soul. Her beautiful spirit enriched the very air that we breathe here at Harmony House." His voice faltered on the last word.

Tears brimmed in Damien's crystal blue eyes. Autumn decided his grief was genuine, but that didn't mean the leader was innocent. "Crimes of passion" was a well-known label for good reason. Such murders happened more often than anyone wanted to believe.

During her Quantico training classes, she'd learned that the U.S. Bureau of Justice Statistics estimated that spouses were responsible for thirty percent of all murdered females, and that number only seemed to rise each passing year.

To have and to hold, to love and to cherish, to murder in cold blood.

Damien Parr hadn't been married to Alice—not in the traditional sense—but he'd certainly displayed an air of ownership over all his female followers. The fact that the women weren't allowed to have any relationships with the other men until Damien banged them in his creepy-ass Ceremony was enough evidence to indicate that Damien considered the females his personal property.

A shuddering sob pulled her attention to the left. Dolly Oleson appeared heartbroken, the force of her grief curling her body into a ball. Almost like her love for Alice had run deeper than mere friendship.

If Dolly had been infatuated with Alice, Autumn was pretty sure those feelings hadn't been returned.

And really, was there any future for the two even if the feelings were mutual? Autumn hadn't noticed any same-sex couples amongst the group. In fact, she hadn't glimpsed a couple of *any* type.

All the women appeared to be fully dedicated to Damien, post-Ceremony or otherwise.

Autumn stared at Dolly's heaving shoulders. Living in denial under the situational restrictions was enough to push anyone to the edge of their sanity.

Had it driven Dolly Oleson to murder?

She didn't think so, but she'd also learned at Quantico never to get tunnel vision.

A choked sob from the opposite direction echoed off the church ceiling. Autumn followed the sound and spotted Evan Blair in a losing battle with his misery.

Evan was another who'd cared for Alice as more than a friend. Maybe the thought of Alice joining and belonging to Damien was too much for the man. Maybe his adoration for Damien was a front, designed to hide a seething hatred of Harmony House's handsome figurehead.

Then again, everywhere Autumn looked, she was met with a grief-stricken face. Any one of them could have also fancied themselves in love with Alice. Hell, Autumn had only known the woman for a brief time, and she was half in love with Alice herself.

Her gaze settled on Chelsea. Maybe she was focusing on the wrong thing. Jealousy was a powerful motivator. What if one of the many women who believed themselves in love with Damien had hated Alice for existing at all?

She rubbed her temples as theory after theory pulsed

through her head. One killer? Two? A group? Were some of the suicides real while the majority were not...or vice versa? Was the killer a sadist who simply enjoyed killing, like Justin Black? Or was the perpetrator under the belief that they were fulfilling a duty of some sort? A calling?

Serial killers traditionally fell under one of several types. There was the visionary, who believed that someone or thing —a god or the devil—was commanding him to kill. This person suffered from some kind of psychosis and was generally disorganized, killing as the voice told him to.

The mission-oriented killer murdered in order to "rid" society of a certain group while the hedonistic killer committed acts for his own personal pleasure, which could range from rape, torture, or money.

Then there was the killer who murdered for power or control. For him, dominating the victim was of paramount importance.

Damien Parr could be a combination of all four of those types.

The room started to spin. Autumn clutched her head, waiting for the dizziness to pass. She'd barely eaten the day before and not at all that morning. Every hour she spent on Harmony House grounds, her surroundings grew foggier when what she needed was for the truth to become clear.

She never could have predicted any of this. The friendship she'd developed with Alice in such a fleeting period of time. The deep agony pumping through her veins at the loss of the bond. How very normal the Harmony House members were.

Part of her had entered into this mission thinking she'd be a rare beacon of rationality amongst a throng of "out there" individuals.

Instead, she'd discovered people. Normal people. And while their "religion" was admittedly unorthodox, they really didn't seem any different from the crowds that filled other churches, mosques, and temples across the nation.

The only major difference lay in the lack of judgment on Harmony House grounds. The total acceptance of one's fellow man was real.

"I know you are all hurting," Damien continued, his voice hoarse, "but what we need to focus on right now is the light that Alice was to the world and the love that she believed all were deserving of. Alice embodied the best of us all. Grace and mercy…compassion and forgiveness."

Murmurs of agreement rippled through the group, and fresh tears streamed down multiple faces. No one could or would argue Damien's statements, least of all Autumn. Alice was the closest thing to an angel made flesh that Autumn had ever encountered.

Damien raised his hands toward the ceiling. "Alice showed kindness to all, regardless of whether or not they knew or understood the way to the light. She felt called to lead others out of the darkness and held firm that all deserved endless forgiveness. A second chance. And a third. And a fourth…" His voice broke, and he cleared his throat, his hands still in the air. "And my friends, she believed with great certainty that we should forgive ourselves as well. *Love ourselves* as well."

Tears spilled down Autumn's cheeks. She didn't bother swiping them away. There was no need to hide her pain from these people who were also in mourning. Everyone here had experienced the streams of never-ending kindness that flowed from Alice Leeson's heart firsthand.

"Please, my brethren," Damien's tears also fell unchecked, "repeat these words with me in honor of our dear Alice and her spotless soul. All possess light. All deserve love. We are the change."

Voice upon voice repeated the words with a steadfast yet

brokenhearted conviction that raised goose bumps on Autumn's arms. She found herself repeating the phrases too. Loud and clear, while the stirring in her chest grew impossible to ignore.

So many years of attempting to be stoic and brave, but she was still essentially just a lost little girl…beaten down and hobbled by her past and unsure of what to do next. All the degrees and badges in the world didn't make her inner torment less real.

A part of her was still that little girl getting slammed into a coffee table, enduring emergency brain surgery, being ripped away from her sister, and sent off to live with multiple strangers who did not love her.

There wasn't a Band-Aid, proverbial or otherwise, big enough to cover those wounds. And a piece of her was exhausted, falling apart, *wailing* from the constant burden of proving she was "okay."

The voices soared around her, raising her up like a thousand beating wings. Buoying Autumn with the courage to finally admit the truth.

She wasn't okay. She never had been.

And Alice had recognized that all along.

Right from the start, Alice Leeson had perceived how broken Autumn was. Why shouldn't she? Autumn's cover story was steeped in painful truths. She was exactly the type of person Harmony House sought to heal. Given a different turn or two in life, she may have ended up somewhere very much like Harmony House all on her own.

She'd entered the cult to spectate the strange and disturbed minds that dwelt with Damien Parr, only to have a mirror held up to her own abnormalities and devastation.

As the meditative chant ceased, Autumn's eyes locked with Damien's. Their silent commiseration, authentic and powerful, threw even more confusion spinning through her head.

Was Damien Parr a killer?

She couldn't be sure.

What she did know was that Damien was a person, and he was in pain.

Don't get sucked into his orbit. You can mourn the loss of Alice, you can mourn the loss of your childhood, and you can witness the humanity in a monster without forgetting that someone murdered that sweet woman and possibly many more unsuspecting souls. You are here to find that person. Find them and make them answer for what they did!

She shuddered, the brief pep talk recentering her just enough to break away from Damien's hypnotic gaze. Conflicting emotions ran rampant through her mind, but one truth remained clear. She had to pull herself together and end this slew of deaths before another cold, stiff body was found.

A visibly uncomfortable Evan excused himself from the group to slink through the back door. As some of the others rose to their feet, Autumn took the opportunity to slip through the crowd after him. Her shoulder blades burned as she reached the exit. She didn't need to turn to guess whose attention she'd snagged.

Deep in despair as he was, the Harmony House leader still kept a keen eye on his devoted followers.

Evan hadn't ventured far from the building. He sagged against a nearby tree, like he was relying on the support to hold him upright.

"Hey." She didn't mask the misery in her voice as she approached. "Are you doing okay?"

He appeared to fight back yet another teary breakdown and shook his head. "No. I'm not okay. I'll never be okay again."

Autumn stepped closer. "You and Alice were really close, weren't you?"

Evan stared at the ground, his chin trembling. "We spent a lot of time together. She was special to me."

"It's hard." As Autumn watched, a tear dripped off Evan's cheek onto the lush green lawn. Her own eyes burned in response. "Suicide…it's so unfair. I've lost a few friends that way over the years too. Lately, I feel like every time you turn around, there's another news report about somebody taking their own life. What's wrong with this world?"

He shook his head, not meeting her stare and unable to respond. Evan Blair reminded her of an abandoned puppy. He truly didn't know what to do without Alice in his life.

Autumn decided to push her luck a little. Any reaction from the grieving man could be informative. "I mean, what is this place doing wrong if someone like Alice is so unhappy here that she just kills herself? I think there was another girl from here that did the same not too far back. Shit. You probably knew her too." She let the very real heartache eating at her chest spill into her voice. "I thought Harmony House was going to offer me peace and love…a fresh start. But I'm beginning to doubt that."

Evan's head whipped toward her, anger tightening his features. "That's blasphemy. You should never say such a thing. Harmony House is a mecca for healing. Damien puts his heart and soul into helping the downtrodden. No one can help everybody. It just isn't possible."

Her focus sharpened. She'd hit a nerve, and she intended to press on the sore spot harder. "But Alice put her heart and soul into helping people too. She was so happy about the changes she'd made in her life and the path she'd chosen to follow by living here. How could someone that full of joy just end it all so easily?"

"Nothing about death is easy." Evan's voice grew raspy,

and his expression returned to a clear image of sorrow. "None of them wanted to go out the way they did." He shook his head, gazing into the sky as though he'd forgotten where he was altogether.

Autumn stiffened, turning the statement over and dissecting each syllable.

"None of them wanted to go out the way they did."

Not just Alice. *"Them."*

Was he referring to Natalie as well as Alice? What did Evan know? What did Evan mean? He was so blindly devoted to Damien that it occurred to her as possible that the younger man would do whatever he was told. He may have loved Alice, but his loyalty lay with his leader.

And Damien Parr only led his devotees down paths that served *his* purposes and gain.

Maybe the almighty authority of Harmony House had acted on his own, and Evan was speaking on a hunch. Maybe they'd both been involved.

Or maybe Evan had simply meant that no soul genuinely wanted to leave this world by taking their own life.

Autumn's head throbbed. Instead of answers, she'd come up with yet more theories to consider.

Evan crossed his arms, hugging himself tight in the July heat. "Damien might know more about what was really going on in her head. I know he went to speak with her last night." He sighed heavily. "I thought I might have seen them getting into one of the Harmony House cars. Maybe they went for a drive so she could talk or whatever. I dunno. They were a lot closer than the rest of us realized."

Autumn's heart stopped at the revelation, but she kept her expression neutral. "They take drives sometimes? Does he do that with everybody?"

"No." Evan shook his head again, his chin trembling. "Just with Alice. She was special to him."

Damien and Alice went for car rides? Alice had mentioned nothing of the sort, but there were two good explanations for that. One, she may have believed the drives to be innocent. Just a couple of friends helping each other through life. Or two, there may have been something going on between herself and Damien that she was embarrassed or even ashamed of.

"Whatever you're thinking, you're wrong." Autumn startled at Evan's comment, wondering what her expression had revealed. "Damien would never do anything to hurt a faithful servant. The faithful have his full protection."

Autumn's pulse picked up speed. "And what about the *unfaithful*? What happens to them, Evan?"

He stared at her for a long, uncomfortable moment before loping off toward the main building. Autumn considered running after him but knew he wasn't going to give her any more intel. Not right now. Evan had probably let more information slip than he'd intended.

Besides, she'd been away from the group for too long. The communal mourning was still taking place. Evan might be able to disappear in such a manner, but he wasn't a brand-new face on the premises. Damien wouldn't think twice about his absence.

Hers, on the other hand, would definitely be noted.

As she'd expected, Damien caught her reentry before the door even closed. His eyebrows drew together as he strode across the room, weaving through scattered clusters of mourners. "Where were you?"

Autumn lifted a shoulder and boldly squared her gaze with his. "This is a super heavy morning, and I'm having a really challenging time processing everything. I needed some air."

Damien's posture remained stiff. "And where is Evan?"

"I have no idea." Autumn gestured toward the back door.

"I spotted him leaving before me and just figured he wanted the same thing. Fresh air. But he wasn't out there."

Her pulse accelerated at the calculated risk. If she'd been honest about speaking with Evan, Damien was almost sure to hunt him down. Demand a word-for-word recounting of what Autumn had said.

But if Damien went in search of Evan anyway and asked if they'd talked...

Damien's eyes narrowed into slits as he stared at the exit, but his expression smoothed before speaking to her again. "I'm sure he's terribly upset. He cared a great deal for Alice."

There was an edge to his voice that inferred Evan's suffering was not his problem. Autumn was struck by the odd impression that Damien might even enjoy the thought of Evan falling to pieces over Alice's death.

Group members began dispersing from the church, some heading for their cabins and others walking toward the main building. As Damien glanced over his shoulder at the commotion, Autumn took advantage of the moment to escape.

"I'm going to the kitchen to help prepare the noon meal. I'll see you in a bit." She strode away from Damien without waiting for permission.

If she were lucky...*very* lucky...Evan wouldn't say a word about their conversation.

She reached the main building and jetted toward the communal kitchen, which was full of puffy-eyed women sniffling and letting out the occasional whimper as they chopped and diced away.

Her pulse gradually returned to normal. At the very least, she was safe here. No one was going to murder her in front of this many witnesses.

Probably.

By now, Chris should have been able to communicate her

lack of a phone to the team. They would surely formulate a plan to get back in touch with her.

Aiden hadn't been keen on the idea of sending her into Harmony House with a working phone. He was more than likely struggling not to come flying through the main entrance and blow her cover to pieces.

An engine rumbled as a car pulled up and parked in front of Harmony House, drawing the attention of the women in the kitchen. Autumn stretched her neck to peer out the window over the tops of all the curious heads.

Chris, Sheriff Frank, and Deputy King exited the police car and approached the building. Autumn joined the sea of other Harmony House members flooding the common room that surrounded the main entrance.

There was no knocking this time. The three law enforcement officials burst into the house with a palpable air of determination. Sheriff Frank scanned the crowd. "Where is Damien Parr?"

Damien barreled into the room from the hallway. "I'm right here. How can I help you?" The question was more of a bark.

Sheriff Frank narrowed her eyes. "We're here to question members of your group. This is not a request, Mr. Parr."

"No one at Harmony House has anything to hide." Damien held out both arms to indicate his fold. "Be my guest."

The sheriff gave Deputy King a nod, and he began to address the group. "No need to panic, folks. We know this has been a distressing day for you all. We're just here to gather some information, and we'd appreciate your cooperation. Anyone who considered themselves close to Alice Leeson, please step to this side of the room…"

While Deputy King droned on, Chris wandered in Autumn's direction. He pretended to study all the faces before settling on hers. "You. I'd like to begin my questioning with you."

Chris's glower and harsh tone were intimidating enough that Autumn had no problem cowering. "O-okay."

"In there." He pointed to the kitchen. "The rest of you wait until the sheriff, deputy, or I summon you."

Without another glance in her direction, Chris marched into the communal kitchen.

The tension in Autumn's spine was real as she followed. She prayed she passed for just another Harmony House resident, emotionally distraught over the horrible events of the morning hours.

And she hoped Chris Parker didn't use this opportunity to toss her under the bus.

29

C hris sat on a stool across from Autumn at a table covered with bowls of fresh fruit and cut vegetables, fighting the urge to grab a few alluring, plump blueberries. They were probably laced with crazy powder, and there was no way in hell he was getting sucked into this cracked-out version of *The Island of Misfit Toys*.

Whackjobs. Total whackjobs.

"Please state your name." Chris checked the doorway, making sure his command was being obeyed.

"U-um. Autumn Nichol." She was doing a bang-up job of keeping her cover, but Chris found her annoying all the same.

Autumn Trent had always irritated him, and he didn't foresee that changing. She shouldn't have ever gotten this assignment over someone like him.

"Okay." He grabbed a small notebook and pen from his jacket pocket, keeping his voice low. "No one is coming in here. Ease up on the performance, Bette Midler."

She flashed him an annoyed look. "Tell me you brought a phone."

He nodded, scribbling random words onto the paper. "Since you've been in here, another body was found. Kenneth Wilder. Heroin overdose. Needle still in his arm and no sign of restraint. He was a member of Harmony House and had recently expressed a desire to leave. His sister says she'd spoken to him the day before on the phone, and he was happy to be going home."

Autumn stiffened. "Another faked suicide?"

Chris eyed the doorway again before responding. He didn't want any of those fruitcakes sneaking up on him. "His sister thinks so. She said Kenneth had some problems with the law but hadn't used drugs in years."

"Damien is behind all of this." Autumn's voice was sharp with anger even as she kept the volume low. "I'm sure of it. I believe he's considered tossing one of his most loyal followers off a cliff. And there are some absurd and frankly unhealthy rituals and rules in place here that make him a veritable king amongst peasants. He thinks he *owns* these people."

"He told you that?" Chris struggled to keep his voice even. "About the cliff?"

Autumn hesitated, clasping her hands together. "Not exactly, but he's a dangerous man."

Voices near the door made them both jump, but the chatter faded away without anyone walking in. Chris fought off an unmanly shiver. "I agree. He's too dangerous. You need to get the hell out of here before you're just another suicide."

"No." She shook her head, her unkempt red hair flying around like Medusa's snakes.

"*Yes.*" He leaned in, scribbling gibberish on his pad. "Make a scene or something. Cause a disturbance. I'll arrest you and take you straight out the front door. Boom. Just like that. Back to safety."

He hoped that Autumn wasn't mistaking his insistence

for actual concern. The only reason he was pushing this so hard was his premonition that if harm did come to this stubborn bitch, Aiden would never forgive him. The old man might even fire him or make him transfer units.

Autumn Trent had screwed Chris's life up enough already. He wasn't going to hand her yet another opportunity to do so.

"I'm not leaving." She calmly grabbed one of the fat blueberries and popped it into her mouth, which only pissed him off more. "I'm going to see this mission through. I have to find justice for Alice and all the others. I'm in good here, Chris. They're buying my story."

Chris ground his molars back and forth, wanting to push her off her stool and leave. "It's a risky plan. I'm not sure I can allow that."

Her cheeks flamed red as she shot him a death glare. *"You* are not in charge of me, Chris Parker. Don't you dare blow my cover. *It's not your damn call."*

He considered the ultimate elation to be found in ruining Miss Ph.D.'s first undercover mission for her. She'd hate him forever, but what the hell did he care?

He'd resented her since day one.

However, there was a far better prize awaiting him if he could just remain patient. Ruining Autumn's entire career would satisfy him in a manner that nothing else on the planet could. Imagining his daily life without this troublesome, know-it-all hag hanging around the BAU was a dream come true that he didn't want to screw up.

Just this morning, he'd received another text from his mystery friend instructing him to purchase a prepaid phone for further contact. Things were about to take off. He could feel it. And while he hadn't had the time to even get near a store because of all this Autumn-centered bullshit chaos, he would *make* the time.

Soon.

Chris considered the cell phone sitting in his jacket pocket. Autumn was being such a pain in the ass about staying in the middle of danger that he was tempted to "fail" to leave the device altogether.

Except, he was almost certain that both the sour-faced sheriff and dumbass sidekick of hers had both witnessed him escort Autumn into the kitchen. Sheriff Frank detested the entire BAU team, but Chris had a dick, so she probably hated him more.

She wouldn't miss any opportunity to throw him under the bus. Or a semi. Or a military-grade tank.

Plus, he had to take into account the fact that Aiden had trusted him with this task. Screwing up the one job he'd been sent to do wouldn't skyrocket his career with the BAU.

Chris jotted a few more notes down, then cursed when footsteps headed their way. He was out of time.

He stood, giving his notes a casual stare and wandering toward the counter. He seized a mug in the dishrack, pretended to give it a good inspection, then slyly pulled the phone from his pocket and slipped it into the mug before replacing the dish on the rack just as one of the cult women approached the doorway.

"Well, Miss Nichol." Chris couldn't remember why the surname seemed familiar. "I'm going to step out for a minute before my next interview, but I do believe we're done here."

He turned away from Autumn and walked through the kitchen doorway back into the sea of screwballs.

AUTUMN MOVED TO THE DISHRACK, grabbing a hanging towel and taking great care to dry a plate sitting near the mug. A few members wandered in and out of the kitchen, having witnessed the big bad law enforcement man's exit.

The trio of officials didn't stay long after that. Whatever questions they had regarding Alice had clearly been used as a cover to get Autumn the burner. She was certain a real investigation would occur in the near future.

She hand-dried several more dishes, waiting for a lull in the activity behind her. When the moment seemed right, she lifted the mug, seized the phone, and tucked it into the side of her bra through her short sleeve.

Her heart pounded as she waited, half-expecting someone to yell at her and demand that she hand over the phone.

When ten seconds passed without a peep, Autumn released the breath trapped in her lungs. Okay. No one had noticed. Now was the time to sneak off to her room to shoot Aiden a text or maybe even call, but she had to do so with convincing nonchalance.

Striving for a casual pace, Autumn strolled in the direction of the hall. She'd just passed the kitchen table when Dolly appeared in the doorway, blocking her escape.

The other woman smiled, but the gesture didn't reach her chestnut eyes. She jerked her chin toward Autumn's shirt. "What's in your pocket?"

Autumn's stomach knotted. Had Dolly peeked in on her conversation with Chris? Or eavesdropped?

Either way, she'd have to bluff her way out of this.

She turned her pockets inside out and raised a defiant eyebrow. "Nothing. What's in yours?" The phone dug into her ribs, the pinch making her brazen attitude easier to fake.

Dolly scowled and put her hands on her hips. "I know you weren't in here talking about Alice that entire time. I could see you through the doorway. He was telling you things, not questioning you."

Autumn made a dismissive gesture. "Oh, he did ask me

about Alice. I just haven't been here long enough to know anything. And then...he told me I was cute and wondered if we could go out on a date. I totally turned him down."

"Ri-ight." The way Dolly drew out the word told Autumn she wasn't buying her story. "We'll just see about that."

After a disgusted snort, Dolly pivoted and headed back toward the hallway. No doubt, running straight to her exalted leader with her suspicions. The question was, would Damien believe her?

That one was easy. *Of course* he would believe Dolly. The brunette was a proven follower, whereas Autumn had just arrived.

The scarier question was, what would he do about the accusations?

Icy dread spread through Autumn's veins as Alice's face flitted behind her eyes. Natalie's as well. Two women who'd almost certainly been killed when they'd upset someone at Harmony House.

Maybe someone exactly like Damien.

As Dolly disappeared around the corner, Autumn bit her cheek, tasting salt as she mentally ticked through her options.

Choice one. Tap out right now by running out the front door and calling Aiden to come pick her up...and pray Damien didn't run her down in a van first.

Choice two. Intercept Dolly before she poisoned Damien's ear against her and try to stick the assignment out.

Alice's pure, joyful laugh rang in her ears, reminding Autumn of her promise.

Her heartbeat quickened, and she hurried for the hallway.

She might have failed Alice in life, but she'd be damned if she'd fail her in death.

✳

MIA JUMPED in her seat as Aiden slammed his phone down. There were only two of them in the Beechum Police Station conference room now, and they hadn't spoken to each other for at least fifteen minutes.

He stood, a touch of smugness in his voice. "I knew it. *We* knew it. Cyber found ties from Stand Strong to the Parr family. They had to jump through a few legal hoops to get there, but the trail led through a series of tax documents and bank accounts that ended with our infamous 'D. Parr.' That bastard is just milking his followers for their money."

Relief coursed through Mia's limbs. They may not have established a direct connection to the suicides, but this was enough to get Damien Parr where they wanted him and uncover the thread that ran from Harmony House to the Grim Reaper.

"And the postmortem donations…" She shook her head, despising the asshole more now than ever.

Aiden gave a heated nod. "He likely had them set up so that even if they abandoned Harmony House, he could still profit from their deaths. Everyone has to die someday."

"Especially if you kill them." She chugged the last of her black coffee. Unfortunately, the bitter flavor did nothing to chase away her disgust.

Aiden's grin turned stone-cold when his phone rang. He hit the speaker button. "Agent Parker?"

"She's okay." Chris started with the phrase that Mia knew Aiden most wanted to hear. "I left her the burner, and she should be contacting you soon. But she's convinced that Parr is behind these deaths. Especially after I told her about Kenneth Wilder."

Aiden frowned. "If she's that sure about Parr, then why didn't you create some sort of distraction and get her out of there? All we needed was an inside look, and it sounds like she got a clear one. Why the hell is she still there?"

Mia wondered the same thing but kept quiet, giving Chris a chance to explain.

Chris's huff translated loud and clear through the phone. "She's there because she made the call to stay. She wants to get justice for Alice and the rest. I think the Leeson woman might have befriended her before she died. Autumn seemed hell-bent on vengeance."

Aiden was as tense as a drawn bow. Mia only hoped he didn't snap like one. The SSA paced a short distance, raking his hands through his hair before shaking his head. "That was *not* part of her undercover detail. You should have gotten her out."

"I got her the phone," Chris reminded the SSA. "That was the mission you gave me, and I did it."

Tension crackled down the line, and Mia braced herself when Aiden's hands tightened into fists. "She better stay okay, Chris. Are you at the meet-up point yet?"

The team had designated a spot about a mile away from Harmony House at the forest's edge.

"On the way with Frank and King." Mia winced when Chris's tone turned emotionless. "Be there soon." She winced again when he ended the call without another word, certain Aiden would take the action as a slight.

The frustrated SSA grabbed his briefcase and headed for the door. "Come on. Noah and Winter are already there. We need to join them and let them know about Stand Strong's ties to the Parrs."

Mia grabbed her purse and strode after him. "You have to give Chris a break on this one."

Aiden spun around. "Do I?"

His icy glare was intimidating, but Mia refused to back down. "Think about it." She tapped her temple with a finger. "This was Autumn's decision. Autumn's risk. How many times have you given Autumn the benefit of the doubt? And how many of those times were before she'd even gone to Quantico?"

She could tell Aiden wanted to argue, but there was no debate. She'd spoken the truth.

"The plan better work." He resumed charging out the door, on his way to rescue the woman who everyone aside from him knew he loved.

Mia mentally crossed her fingers for Autumn and Chris's sakes. The plan, foggy as it was, would work.

She refused to entertain the alternatives.

30

Autumn hurried down the hallway after Dolly, her pulse a frantic drumbeat in her ears.

If Dolly spoke to Damien, the best-case scenario was that her cover would likely be blown. As for the worst?

She moved faster. She didn't want to think about the worst.

As she narrowed the gap, she realized she didn't have much of a plan. Or any plan, really. Just the burning need to stop her house of cards from collapsing.

Remember, you're supposed to be a person without a place to go. Desperate. Willing to fight to keep this newfound shelter and food.

Desperate, okay. Good. She wouldn't even have to fake that.

Dolly was less than fifteen feet from Damien's door when Autumn turned on the speed and burst ahead of her. She had no real objective beyond reaching Damien first.

She only made it a step when Dolly snagged the back of her shirt, yanking her to a stop.

"Where do you think you're going?"

Crap. Autumn had hoped the pacifist, Kumbaya culture of

Harmony House would prevent Dolly from placinghands on another member, although technically, her shirt wasn't human.

Then again, the whole reason she was here was to flush out a murderer, so that might not have been her wisest assumption.

Think, Autumn. Remember, you're desperate. Someone who lives on the streets and has to fight for every little scrap.

She growled at Dolly over her shoulder. "If you rip my shirt, you'll be sorry. And not that it's any of your business, but I'm going to speak with Damien in his office. We have important matters to discuss."

"Nice try, but I don't think so." Dolly released her shirt. The next moment, she was barging past Autumn, bumping her shoulder in the process.

Heart pumping wildly, Autumn's hands shot out, and she shoved Dolly. Hard.

Never underestimate the power of distraction. One of her takeaways from Quantico.

"What the…" Dolly stumbled sideways before whirling on Autumn with all the fury of hell on her face. "How dare you!"

She lunged forward and pushed Autumn into the wall.

"Bitch," Autumn hissed. *Come on, Dolly. Keep taking the bait.*

Dolly's mouth tightened, but she stayed right where she was. "There is *no violence* on Harmony House grounds."

Autumn laughed and continued walking. "That's funny 'cause I'm pretty sure *you* just shoved the crap out of *me*."

They were side by side again within seconds, and Damien's office door was within sight.

"You don't belong here," Dolly muttered as she stomped. "And I don't trust you *at all*."

Autumn pounded a fist on Damien's door before turning to bat her eyes at Dolly. "That's funny because Alice sure did."

She sucked in a breath when the barb hit. A little too well, based on Dolly's rage-contorted face. If looks could kill, Autumn would be dead already. No fake suicide necessary.

Could Dolly be the killer?

The other woman bared her teeth. "Don't you say her name. Don't you *ever* speak her name." She grabbed Autumn's t-shirt collar and yanked the material taut to her neck.

The door swung open, and Damien's head appeared in the crack. His already troubled brow creased more as he took in the scene. "*What* is going on?"

Dolly gasped and released her grip. "I...I..."

Autumn seized the moment to press her advantage. "Damien, I'm so sorry to bother you, but I need to talk to you, and she's trying to stop me."

"What? She's a liar! She knows I was coming to talk to you first."

Autumn whimpered when Dolly spoke, scooting closer to Damien like she sought his protection. Nothing stroked an egomaniacal male's ego like a damsel in distress. "See what I mean? I don't know why she's acting like this. I think maybe she's just really upset. It's been such a hard afternoon...for all of us."

"For all of us? How *dare* you." Dolly threw an arm out and blocked the office entry. "You barely even knew her."

"Silence!" Damien raised a hand, causing Dolly to bow her head with immediate obedience. "This is not the way we treat our honored guests."

Autumn's eyes widened at the woman's sudden change of demeanor.

Dolly Oleson was not a weak woman, yet she folded in front of Damien like a blade of grass in the wind.

For better or worse, Damien's followers truly believed in him. They'd granted him authority and power over their lives as though he was their *god*. Dolly bowed to Damien because, at some point, she'd made the decision that he was "the answer." He was *the way*.

The only true path to light.

Autumn peeked up at Damien's face. "I am *so* sorry. I didn't mean to cause any trouble. I just have some important business matters to discuss with you, and I didn't want to wait any longer."

Interest sparked in his translucent gaze. The term "business" most often implied money, and Autumn was well aware that money was Damien's favorite word. And topic. And reason for waking each morning.

He smiled. "I've been wanting to talk to you as well. To check in on how you're doing in the wake of Alice's death. I know you two were close."

A strangled laugh escaped Dolly's mouth. Autumn experienced a pang of empathy, knowing what a gut punch Damien's sentiment must be. *He* was the reason Dolly had never been able to pursue Alice, yet the woman had still given him her full allegiance.

And now, he was passing her over for a chat with a veritable stranger.

Autumn didn't think for one second that Damien had made the comment about her friendship with Alice on accident. Those odd, magnetic eyes of his missed next to nothing. Dolly may have never vocalized her love for Alice, but she'd bet money Damien knew anyway.

Dolly's voice grew shaky. "What I have to talk to you about is also of great importance, Damien. Does that not matter?"

He pulled Dolly into a hug, surprising Autumn. She'd expected him to give a sharp reprimand, but the man seemed to know how to pick his battles. He caressed Dolly's brown tresses as though she were a baby. "We will have time together soon. There's no need for jealousy. I have infinite love to give."

Autumn held down a powerful gag reflex while Dolly pulled away from Damien. Anger distorted her pretty features.

The other woman glared and shook her head. "I need to talk to you *now*."

Dolly's insistence appeared to push Damian over the edge. His face went blank, almost scary. "I do not enjoy having to repeat myself so many times to a grown woman. You understand my words, so take that knowledge and go back to your work. We will speak later, after you've had time to ponder your transgressions."

Dolly's posture sank into docile defeat, but she still managed to throw an intimidating "I'm going to get you and get you *good*" stare at Autumn as she turned and marched from the office.

"She'll be fine," Damien assured Autumn, walking to his desk. She took the swift moment of privacy as her one chance to slide a hand across the burner in her bra and press its outer audio-record button.

He sat and gestured to the empty chair across from him. Autumn obeyed, giving the door a timid glance. "I hope so. She…she scared me a little." She lowered her eyes in embarrassment.

"Oh, Autumn." Damien leaned across his desk, no doubt hoping she would do the same. "You have nothing to be scared of at Harmony House. Dolly isn't dangerous. She's simply had a rough day. Between you and me, I think Dolly may have harbored some misguided feelings toward Alice."

You bastard. I knew you knew.

"Misguided how?" She kept her tone innocent…almost childlike.

Damien gave her a sad smile and gazed at the ceiling. "We

accept all people here. Everyone is free to love whomever they love. There is no judgment on this land, but Dolly failed to understand just how devoted Alice was to me. Alice and I shared an extraordinary type of love. I believe Dolly may have wished that Alice felt the same toward her."

Autumn was simultaneously shocked and not surprised at all. His flippant attitude toward Dolly's tortured affections was harsh. But had she really expected anything else?

The important question, of course, was whether *Alice* had harbored romantic love toward either of them. A mystery that would remain forever unsolved now.

"Her passing must be awful for you." Autumn's lower lip trembled. "I am so sorry that you're experiencing such a great loss."

Damien nodded and stared at his desktop. "She was a good person. The best person I have ever known."

"I agree." Autumn straightened in her chair. "Alice inspired me so much in such a short period of time. I would really like to follow her example and reconnect with my family. They live all the way on the West Coast."

"That is very far away from our dear, sweet Virginia. How exactly would you pay for a plane ticket? I had assumed you'd been out of work for quite some time…" He trailed off and lifted a perfect eyebrow, inviting Autumn to fill in the gap.

Autumn shrugged. "Well, I have money in a trust fund that I couldn't access until my twenty-fifth birthday. And *today* is my twenty-fifth birthday."

She gripped the chair edge as she waited for his reaction. What if he saw right through her ruse?

Damien's smile was Cheshire Cat worthy. Her fingers relaxed. Lucky for her, the Harmony House leader's greed appeared to exceed his astuteness.

He pressed a hand to his chest. "Happy birthday to you,

my friend. What a wonderful gift to receive. There is *so* much good that can be done in this world if people would simply open their hearts to giving."

And open their wallets...and legs...to you. Jerk.

"So," she continued spinning her web of lies, "I think this is a perfect time to go home. I can reconnect with my family and claim what is mine. Then I will be able to do what I want with the money."

"And what *do* you want, Autumn?" Damien purred the question, his crystal blue eyes sparkling with excitement.

She sobered and clasped her hands together. "I want to honor Alice's memory. I want to make a sizable donation to Harmony House. This place has changed my life in such a short period of time...and Alice. Alice changed my life." She choked back the wave of genuine emotion that arose with the statement.

The only real part of her experience at Harmony House had been her instant adoration for Alice. And that friendship was the piece almost immediately stolen from her.

"Wow." Damien put a hand to his heart. "Autumn, that is an incredibly generous gesture. I can't even begin to tell you how touched I am that you would make such a decision. *And*...happy birthday to you. My goodness."

Greed took hold of Damien Parr, morphing him into the slimy creature Autumn had known he was before ever setting foot on Harmony House grounds. As much as he "loved" Alice Leeson, he'd entirely forgotten the woman at the first hint of a dollar sign.

Damien reached for a nearby notebook, his hand shaking with what Autumn assumed was anticipation. "Since there's been a bit of...strife...between you and your family, perhaps the safest route to take in the present moment would be to put your wishes in writing. Solidify your true and noble intent."

Autumn flashed him a bright smile. "I think you're right. I'm going to do my very best to make amends with my family, but I guess I can't guarantee that everything will work out the way I want it to. I wouldn't want them to interfere with my intentions out of anger or anything like that. How about I do you one better and leave instructions...in writing...that the trust in its *entirety* should go to Harmony House should something happen to me?"

This wasn't her first time being in such close contact with a psychopath. In fact, Damien Parr was just one man on a long list of deranged individuals she'd voluntarily worked with. But the curtain of evil that dropped across his *GQ* magazine features was new to her. He hadn't even tried to cover his gluttony.

The blue eyes that had glistened with tears for Alice's ruination just moments before now gleamed with sadistic, self-serving radiance. Autumn's stomach turned. She envisioned Alice. Pure, compassionate, and *good*.

Damien hadn't deserved to know Alice, let alone enjoy her subservience and gratitude.

Pay. You are going to pay for this.

"I have experience in this type of documentation." Damien's pen moved swiftly across the paper. "If you'd like, I can help write up a proclamation that would satisfy both you and any court, should your desires ever be challenged. I invested the time required to become a notary public recently. I cannot tell you how important it is to have someone like me legally notarize your documents."

Her skin itched with the need for a shower. She wondered how many times he'd been forced to fight for the sums of money that had been happily signed over to him by enchanted followers. Enough that he'd taken the matter into his own hands and could now ensure his legal receipt of the funds should anything "unthinkable" happen to a member of his loyal fold.

Like an untimely suicide, for example.

She watched him expertly draw up a document that would no doubt give Harmony House full rights to Autumn Nichol's trust fund dollars. The pleasure on his face was equal to the savage joy in her heart. Those papers he was preparing would never get him that money because Autumn Nichol didn't exist, and neither did her trust fund.

What they would do was provide compelling evidence as to his motives for killing his members. The bastard was assisting her and the entire Bureau in taking himself down.

Satisfaction coiled inside her, enabling her lips to curve into a heartfelt smile.

Her lack of a team wouldn't impede the blaze of retribution.

Even on her own, victory was on the horizon.

BENEATH THE CANOPY OF LEAVES, Aiden's gut clenched as he checked his phone screen for the millionth time. Autumn should be calling. Texting. Reestablishing a line of communication with him and the team.

Yet so far, not a peep. Was it possible that her contraband phone had already been discovered?

The knot in his stomach tightened. To relieve some of the nervous energy, he shuffled his feet along the forest floor.

Snap!

A twig cracked beneath his boot, reverberating like a gunshot in the quiet, wooded air.

He stilled his antsy legs and slowed his respirations until his nerves were back under control.

Get your shit together, Parrish. You won't do Autumn any good if you blow this whole mission up by charging in like a rabid bear.

Noah waded through the trees toward him, with Winter close behind. "Nothing?" The other agent stared at Aiden with a grim expression that triggered his own adrenaline levels to spike again.

Get. Your. Shit. Together.

Aiden inhaled a long, slow breath. Released it. "Nothing." He noted the concern also embedded in Winter's tight-lipped features. "We need to move in closer."

Sheriff Frank leaned against a tree trunk and nodded. "I agree. It's possible that someone eavesdropped on Chris and Autumn's conversation or was just suspicious of their inter-action in general. Or maybe they found her burner right away. We have no idea what the consequences are for that type of betrayal."

Aiden's jaw set. Not what he wanted to hear, even if he'd flipped through all those same possibilities.

Also, what the hell was Frank's deal with leaning? He was starting to believe she was incapable of standing without something to prop her up.

Chris crossed his arms. "I'm guessing the consequences for betrayal have something to do with Autumn's impending suicide."

Aiden contained the growl rising in his throat. Barely. His hands itched to latch onto Agent Parker's neck and throttle him. Lucky for Parker, he needed every hand on deck.

"We move now. Sheriff Frank, Agent Logan, you will come with me. We will move northwest to the middle of the property. Agent Parker and Deputy King will circle to the east. Station yourselves as close to the entrance as possible but stay hidden. I do not want anyone leaving this damn hell-hole until Parr has been arrested."

King nodded. Parker's hand went instinctively to his holstered Glock.

"Agents Dalton and Black," Aiden eyed the pair, "you're going to circle west to the south side and make your way inward. You're going to have a steep incline, but you'll also have the most unobstructed view, considering the west side of the property is almost entirely the cliff and the outlook. Fewer trees."

Everything about this scenario plucked his nerves like guitar strings. No word from Autumn. They were charging in through unfamiliar terrain. He had serious doubts as to Agent Black's current ability to handle both the hike and the stress of the situation.

He inspected Winter one last time, taking in her flushed cheeks, squared shoulders, and glittering eyes. Was she ready for this? Impossible to say. However, leaving her in the car wasn't an option. She would raise all sorts of hell, and he didn't have the time or mental bandwidth for a standoff right now.

Not with Autumn's life potentially hanging in the balance.

The truth was, he needed the extra bodies...and Winter needed to believe *he* believed in her ability to do the job. She was struggling, but she was here. Pulling her out of action now might do more damage than good in terms of her recovery.

Agent Dalton met Aiden's eyes, gave him a slight dip of his chin. His tacit agreement to keep his partner safe. If anyone could protect Winter Black, it was Noah. Aiden only prayed he wasn't making an irreversible mistake.

His attention was ripped away from the duo when Mia approached. "We're not waiting for HRT?"

He shook his head. "They can follow us in when they get here." He'd called in the Hostage Rescue Team from Richmond, but there was no guarantee that they would arrive before something awful happened to Autumn. Parr's victims deserved justice, but Aiden wasn't willing to sacrifice Autumn to get it. "We may not have the time to wait. Everyone gear up. Now."

A flurry of activity followed. Aiden pulled on his own ballistics vest.

There was a chance that every member of Harmony House had their own firearm and were under orders to shoot intruders on sight. The theory seemed out of line with their professed desire to spread peace and love, but so did the string of suicides that all led back to their community.

Aiden sent up a silent prayer that Harmony House wasn't a gun kind of cult. The last thing they needed was another Waco.

Although, unlike with the FBI's standoff with the Branch Davidians, if this cult was armed, Aiden's team might easily be outnumbered in terms of firepower.

Stealth would be their most effective weapon.

"Keep low." He circled the group, giving each team member a last glance. "Observe and *only observe* unless you have direct reason to act. Earpieces in and on. *Communicate.* Go."

They spread like silent wildfire through the woods, heading toward their separate destinations. Aiden crept toward his own target location, careful of every foot placement. They had no idea when or if any cult members might traipse into the surrounding woods, so he peered around each tree before moving, half-afraid he might stumble upon people performing some weird hippy ritual involving leaves and squirrel scat.

Closer and closer they crept, freezing with every rustle in the bushes and every snap of a stick. He paused multiple times to swipe the sweat from his forehead, which had more to do with anxiety than heat.

When they were as close as they dared to get, he ordered Mia and Sheriff Frank to stop.

The heart of Harmony House grounds lay directly in front of them, protected only by an old-fashioned log fence. As he waited for the other agents to check in, he cycled through all the things that could go wrong.

What if unanticipated obstacles kept the other agents from reaching their posts? What if they were caught? What if comms went down?

What if they were too slow to help Autumn?

His earpiece crackled.

"Agents Dalton and Black reporting in. We reached the cliff base. No sign of suspicious activity. Over."

A tiny bit of the tension eased from his chest. So far, so good.

The next fifty minutes were torture. Aiden was close to crawling out of his own skin when Agent Parker's urgent whisper carried through the radio.

"Sorry, boss. I've been made."

Aiden clenched his hands. *Dammit.* Their timetable had just moved up.

The weight returned to his chest. "Stay calm, Parker. Tell them nothing." He nodded to Mia and Sheriff Frank. "If Chris has been compromised, Parr is smart enough to know more trouble is coming. We're not giving him time to slip through our fingers. Everyone move in. Locate and secure Damien Parr, *now*. We're taking him into custody. *Go.*"

31

Once Autumn's signature graced all the drawn-up documents, Damien's good mood returned like magic. She had to fight to keep from smacking the pleased smile right off his smug face.

Alice's body had barely grown cold, yet her leader had moved on to sunnier days.

Days full of profit...and possibly murder.

Her gaze dropped to where her name was scrawled in blue ink, and a shiver danced across her skin. Had she acted too hastily? Now that Damien believed he was the benefactor of her estate, what was preventing him from offing her sooner versus later? Provoking the killer into another murder without discussing her intentions with Aiden first might not have been her smartest plan.

Then again, Dolly had forced her hand.

She wrapped her arms around her waist. Too late to second-guess now.

"Come." Damien stood, holding a hand out to her. "Join me in my meditation on the outlook. We will make today beautiful in spite of our suffering."

Eww. Autumn really hoped he wasn't implying what she thought he was. Her recent peek into his lust-filled head wasn't reassuring, though.

Her disgust was second only to the alarm bells clanging in her skull. Reminding her about the big, fat target she'd just slapped on her own back.

Essentially, she'd turned herself into a walking dollar sign. The only thing worse than strolling to the edge of a cliff with an evil, greedy man who wanted to add her to his harem was strolling there with one who intended to murder her to inherit her trust fund.

Her mouth went dry. Forget cliffs. She needed to find Dolly. All her time at Harmony House would be wasted if the woman went to Damien and shared her doubts.

Autumn was too close to finding Alice's killer to give up now. The wheels were all in motion.

Somehow, someway, she had to convince Dolly to zip her mouth.

"Sorry." Autumn stood as well, backing toward the door with swift steps and an apologetic smile. "I have so many things to do. Chores to finish. The teamwork here is so important and such a touching design. I wouldn't want to mess that up."

Damien smiled and opened his mouth to speak, but Autumn waved and exited his office. The arrogant superior of Harmony House was no doubt insulted by her second rejection since arriving at his estate, but he'd forgive her while under the influence of his cash-happy haze.

She paced the first floor, checking the kitchen and dining rooms, as well as the communal entry. There were many members still clustered together in mourning, but Dolly wasn't among them.

Autumn headed for the second floor, forcing herself to move at a normal speed. The second floor was nearly empty, only a few newbies peeking out from their rooms or wandering the hall.

Half-suspecting to find Dolly hunting through her backpack in the closet-room Alice had shown her to, Autumn jetted for the third floor. But the hall and the rooms—hers included—were deserted.

Her cool began to wane as she flew down the flights of stairs. She nearly crashed into Roberta when reaching the first floor.

"I'm sorry, I wasn't paying attention." Autumn put a hand to her chest. "I'm trying to find Dolly. You haven't seen her around down here, have you?"

Roberta managed a weak smile despite her swollen, red-rimmed eyes. "I saw her go outside just a few minutes ago."

After a grateful nod, Autumn jetted out the back exit of Harmony House. She circled the main building, eyes darting in every direction. No sign of Dolly anywhere.

Her nerves clamored like cymbals in her ears.

She's with him. She found him on the outlook, and she's telling him all about your sneaky ass right now.

Autumn took off at a jog toward the outlook, too anxious to worry about who witnessed her bizarre behavior. When she reached the wide deck, she found a single occupant. Damien sat alone on the wooden floor with his legs crossed and eyes closed, performing deep breathing exercises.

Relief flooded her body. Just Damien. No Dolly.

Unless she caught him already.

Autumn was about to creep away when his eyes snapped open. His eyebrows rose before he gestured for her to come closer.

"You changed your mind? Excellent!" Damien's smile helped her breathe a little easier. Dolly obviously hadn't succeeded in throwing Autumn under the proverbial bus just yet.

The smart move was to decline. Instead, she hesitated. She could leave and continue her search for Dolly...or stay and ignite another fire under the killer's ass.

The first part of her mission was complete. She'd checked off the boxes of praising Harmony House, signing over her trust fund, and ingratiating herself with the leader of the operation.

All that was left to do now was mention her intent to leave and not come back. That was the trigger.

She just needed to know who was holding the gun.

As Damien smiled up at her expectantly, she chewed her cheek. Aiden would hate the plan. He would forbid it. Making herself a target for a proven killer was not something he'd ever sign off on.

Undercover? Sure. Bait? No.

Autumn threw her shoulders back. Aiden *wasn't* here. And before another sweet soul like Alice was found swaying by her neck, Autumn had to find...and *stop*...the psychopath living within the peaceful, loving borders of Harmony House.

She'd made a vow to Alice.

"I didn't come to meditate," she confessed. "I thought about things after our meeting...and I realized that if I can make things right with my family, I want to stay with them. This is a beautiful home, Damien, but it's not mine."

Damien sprang to his feet. "No, no, no. This *is* your home. Harmony House welcomes *all*. You *belong* here. That's why you found us. Don't you understand that? There was no accident in the matter."

She frowned, shaking her head. "This is a place for the lost. I'm financially independent now, and I feel like my head and heart have been straightened out. Those beds in that building belong to the next troubled soul who seeks shelter. I could never stay and take the space of someone in actual need."

"We're a family, Autumn." He stepped closer. "We don't just doctor people up and send them on their way. Need isn't solely based on finances. There are parts of you that no trust fund will ever mend. You need love. Support. People who stand by your side through anything."

The sincerity ringing in Damien's voice enraged her. He was preaching the limits of money while simultaneously trying to take everyone else's. Including hers.

Did the man ever mean a damn word he said?

"I'm hoping my family...my *real* family...will be the ones who stand by my side." Flashes of Sarah assailed her psyche.

Damien emitted a heavy sigh of exhaustion. "If your 'real family' cared enough to stand by your side, you would never have ended up here. They would have been there to catch you when you fell on hard times. I don't see them anywhere, do you?"

"I-I'll still send a large gift to Harmony House." Autumn avoided his eyes. "And I really like this part of the country. Maybe I'll buy a house nearby so that I can visit often—"

"What?" Damien's alarm echoed across the gorge. "Why would you waste so much money on something so superficial? You have everything you need right here, and you always will. You don't want to place yourself on the government's grid where they'll just tax and track your money as though it's their own. That's foolish, and you strike me as a very intelligent woman."

She met his eyes, wishing they weren't so gemlike and inviting. "There's a whole world out there, Damien." She gestured toward the forest, the mountains, the sky.

"Yes." He didn't break eye contact for a second, lulling her with his hypnotic stare. "And what has that world ever done except chew you up and spit you out? Why would you turn away from an absolute haven? From a family who will never abandon you?" His voice softened. "What are you scared of?"

Autumn gulped without intending to. She pictured sweet little Toad and Peach, innocent little creatures who loved her without question, yet she willingly left them behind. Often.

And even the BAU team...

Had she *wanted* to go undercover or had she not known how to settle into her new "family" as a fellow agent and comrade? She'd returned from Quantico, joined her colleagues, and extricated herself from the safety of her team almost immediately.

Aiden...there was something so obvious and loud between them, but she refused to give it a voice.

Her best friend was suffering in a way that she wasn't sure how to help, but she wanted to try.

There was a level of dependence she wasn't willing to enter into for anyone or anything. Nothing in this world was permanent, and the people you could trust with every last fiber of your being was a simple, sad count of one.

She trusted herself. Not to always be right or good, but to always be there. Everyone disappeared at some point. Every living thing. The only person who would hold her hand the day she died stared back at her from a mirror each morning.

The easiest way to remind herself that there were no guarantees in life was to promise herself no guarantees. No endless love. No timeless friendship. No immortal furry creatures at her side.

A series of gains and losses...that was life. If she could help others during her particular run of days on this planet, then she hadn't wasted her life. This was the reason she'd chosen her career path.

Who allowed their heart to be broken if there was an obvious way to protect it?

An intelligent human being understood that all security

in life was a farce. A beautiful lie. She'd had her fill of those falsities and disappointments before even reaching her teenage years.

No more.

"Autumn." Her name was a seductive whisper on Damien's lips. "Put all physical beauty aside, and you are still a beautiful *soul*. You are capable of doing so much good in this world. More than you seem to realize. If you let me, I can guide you through the noise of your former life. I can escort you to a state of existence where you are free. *Free*. No pain. No regret. *Just love.*"

She was aware that he was reading her every movement. Her emotions and turmoil played out for Damien like a movie reel. He saw that she was beginning to bend his way, and he would grasp and refuse to let go.

And would that be so bad? Was Damien Parr's world really such a terrible place?

His words sank in and peeled back her protective outer layers, revealing the vulnerable woman underneath. One that he promised to nurture. To soothe her pain away and help her grow.

Autumn swayed toward him, captivated by those translucent blue eyes. The people on this estate were *happy*, and they *weren't* faking it. She'd witnessed that with her own eyes over the last twenty-four hours. Alice had been genuinely rapturous just to be alive each day.

What would Autumn truly leave behind if she were to settle in a quiet space such as Harmony House? A dangerous job? Regular encounters with the darkest minds mankind had to offer? A continuous string of personal failures that cost others their lives?

She could do no harm to others here, *and* she could be safe from harm herself.

Temptation tugged at her defenses. Whispered soft, honeyed words in her ear.

Alice had only become unhappy when her past invaded her present. Her parents had barged into her utopia and poisoned it. That was when it had all gone downhill for her. When she'd lost sight of her previous decision to stay and be and breathe and smile.

Damien's voice was in her ear now, his hot breath tickling her skin. "I know you say you want to leave, but I'm not so sure you do. And I, for one, would never send you away, Autumn. I would never abandon you. That much I can promise. I would keep you safe for the rest of my days."

He meant the vow. She could discern that much.

The knowledge settled on her skin like a warm, protective blanket. No one here would judge her. No one here would care who'd she'd been up until now. They would only want to help her find peace. Bliss. Joy.

Damien placed a gentle hand on her cheek. She jumped as the mental imagery surged into her head.

His hands, pulling off her clothes. His naked body grinding on top of hers within the circle of fire.

Oh, he wanted to "guide her" toward bliss, all right. Just not in any sort of spiritual way.

Her stomach revolted. The man truly was a master manipulator. Even for someone as educated as her.

You should bow down and praise the special ability your brain injury gave you, because without it...

She shuddered as she acknowledged the truth. Without her ability, she likely would have succumbed to this man's charms. Damien Parr preached a dream while embodying a nightmare.

Autumn pushed him away without thinking.

"Are you all right?" Damien's concern could have been real. Or fake. Or half and half. She no longer cared. She had to get out of this mindfuck blackhole before...

Before what?

She stumbled a step back, shaking her jumbled head. She had to escape before she forgot who she was and simply became another pretty face amongst Damien's harem of gentle hearts.

"I have to leave." She wasn't attempting to poke the bear at this point. She *did* need to leave. She shouldn't have ever come. Aiden and Winter had both called this, and they'd both been right.

Her life experiences made her too vulnerable to this man right now. She'd been the wrong choice for this mission.

"Please," Damien pleaded, his performance so convincing she'd ceased to analyze it. "Please let me help you. You need Harmony House. You need me."

Autumn envisioned the altar that Roberta had laid upon. She pictured Damien crawling over Roberta's youthful body like a predatory animal.

Fire kindled in her chest.

What Autumn *really* needed was to castrate this asshole before he preyed upon anyone else.

"No. I don't need you at all, Damien."

When Autumn turned her back on the Harmony House leader, she immediately felt lighter. She crossed the wooden planks with a new bounce in her stride.

From here, she'd walk straight to the front gate and leave Harmony House forever. Aiden would understand. The team could return and apprehend Damien Parr and anyone else they wished to question with a proper warrant.

Instead of solving the mystery alone, seeking justice for Alice alone, Autumn was making the choice to join the agents who had her back. She didn't *have* to continually fling herself in the face of danger.

She didn't have to attack every problem independent of all assistance. Her team was there. For her and each other.

Autumn stole one more glance over her shoulder at a slack-jawed Damien before turning to exit the overlook for good.

Her plan was cut short when a woman with wild chestnut hair and manic eyes flew right at her.

Dolly.

There was no time for Autumn to do more than brace for impact. Her muscles tensed, but at the last second, Dolly swerved and charged past her. "Dami—"

"I thought I was clear with you, Dolly." Damien's voice boomed in the otherwise quiet afternoon air. "We will talk *later*. This obsessiveness you're displaying…I do not appreciate it. Do you understand?"

Dolly's face flushed a deep red. "Feds! There are federal agents here!"

"What?" Damien's face paled, even as Autumn's heart leapt.

Her team was here.

"I took a walk," Dolly rushed on, "and noticed a man lurking near the front entrance. He thought he was hidden in the shrubs, but I saw him. It was the man who came with the sheriff and deputy to question us earlier. And this time, he's wearing an FBI jacket."

In the short time that Dolly had been speaking, Autumn's initial excitement had given way to the apprehension pulsing through her limbs.

Her cover was seconds from being blown.

Keeping her eyes locked on the others, she began to sidle toward the exit.

Damien's chest rose and fell in rapid succession. He lunged for Dolly and grabbed her arms. "Are you sure?"

"Yes!" Dolly shouted in his face. "I'm positive! And *Autumn* was alone with him for quite a while in the kitchen. I couldn't hear, but I could see." Autumn froze when Dolly turned and pointed at her. "He was *telling* her things, not questioning her. And he left her something in the dish drainer. A phone maybe, I'm not sure."

Autumn crossed her arms and pressed what she hoped was the programmed call button through her shirt.

If she was pushing the wrong button, she'd know soon enough. Either Aiden would send help, or he wouldn't.

Damien remained focused on Dolly. "Do not take your eyes off this blasphemous woman. Keep her right here while I figure out what in the hell is going on." Then he took off running for the main house.

Autumn's eyes slid to meet Dolly's hateful glare.

The other woman smiled the dark smile of a deeply disturbed soul. "I won't let you hurt Harmony House. I won't let you ruin all the good Damien does. You're *done for*, you lying bitch."

She stalked toward Autumn, chestnut eyes aflame.

32

Pounding. Incessant pounding.

The constant, unforgiving pain throbbed at Winter's temples, threatening to beat her into unconsciousness. Sweat beaded on her face, between her breasts, and ran in streams down her back. Her shirt was soaked through.

If Noah noticed, she planned to blame the July heat for her condition. Hopefully, he wouldn't guess the real reason.

Withdrawal was a bitch.

She gritted her teeth and fought to stay on her feet. She'd tried to wean down, even just a little. Baby steps would eventually amount to giant leaps regarding her addiction. She knew this. She'd said those words to other addicts before.

But that was when you were tough, Sissy. No one would listen to a damn word you said now. You look like a Skid Row reject. Just embrace it already. Take a damn pill.

She glanced at her watch. Nearly two hours had passed since her last dose. She'd promised herself three. Three hours. She'd even left the pill bag behind to ensure she didn't cave to the cravings.

"Dammit. Dammit. Dammit." Winter whispered the

words, hating herself for not bringing her stash just as much as she hated herself for needing it to begin with.

The sweat pouring nasty rivers down her skin was nothing compared to how slimy she felt on the inside. Her best friend was in danger, yet here she was. Counting the minutes until her next fix like a damn junkie.

You know, if you don't take one, I'm gonna get louder, and louder, and louder. Do you really want me in your ear while you save your idiot friend? Check your pockets. Check your boots. You hid one in there a while back. Check it, Sissy. Do it.

"No!"

She flinched. She'd been way too loud.

Noah hurried over. "No, what?"

Winter tensed, and her mind went blank.

Go ahead, Sissy. Tell him. He definitely won't think you've lost your mind. See? You should have taken a pill.

"Winter?" Noah prodded.

Chris's raspy whisper in the headset saved her. "Sorry, boss. I've been made."

Aiden's sharp intake of breath was a hiss in her ear. "Stay calm, Parker. Tell them nothing. If Chris has been compromised, Parr is smart enough to know more trouble is coming. We're *not* giving him time to slip through our fingers. Everyone move in. Locate and secure Damien Parr, now. We're taking him into custody. *Go.*"

The urgency in the SSA's voice stoked Winter's own fear. She inferred what Aiden had stopped short of saying.

Parr was smart enough to realize more trouble was coming…and clever enough to make Autumn too. If the cult leader was killing off devoted followers, then he wouldn't bat an eye at offing a spy.

"Shit." She shook off an image of Autumn's body, broken at the bottom of Dogwood Falls. No. That couldn't be her friend's fate. They'd get to her in time. They had to.

Noah pointed toward the rocky incline that met Harmony House's southwest corner. Following his finger, a flash of red took her eyes farther west.

The outlook.

Winter lifted her binoculars, her stomach lurching as she focused. Autumn and Damien stood alone on the wide, man-made deck. Far too close to the edge of the cliff. "I've got eyes on Parr. He's on the overlook right now, and Autumn is with him."

"Move in. Now." Aiden's command was terse.

Before Winter could comply, another woman entered her field of vision. Her grip tightened on the field glasses. "Hold up, there's someone else. A woman."

She walked right up to Damien and Autumn. Based on body posture and movement, Winter deduced they were arguing. The new female arrival seemed particularly angry.

Winter's blood ran cold. Two against one. "Get off the damn outlook, Autumn," she whispered, unable to look away from the scene. "Get onto the land."

To her surprise, the person who left first was Damien. The man stalked off, disappearing onto a wooded path. Winter barely had time to register her relief when another man came out from behind a tree. His slow pace as he crept up behind the women made the blood drain from her head.

On his next step, the man's outline glowed an angry red, like an ember of hellfire.

"Noah." While low, her voice crackled with urgency. "Parr isn't the killer. It's another man. And he's headed straight toward Autumn."

"Are you—"

"I'm sure!" Winter took off up the steep incline without another word.

Oh, look at you, running off to save your BFF. That's cute. But don't forget, Sissy, even if you save the good doctor, you are still a bona fide killer. A murderer. Nothing changes that. You're juuust like me now.

Winter grunted and moved her legs faster. "You're right. I'm a killer. And I'm going to kill you next, little brother."

Her promise was carried away with the mountain breeze.

AUTUMN PREPARED FOR BATTLE.

Dolly prowled toward her, madness in her eyes. "You thought you could simply walk onto this sacred ground and ruin everything we've worked to build here? Are you that stupid?"

Evan Blair popped into view behind Dolly, appearing from the trees bordering the outlook's northern edge. He caught Autumn's eye and put a finger to his lips as he crept up on the enraged woman.

Some of the tension eased from Autumn's neck. For a second there, she was afraid she'd end up in a fistfight with Dolly. Whatever the other woman lacked in training, she'd probably more than make up for in unadulterated fury, and Autumn would prefer to escape this hellhole with all her hair intact.

Even now, Dolly's hands were curled into claws. Ready to inflict damage. "You know, when I first met you, I thought you were such a strong woman, but I was wrong." Autumn shook her head. "You follow Damien around like a puppy. You let him speak to you like a child. He's not special, Dolly. Damien is no better than Charles Manson or James Jones or all the other cult leaders who tried *and* failed to build their own kingdoms."

Dolly halted, her face a twisted mask of devotion. *"You don't know Damien.* You say that because you're not one of us. You don't belong here. You never belonged here. You're just a whore who happened to get a lucky break, but that break is over. Damien *loves* us. All of us. You don't deserve to even breathe the sacred air around you!"

"Well," Autumn held up her hands, "sorry. As you can see, I'm still breathing. Although, hopefully, I won't be sharing air with you for much longer. Oh, and when you say 'Damien loves *us*,' you do realize that he loved Alice just a teensy-weensy bit more, right? And from what I've been told, she loved him back."

"*She did not!*" Dolly screamed, her face contorting in agony at the mention of her beloved Alice. "Alice loved *me*! *Me!* She wouldn't join to Damien because she loved *me* too much!"

The woman's rage echoed through the valley. Loud and wild enough to convince Autumn that she was the killer they'd been hunting all along.

Autumn frowned. The profile indicated a man. Plus, Dolly wasn't strong enough to fake a hanging, was she? Unless she'd had help?

As Autumn peered over Dolly's shoulder, an icy fist squeezed the oxygen from her lungs. At ten feet away, Evan's docile, shy features had changed. There was no longer any sign of the awkward young man from their previous encounters. His eyes now glittered with an awful delirium that she'd encountered only once before.

In Justin Black's vivid blues.

She opened her mouth to scream a warning, but Evan was quicker. He lunged forward, grabbing Dolly by her arms.

"Evan, stop!"

In his wild state, Autumn wasn't even sure Evan heard her as he dragged Dolly toward the outlook's edge.

"*She didn't love you!*" he screamed, no longer sounding like soft-spoken Evan Blair.

No longer sounding human at all.

Evan whirled and shoved Dolly forward, pushing her against the railing. "You stupid bitch! She didn't love you! And she didn't love Damien! *She loved me!* Just like I loved her. That's why I had to release her from this world and end her suffering! She was too pure for us!"

A wave of dizziness rooted Autumn to the deck. Wrong, she'd had it all so, so wrong.

Damien wasn't the killer. Neither was Dolly.

Bashful, socially awkward Evan Blair was the murderer they'd been hunting. He'd never intended to help Autumn. In fact, he'd probably planned to kill her before Dolly's commentary about Alice's love sent him into a rage.

Dolly.

Autumn edged forward slowly. Fully aware of the abyss yawning beneath their feet. One wrong move and she had no doubt Evan would launch Dolly over the side. "Evan. Why don't we all take a moment to calm down?"

If Evan heard her, he gave no indication. "You're going to *die!*" he screamed in Dolly's face as she struggled to free herself from his grip. "You're going to die knowing that Alice was *mine!* Think about that while you're falling, you stupid whore!"

Shit. This was escalating way too fast.

Sweat dripped down Autumn's chest. She wished like hell she had her service gun. "Evan, please. Let's talk this out. Alice wouldn't want you to hurt Dolly. You know that."

She crept closer. She could do this. She could talk him back from the edge. Distract him with her soothing voice and reassuring words, like she'd done with so many patients before.

He craned his head in Autumn's direction. She froze, pinned in place by those maniacal, wild eyes. Her heart crashed against her ribs. So close now, but she didn't dare move. Not with Dolly's legs pinned against the safety barrier while Evan forced her upper half to lean over the sheer drop.

The other woman no longer fought Evan's tight grip. Probably realizing that one wrong move would end in her skull cracking open on the rocks below.

"Don't you dare tell me to stop. I *won't*. *I can't.* This is what I was put here to do. I am the *protector* of Harmony House, and there's no room here for liars."

Autumn was still formulating a response when he slammed both hands into Dolly's shoulders and shoved her over the railing.

A shrill scream rent the air as her body somersaulted over the waist-high beam, like a kid on the playground bars.

Adrenaline shot through Autumn like a bullet. She dived for the parapet, panic lending her speed. As she slid forward, Dolly made one last, desperate grab for a beam.

Her fingernails skimmed the surface. Clawed at the wood.

Began to slide out of view.

Autumn managed to capture Dolly's wrist a split second before she plummeted out of reach.

The full impact of Dolly's weight snapped at Autumn's shoulders. Pain screamed through her joints and across her back. Her stomach slid along the wood as gravity fought to claim its prize. When her hands slipped on Dolly's skin, she tightened her grip.

Do not let go.

Five months of weight training paid off as she dug in and worked her way back to her knees. Slowly, she hauled Dolly up, inch by excruciating inch.

Her body shook with the strain, but she gritted her teeth and worked harder. She could do this.

There was a blur of motion in her peripheral vision as Evan appeared, dropping down by her left side. His strong hands clamped over hers. Worked to pry her fingers loose. "You can't save her! She's an evil liar! Alice didn't love you! *She didn't love you!* SHE DIDN'T LOVE YOU!"

Pain seared Autumn's arms and her grip weakened. She couldn't fend Evan off for long. With a last, monumental effort, she dug in hard and pulled Dolly up enough to push the woman's fingers around the railing.

Just in time. As if he could read her mind, Evan abandoned Dolly and turned on Autumn, punching her in the rib cage.

The hit knocked the breath from her lungs. She panted and curled onto her side as Evan sprang to his feet.

Through her haze of pain, a fire ignited deep inside her. A blaze that infused her with fresh strength.

She called upon that strength when Evan raged toward her, pulling both knees in at the last second. The next, she lashed her feet up and out and kicked him square in the balls.

He shrieked and doubled over before collapsing to his knees. The blood continued to whoosh in Autumn's ears. His insanity likely would have him back up again in no time.

"Help me, please!"

Dolly's terrified scream sent an ice pick slamming into Autumn's spine. She flipped over, checked the railing for those pale fingers.

They were there. Bloody and trembling from fatigue, but there.

Barely.

On hands and knees, Autumn crawled over. She was inches away when a hand circled her ankle and yanked her back.

Her foot lashed out on reflex. She scrambled up to her knees. Before she could climb to her feet, he'd grabbed her from behind. A wiry arm clenched around her chest and squeezed. His other hand latched over her mouth and nose.

Autumn bit down hard on Evan's palm until she tasted blood. The second he shrieked and released her mouth, she threw her head back.

Crunch!

He shrieked and fell away, but his rage was a powerful stimulant. Before Autumn could do more than blink, he was struggling to raise himself onto his hands and knees. "I'm not going down that easy, you bitch. You'll die for this. You can't break the Circle. No one has that power. You'll—"

Autumn leapt to her feet, raised her right leg in the air, and slammed her heel down on Evan's back. He hit the ground with a satisfying thud.

After checking to make sure he wasn't going to pop up again, Autumn slid over to the edge and grabbed Dolly's wrist. With a lot of effort on both their parts, she managed to pull Dolly high enough to fit her through the open slats. Calling on her failing reserves of strength, she hauled Dolly the rest of the way to safety.

They both sprawled on the deck, panting for several moments. Autumn finally summoned enough energy to kneel by Dolly's side. "Are you okay?"

The woman couldn't respond as she fought to regain her breath. Autumn stood, turning just as Evan went sprinting toward the overlook's edge. His hands reached for the railing, beginning the vault that would send him soaring to certain death.

A blur of motion came out of nowhere and tackled him from the far side. Instead of leaping over the railing, he flew to the right, smacking the deck so hard the entire structure shook.

This time, he didn't move. Probably because Winter stood over him with a shiny gun trained on his chest. "Geez, Trent, were you going to save any of the fun for me?"

There was a moment of shocked silence before a giggle

escaped Autumn's mouth. She wrapped an arm around Dolly and pulled the dazed woman to her feet. "Well, you know. I figured I'd make it a solo party this time."

Their eyes locked for a moment, and Autumn's chest clenched. Not from the fight she'd just survived, but from the love shining from her friend's face.

Winter inclined her head. "I knew you had it in you."

Autumn's laugh was shaky. "That made one of us, then."

The team, along with Sheriff Frank, Deputy King, several Beechum police officers, and the Bureau's own Hostage Rescue Team flooded the deck, spreading across its expanse like one large flame.

Evan was handcuffed and dragged away, sobbing with no fight left in him. Autumn took a moment to process what she'd just learned...that Evan had killed Alice himself.

The anger burning through her was tempered by a familiar wave of empathy. She hated him for taking Alice from the world. For being so selfish in his obsession with the sweet, innocent soul who had befriended Autumn within moments of her arrival at the soup kitchen.

Yet mad as she was, a part of her also ached for him. Evan Blair had loved Alice in his own, messed up way, but he wasn't mentally sound. The man had probably suffered from a chemical imbalance long before he was sucked into Damien's black hole of brainwashing.

Her hands shook. With the proper treatment, Evan might have recovered, or at least, led a productive, healthy life. Only he'd never had the chance because—

Damien's voice carried through the air. "Get the hell off my property, you damn goons! You have no right to be here! I'll have every last one of your badges for this! Who do you think you are?!"

Autumn caught sight of the ranting Harmony House leader just as Aiden came face-to-face with him. The SSA pulled a piece of paper from his pocket and waved it under the cult leader's nose. "Hello again, friend. This here is what we call a warrant, and it gives us *every* right to be here. We will be searching the entirety of your organization's grounds, Mr. Parr. And I've got to say, based on the information we already have, this doesn't bode well for you."

Sheriff Frank walked over and snatched the extended warrant from Aiden's hand. "We've got this, Agent Parrish." Her deputy stood by her side, legs wide and planted, with a menacing expression on his face.

Good for you, Deputy King.

Aiden smiled, a rare public sighting that deserved paparazzi attention. "I've no doubt that you do, Sheriff."

Damien blanched. There wasn't a single thing he could do to stop the search—and his subsequent downfall—from taking place. He allowed a few of his frazzled followers to guide him back toward the main house, which was currently being swarmed by agents.

After relishing his walk of shame, Autumn turned back in time to witness a harried-faced Noah embrace Winter and lift her off her feet. "Don't you ever leave me behind again, darlin'."

Winter laughed and squeezed back. "It's not my fault that you can't keep up."

Her heart warm, Autumn turned to scan the crowd for Aiden. She jumped to find him standing not a full foot away. Until that moment, she hadn't realized how much she'd missed his solid, comforting presence. Like a giant boulder in the midst of a hurricane.

He edged forward, closing the distance between them. "Parr's in some deep shit. We've connected him to several shell corporations, as well as a nonexistent charity. He's been funneling and laundering money for years. But I'm guessing the intel we have right now is just the tip of that iceberg."

Autumn nodded, not surprised in the slightest. "He's a despicable man. But...he's not our killer. I was *sure* he was the one behind the suicides, Aiden. I was wrong."

Aiden put a hand on her shoulder. "We all were. But *you* were the one who found out who the real killer was. You should be proud of yourself, Autumn. I'm *damn* proud of you."

There was a familiar and overwhelming current emanating from Aiden's hand on her shoulder. It raced through her body with electric speed, a shock to the system like always.

But for the first time since meeting Special Supervisory Agent Aiden Parrish, Autumn didn't fight the flow. She relaxed into his touch, allowing herself to savor the sensation and ponder the fact that maybe there were certain walls worth letting down.

Maybe.

33

Autumn sank into the cushions of her couch, holding a face-licking Toad in her arms. Peach glared at her from the kitchen counter. "Goin' for a little déjà vu there, Peachy? You can't hate me *every time* I leave." The feline stared back with a look that clearly indicated she could do whatever the damn hell she wanted.

Arriving home just yesterday evening, Autumn had greeted and tended to her pets before collapsing into bed. She was asleep within seconds and only woke the next morning because Toad was running hot laps, whining, and doing his general best to alert her to the fact that he had some business to do outside.

"How about a big Saturday morning breakfast?" Autumn gave Toad's belly a good scratch. "You know I'll share." She flipped the local radio on, dancing around to *Today's Greatest Hits*, and whipping herself up an impressive meal.

Scrambled eggs, a load of slightly burnt bacon—this was the only kind worth eating in her opinion—and some toasted English muffins dripping with butter and blackberry jam. Toad inhaled whatever he could guilt-trip her into giving him with his puppy dog eyes, and Autumn managed to earn back a little favor with Peach by slipping her scrambled eggs and bacon under the table.

When they were all three stuffed, Autumn pulled out her laptop. No more delays. She was going to find her sister.

Bam! Bam!

After she sent whoever was banging on her door away.

With a sigh, Autumn rose and walked to the entryway and peered through the peephole. Her heart skipped a beat.

Aiden stood on the other side, dressed in his usual crisp suit. Apparently, Saturday meant business as usual to SSA Parrish.

Swinging the door wide open, she granted him a smile while blocking Toad's attempt to door dash with her foot. "Hey, stranger. Haven't seen you in so long. Did you get taller?"

He grinned and entered, shutting the door behind him while Autumn placed her dirty dishes into the sink. The grease-filled bacon pan would just have to wait.

"Do I smell," Aiden lifted his nose high and sniffed, "actual home-cooked food?"

She walked past him and plopped onto her couch. "You do, and you just missed it."

Aiden followed and sat beside her. "Another day. Another tragedy."

Toad took the liberty of jumping back onto his owner's lap and unabashedly gazed at Aiden while Peach perched on the couch arm and did the same. Autumn laughed. "They've got you surrounded, Agent."

"I surrender." He held up his hands. "How're you holding up after your first official case, Agent Trent?"

She was exhausted and more than a little saddened by the passing of such a fantastic spirit as Alice Leeson, but she was alive. Solid. "I'm terrific, given the circumstances."

That wasn't even a white lie, for the most part.

"Well, I brought you something." Aiden reached a hand inside his suit jacket and pulled out a small plastic baggy. An evidence bag.

"What the heck, Parrish?" She grabbed for it, but he held it out of her reach, playful and, unfortunately for her, handsome as hell.

He grinned. "This is official evidence. I have to get it back to the field office stat, and I shouldn't have 'borrowed' it in the first place. But…you seemed to have grown rather fond of Alice Leeson during your short stay. This will more than likely end up with her parents after the whole Harmony House mess has been sorted through. It was the only 'belonging' she seemed to have had, and even then, it was hidden away under her mattress. I just thought maybe you'd like to read it. Gain a little more insight to your friend."

Autumn hesitated. Would Alice be okay with her reading whatever Aiden had found? She pictured Alice's eyes, sparkling with her innate, inner glow, and reached for the evidence bag.

Inside was a small, wrinkled sheet of notebook paper covered in delicate, feminine script. Autumn held the clear plastic up to her face and read.

I cannot tell a single soul
So tell it to the wind
I love her deep and strong and bright
I'll love her 'til the end
And even as we spend our days
Together yet apart
This page will tell how I loved Dolly
Every beat of heart

Autumn's eyes stung. She swallowed hard to hold back the tears, but a few slipped down her cheeks as she recalled the desolate ache on Dolly Oleson's face the morning they were told of Alice's murder.

"They were both hiding it," she murmured, looking up at him. "They were hiding their feelings because of Damien and his rules."

Aiden's intense gaze locked her in place. "Well, we thankfully don't all answer to Mr. Parr."

A buzz from Aiden's jacket pocket broke through the trance that had overtaken them both. The SSA pulled his device out and held up a finger of apology before walking to the kitchen.

The job never stopped for Aiden Parrish.

She was aware that his tireless drive was a permanent part of who he was, just as her endless empathy could never be completely shut off.

They were as opposite as two humans could be, but the balance…the balance between them intrigued her.

Aiden walked back to the couch but remained standing this time. "There's a series of home invasions in D.C. that we'll be looking into, but we wouldn't be leaving until Monday if we take the case."

"*Murderous* home invasions?" Autumn cuddled Toad close to her chest.

"Of course. Only the best for the Feds. Or worst, more accurately." Aiden ran a hand across his eyes. "How about it, Agent Trent? Are you up for another trip?"

She'd been hoping for a nice quiet week of paperwork, but the truth was, they'd all be going out of their minds with boredom if that were to happen. She glanced down at Toad, mentally promising him a hundred walks and infinite treats.

"I'm up for anything." She smiled at Aiden, earning the same in return.

He reached a hand out for the evidence baggy, and

Autumn placed it on his palm. Their fingers touched for just an instant, infusing her body with hunger.

Hers or his, though? The contact ended before she could be sure, leaving her skin humming and a curious ache in her chest.

There was a moment of hesitation before he turned toward the door. "Get some rest, Agent Trent. I'll see you Monday morning."

"You betcha."

After he left, Autumn stared at the closed door. The ache in her chest grew.

Stepping forward, she leaned her cheek against the wood, reminding herself that the *symbolic* door was still wide open.

She only had to walk through it.

34

From the driver's seat of the parked car, he sneered over his to-go coffee as he watched Autumn's dick of a boss exit the apartment building. He'd heard every damn word they'd exchanged. Listening to the two of them interact turned his stomach.

Dropping by on a Saturday morning with some bullshit excuse? Pathetic. And he *still* hadn't gotten the job done.

The SSA obviously wanted to fuck his little protégé, and a real man would have grabbed her by the hair and made her scream by now.

Though, from the sound of things, they'd be fucking soon enough. She'd drop her panties...bare her tight ass...spread her long legs...

Blood surged into his groin, and he started to get hard.

You can jerk it to thoughts of her later. For now, focus on the plan.

With effort, he pushed the redhead's perky, bouncing breasts from his mind. The plan. Everything was coming together beautifully.

After another gulp of coffee, he traded the cup for the burner phone in the center console.

His call was answered on the first ring.

"Whadya got for me?" Justin Black didn't answer the phone like a normal human being because he wasn't one.

He smiled, knowing Autumn would be coming out soon with her mutant dog. "Just letting you know that the bugs you had me plant while the little whore was gone are working like a charm."

Justin snorted. "Stick with me, and I'll teach you everything you need to know. You'll be a world-class serial killer in no time. Nothing close to *my* genius talent, but *notable*. Ready?"

The Greatest Fan smiled. "Oh yeah, I'm ready. Just tell me what I need to do next."

The End
To be continued...

Thank you for reading.
All of the Autumn Trent Series books can be found on Amazon.

ACKNOWLEDGMENTS

How does one properly thank everyone involved in taking a dream and making it a reality? Let me try.

In addition to my family, whose unending support provided the foundation for me to find the time and energy to put these thoughts on paper, I want to thank the editors who polished my words and made them shine.

Many thanks to my publisher for risking taking on a newbie and giving me the confidence to become a bona fide author.

More than anyone, I want to thank you, my reader, for clicking on a nobody and sharing your most important asset, your time, with this book. I hope with all my heart I made it worthwhile.

Much love,

Mary

ABOUT THE AUTHOR

Mary Stone lives among the majestic Blue Ridge Mountains of East Tennessee with her two dogs, four cats, a couple of energetic boys, and a very patient husband.

As a young girl, she would go to bed every night, wondering what type of creature might be lurking underneath. It wasn't until she was older that she learned that the creatures she needed to most fear were human.

Today, she creates vivid stories with courageous, strong heroines and dastardly villains. She invites you to enter her world of serial killers, FBI agents but never damsels in distress. Her female characters can handle themselves, going toe-to-toe with any male character, protagonist or antagonist.

Discover more about Mary Stone on her website.
www.authormarystone.com

Connect with Mary Online

facebook.com/authormarystone

goodreads.com/AuthorMaryStone

bookbub.com/profile/3378576590

pinterest.com/MaryStoneAuthor

Printed in Great Britain
by Amazon

75328166R00220